Praise for

"Judy Kerr may be the new mystery kid on the block, but *Black Friday* is a crime novel you won't want to miss. This engaging debut will not only have you guessing as you move deeper into the story, but perfectly sets up the next in the series. Highly recommended!"
~MWA Grandmaster Ellen Hart, author of the award-winning Jane Lawless series

"A gripping debut novel, expertly crafted and impossible to put down. I loved, loved, loved this book!"
~Pat Dennis, author of the Betty Chance mystery series

"*Black Friday* is very good. Mainly it has that very important quality that keeps me wanting to read: wanting to know what will happen next. Second, it has loving relationships from the beginning. Usually we have to wait until the end. I think Judy Kerr has written a winner!"
~Sue Hardesty, author of the Loni Wagner mystery series

"An exceptional debut novel from Minnesota author Judy Kerr. Deftly plotted with rich settings and well drawn characters you'll come to care for deeply. I will be first in line for the next in this series."
~Timya Owen, editor of *Dark Side of the Loon*

"A story that will amuse you, touch your heart, and make you want to share a cup of coffee with cheeky Postal Inspector MC McCall, a woman committed to hunting down Truth, even through her own personal heartache. Dry humor and a strong sense of place add special sauce to this spirited adventure."
~Michael Allan Mallory, co-author of the Snake Jones mysteries

"In her debut, Kerr has penned a satisfying, suspenseful multi-agency police procedural with a protagonist touched by tragedy who has to battle her own demons while she fights for justice."
~Greg Dahlager, Writer's Digest award winner and contributing author of *Dark Side of the Loon: Where History Meets Mystery*

Black Friday

An MC McCall Novel of Suspense
Book One

Judy M. Kerr

Judy M. Kerr

LAUNCHPOINT
PRESS

Launch Point Press
Portland, Oregon

ISBN: 978-1-63304-203-2
E-Book: 978-1-63304-215-5

FIRST EDITION
First Printing: 2019

Copyediting: Sue Hardesty, Sandra de Helen
Formatting: Patty Schramm
Cover: Lorelei

Published by:
Launch Point Press
www.LaunchPointPress.com

Author's Note

Dear Reader: No law enforcement agency can provide all its investigative techniques and secrets to outsiders. I've taken liberties with duties and protocols of all the law enforcement agencies mentioned in this book. The agencies mentioned are real, but the circumstances, characters, procedures, and some locations are fictitious. While I did research, please know that any mistakes are my own. Fiction writers make stuff up and at the same time work to ensure believability—it's what we do in the name of entertainment. I hope you are all entertained.

Acknowledgments

The US Postal Inspection Service (USPIS) is rarely mentioned in everyday life. Long known as "the silent service" by some and looked at as simply guardians of the US Mail by most, it's past time that the hard work and dedication of the oldest federal law enforcement agency in the US be recognized. The value the USPIS provides to postal employees and customers is far-reaching. The US has over 200 laws regulating mail, and USPIS is responsible for enforcement of those laws. The inspectors work hard to keep the mail, employees, and customers safe. They investigate crimes such as identity theft, mail fraud, robbery, mailbox destruction, obstruction of stamps, and child exploitation. While much of their behind-the-scenes action and procedures must remain confidential, people should know about the great work the USPIS does.

I thank USPIS Media Inquiries staff for providing me historical background and references to *The Inspectors*, a TV show about the USPIS. While they were not able to share investigative information or techniques, I appreciated that they took the time to respond to me at all, and I respect the need for them to remain tight-lipped about the inner workings of USPIS.

Research in general is tough, but research in writing about a specific law enforcement agency brings more challenges. In order for my book to pass the believability test, I was lucky enough to have the help of a retired postal inspector. He shared background and basic investigatory information and allowed me to bounce scene ideas off of him to ensure I formed them into a plausible story. I am forever grateful for his time and patience in answering my many questions. Keeping in mind that this is a work of fiction, all credibility of detail is thanks to my resource and any mistakes are my own.

I have a long list of people to thank for helping and guiding me down the long and winding road of writing a novel. First and foremost, I thank my family: my dear partner, JJ, who supported me, especially when I doubted myself. I love you. Also, our kids: Jeremy and Erin, you two are my heart and soul. I'm so proud of you and I love you so much. I feel lucky to be your mom. Rickey and Javi, you guys are so talented and have made this stepmom's life a richer experience—love you both. And Mom, you've loved and supported me all my life. I love and respect you so much.

Next, I thank my Minnesota Minions: Jessie and MB. You are shining examples of great writers, and I admire and love you. Thank you for reading many, many drafts and providing me with excellent feedback and "tough love" when needed.

Thanks to Sue Hardesty and Sandra de Helen for timely and helpful editing and advice.

And lastly (but not least), my editor and publisher—the guru of good writing—Lori L. Lake, thank you for believing in me and giving me a shot at this wild world of publishing.

Judy M. Kerr
Minneapolis, Minnesota
June 2019

Black Friday is my first novel, and I
wouldn't have even attempted to write at
all without encouragement from my partner.
JJ, this one's for you.

Chapter One
Friday, October 31

White! McCall! Where are you?"

The gravelly voice of her fearless leader (dreadful butthead, in Inspector MC McCall's opinion) grated on MC's last nerve. Roland Chrapkowski (pronounced Trap-kow-ski a/k/a "Crapper" to most inspectors in the office) was the last of the misfit toys in the USPIS or IS, otherwise known as the US Postal Inspection Service. The Twin Cities Domicile fell under the command of the IS Denver Division.

Pushing sixty, Team Leader Chrapkowski sported caterpillars for eyebrows, and wiry sprouts issued forth from his ears. MC swore if he were tilted sideways, the sagebrush coming out of his ears could be used to scrub the tile floors. He was of the old guard and disliked women in law enforcement. The majority of her team's work was mail theft and destruction cases and Chrapkowski rode MC's ass every chance he could. More often than not, MC wished she were assigned to the other team in their office which was supervised by Team Leader Jamie Sanchez. His team handled mostly fraud and money laundering investigations.

MC rolled her eyes at fellow inspector Cameron "Cam" White. "You're lucky to be slotted onto Jamie's team," she said to Cam, then cringed when she caught sight of Chrapkowski steaming toward them.

Her office was barely large enough to accommodate her desk, a couple of WWII-issue five-drawer metal file cabinets, an old wooden coat tree, and two chairs in front of the desk, one of which Cam occupied.

Chrapkowski's bulk filled her doorframe. "What are you doing?"

"Discussing the possible next moves on the Stennard thing. And getting caught up on other work." What the hell did he think they were doing, plotting world domination? MC hated the old dinosaur hovering, filling her space with his halitosis. She could almost taste the *eau de* stale cigarettes that oozed from his clothes, a skanky cologne.

"That's what I'm here to tell you, McCall." He huffed a breath, and even from across the postage-stamp-sized office, MC swore it smelled like something had crawled inside him and died.

"Both of you need to go to Wayzata." He wheezed another breath, his five-foot-ten bowling-ball frame oozing out of his too-tight suit. "For some godforsaken reason, the FBI wants to send you into Stennard's to talk to the staff. Apparently, the whistleblower is getting cold feet and needs some handholding or warm, fuzzy reassurances. Whatever. Meet Assistant Special Agent in Charge Oldfield at the Command Center, and he'll fill you in on the particulars." Chrapkowski coughed, emitting a sound like a grizzly bear clawing its way from his lungs, up his throat, and out his mouth. He waved a hand at them and disappeared, hacking away down the hall.

MC figured Chrapkowski wasn't long for this world. He wasn't worth wasting another brain cell on. Time to get psyched for the day's assignment.

Cam grabbed the edge of MC's desk and pulled up his six-foot-three frame. "I'll grab the keys and my phone, then I'm ready to roll."

"Me, too." She dropped her phone, a pen, and a pocket-sized black Moleskine notebook into her messenger bag.

Cam liked to tease her about her special notebooks, but she had a thing for fine writing tools and stuck her nose up at the government issue stuff. She double-checked her shoulder holster to ensure her SIG Sauer and the two fifteen-round magazine clips were secure.

Nerves sizzling with expectation, she snapped her ID badge to her belt under her jacket. Her mind whirred with questions and bits of information, working on the beginning of the puzzle, and oh, how she loved to solve a puzzle. "Let's blow this pop stand."

Cam pushed a flop of sandy hair off his forehead and dangled the keys in front of her as they headed for the door. "Wanna drive?"

"You're losing that G-man image partner."

"I haven't had time to get to the barber, so cut me some slack. No pun intended. You want to drive or what?"

"Nah. You drive. I want to update my notes and jot down a few questions for ASAC Oldfield." They exited to the parking lot on the west side of the carrier annex building in a suburb south and west of downtown Minneapolis.

Inside the car, a dirty gray Impala almost as old as the building they worked in, Cam switched on the heater, which blew frozen air at them as exterior wind buffeted the car. "Damn frost. I'll clear the windows." He grabbed a scraper from the backseat.

MC pulled out her notebook and turned to a blank page. She missed the parking at the old building. At least there they'd been out of the wind and didn't have to scrape the windows.

Cam hopped back into the car, blowing on his hands. He glanced at her. "Do you think it's a waste of time writing down questions before we know what Oldfield has planned?"

"Maybe. But I want to be prepared just in case."

"I'm worried Arty will flake out. I know he had the balls to come forward, but my first impression of him was he seemed squeamish."

MC considered Cam's assessment of Arty, the whistleblower. "He's bullish enough to handle the CFO job. Top dog in finance. Don't let his mousy demeanor mislead you. The guy has been in the muck right along with Stennard and Thomson. He's stronger and smarter than he appears. My two cents."

"I'm sure you're right. I'll chat him up. Give him plenty of reassurance. Let's push this plan with Oldfield. He seems like he trusts his team to do what needs to be done without micromanaging."

"Sounds good. Let's rock it so I can get home to Barb and all the good Halloween candy—Reese's Peanut Butter Cups."

"But doesn't the chocolate and peanut butter combination give you cold sores?"

MC whapped Cam's thigh. "Shut up, Barb."

The Command Center they were headed to had been installed over the previous four days in a vacant end unit of a four-store strip mall off of Wayzata Boulevard. The whistleblower, Arty Musselman, CFO of Stennard Global Enterprises, had visited the US Attorney's office in Minneapolis with his attorney to report his role in aiding Michael Stennard and his co-conspirator, Gavin Thomson, in a multi-million-dollar Ponzi scheme.

Arty Musselman gave up the goods on his boss when he realized there was no way Stennard Global Enterprises would ever be able to come up with the funds needed to pay the investors. The scheme was about to crash and burn, and Arty decided to grow a conscience. His lawyer brokered a deal with the AUSA, Assistant US Attorney, in which only one charge would be filed against Arty—a charge for conspiracy—to which Arty would plead guilty. The maximum sentence was a seven-year prison term and restitution, with sentencing to be handled at some undetermined date in the future. Within hours of Arty's agreement to cooperate, the AUSA brought in the FBI, the IRS Criminal Investigation Division, and the US Postal Inspection Service.

The FBI was appointed to lead the task force, and in the spirit of covert operations, the storefront windows of the strip mall space had been covered with brown butcher paper and a sign on the front doors proclaimed "EZ Financial Planners Coming Soon."

The interior had been converted to a NASA-like operation. Hi-res flat screens hung from the ceiling, displaying surveillance video feeds of the exterior from Stennard Global Enterprises and several subsidiary operations, along with exterior video of Stennard's home. The techies installed state-of-the-art sound and recording equipment in one corner.

No vehicles were parked in the barren strip mall parking lot as Cam cruised past the storefront. They drove to the rear of the building and found several nondescript grimy sedans and a couple of panel vans parked in the loading area. Cam maneuvered into a space between a gunmetal gray Impala and a dirty white panel van with Office Supply Store logos on either side.

MC opened her door. "Do you think people from the two businesses at the other end of the mall suspect the law enforcement presence when they see these cars and vans?"

"Depends on who's watching. If this operation were in the middle of Minneapolis, I'd say in a heartbeat everyone in a two-mile radius would know. But out here in the land of plenty, I don't think anyone even drives past this mall, especially not the back. It's like the slums of Wayzata, a place to avoid."

They climbed the flight of metal steps to the rusting delivery door.

"Remember the secret knock?" MC asked.

"Ha ha. Funny, Inspector Clouseau. Whaddaya think, I'm a rookie? Secret knock. Geez." Cam pushed the white button next to the door.

A tinny disembodied voice wrapped in static came through the speaker below the button. "What's the password?"

Cam faced MC, mouth agape.

MC said, "What're you looking at me for? You're not a rookie, remember? I'll let you handle it." She hummed the tune from the game show *Jeopardy*.

The voice squawked again. "I'm messing with ya, White." The door opened and they entered another dimension.

"White. McCall." ASAC Philip Oldfield greeted them. "I couldn't help but play with ya, White." He clapped Cam on the shoulder and grinned. Oldfield was a black man with close cropped gray hair, who stood a couple inches shorter than Cam. He was strong and sinewy. Oldfield had been with the FBI since his discharge from the military fifteen years earlier. At age fifty-five, he could easily pass for forty. Oldfield was a brilliant leader, engaging his people instead of commanding them.

"I heard McCall ask you about the secret knock, so thought I'd play along." He led them to his makeshift office, which probably had been the store manager's office at one time. "Grab a couple chairs and I'll get you up to speed."

Oldfield settled into a creaky leather office chair which had seen better days. MC and Cam sat across the desk from him.

He opened a thick three-ring binder and skimmed a couple of pages. "Arty Musselman, CFO. Old college buddy of Stennard's. In fact, Mike, Gavin, and Arty all went to college together. As you know, he's agreed to a wire and will attempt to convince his cohorts to spill the beans. Our guys will get him set up a couple hours before his scheduled meeting next Friday with Stennard and Thomson.

"He's a bit green around the gills and we can't afford to have him blow it now. Things are moving quickly and we need to get as many conversations recorded as possible.

"When I had you two here last Friday I'd hoped to send you out to the Stennard offices, but as I told you then, we had a conflict. Today should be much better for us.

"White, I want you to talk to Musselman. Give him the lowdown on the repercussions should he bail. Mail fraud and money laundering convictions will put him away for quite a while. Give him a friendly reminder of what life in prison might mean for a wee man like him." Oldfield's ebony eyes glinted.

Cam leaned forward. "I can definitely convince Mister Musselman of the wisdom of his full cooperation. I'm very persuasive."

"Good." Oldfield focused his attention on MC. "I want you to work on the receptionist."

"Taylor Pederson," MC said. "According to my information, a young woman, a few years out of high school. No college degree. My guess is Stennard hired her for front desk eye candy. Of course, I could be completely wrong. She could be a conduit to the big boss, but it seems unlikely."

Oldfield leaned back in his rickety chair and folded his hands over his midsection. "I like when my team is thinking ahead. Makes my job easier."

"We're definitely team players." Thoroughness and tenacity weren't qualities exclusive to FBI agents, MC thought.

"Speak with Ms. Pederson. See what she might know or might have seen, without letting her know anything is wrong. Think up something postal-related. The mail wasn't getting delivered or whatever. White needs time alone with Musselman in the second floor Accounting office, to work his magic. And remember the fewer people who see you, the better. Got me?"

"Yes," MC said.

"Good, head on out." Oldfield rose. "Report back here afterward."

They were headed toward the rear exit when Agent Steve Braun, one of the FBI surveillance equipment specialists they'd met the previous week, hollered, "Hey, McCall. White. Hope you get Musselman nailed down. We installed some sweet equipment in Stennard's office for the meeting."

MC said. "What'd you guys rig up?"

"You'll love this." Agent Braun scooted his chair closer to the two inspectors. "We sent Bill in disguised as a contractor to check out the smoke detectors in the building. Blondie at the reception desk bought it and gave him the run of the building."

MC said, "And?"

"He swapped the ceiling-mounted smoke detector in Stennard's office for a fake with a video recorder in it. We downloaded software from the computers." He pointed toward the bank of PCs where he and three other agents sat working. "All we do is click on a web link, and we can watch it live stream and record it, too."

Cam said, "No shit."

"Check it out." He rolled his chair over to the long table where four PCs and a couple of printers sat in a nest of cables. He navigated to a web site, and the image of an everyday household item filled the screen.

MC said, "It's a smoke detector."

Agent Braun used the mouse to flip to another image. "Outside it's your basic plastic smoke detector. But abra cadabra—open it up and inside is a camcorder the size of a deck of cards. There's a slot for a one-hundred-and-twenty-eight gigabyte SD card and the option to watch live. The recorders allow for voice activated recording, scheduled, or continuous recording. It's set on a schedule so we won't have a lot of dead air to wade through or have to swap out SD cards."

"Impressive," MC said.

Cam stepped closer to the computer. "Amazing what they've done with recording equipment."

Braun picked up something from the table. "We also have this little beauty."

Cam gazed at the object. "I assume this isn't a typical flash drive."

Steve laughed. "This baby is a sixteen-gigabyte voice-activated recorder, too."

MC picked up the small black USB drive and rolled it over to show them an on/off switch. "James Bond is drooling."

"We've given Arty a similar USB drive so that he can record phone conversations with Stennard and Thomson. High quality audio. The more the better." Braun retrieved the device from MC. "So, you guys need to make sure our boy gets himself to Stennard's office for the meeting and leave the rest to us."

Cam said, "You can count on us."

Back in the car, Cam checked his watch. "All the spy stuff made me hungry. I didn't have time for breakfast this morning. Had to drop off the kids at daycare."

MC scribbled some notes in her ever-present notebook. "Let's grab a bite to eat. I think there's a Perkins a half mile from the Stennard building."

Cam put the car in gear. "Sounds like a grand plan."

H

MC and Cam arrived at Stennard's Lake Minnetonka offices at eleven a.m. They'd taken their time over breakfast in order to go over their action plan. The Stennard compound sat tucked into a cul-de-sac at the end of a three-quarter-mile-long section of commercial buildings. The windows in the brown brick four-story building were dark tinted. The surrounding grounds were parklike, all picnic benches and lush green grass turning a winter yellow-brown.

The section of the parking lot to the left of the building was labeled "Employee Parking" and provided a glimpse of how much money sat in the CEO spot. The shiny obsidian black Mercedes-Benz G-Wagon had to be Michael Stennard's ride. Stennard was known to flaunt his wealth. Several other high-end vehicles were on display as well. Cam parked their shabby Impala in a visitor parking space, and they entered a plush lobby, skirted around a zen rock water fountain set in the center of the entryway, and made a beeline for a reception desk that looked made for the likes of Paul Bunyan.

"Nice digs," Cam said as they crossed the cushy merlot-colored carpet. "Gives a whole new meaning to 'roll out the red carpet,' eh?"

"Too true," MC said as they arrived at the desk. Three hallways branched out from the desk; one leading toward the back of the building behind the desk; and one to the right; the last to the left.

A blond-haired, blue-eyed receptionist perched behind the desk. "May I help you?" A blazing white smile followed her greeting. Taylor Pederson's name was stamped on a plastic faux gold nameplate displayed prominently front and center on the desk.

"I'm Postal Inspector MC McCall, and this is Inspector Cameron White." MC gestured toward Cam.

"What can I do for you?" Taylor's eyebrows drew together over a nose that may have been cute at one time, but now slanted right and sported a bump on the bridge.

"We need to speak to Arthur Musselman," MC said. "I believe he's expecting us."

"One sec and I'll buzz him." Taylor pressed a couple buttons on a black phone system, which ate up about a third of her desk space. "Mister Musselman, there are a couple of Postal Inspectors here to see you? Uh-huh. Okay." She hung up the handset. "You can go ahead. Take the elevator to the second floor. His office is the first one on the left." She swiveled her chair slightly and pointed out the elevator alcove behind the reception area.

MC said quietly to Cam, "I'll hang here and chat with Taylor." She dug out her notebook and pen.

"Sure thing." He made for the elevator.

MC set her bag on the floor and leaned against the reception desk, forearms resting on top, and smiled. "Mind if I ask you a few questions?" She didn't want to freak out the young woman.

"Me? Questions about what?" Taylor's eyebrows drew together again, and she began repetitively clicking a ballpoint pen.

"My partner and I are investigating a complaint of mail theft in the area. We're talking with as many businesses as we can to determine if it's a widespread problem."

"Really?" Taylor visibly relaxed, though she continued to click the pen. "I don't think we've had any problems."

"Are you the one who handles the mail? Is there a mailroom?"

"I handle the mail. We don't have a mailroom. The mailman drops off the mail here and if there is any outgoing I give it to him, or if I'm not here, one of the accountants will give it to him."

"Good. That way there's less chance anything would be missing. I'd be more concerned if the carrier was delivering the mail to a box curbside."

MC wrote Taylor's answers and reactions on her note pad. She unobtrusively scanned the surroundings as the receptionist continued with her click-click-clicking. MC wanted to rip the pen from Taylor's hand and jam it into the young woman's eye. Instead she asked, "Have you noticed anyone behaving unusually around the place? It could be employees or anyone coming into the building who you think doesn't belong."

Taylor frowned. "No, I don't think so."

MC hoped Cam wouldn't have to spend too much time with Arty because she was running out of questions to keep Taylor occupied.

"Nothing unusual lately, then?"

"Nope. Nothing weird at all." Taylor finally set down the pen. What a relief. "Why would anyone want to steal the mail, anyway?"

"Believe me, there are a multitude of reasons. Money and fraud are at the top of the list." MC met the younger woman's gaze, wondering if the word fraud would draw a reaction.

A loud male voice bellowed from behind one of the office doors, "Because I said so!"

"Oh, geez." Taylor jumped, hand to her chest.

"Trouble?" MC asked.

"I dunno. That's Len. Len Klein—the head of security." Taylor leaned forward. "To be honest, he gives me the heebie-jeebies."

A door halfway down the hall, just past the elevators, flew open and a man with a cell phone clamped against his ear strode out. He stopped and glared at the reception area and then the opposite way toward the rear exit before deciding to head toward MC and Taylor.

"I'll deal with you later." He pulled the phone away from his face and dropped it into a pocket of his black cargo pants. Black was apparently his color since he was dressed in all black, right down to his combat boots.

"Taylor?" Klein barked. He appeared to be a couple inches taller than MC, barrel-chested, and sported the standard military buzz cut. Black eyes blazed at MC, even though he was speaking to Taylor.

"Yes, Mister Klein." Taylor's voice quivered.

"Who do we have here? A new client? You sound nervous, Taylor. Is there a problem?"

"Uh, no. No problem."

"Is there something I can help you with?" He ignored Taylor's response and came around the desk toward MC.

"I'm speaking with Ms. Pederson about a matter." MC pulled aside her coat enough to display the badge clipped to her belt.

His eyes widened slightly. "Postal Inspector, huh? What brings you here?"

MC wanted this guy gone before Cam returned. "We've had a report of stolen mail in the area so we're checking with all the businesses to see how widespread the problem may be."

After she uttered the word mail, he lost interest, kind of like a balloon deflating. "I don't know nothin' about no mail being stolen. Taylor's the best one to answer questions about the mail." The air was less charged with friction as he hustled back down the hall from which he'd come.

MC watched him disappear. "Nice guy."

"I guess you can see why he kinda scares me." Taylor began clicking the pen again.

Before MC could respond, a soft ping sounded and Cam exited the elevator with another man, who MC recognized as Arty. They chatted in hushed tones as they made their way toward the front desk.

"We're done here for now," MC said to Taylor. She stowed her notebook and pen and buttoned up her coat, thanking her lucky stars Cam's timing was right on. If Klein had seen him coming out of the elevator with Arty, he may have become suspicious and their cover story about mail theft would've been blown.

"Okay." Taylor shuffled papers around the desk. She'd definitely relaxed after Klein was out of sight.

"Thanks for your help." MC handed her a business card. "If we have any more questions we'll call or come back. And please let us know if you have any problems with your mail."

"Will do." Taylor took the card and pushed back from the desk. "I've got some filing to do. Have a nice day." She wandered down the hallway where Cam and Arty had come from.

"I think you're all set." Cam clapped a hand on Arty's shoulder. "Right?"

Arty nodded. "I'm fine. All set." He peered around nervously. "I'll be glad when it's all done." His Adam's apple bobbed up and down as he swallowed. "Mike, Gavin and I have been friends for a lot of years."

Cam said, "I know it's rough, but hang in there. Remember, you need this or your deal with the US Attorney falls through."

Arty fidgeted and glanced around again. "You're right. I'm tired is all."

"You'll be okay." Cam cast him a last glance as he and MC left.

"Damn. You sure he can handle this?" MC checked back over her own shoulder at Arty, who was retreating toward the elevator.

"He's nervous as hell. Something or someone spooked him, but I believe he's determined to do the right thing. And to save himself from a harsher sentence."

"Partner, you have impeccable timing."

"How so?" Cam pushed the door open and motioned for MC to precede him out.

"While you were with Arty I had the pleasure of meeting Len Klein, head of security. A Rambo wannabe. He was interested in who I was and why I was talking with Taylor. She was freaked out by his mere presence."

"Shit. Could've thrown a wrench in things, if he'd seen me and Arty together." Cam fished the keys out of his pocket. "Let's get the hell outta here before anyone else sees us."

ℋ

Klein exited the Stennard building via a rear door leading to a parking lot with barely enough space to accommodate the five security vehicles. He lit a cigarette and smoked as he paced back and forth in front of a five-gallon plastic bucket of sand which served as the butt receptacle. The postal inspector pinged his radar. She'd remained cool and alert during their encounter. Most women feared him. Not her, though. Stolen mail, he thought. He didn't for one second believe that story.

Klein stubbed his half-smoked cigarette in the sand and yanked his Blackberry from his pants pocket, putting his suspicions about the inspector on the backburner. He texted Nick Wooler: *Do you have the goods for tonight's party at Stennard's house?*

Nick responded: *Yep.*

Klein sighed and rubbed his chin. Communicating with Nick could be frustrating. He was a man of few words, which Klein respected, but sometimes he wished he didn't have to drag every single word out of the guy.

And you and Quentin will be there at nine o'clock?

He had scheduled Nick Wooler and his shadow, Quentin Laird, to serve as security at a private party at Michael Stennard's Lake Minnetonka home. Sex, drugs and rock-n-roll were imperative for all of Stennard's private gatherings. Klein, as head of security for Stennard Global Enterprises, was responsible for providing the security for all job-related and personal events. Though not part of his official job description, he oversaw the booking of all entertainment. On tonight's agenda: a local DJ, cases of booze, and an array of drugs—everything from pot to cocaine—along with several ladies of the lush and lascivious variety.

Klein liked Nick, a local thug with connections to a fairly prosperous drug ring, and his buddy Quentin Laird. The two men were in their mid-twenties, streetwise, both having grown up in the rougher parts of Minneapolis. They held no official positions of employment with Stennard Global Enterprises. Instead Klein paid them cash, and lots of it, for their services. They provided the drugs for all parties as well as patrolling the residence and escorting rowdies out before they could make a scene, thus keeping local law enforcement from coming down on Mr. Stennard. They packed heat, and Klein never asked if they were registered or not. What he didn't know couldn't come back to bite him in the ass later.

Nick texted: *Chill. We got this.*

Famous last words. Nick's agenda didn't always coincide with the needs of the company. Quentin pretty much followed Nick's lead in everything. Hopefully, Nick had everything under control for tonight's event. Mr. Stennard was depending on some quality pot, a mound of cocaine, and a colorful assortment of pills to ensure everyone partied to their hearts' content.

Klein stuffed the device back into his pocket and stomped around the side of the building. He rounded the front corner in time to see the woman postal inspector in the passenger seat of a dirty sedan. The sunlight obscured the driver from Klein's view. He backpedaled around the corner of the building and poked his head around. The car exited the parking lot and sped off down the road. While that woman's presence still bothered him, he decided he had more important things to worry about.

Klein reentered the building through a side door and headed toward his office, his thoughts focused on the upcoming party.

The elevator dinged and the doors slid open. Arty Musselman emerged and scurried past Klein without a glance.

"Hey, Musselman," Klein said, with no response from Arty, which Klein found odd. The pipsqueak was usually so polite.

Klein followed him to the reception area to ask Taylor if she knew what was bothering Musselman, but she was nowhere in sight. He stood behind the desk and watched Arty, hunched over and mumbling to himself, as he passed through the glass front doors.

Klein noticed a white business card on the floor near Taylor's chair. He picked it up. Embossed in blue lettering was, *MC McCall, US Postal Inspector, Twin Cities Domicile, 612-555-2200.*

He tapped the card on the desk. That feeling of unease crept in. This woman inspector was bad news, and he needed to find out why. He typed her information into his Blackberry contacts and tossed the card on the desktop.

Chapter Two
Friday, October 31

Barb Wheatley sat stiffly, deliberately sipping her very full mug of hot tea with care. She wore a black felt witch's hat, her refined version of a Halloween costume, compared to MC's more comical Batman getup, which consisted of a black plastic mask with pointy "bat ears" and a black cloth cape tied around her neck, the yellow and black oval-shaped Batman logo ironed on the back.

Wisps of cinnamon spice tickled MC's nose. She rested an arm across the back of the couch, not quite daring to touch her partner's shoulders for fear of an awkward tea spill. They both ignored the low drone of the TV, which was tuned to a favorite crime show. Wind-whipped leaves scratched eerily at the window behind them.

"I'm always careful in the field," MC said, her tone soothing and carefully modulated. "It's not like we're investigating a murder or something."

Barb set her cup on the coffee table, the tiny string from the teabag straggling down the side. "Murder? Why would you even say murder?"

MC did a mental palm smack to her forehead. "A poor attempt to allay your fears. My point is, postal inspectors don't face imminent threats like street cops do on a daily basis. At least not normally." She pushed the Batman mask higher up on top of her head.

"But there are so many different agencies involved. I don't remember you ever being involved in such an expansive investigation." Barb finally met her eyes. "I know you're a perfect choice for the assignment, but..."

MC shifted to face her. "I love you. You're my staunchest supporter. I promise I'll do my best to stay safe. And I'll come home to you at night. But seriously, this is fraud. Bigger-than-I-ever-imagined fraud." MC felt her face heat up with excitement. She envisioned this was how Batman must feel every time he took down the Joker or the Riddler.

Barb nudged her in the ribs. "What are you grinning about?"

"Do you think Batman felt like I do right now every time the Bat Signal flashed in the sky above Gotham City? Ready to make the world a safer place?"

The doorbell sounded and fists pounded on the front door followed by a muffled cacophony ending in, "Trick or treat!"

Barb rose. "I've got 'em this time."

MC watched the closing credits roll as she listened to Barb open the door.

The scent of melting candle and scorched pumpkin floated into the living room along with the tang of wet leaves.

Deeper voices hollered, "Trick or treat!"

Uh, oh, she thought. She knew how Barb felt about the "big kids" begging candy on Halloween.

At that moment the little bird in the old cuckoo clock on the wall appeared nine times, each punctuated with a call of 'cuckoo.' Nine o'clock was the witching hour, ending their handing-out-candy ritual.

Barb blew out the candle and shut and locked the front door of their one-and-a-half story bungalow in Saint Paul's Highland Park. Their humble abode was eclipsed by expansive two-story homes throughout the neighborhood, some with distended appendages sprouting out the back, the coveted four-season-porch eating up the yard.

MC loved the locale. They were close to main freeway arteries and to the Mississippi River, where she loved to run.

Barb shut off the outside light and wandered back to the couch. "I refuse to give those big lugs candy."

MC raised her eyebrows and nodded toward the green plastic bowl. "I'll take care of the leftovers."

"I think not."

The opening scene from the show *Blue Bloods* filled the TV screen. MC reached for the bowl, which was about a quarter full of Reese's Peanut Butter Cups, her all-time favorite candy bar.

"No way. I know exactly what you'll do." Barb slapped MC's hand. "You'll start and won't be able to stop. Then two days from now you'll be moaning about another cold sore." Barb held the bowl tight against her middle and sidled away.

"C'mon." MC stood and reached again for the bowl. "You don't want to give them out, and I know *you* won't eat them." She knew she sounded like one of Barb's second grade students, but it was too much fun to tease.

Barb held the bowl aloft. "I refuse to give them to overbearing teenagers. Halloween is for young children who are excited about wearing a costume. Those older kids don't have any Halloween spirit. I swear it's about greed. Well, maybe not exactly greed, but—"

"I know. After nine o'clock nothing good happens. The troublemakers are on the streets and the fun is over. So, why not hand over the candy to a responsible adult?" She maneuvered closer to her partner, eyes glued on the neon bowl.

Barb held up one hand in the "halt" position. "You don't need any more chocolate tonight." Barb spun and beat feet down the hallway toward the back of the house. She was quick—MC had to give her that. Barb's twenty years as a second-grade teacher had provided lots of practice chasing down rambunctious kids.

MC pulled her mask in place and bolted after Barb, black cape flapping behind her. "Hand over the candy, you evil wench."

Barb held her black pointy hat atop her head with one hand and the plastic bowl of leftover candy in the curve of her other arm. "I'm not evil, I'm Glenda the Good Witch, and you don't need any more sugar. You've already had three, for Pete's sake. You know your limit is one a day. And you know I only say this because I love you and don't want to see you suffer. Stop your whining."

"Batman doesn't whine. He saves the day." MC grabbed the end of her black cape and snapped it around. "And all the expended energy needs to be replaced somehow. Peanut butter cups are the perfect energizers." MC whipped off her cape and mask. "And US Postal Inspectors need sustenance, too. Hand over the candy or I'll be forced to take you into custody, maybe even use my handcuffs on you." She grabbed Barb and pulled her tight. The plastic bowl went flying and candy bars skittered across the kitchen.

Screw the candy. MC snuggled into Barb's warm skin and familiar scent. "Give me a kiss, my lovely witch." She pinned Barb against the counter and captured her lips.

"Mmmm." Barb wrapped her arms around MC. The witch's hat fell off her head into the sink behind her. After a few long seconds she said, "Well, that's certainly better than fighting over candy. How about we make a run to Flannel and see how Dara and Meg are holding up?"

"You're on, my beautiful gal." MC loved hanging out at Flannel, the coffee shop owned by their two closest friends, Dara Hodges and Meg Daley. The foursome had been best friends for nearly twenty years. MC and Barb helped out at Flannel often and in return they never had to pay for coffee or food at the cozy shop.

Candy bars and costumes forgotten, MC tugged Barb by the hand to the front closet to grab their coats.

⚓

"Trick or Treat!" MC hollered at Dara and Meg as she and Barb hustled into Flannel, where only two patrons sat in the back.

MC drew in a long slow breath, allowing the aroma of steamy java joy to tickle her senses. "Ah, the toasty goodness of caffeinated heaven. Where's the candy?"

The warm golden brick interior created a homey atmosphere. Framed art, all by local artists, lined the walls. Three-by-three-inch placards displayed the price and artist info. MC admired Dara and Meg's support of locals. The art was interesting, ranging from pencil sketches to abstract oil-on-canvas paintings.

And, of course, what tied the whole scene together nicely was Dara in her ever-present flannel shirt and cargo pants, hence the shop's name.

Dara and Meg bought the place a few years after college more than twenty-five years earlier and made it work through thick and thin, including during the latest recession when many small businesses sank into the economic black hole. Despite the big-name chains, Flannel powered on, anchoring the neighborhood.

"Don't listen to her," Barb said. "No more candy. She's about to change into a giant peanut butter cup." Barb kissed MC's cheek.

Meg came around the counter, tossing the rag she'd been using at Dara. "It's our two favorite people. Sorry, MC, we're all out of candy. But we do have some biscotti. Your favorite—chocolate and salted caramel. That shouldn't make you into a big bad chocolate monster."

Dara took the rag, threw it below the counter, and followed Meg. "What's up?"

MC gazed around the tiny cafe. "Thought we'd stop by and see if you needed any assistance corralling rowdy customers." She noted the only two customers were a couple of young women in the two overstuffed easy chairs in the back corner. They were oblivious to the world, hands touching, heads bent toward one another. Two giant mugs sat on the coffee table in front of them.

Dara did an exaggerated scan of the space. "Sure, tough gal, we definitely need some strong ass law enforcement type keeping the peace in here tonight. The customers are totally out of control. Cuff 'em all."

MC said, "Sarcasm will get you nowhere. However, your coffee will buy my undying love and protection forever and ever."

"Amen," Dara said.

"Dara," Meg said, "for gosh sakes would you be nice for once?" Hands on her hips, she gave Dara the evil eye, which inevitably kept Dara in line.

Barb laughed. "Always picked on, poor thing." She gave Dara a squeeze. "We love you."

"Whatever." Dara straightened, ran a hand around the waistband of her cargo pants to ensure her soft, well-worn flannel shirt was tucked in, and ambled toward the counter. "What can I get everyone?"

MC followed Dara, and Barb and Meg sat at a table nearby, already deep in conversation about holiday decorations.

MC said, "We'll take two coffees, dark roast, if you have it. And one of those biscotti your spouse mentioned."

Dara glanced at Barb and Meg, clearly amused by their yammering over when to change themes from Halloween to Thanksgiving.

"It's a good thing they have a knack for prettifying, or this place would be an eyesore." MC accepted the steaming mugs from Dara, balancing a biscotti on top of one. "Thanks."

"Always." Dara grabbed a half-inch high stack of envelopes in one hand and two mugs in the other.

MC and Dara joined their partners

"So," Dara asked, "have the two of you solved the decorating dilemma of the moment?"

"You know we have. No one else around here can be bothered to do it." Meg stuck her tongue out at Dara. "I'm only teasing, so don't get your panties in a twist."

"What's new with you guys?" Dara asked, peering at MC and Barb before tearing open the top piece of mail.

Barb scooched her chair closer so she could link her arm through MC's. "MC has been assigned to a big investigation with the FBI and some other alphabet agencies. Honestly, it makes me nervous, but I know that's not exactly a rational feeling. They want the best and brightest, and that's my gal in a nutshell."

MC felt the blush creeping up her neck. "Um. Yeah." She wasn't usually at a loss for words, but the pride Barb displayed in front of their friends left her *verklempt*.

"Do tell." Dara let the envelope fall to the table.

MC glanced at the half-opened mail piece. "Dara, you do know it's a federal offense to open mail not addressed to you, right?" She took a bite of coffee-soaked biscotti.

"What are you talking about?"

MC pointed to the stack of envelopes. "That envelope you opened is addressed to Meg Daley, not Dara Hodges. I could slap the cuffs on you right now."

"Right, but you won't because we're friends and anyway you have bigger fish to fry. Give us the scoop and stop with the idle threats." Dara slid the stack of mail toward Meg.

MC said, "Okay, but I can't give any explicit details."

"We understand," Barb said. "Just tell us what you can. You're so amazing at what you do."

MC leaned forward. "The US Attorney's office had a visit from a reliable source from this huge company, and he brought along his lawyer. The company is a local conglomerate, has worldwide subsidiaries, and this source confessed that the head of the company, the chief operating officer, and the source himself had been working a Ponzi scheme for more than five years. They hatched a plan that garnered millions for sure, possibly billions of dollars for the parties involved. They've bilked unsuspecting investors of their funds. We think some really big-name investors and even small-time mom-and-pop types may have risked their retirement nest eggs on this deal and lost massive amounts of money."

"Holy shit!" Dara's eyes were wide. "Are you freaking kidding? But, wait. What's the Postal Inspection Service got to do with financial stuff?" Dara's voice was one decibel below an outright bellow. "Ponzi schemes don't have anything to do with mail. I don't get it."

"Shush! Keep it down." Meg squeezed Dara's arm for emphasis and peeked over the top of Dara's head at the two women in back. They appeared unaware of the outburst.

MC grinned. "Not kidding. We got involved because financial documents directly related to the scheme have been sent, via US Mail, to the investors. All it takes is one piece of mail to make a case like this the jurisdiction of the Inspection Service. Check this out: even if they'd used FedEx or UPS, federal statute gives us jurisdiction to investigate."

Dara said, "Still seems odd for the Inspection Service to be investigating an alleged Ponzi scheme."

MC retrieved the rest of her biscotti from Barb and finished it off. "Not at all. In fact, the Inspection Service was the investigative force in the first ever Ponzi scheme."

Dara whistled, "Shut the front door."

MC said, "I'll enlighten you on the historical context. Post World War One, a Boston man named Charles Ponzi—"

"Seriously?" Dara said.

"Yes! He started a pyramid scheme using International Reply Coupons. Those coupons were a way for people in different countries to send return postage to one another. You'd purchase an IRC in one country and they would be redeemed in another for the value of that nation's stamps. He noticed that because of the exchange rates these coupons purchased in Europe were worth more in the US than their original costs. He started buying and reselling them and convinced investors to pony up money promising them a fifty percent profit."

Meg set aside her mail. "Did he make them rich?"

"At first. But then the postal inspectors got suspicious because they could see that International Reply Coupon sales weren't high enough to back up Ponzi's tale about trading them. They were certain he was doing something illegal. He was even using the US Mail to communicate with his investors, but the inspectors couldn't arrest him because no one was complaining about being cheated . . . yet. Eventually, Ponzi's luck ran out. The new investors trickled out and he didn't have the funds to pay out to old investors."

Dara said, "So they arrested him and threw away the key!"

MC said, "Not quite. It took until August of 1920 before investors cried foul and Ponzi was charged with using the US Mail to defraud and then in November he pled guilty and got five years in prison. Eventually he was deported back to Italy. But he left his mark in that the fraud he committed was named after him, 'Ponzi Scheme.' "

Barb said, "I had no idea. We learn something new all the time."

MC swallowed a gulp of lukewarm coffee. "Anyway, back to current day. The whistleblower in our case, see, he's agreed to wear a wire and try to get the CEO and COO to admit to everything. It's gonna be big—I'm talking tidal-wave impact—when it hits the newswires, which could be soon. We're moving fast. The FBI has the lead on the joint task force which includes the Inspection Service, the IRS, and the US Attorney's Office."

Dara whistled. "Impressive shit. You're gonna be famous, I suppose, and then forget about all us insignificant people in your life as you move up to the big time."

"You know better." MC leaned on the table. "You're my best friends. And I seriously doubt there's any fame in this for me, but I'm stoked about busting these assholes. I mean, really, who does shit like that and sleeps at night?" MC stood. "Mind if I grab a refill?"

"Go for it," Dara said.

"Would you top me off, too, sweetie?" Barb asked.

"Anything for the love of my life." MC retrieved her mug and planted a soft kiss on her lips.

A huge smile lit up Barb's face.

Meg said, "The two of you are beyond cute."

Dara stood up and kissed Meg smack dab on the lips, taking her time to make sure it was a good one. Then she asked, "Can I get *you* anything, honey?"

"Um. No. Oh, my." Meg fanned herself. "I'm quite good. Thank you."

Everyone broke into raucous laughter.

The clank of coffee mugs caught their attention as the couple in back stood and bundled up. They carried their empty mugs and plates to the gray plastic bin at the end of the counter, and ambled hand in hand toward the door with a friendly wave. The brisk night whipped into the shop as they exited.

"Ah, young love." Meg sighed and gazed out the window.

Fingers of cold air swirled around their legs. "Brrr." Barb shivered and pulled her jacket tighter. "Winter is definitely rearing its ugly head."

Dara asked, "Were we ever so young we were unfazed by cold, wind, and snow?"

Barb blew into her hands. "Yes, believe it or not. And now we're middle-aged and living the dream. And quite a lovely dream it is."

MC and Dara returned to the table with freshly topped off mugs. MC handed Barb a coffee. "And I'm digging it, this lovely dream."

"Thanks, babe." Barb wrapped her hands around the cup.

Dara said, "Here's to middle-aged love." The four clinked their mugs together and they sipped, enjoying companionable silence.

"How about we help you close up?" MC asked.

Meg said, "Fabulous idea. You two are the best."

#

MC and Barb arrived back home at ten past eleven, both pleasantly tired despite the late-night caffeine consumption, which they had effectively burned off cleaning up and restocking at Flannel. MC helped Barb out of her jacket and led her up the stairs to their bedroom for a romantic end to a night celebrating hobgoblins, superheroes—and major cases.

Later, after Barb was asleep, MC left the warmth of their bed and tiptoed downstairs to clean up the Halloween mess in the kitchen. Then she went in the living room and flicked on the TV. *The Last Call with Carson Daly* was ending. MC stood munching a peanut butter cup, hoping this final treat wouldn't be the tipping point to a cold sore outbreak. On the screen an as-yet-to-be-discovered band named Dolores, from Madison, Wisconsin, performed a song, "Philly's Got a Plan." According to the text on the bottom of the screen, the cut was from their album, *Nectar Fields*. The four twenty-somethings were pretty good. She tapped her foot to the beat as the credits rolled and hit the off button when a commercial for Oxy-Clean blasted from the speakers. Why did some commercials have to be so obnoxiously noisy?

She snuck into the kitchen for another peanut butter cup, though she knew she was tempting fate. Then she grabbed her water bottle from the fridge and her laptop from her messenger bag and curled up on the couch. She wanted to go over the notes on the Stennard Global Enterprises case. The case was, without a doubt, the most complex she and Cam had ever worked. She was incredibly fired up about the collaboration with other agencies.

Even though Barb was fully aware of the case, MC liked to keep her time at home separate from her time at work. She usually tried to wait until Barb was asleep or away before poring through case files.

She double-clicked to open the file at the same time Barb's voice floated down from upstairs.

"MC? Come back to bed. I know you're on your laptop. It's the weekend."

MC hadn't been quite as stealthy as she'd thought. She gazed longingly at the computer before shutting it down. She doused the lights.

"Coming."

God, but she loved Barb. MC was skittish about loving anyone. Her track record was horrible—seemed if she loved people they were horrifically ripped from her life. Her older sister Cindy died when MC was not quite four and Cindy was eight. They'd been at a July Fourth picnic at Minnehaha Falls. MC remembered Cindy, her idol, skipping off with a group of big kids—MC too young to tag along. Soon traumatized kids screamed. Parents panicked. And MC was whisked away by a neighbor without explanation. She'd never seen her big sister again. A vacuous space took up residence in her stead.

MC didn't hear the full story behind her sister's death until she was almost ten. A classmate, Teddy, whose older brother had witnessed Cindy's death, told MC that Cindy's head broke open like a watermelon on the rocks. MC's parents told her the whole story about Cindy falling from a bridge, an accident, nothing to be done but to move on. They never spoke of the incident again.

Fast forward to her parents' tragic death in a car accident a year after she'd started working for the Inspection Service, and she feared she'd never again know the closeness of family. She'd lost herself for a while, searching for answers in bottles of vodka. Eventually she sucked it up and decided she didn't need family.

Now her heart swelled, and she thought about how lucky she was to have spent the last nineteen years with the love of her life, and how lucky they were to have solid loving friends like Meg and Dara.

She hoped for many more years together, maybe even a summer wedding now that it was legal. Barb had been hinting, strongly, at the idea since the same sex marriage law passed. MC shied away, though. All the fanfare and crowds of people dropped her right back into that fateful July Fourth picnic memory. She had an irrational fear that Barb would be severed from her life, like Cindy and her parents had been. And she couldn't bare that deepest darkest memory to anyone—not even Barb. No, Barb hadn't a clue—in fact she believed MC was an only child.

If MC could convince Barb to keep the celebration small—very small, like the two of them and Dara and Meg—then they'd all survive. Maybe they could safely make plans.

Maybe.

Chapter Three
Friday, November 14

Mister Anal Retentive Early for Everything Cam wasn't in the office yet. A miracle that MC beat him in.

She shook off the wisps of angst over Barb's reaction the previous night to being told MC was on call during Thanksgiving. Normally, Barb took it in stride when MC had to work, even on holidays, so her cryptic reaction this time puzzled MC.

They'd helped Dara and Meg at the café, and later she'd tried to draw Barb out on the drive home to find out why she'd reacted so negatively. Barb changed the subject, which MC knew to be the end of any discussion until Barb decided otherwise.

MC had learned early on how Barb's mind worked, percolating thoughts like fine coffee before laying them out like neatly organized lesson plans. The school teacher was used to dealing with second graders and she had the patience of a saint.

Gnawing on a thumbnail, MC powered up her desktop and pulled a stack of folders from a drawer in her desk. The Stennard Global Enterprises investigation file had grown over the past two weeks.

"Morning!" Cam entered MC's smallish, utilitarian office. He dropped his coat into one of the chairs and paced back and forth.

"What's on the agenda for today?" MC asked.

"Last I heard, Arty was going into a meeting with Stennard and Thomson late this afternoon. We're to be at the command center by two, and we'll listen in with the team." Cam rubbed his hands together. "Should be good."

"I hope Arty keeps it together."

"He'll be fine. He told me he's really pissed off by the shit Stennard and Thomson have been doing, even though he's been helping out. Swindling folks—retired folks, especially. They're gonna go down and go down hard."

"I can't wait to put the assholes behind bars where they belong."

Cam said, "I think about my own parents and how they could've been scammed by shits like Stennard. Offering huge returns on investments which never pan out. Burns me to think about the people losing everything. Life savings. Retirement."

"We'll get them. Even though those people probably won't get their money back, at least we'll put these guys out of commission and prevent them from scamming others." MC deleted a couple emails. "I think I'm up to speed on my other work. Nothing needs attention today, anyway."

"I told Jane I'd be late tonight."

"I told Barb the same."

"All right. Wanna grab lunch at Punch Pizza before we report to Oldfield?"

"You bet."

♯

MC and Cam pulled into the back lot of the command center. Bellies full of Punch salad and pizza, they were ready for the big show. The white panel van with the Office Supply Store logos was missing.

After one of the FBI agents let them inside the command center, ASAC Oldfield directed them to a rickety table. "Things are moving along. The team's in place, and everything is set. If all goes as planned, we should get a good start on compiling the evidence needed to obtain search warrants."

MC felt a thrill go through her. Shit was about to get real. She pulled up a metal folding chair and dropped her messenger bag on the floor.

Oldfield's cell phone rang. "What? Where is he? Great. Just dandy." He thrust the device into his suit coat pocket. "We've got a glitch. According to one of the agents on site, Mister Musselman has gone home sick and will not be attending the meeting this afternoon. Dammit all to hell." He leaned on the table. The four agents working the equipment made themselves busy and stayed out of the way.

"Is he really sick?" MC asked. "Or is it cold feet—again?"

"Question of the hour. I'm tempted to send you and White to pay him a visit at home. Keep things unobtrusive. People seem to sniff out FBI from a mile away."

MC grabbed her messenger bag. "We can do that."

Cam said, "We'll use the mail theft cover if anyone gets curious. I can't believe he flaked out—if he did. I'll get him to see reason."

Oldfield said, "But if he's already told Stennard he won't be at the meeting and suddenly changes his mind, that could be problematic, create suspicion. The last thing we need at this point is to let the cat out of the bag and put Stennard and Thomson on alert." Oldfield stopped, hands on hips.

MC said, "On the other hand, if Arty is sick, chances are Stennard will already be rescheduling the meeting."

"True." Oldfield sighed. "Here's what we're going to do. You two go to Arty's home. If he's sick, and I mean really sick, then find out if the meeting has been rescheduled. If he's not sick, then I want you to drive home the importance of him getting back in the saddle." Oldfield scrolled through his cell for Arty's address and showed MC the screen. "He lives in a condo in downtown Minneapolis."

MC typed the address and phone number into the contacts on her phone. She saw the make and model of Arty's car listed, so she tapped that in too. "We're on it."

H

Cam pounded a fist on the steering wheel. "Sonofabitch! I thought Arty was set." He blew out a breath. "Shit. I get all turned around in downtown Minneapolis. I'm directionally challenged, according to my wife."

"Relax. I got this. The Arch Lofts is over by the river near the Stone Arch Bridge." She directed Cam to the quickest route and soon they were eastbound on Interstate 394.

"What's Arty thinking?" Cam asked.

"Maybe the guy really is sick. 'Tis the flu season." She took another peek at the address. "Swanky place he lives in. Not over the top, but definitely outside my price range. One of those complexes made to resemble old warehouses, but all new construction. Basically, wannabe lofts instead of the real deal."

"Wonderful. Not how I wanted to spend my afternoon, in the lap of someone else's luxury."

MC glanced at the info on her phone. "Arty drives a light blue BMW 328i, four-door sedan. Funny, I envisioned Arty driving a Prius, not a BMW."

"With the shitload of money he's made, he could be driving a freakin' Tesla if he wanted." Cam switched into the lane for downtown Minneapolis and was soon approaching the neighborhood.

The four-story newly constructed lofts loomed in front of them. The Arch Lofts logo, situated over the front entrance, wasn't fancy but was a rich gold color, perhaps an attempt at understating the real estate value.

"Underground parking," Cam said. They parked on the street a hundred feet from the parking entrance. "Options for breaching parking security to check for Arty's car?"

"We could wait and follow a tenant in . . . or call Arty's cell."

"Go with the latter. Gimme the number." Cam pulled his phone from the breast pocket of his coat and as MC read him the number, he programmed it into his contacts. Then he tapped to call.

He mashed the iPhone against his ear. "Arty, this is Inspector White. Please call me ASAP. We need to talk." Cam ended the call and tapped the phone against the steering wheel.

"Heads up. Car coming up the street." A squat shiny silver Lexus sport utility slowed and signaled a turn into the parking entrance.

Cam put the car in drive. "Wait for it," he said. The Lexus's taillights flashed once as the vehicle entered the garage. Cam drove in behind the SUV. "Slick as frogshit. You watch the cars on your side, and I'll check out those on mine."

The SUV pulled into one of the first spots and the driver hopped out and hobbled to a nearby door. The woman had bags in both hands and struggled to get the door open before disappearing inside.

"She didn't even notice us," MC said. "I swear people are so self-involved, we could be axe murderers and they wouldn't notice."

He trolled through the dimly lit two-level garage. At the end he pulled into an empty numbered slot and left the engine idling. "Nada."

"Maybe we'll get lucky and find him as we go back up. If not, then we set up shop on the street. He's got to come home sometime and there's only one entrance to the garage."

Cam pulled out of the parking spot. "Lots of empty spaces here." He inched along the subterranean concrete cave toward the exit. "Have you noticed any security cameras?"

"No cameras. Hold it!"

Cam stepped hard on the brakes and leaned over to scrutinize the car MC pointed to. "Right color and size, but it's an Audi."

Back where they'd started, Cam navigated across the street from the garage entrance and put the car in park facing toward the river. He picked up his cell and called Arty again. He put it on speaker, and the sound of ringing mingled with the low rattle of the heater inside the car. Arty's tinny voice came through telling the caller to leave a message and he'd return the call. Cam left another message.

"We should check in with Oldfield." MC retrieved her phone from her messenger bag. "Maybe he's heard something." MC scrolled to Oldfield's contact and reported in. After a brief conversation, she ended the call.

"What's the scoop?" Cam asked.

"Someone called Stennard's office and found out today's meeting has been rescheduled for Monday the seventeenth. Oldfield wants us to sit tight and see if Arty shows up. Then we can nab him and find out what happened."

"We cool our heels some more. That sucks. I want action."

"Come on, Cam, it's not that bad."

MC took stock of their location. A new building one block down and close to the river boasted retail space for lease. A colorful neon Izzy's Ice Cream sign lit one set of plate glass windows, and a more austere sign in the next space advertised a Dunn Brothers coffee shop. "How about some caffeine?" She pointed down the street.

"Good idea. Who knows how long we'll be sitting here."

"I'll make the run. Coffee?"

"Make it a large. Black."

"You got it. Call me if anything happens." MC shoved her wallet and phone into her coat pocket and opened the door. MC entered the coffee shop, and the scent of warm java enveloped her. She took a deep breath and enjoyed the nutty roasted aroma. The barista took her order, and she was out the door in under five minutes. Filaments of steam led the way back to the car.

"You're quick." Cam accepted the cardboard cup from her. "Thanks."

"Not much business at this time of day. Arty call?"

"Nada." Cam sipped his coffee. "This is good."

"Colombian. One of their better blends, in my opinion." MC blew into the sip hole in the plastic lid before taking a cautious taste.

They chatted about coffee, about weather, about Arty. After almost an hour, three more vehicles had entered the garage, none of which were Arty's.

"You don't suppose he has more than one car?" MC asked.

"Nah. Oldfield had someone run his name through DVS. Unless he's driving someone else's vehicle."

The thought hung out there and they continued to monitor the traffic.

"When do you think your supervisor will take a hint and retire?" Cam ran his finger around the rim of his empty cup.

"Not soon enough." MC scanned the street. "I'm sick and tired of him in my face all the time. I swear it's getting worse."

"Have you considered asking him for a transfer to Jamie's team?" Cam shifted to face her.

"I probably should, but I think he'd expect a woman to complain, and I don't want to give him the satisfaction of fighting me. He's so worthless it's hard for me to believe he was ever a good inspector. Though Jamie tells some stories about the days when his dad was partnered with Crapper and they made quite the team." MC couldn't understand how anyone on the job could become incompetent, the way Roland Chrapkowski had. "Maybe the supervisory role flipped some kind of switch inside him."

"I heard that his ex-wife will get half his pension when he retires. That could make for a cranky Crapper. And explain his attitude toward women, in general. Not that I condone such behavior."

"Uh huh," MC said.

Cam continued, "Could you talk to Jamie about transferring to his team? He's a more effective boss than Crapper. And he respects you, at least in my estimation."

"Thanks for the vote of confidence." MC was warmed by her partner's opinion of her. "I know you guys were in training together. Was he fair and honest from day one? I'm curious about whether he's a legacy because of his father. What's his story?"

"Oh, man, Jamie, he's always been at the top. One of those exceptional inspectors, great in the field and a phenomenal leader. He's got the charisma and the brains. A guy you can count on as long as you're on the right side of the law."

"Good to know. The last thing we need is someone to follow the trail Crapper blazed. Whoa. Hold up. Check it out." MC pointed to a car crossing the intersection and coming toward them. "Is that him?"

Cam leaned forward, peering through the windshield. "Yep, that's Arty's car." He reached for the gear shift, ready to drop it into drive. "Signaling to go into the garage."

A sleek compact BMW the color of a cloudless winter sky glided into the downward sloping ramp for the Arch Lofts building.

MC buckled up. "Let's do this."

Cam waited until a Jeep flew past them on the street and made a quick turn into the ramp. The door shuddered as it began a slow roll downward. Cam hit the gas and the Impala slid under in the nick of time. "Holy shit."

"Up ahead. To the left. A splash of red light reflecting off the cement."

Cam accelerated.

A blue car backed out of a slot and pulled forward again, straightening its position.

"Got him." They unbuckled their seatbelts in anticipation.

Cam pulled the car behind the BMW, blocking any chance of escape. He threw the gearshift into park, left the engine idling, and they exited, meeting at Arty's rear bumper.

Cam leaned against the side of the Impala and MC impatiently tapped her thumb against her arm. The man shuffled like a sloth on Valium.

Arty pulled a battered brown leather briefcase from the backseat of his car and fobbed the locks. He pivoted and stopped dead in his tracks. "What?" He swiveled his head left and right.

MC wondered if he was searching for help or making sure no one saw them together. "Hey, Arty. What's new?"

Arty shuffled forward, stowing his keys in a big pocket of his overcoat. "What are you doing here? How'd you get in?" He sniffled, sneezed, and groaned.

MC made a mental note that Arty had all the earmarks of being unwell, possibly even contagious.

Cam straightened from his sloppy lean against the Impala and put his fists to his hips. Scuffing a toe on the dirty concrete floor, he said, "Arty. Arty. Arty. You didn't show up for the pre-meeting rundown this afternoon, and all hell's broken loose tracking you down. What's the story? I'm sure you have a really good excuse for not showing."

"I called in," he croaked. "I told my attorney I couldn't do it today. I'm sick. I went to the doctor. I have strep and an ear infection. I feel like I swallowed glass and someone jammed a wad of cotton in my right ear."

"Did you call anyone besides your attorney?" MC asked.

"Yes. I called Mike's secretary, Linda, while I was at the pharmacy waiting for my prescriptions to be filled. I told her I have strep and the doctor recommended I go home for a couple days so as not to infect others. She put me on hold, and then Mike came on the line. I repeated the information and he told me not to worry, we'd do the meeting on Monday instead." Arty coughed, a painful-sounding bark. "He said he and Gavin would take advantage of the change and make a quick trip to Las Vegas over the weekend. They're lining up some cash with a couple of guys out there."

Cam stepped forward leaning over the cowering man, finger poking in the air in front of his face. "You better be telling us true, Arty. Because if you back out now, it will not go well for you. You need to confirm the new date and time. Get the information to your attorney. Call us. Don't mess with this, I'm warning you."

"I swear." Arty's voice was raspy and nervous. He was speaking quietly, every word an infliction of pain. "I'm not messing with anything. Believe me, I'm done with all the conniving, falsifying, and lying. I want it to end as much, if not more, than you all do. In the weeks since we talked on Halloween, I recorded phone calls on the USB drive the FBI gave me. Calls with Mike. I *am* working on it." Arty raised his hand. "But right now, all I want to do is go upstairs and take some medicine and sleep."

Cam stepped aside.

Arty scooted past, hacking into a gloved fist.

"We'll be waiting for your call, Arty. Feel better."

Cam and MC climbed back into their car and drove out of the parking garage.

MC said, "We best give Oldfield the news in person." She called Barb to let her know she wouldn't be late, as originally expected. The news drew a happy response from her partner. At least something positive came out of the day's clusterfuck.

H

Ghosts and goblins and monsters, oh my!" Barb removed Halloween decorations from behind the counter at Flannel and placed them in a cardboard box on a nearby stool.

Meg clapped her hands. "I like that." She added an armload of decorations she'd retrieved from the front windows. "I can't believe

Thanksgiving is two weeks away. I'm glad you two were able to help tonight because I'm behind on changing the decorations."

Dara and MC rolled their eyes at the antics of their partners as they drank cups of Flannel's best coffee.

"MC, how's the big case going?" Dara nudged her buddy with an elbow. "Give us the dirt."

"You know I can't talk about it."

Dara sighed. "Company line. Spill it."

"I will tell you this. We're close."

Dara said. "Who? What? Where?"

"I can't give you specifics, but once things break, it'll be all over the news."

"Sounds impressive. Stay safe." Meg sealed up the last box of Halloween decorations. "Barb, will you help me bring these down and haul up the Thanksgiving stuff?"

"You bet." Barb picked up two stacked boxes.

"Do you need help?" MC asked.

Barb kissed MC on the cheek as she slipped past. "You help Dara wait on customers while we're slaving away. Earn the free coffee you're gulping down by the bucketful."

Dara slapped a hand on the counter. "Slaving away. Ha! You both live for decorating for the holidays—every holiday. You'd decorate for each day of the week if it wouldn't appear too obsessive."

Barb and Meg presented Dara with their backsides. "Kiss my grits, Dara," Barb said over her shoulder. They giggled and disappeared to the back of the shop.

"Those two would be entertaining in a burlesque show." MC finished her coffee.

"Don't give Meg any ideas."

"Slow tonight."

"Yes, but we were swamped all afternoon. Shoppers. Kids after school. Nonstop customers from before lunch until supper." Dara poured another cup of coffee for herself. The wind buffeted the windows.

"Getting colder by the day."

Coffee aroma wafted through the air, a warm invitation MC couldn't resist. She held out her cup. "I dig this dark roast, rich and smooth." She added a splash of cream and a packet of sweetener. "What are you and Meg doing for Thanksgiving?" MC dropped in a chair at a table close to the counter.

Dara sat across from MC and picked at a glob of goo stuck to the table top. "We're biting the bullet and going up to New York Mills to my parents' house. My sisters will both be with their husbands' families, so Meg practically forced me to acquiesce to my mother's insistent invite."

"Your parents aren't bad. They've come a long way over the years. They seem to really love and accept Meg."

"I'm fifty and my dad still won't say the word gay, much less lesbian. He'll go to his grave without ever uttering either." Dara got up and pushed chairs under tables and tidied up the shop. This was Dara's go-to chore whenever she wanted to avoid a conversation about an uncomfortable topic. Back in her heyday, Dara would've resolved her unease by bellying up to the bar and pounding down whiskey. Those days were long gone.

Meg laid down the law about twenty years earlier—around the same time MC met Barb—either Dara stopped drinking and attended AA meetings or they would sell the shop and Meg would leave. Leave Dara. And leave the Twin Cities.

Dara was at an AA meeting the very next evening.

"Yo! MC!" Dara snapped her fingers in front of MC's face.

MC batted her hand away. "What?"

Meg reappeared carrying two boxes with turkeys stenciled on the sides. "What are you two bickering about now?"

Barb set her boxes on the floor next to Meg's. "You can't be left alone for two seconds without sniping at each other." She opened a box, pulled out a string of turkey lights, and stood on a chair to hang them over the front counter. "Dara, Meg told me the two of you will be spending Thanksgiving with your parents. I'm happy for you."

MC said, "What she really means is it sounds better than what we're doing, which is staying home and having a turkey breast and some of the fixings because we can't go anywhere. I'm on call. And Barb's brother invited her folks to Mankato, so it's just us."

"Which brother?" Meg asked.

"The priest, Father Tom," Barb said. "He's assigned to St. Ignatius parish in Mankato."

"You're both welcome to come along to my parents," Dara said, "but I can see that's not an option. It would've been so much better with you guys along."

"Barb, you could go with them," MC said. "I'd miss you like a fool misses the point, but think how much you'd enjoy a fun family gathering on Turkey Day!" Her smile belied the truth. She didn't want Barb to go. Barb was her family.

"Oh, hell yes!" Dara said.

"Thank you, Dara. But I'm staying home." Barb gave MC her "do not dare question me" teacher face. "We'll spend the holiday together. It will be a quiet one, but at least we have each other." Her tone left no doubt in anyone's mind that her decision was final.

MC said, "I know it's not easy being with me. The job gets in the way, as does my quirkiness about family. But you'll be able to hit all the sales on Black Friday, and Meg will have to miss them." MC's attempt to cheer her partner was met with a frosty stare.

"There are more important things in life than shopping." Barb pulled away and returned to decorating.

The response seemed odd to MC. Barb loved shopping, especially the sales. Something else drove this sudden brusqueness. Perhaps their recent discussions about a wedding were weighing on Barb. MC made a mental note to broach the topic when the opportunity presented itself, which was not at the moment.

Dara cleared her throat and went back to cleaning up behind the counter.

Meg lugged a box to the front of the shop and stuck decals on the plate glass windows creating a toasty, cozy world inside while keeping the cold dark outside world at bay.

MC wandered into the office and found the portable CD player on a shelf and dragged it out front. Determined to cheer the troops, she loaded an Indigo Girls CD. Soon the foursome was singing "Closer to Fine" at the top of their lungs. The music gobbled up all the bad mojo, and the boxes of Thanksgiving decorations came home to roost.

Chapter Four
Monday, November 17

Early in the afternoon MC grabbed her notebook and pen and strolled down the hall to Cam's office, an almost exact replica of her own.

Roland Chrapkowski's voice boomed from behind her before she'd reached Cam's door. "McCall. My office. Now."

MC swallowed a retort and wondered what she'd done to rile the old bastard this time. She stopped in the doorway leading into his office. "Yes?"

"Close the door and have a seat."

Oh, crap, she thought as she settled in front of the gold nameplate with "Team Leader, Roland Chrapkowski" embossed in black lettering prominently set front and center on the tidy oak desk the size of a small island. Not a speck of dust or drip of anything marred the glossy finish. The persnicketiness of his office clashed with his personal appearance, which was disheveled and rumpled on a good day and gave the appearance he'd crawled out of a sewer on bad days.

Chrapkowski slid a file toward her. "This is shoddy work. Doesn't surprise me, coming from you. How many times do I have to explain to you how to do paperwork?"

MC reached for the manila folder and opened it, thinking he'd never told her how to "do" paperwork. She skimmed the documents, which were standard forms along with a written summary signed by her and Cam.

"All the required documentation is here, along with the summary. Everything is digitized, too." Why they were still required to do a hard and a digital copy of everything perplexed her. A couple years earlier, the agency had spent a lot of money in software upgrades. Witness statements, memorandums of interviews, investigative memos, affidavits, search warrants, arrest warrants, photographs and even handwritten notes were all scanned or entered electronically. This allowed for cross-referencing and case-sharing by all inspectors.

"All the required documents are there. However, the required documents are supposed to be in duplicate. My eyesight isn't twenty-twenty, but unless I've gone completely blind, I'm not seeing duplicates. Care to explain?"

Shit. An oversight on her part? Then she remembered: Cam had taken the copies. She'd placed the originals in the file, but he wanted to read through everything one more time before providing the records to management, so he'd taken the dupes out. He probably forgot to put them back in, and she'd submitted the file this morning without double-checking.

Why was Chrapkowski concerned with these files? MC took it as another sign he didn't like her, but she refused to allow him to see her discomfort. She'd play along. For now.

"Cat got your tongue, McCall?"

She swallowed the biting response clawing its way between her lips, thinking his ex-wife deserved more than half his retirement. "I believe Cam has the duplicates. I was heading to see him when you caught me. I'll verify with him and get the paperwork to you ASAP."

Chrapkowski stood and leaned over his desk. "Now, McCall. ASAP is now!" His bellow reverberated, and it was all MC could do to stop from fanning the rancid air. For God's sake the man's breath smelled like a stale barroom—all whiskey-soaked dead ashes.

MC shot out of the chair and yanked open the door. She stormed down the hall, stopped in front of Cam's office, and took a deep breath. A sideways glance confirmed Chrapkowski stood outside his door, meaty arms crossed. She knocked.

Cam's voice sounded. "Come in."

MC entered the office and closed the door at the same time Cam set the phone handset back onto its base. "Sorry to interrupt." Her voice shook, and she wiped sweat from her forehead with the back of one hand, notebook and pen grasped in the other hand.

Cam slid his chair closer to his desk, wheels squealing in protest. "No problem." He raised his head and did a double take. "You okay? You look heated."

"The file I gave Crapper this morning. Do you, by chance, have the duplicates? The sonofabitch is on my ass because I gave him the file without dupes. Like this is the end of the world or something. Jesus flipping Christ." She wanted to pace but there wasn't enough room. Instead, she tapped the notebook against her thigh.

"My bad. I'm sure they're here. Damn. I'm sorry. I meant to stick them back in the folder before I went home on Friday." He dug through a stack of papers on one side of his desk. "Yep. Right here." He handed her the pages, neatly clipped together. "I can bring them down to him."

"No. If you do, he'll find something else to get on my case about. I'll be right back." She opened the door as Chrapkowski waddled up. "Here you go," she said, loud enough to warn Cam of Crapper's presence.

"You might want to be more vigilant in the future, McCall. I don't like when inspectors on my team do half-assed work. Keep that in mind." He snatched the papers from her hand and stalked away.

Red-hot anger skewered her.

Cam came up behind her. "You really should report him to the Assistant Inspector in Charge out in Denver." He stood aside, let her inside, and shut the door behind her. "Seriously. Or talk to Jamie. Do something. He treats you unfairly, not to mention unprofessionally."

"I thought I could ride it out, but I think you're right. I'll talk to Jamie."

"I'm here for you if you need any corroboration." He sat down behind his desk.

"I appreciate your support." She sighed. "Before we were so rudely interrupted, I was coming to see if you had any updates on Stennard."

"I checked in with Arty. He's feeling well enough to show up for this evening's meeting."

"Hopefully, he won't have a relapse and send us on a wild goose chase like last week."

They spent the next hour hashing over their individual caseloads. The inspectors in the Twin Cities Domicile were divided into two teams: a mail fraud and money laundering team, which Cam was assigned to and a miscellaneous team that worked all types of cases, but mostly mail theft, which MC was assigned to. Even though they were both working the Stennard case, which was time-consuming, they also had their own caseloads, fifteen to twenty cases apiece, varying from mail theft to narcotics and money laundering to dangerous mail, including violations like shipping guns via US Mail.

Once they finished, MC stood. "Can we meet at three?"

"Perfect."

MC returned to her office, still stewing over Chrapkowski's relentless harassment. She loved this job. And she was damn good at it. But when Chrapkowski got a wild hair up his ass she thought about a transfer to another domicile, or even considered applying to other agencies. But then she resolved to not give him the satisfaction of driving her out. She'd definitely find some time to meet with Jamie and report Chrapkowski's behavior, though she probably should hash it out with Crapper first. If she was lucky the jerk would retire—or drop dead.

⑂

Cam merged onto the freeway and tucked the Ford Explorer in between a semi and a minivan. They were on the way to the meeting, and both of them were slightly nervous.

MC said, "I hope this meeting goes better than last time."

"No kidding. I thought Arty was solid. Now I have doubts, even after his reassurances."

"Something's not quite right. I can't put my finger on it, though."

"Do you think someone spooked him? Found out he was working with us?"

MC thought about that. "I don't know who could've found out. The whole team has been cautious. You and I are the only ones seen on Stennard property, as far as I know, and we had a plausible reason, but something is hinky."

"Right?"

They made good time going across town and arrived at the task force command by four.

Oldfield granted them entrance. "Good afternoon. Go in and pull up a couple of chairs. Arty is due to be briefed in the van at four-forty-five, and by all appearances things are on track today."

MC said, "That's a relief."

Cam added, "I'm glad he didn't flake out again. I was seriously concerned he wouldn't follow through. By the way, he mentioned last week he had a USB drive with recorded phone calls he'd be turning in. Has he handed it over?"

Oldfield checked a sheet on a clipboard. "I don't see it noted on the evidence list yet. Braun?" He waved his hand at one of the four surveillance equipment techs seated across the room in front of a table lined with PCs.

Steve glanced up from a monitor. "Yes, sir? Hey, McCall. White."

MC and Cam returned his greeting.

Oldfield asked, "Have we retrieved the thumb drive from Musselman and issued him a new one?"

"He was supposed to make the trade-off last week, but then things got hosed. My understanding is the guys will get it today. I gave one of them a fresh recorder before they left here earlier. Anything else?"

Oldfield waved a hand at him. "Carry on." He rubbed his two o'clock shadow. "We'll get that USB drive today." He clapped a hand on Cam's shoulder and steered him over to the surveillance area.

MC followed, bothered by the fact the USB recorder hadn't been retrieved the previous week. Those recordings would be important in obtaining search warrants.

ℋ

Arty Musselman parked his blue BMW in his assigned spot in the Stennard company parking lot. His meeting with the FBI had both eased his mind and put him on edge. They'd foregone putting a wire on him because they'd installed a camcorder in Stennard's office.

His mouth felt like a cotton ball had taken up residency, and he had an empty feeling, the size of the Grand Canyon, in his stomach. He knew he was doing the right thing. After recording phone conversations with Mike over the last couple weeks he'd become even more determined to put an end to the lunacy. What they were doing was wrong on so many levels that if he were Catholic he'd find the nearest priest and drop to his knees and confess all his sins.

"Hey, Musselman. Going the wrong way, aren't you?" Len Klein was on his way out the front door as Arty entered. Klein laid a hand on Arty's shoulder, halting him midstride. "What's up? You can't be bothered to say hi?"

Arty shrugged the hand off his shoulder. "I'm on my way to a meeting with Mike and Gavin, if it's any of your business." He pressed his lips together and ground his teeth. The security guy was always pestering him.

Klein leaned in, arms folded across his barrel chest. Arty tensed and pulled his coat collar together. The guy was malevolent in a Black Ops kind of way. He made Arty's blood run cold.

"Meeting? Really? Mike didn't mention it. Maybe I should hang around."

Arty frowned. "I'm sure if Mike wanted you to stay he'd have told you. Just leave me alone." Arty proceeded toward the hallway behind reception where the elevators were located. The last thing he wanted or needed was to deal with Klein.

Dude of darkness followed Arty to the elevators. "No point in leaving only to have to come back later. I got no plans for tonight, anyway."

"Do what you want." Arty pushed the up button for the elevator and pocketed his car keys.

Klein mumbled, "I'll do what I want." He pushed past Arty and the elevators, used his keycard to access the security office down the hall. The door slammed shut behind him.

Arty's pulse hammered in his temple. Great. Now he's pissed off at me. More stress. A ping sounded, and the brushed steel doors slid open. Arty stepped into the car and was whisked up to the fourth floor where Mike and Gavin's posh offices, along with a mini kitchen and several conference rooms, were situated. A theater of sorts with a giant screen for use in meetings and training sessions occupied one room, although the room was rarely used.

Mike's secretary, Linda, was packing up for the day when Arty entered the outer office. "Hey, Linda. Heading home?"

Linda jumped. "Oh, my, you scared me." A hand with bright red perfectly manicured nails fluttered over her chest.

"Sorry." Arty wasn't used to having such an effect on people. He was the type to melt into the woodwork, and usually they didn't notice him.

"Don't worry. I knew you were coming, but I'm running late, and I've got to get home and get supper on the table before Charles gets there. Mike and Gavin are inside waiting." She pulled her coat on and grabbed her purse.

"Enjoy your evening," Arty said.

She lifted a hand in acknowledgment.

Arty unbuttoned his coat and pulled a white cotton handkerchief from his pants pocket. He wiped his forehead and sucked in a deep trembly breath. As he let it out, he checked his watch. Right on time.

Arty knocked on the solid oak door leading into the inner sanctum.

"Come in," came the sound of Mike Stennard's muffled voice.

Arty entered. A lavish walnut desk, roughly the size of a small yacht, held a desktop computer, laptop, and a phone. Off to the left of the desk was a coffee table, sofa, and two leather armchairs. A floor lamp stood like a watchman between the chairs. To the right of the desk was a mini conference table with six plush, black leather chairs on wheels.

Mike, on the phone as usual, waved Arty over, pointing to an empty chair across from him. Apparently, tonight they'd be sitting around Mike's desk.

Arty set his briefcase on the floor and tossed his coat over the back of the chair.

Gavin was already in the other chair facing Mike's desk. He raised a cut crystal highball glass with about an inch of amber liquid. "Want a drink?"

"No thanks."

Mike also had a drink, probably the same liquor, sitting on a cork coaster on his desktop.

Gavin tossed back most of the booze and stood. "You sure you won't have one?" He tilted his glass towards Arty. "I'm happy to hook you up. Single malt. Good stuff. I hit the boss's private stash."

"No thanks on the Scotch. I'll take a bottle of water, though." Arty tried to concentrate on Mike's phone conversation but Gavin was distracting.

Mike said, "No. No. We're good. I promise you, we'll get those to you ASAP. You won't be disappointed."

Arty got up and wandered over toward the dark wood half-circle shaped portable bar located behind the sitting area of the office. "Who's Mike talking to?" he said quietly.

Gavin retrieved a bottle of water from the mini fridge behind the bar and gave it to Arty. "Dunno. He was on the horn when I got here a few minutes ago."

Gavin seemed uninterested in anything other than his next drink. He poured a neat two inches into his glass and gently swirled it. Light reflected off the golden liquid.

"You okay, buddy? You're practically hyperventilating, like you've just run a marathon." He sipped the Scotch, eyes locked on Arty's face.

Arty twisted the top off the bottle of water and took a couple gulps. "I'm fine. Still getting over a bug." He leaned against the bar and rested his foot on the brass rail along the bottom, trying to maintain his cool. "What's on the agenda tonight?" He fingered the cell in his pants pocket and got the bright idea to record Gavin before the actual meeting.

Arty found Gavin creepy. He'd never trusted him, even back in college. Gavin was always calm and collected, but his eyes were like staring into an ash encrusted volcano. Arty figured they may be out of camera range for the task force recorder setup because the smoke detector/camcorder was on the other side of the office above the conference table and angled toward Mike's desk.

He wasn't sure if the sound would pick up, and was pretty sure the video wouldn't. Before he lost his nerve, he pulled the phone from his pocket. "Wanna make sure this thing's on silent mode so our meeting isn't disrupted." Arty hit the touch screen and quickly tapped the voice recording app, then tilted the phone sideways and made a production over sliding the switch to vibrate mode before slipping the device into the side pocket of his suit coat.

Gavin barely paid him any attention. He was focused on his beverage. "Good idea." He headed toward Mike's desk.

Mike hung up the phone. "Holy shit guys. I was talking with Marco Radcliffe from Skylark International. Sit down. Sit down." He took a slug of his drink and smacked his lips together. "Damn fine single malt." He raised his glass to Arty and Gavin. "They're functioning as the pass-through. I got a guarantee of two hundred million dollars last week in Switzerland."

Arty sat up straight in his chair. "Wait. I don't understand. If you got the two hundred mil from Switzerland, why do you need Skylark International?"

Gavin leaned to his left and nudged Arty's arm. "So, Skylark can buy the receivables back at a discount."

"Fuckin'-A!" Mike hoisted his glass and drained it, then jumped up to get a refill. He danced across the carpet to the bar, saying over his shoulder, "There's a couple stages involved here. First, I gotta get an extension from Fast Eddie. I need three weeks to get the money from Skylark International. Then I gotta get money to a couple other investors screaming for payment. Fifty million and forty-six million. Keep 'em quiet, for a while anyway."

Arty twisted in his chair and watched Mike replenish his drink.

"I've got to sew this one up," Mike said. "Some of the investors have been making waves. There's been talk about notifying the authorities about fraud. We can't allow anyone to tattle. Right?" He threw back the liquor.

Gavin said, "The last thing we need are cops breathing down our necks. We have to be sure there's an exit plan in place. Passports ready. You know the drill. Hopefully, it won't get to that point because of the commitment from Skylark." He regarded Arty and then Mike.

"Right you are, Gav." Mike rubbed his hands together like a kid ready to dive into a pile of presents. His face was candy apple red. "Arty, I need you working on funneling the money to different sources. A couple two, three, no, make it four different sources. Focus on moving money instead of making up purchase orders. You need to move the money to get it cleaned or we're dead in the fuckin' water guys. Dead as damn doornails. And then we'd need to get the hell outta the country. I got my place in the Caymans, so I'm not too worried, but I'd rather stay here."

Arty said, "Good. I'm sick of doing fake purchase orders." He watched Mike standing by the bar, lost in his own semi-inebriated world. "But I'm still not clear what my part is on this new deal." Arty blotted his forehead with his handkerchief as he waited for Mike's reply.

"You bailing on us, pal?" Gavin swung toward Arty. "Mikey, suddenly our guy here is all worried about doing fake purchase orders when up until now he's whipped them out faster than a Nascar race driver whizzing around the track."

Arty's radar blipped. His lungs seemed to have stopped functioning. He felt like he was watching a bad episode of *The Twilight Zone*. Waiting for Mike to defend him, he melted like a wilted flower, sweat dripping down the sides of his face.

Mike didn't hear, or maybe he'd had a hit of cocaine before Arty got there, because he was off on another tangent. "I went to see one of the investors last week, as a precaution. Wanted to cover our asses. Told him I'd probably go out of business and maybe even end up in jail because we bought a whole lot of bad paper—the POs—similar to when people got caught up buying bad mortgages. That was how I put it to him. A great excuse to get us out of this mess, if it becomes necessary."

Arty said, "We didn't buy the POs. I *created* the POs. You told me to make up all the POs."

Mike returned to his desk. "I know. But I told *him* it originated from someone else, not us. We didn't know who, we just bought them."

Gotcha, Arty thought, covering a twinge of exhilaration. He felt perspiration sliding down his back and was grateful he'd kept his suit jacket on so Gavin and Mike wouldn't notice. "Okay. But we didn't buy the POs from anyone, Mike. And I don't understand why we'd say we bought bundles of bad POs from people. Who would we have bought them from?"

Gavin asked, "Why are you so hung up on an inconsequential fib, Arty?"

Arty's heart palpitated, but he concentrated and kept his speech steady to make sure the recording was clear. "I mean, we all gotta be on the same page, right? Tell the same story."

Gavin pointed a finger at Arty. "You, especially, better make sure you're telling the *right* story."

Mike switched gears. "If we don't cover our asses now, I'm afraid one of the investors will sniff out the scam and throw us under the bus. Gavin thinks we need to talk more, Arty. Get our story straight. I don't trust Fast Eddie or one of the others if something starts to go south. And it could. I know Eddie's thrown others to the wolves to save himself."

Gavin said, "It's like Mike said earlier, our situation is similar to those guys who were buying bad mortgages. Brokers all over the place writing up bad mortgages and these guys buying the paper. Some people didn't pay. Couldn't pay up, so they covered their arses. 'Oh, we had no idea we were buying bad mortgages.'" He stood. "My opinion is we have to play our defense similarly, should it become necessary. We were the buyers of these bad POs. The only ones we may have risk on are one or two where you say you did it yourself, wrote up the fake POs yourself. Memorize the details, buddy." He clapped a hand on Arty's shoulder. "Understand?"

"Our risk is higher, though," Arty said. "All of the POs are fake. Not some, *all*. Which obviously means we have more risk. And by admitting we conjured fakes on one would only substantiate our complicity in everything." Arty reached, again, for his handkerchief and mopped his forehead. He chanced a quick glance up at the smoke detector/recorder and wondered how anyone outside the room would be able to make sense of the many-faceted scheme.

Gavin leaned into him. "You sure you're all right? You're sweating up a storm and it's actually chilly in here. Getting cold feet?" Gavin's stormy gaze fixed on Arty.

Arty swallowed, shrank under Gavin's scrutiny. He didn't trust his voice for a moment.

"Oh, come on Gav, you know our boy is in the thick with us. He's got our six. Loyal to the end."

Arty jutted his chin at Gavin. "I'm still recovering from an ear infection and strep." He wiped his damp hand down his pants leg, smoothing the fabric.

Gavin shifted backward in his chair. "What the hell? You contagious?"

Arty stuffed the soggy square cotton cloth into his side pocket and briefly touched the phone inside. "No, but I've still got a slight fever. That's why I'm sweating. Can we get on with the business and forget about my health?"

Gavin laid a hand over his heart. "But, Arty, your health is of the utmost concern to us." He smiled, but the emotion didn't reach his eyes.

Mike stood and moseyed over to the bar again to pour himself another drink. "Arty's right. We need to focus on the situation. Let's wrap this up. I've got a date later."

Gavin rolled his eyes at Arty. "How old is this one, Mike? You need to be careful. The last one was barely out of high school. We don't need any unwarranted media attention, my friend."

For once, Arty agreed with Gavin. "Be careful, Mike."

"You guys are jealous. Tori is suitably past the age of consent. Trust me." Mike leaned against the bar and took a swallow of booze. "Arty, you know what to do? Forget the purchase orders, for now. Focus on channeling the funds we got coming in to keep the investors fat and happy. Oh, and also prepare for an audit because Skylark International might want an audit of our financials before they release funds to us. I'm certain I can talk them out of it, but just in case, you gotta have copies of the PO files ready for them to review."

"Wait! What?" Arty jumped up. "Mike, have you lost your mind? We won't withstand an outside financial audit. We *have* no files. We have stacks of fake POs. Nothing to back up the money going in and out of this place. Zero. Zilch. Nothing." Waves of adrenaline and fear surged through him.

Mike laughed. "Calm down. We'll be fine." He waved his glass in the air. "You got your tightie whities in a bundle for nothing."

"This is not good, Mike. Not good."

Gavin stood and drained his glass. "I told you he was a weak link, Mike." He eyed Arty. "You gotta do what you gotta do here, buddy. Cover our asses. Which means covering your own too because you're in this manure pile just as deep as we are." He crossed to the bar and set his empty glass on the bar top. "I've gotta get home to the missus. We good here?"

Arty dug his hands into his pants pockets and faced Mike and Gavin. "Dandy."

Mike clapped Arty on the back. "See, Gav, I told you he'd be fine. Arty's tough enough." He swilled the remaining liquid from his glass. "I think we all oughta head out." He laid a hand on Arty's shoulder. "Chin up. We're gonna make another boatload of money!"

Gavin said, "Mikey, you sure about him?" He tilted his head toward Arty. "Maybe we should put someone on him? You know, make sure he doesn't flake out on us? Let me put out a call."

"Still in the room, Gavin." Arty retrieved his coat from the chair.

Mike squinted at Arty. "He's trustworthy, Gav. We've had each other's backs since college. Nothing's changed, except we're all older and richer."

"It's on you, Mike." Gavin pointed a finger at Stennard. "You make sure he sticks with the script. Because if you don't, I will. G'night guys."

Mike closed the door and leaned against it for a moment. "You've got him worried. Are we solid? I need to know. I need you to tell me you're with us."

"I'm on board." Arty picked up his briefcase. "I hope you're right about the money, Mike. Seriously."

Mike guided Arty toward the door. "I am, my man. Have faith. You know I reward loyalty."

His assurance did nothing to soothe Arty's nerves.

"Haven't we always come out smelling like a rose?" Mike pushed Arty through the portal.

Arty was hot beneath the cold sheen of sweat coating his body, his mind bouncing like popping popcorn. He pulled his phone from his suit coat with a shaking hand as he left Mike's office and moved toward the elevator. He thought about stopping the recording, but replayed Gavin's comments over in his head.

The distinct snick of the stairway door, to the right of Mike's office, brought him out of his reverie. Had someone been lurking? Len? Maybe Gavin? Who else would be up here? The cleaning crew didn't come in until ten o'clock.

He jammed his phone back into his pocket. Sucking in a lungful of determination, Arty stepped toward the stairway door, once through, he guided the door closed quietly behind him. He stood, taking shallow breaths, listening. His pulse thundered in his ears. He thought he heard a distant shuffle of footsteps followed by another click as a door below closed.

Arty retreated through the door into the fourth-floor hallway. He took the elevator down so as not to let on he'd noticed the snoop. Arty suspected Klein was spying. Or maybe his imagination was working overtime. He sighed and dug his phone from his pocket again. Setting his briefcase on the elevator floor he fumbled to stop the recording app. The elevator reached the main floor and the doors glided open. Arty dragged the briefcase out onto the hallway floor intending to finish his business with the phone.

"Heya, Arty!" Klein sidled up to Arty and slammed a meaty paw onto his shoulder.

Arty jumped and his phone squirted out from his sweaty grasp. "Jesus H. Christ, Len." He grappled with the phone in midair and managed to cup it in both hands. "What the hell is wrong with you?"

"A bit jumpy, aren't we?" Klein said.

Arty's heart plummeted. "No. Now, if you don't mind, I need to be somewhere." He retrieved his briefcase and fled the building.

Arty paused at the glass doors and craned his head to make sure Klein wasn't following. He observed Klein take out his cell phone. Arty felt sick. This whole mess was wreaking havoc with his immune system. He couldn't wait for everything to be out in the open.

He tossed his briefcase onto the back seat and got in his car. A marching band blared inside his skull so he took a couple aspirin dry, and with shaking hands started the engine. The FBI was waiting for him, and while they'd be pleased with the info he'd recorded tonight, he was certain they'd not be pleased he didn't have the thumb drive on him. Tomorrow he'd retrieve it and give it to his lawyer.

He shifted the gear stick into drive and eased out of his parking space and toward the exit. The blaze of headlights reflecting off his rearview mirror burned his retinas. A large vehicle pulled in behind him. Arty maneuvered to the side and flipped the overhead light on, pretending to search for something in the glove box, hoping whoever it was would get impatient and go around him.

No luck.

The monster patiently idled at his rear bumper. He couldn't make out the driver in the rearview mirror because the light refracted like a sunburst. Arty found his phone and hit the app to start a new voice recording. He wasn't taking any chances—he'd cover his ass.

He muttered, "Goddamn, Len, if you're following me . . ." His throat burned with the acid taste of pain reliever and fear. He swallowed it down and put his foot on the accelerator and spoke in a clear even tone.

"It's a few minutes after seven o'clock and I'm leaving the Stennard parking lot. An SUV or truck—I can't see color or driver because of the glare of headlights—is behind me. I'm going to drive around and try to lose them. I can't chance the scheduled rendezvous with the FBI. Damn." He drummed his fingers nervously on the steering wheel as the SUV remained about five feet from his rear bumper.

Arty drove aimlessly around Wayzata, passing strip malls and gas stations and restaurants. He kept his speed at the posted limits, making random turns. Still the SUV stuck with him.

"This town needs more street lights. I think the vehicle is dark, maybe black. Could be one of Stennard's fleet. Might be Len Klein. We've been going 'round and 'round for thirty minutes. Time to end this game."

At a stop sign on Main Street and Bay Avenue he considered his options: find a cop or return to work.

"I'm heading for the police station. Seems safest." Arty navigated right, intent on taking a shortcut across town to the police. He signaled onto a dark frontage road that wound through an industrial area and would dump him close to his destination.

The SUV accelerated and tore around him on the unlit, curvy road. He swerved and hit the brakes as the vehicle planted itself in front of his BMW.

"Now you decide to pass?" His voice squeaked. The SUV brake lights painted the night in bloody hues and Arty made sure his foot was firm against the brake pedal. "Black SUV. Passenger door opening. Shit." A shiver of foreboding scuttled down Arty's spine. The SUV tore off leaving a villain dark as doom behind.

"The SUV left. Guy wearing a black knit mask. He's also holding a . . . I think it's a gun." Arty's voice trembled and his mouth went dry as a rain-starved farm field. "Person standing in front of car pointing a gun at me." Arty slipped the phone into his coat pocket.

The gunman pounded on the passenger side window. "Unlock the fucking doors. Now."

Arty hesitated. He considered taking off. Maybe he should just open his door and run for it.

The guy took a shot overhead. Arty's foot slipped off the brake pedal. The car inched forward.

The gunman pointed the gun at Arty's head. "My next shot goes right through the fucking window."

Arty stomped on the brake and fumbled to comply. "Shit. Shit. Shit. Who is this? Why's this happening?"

The masked gunman jumped into the passenger seat, still brandishing the gun in his black-gloved hand. The weapon was stubby and chunky and aimed at Arty's head. "Drive and don't do anything stupid."

Arty's hands gripped the wheel, knuckles white in the dash lights. "Where?"

"Fucking drive!" Cold metal pushed against Arty's ear. "I'll tell you when to turn."

He didn't recognize the guy's voice. At this point he was ready to hand the car and his wallet over to his captor.

Arty hit the accelerator, and the BMW jumped forward. "What do you want? My wallet's in my back pocket. I've got some cash—"

"Shut the fuck up and drive." The man kept the gun at Arty's head until they got onto a street with lights, then he dropped it to hip level and kept it firmly against Arty's side. "Turn right two blocks up."

Arty followed directions until he pulled into a hard-packed gravel service road parallel to a boat and RV storage business. He didn't recognize the place. His fear intensified as he realized the road was a dead end, and the only lights were those inside the fenced area where behemoth boats and RVs sat covered for their long winter's rest.

"Get out. Leave the car running," the man said.

Arty did as instructed. He stood next to the open door. The gunman joined him. Arty had no clue who the guy was, but a sense of dread dropped over him. The dude stood several inches taller than Arty and appeared bulky beneath his winter jacket. Had someone discovered he had turned whistleblower?

He again tossed out the offer of his wallet, hoping to entice the guy into taking it and leaving him.

The man said, "Move it." He motioned to the impenetrable blackness where dense shrubs lined one side and chain-link the other. The end of the road. "No place to run, so don't even think about it."

Arty shuffled to the designated spot, his mind spinning. Leaves covered the ground behind him in a pre-winter blanket. His fucked-up life was a slideshow in his mind. "Why are you doing this? Tell me what you want."

"Shut the fuck up, asswipe. Down on your knees. And while you're at it, I'll take your wallet. Drop it on the ground." The guy waved the gun at Arty.

Arty pulled his wallet from his back pocket and tossed it on the ground. "Is that a friend of yours in the vehicle pulling in?"

The gunman whipped around peering back down the road.

Arty took the phone from his coat pocket and tossed it behind him into the leaf covered shrub-filled area. He coughed loudly.

"Shut up." The gunman glanced back and forth between Arty and the approaching car. "Fuck."

The driver pulled in behind Arty's car. The mystery SUV only had running lights on. Was this the same vehicle from earlier? Arty watched the driver's side door open, and the driver hurried toward them.

Arty sucked in a breath. "You."

The driver grabbed the snub-nosed weapon from the masked guy and aimed it at Arty. "You couldn't keep your yap shut. Loyalty, Arty, is all I asked."

Arty said, "But—"

The loud click of a hammer echoed, followed by an incredibly loud explosion. The alarm bells screeching in Arty's head abruptly stopped.

⚓

The shooter tossed the weapon back to the gunman. "Needed to be done." He kicked gravel at Arty's sprawled body.

The gunman said, "Shit, man. What'd you need me for if you were gonna do it yourself?"

"Clean this up and take care of his car," he said. He slapped his black leather-gloved hands together. "Remember, I reward loyalty. You'll get the rest of your money after you finish the job." He sauntered back to the giant vehicle and reversed down the road.

The gunman picked up the wallet, killed the engine on Arty's car and doused the lights. The night was blustery enough he doubted anyone would be out wandering around, but better safe than sorry. He strode to the fenced area, climbed over, and jumped onto the nearest stored boat. The vessel was the size of the SS Minnow from the old-time show, *Gilligan's Island*.

He lifted a corner of the canvas cover on the back of the boat. Beneath it, blue plastic tarps were stacked up, along with a bolt cutter and some rope attached to an anchor. Fuckin'-A. This is better than if I'd planned it, he thought.

The bolt cutter went through the chain link like butter. He dragged Arty's dead ass through the hole, thankful he wasn't heavy. He rolled Arty in one of the blue tarps and tied the bundle tight with the rope then hoisted him into the vessel. The canvas cover was easy to resituate over the rear of the boat, and he was ready to go, but then he noticed the bolt cutter lying on the ground next to the fence.

"Aw, fuck me," he mumbled. He hopped down from the boat.

As he grabbed the tool, his burner phone bleated in his jacket pocket. He took stock of the area, and seeing no one around he tossed the bolt cutter under another boat and pulled the chain-link back into place.

"What?" he barked into the cheap plastic device and hustled to the car.

"Do not use that tone with me. You don't want to piss me off. Have you finished?"

The smooth voice on the other end made his blood run cold. "Sorry. Didn't know it was you. It's done. But I need to get outta here like right now. Geez, you barely gave me time to get it done. I did what the boss said and cleaned up really good."

"Boss? What are you talking about? Never mind. I'll call later. Be thorough."

The call ended and he stuck the small phone in his pocket. He started the BMW, then remembered he needed to check for footprints. He ran back and tried to scrape away what he thought might be imprints in the hardscrabble ground. Blood and brain matter were harder to get rid of. He tried scuffing it with his shoes.

"Good enough," he muttered. Back in the car he kept the lights off until he was on Main Street in Wayzata. He dug the phone out of his pocket and hit the speed-dial for a buddy in Minneapolis. "Meet me at the park in twenty. I'm in a light blue Beemer."

"Man, you rolling high these days."

"Fuck you. Be there. Tell no one, not even Quentin."

"I know. Chill out."

He jammed the phone back in his jacket. "Chill out. He tells me to fucking chill out." He hit the seat with his fist. Killing didn't bother him, but damn, the business man was eerily calm, and the gunman knew enough to follow orders and not mess around.

And then the boss showed up and took the shot. He'd almost shit his pants right then and there. Not like when he worked with Klein. No. This guy was serious evil and paid mega coinage for the dirty work. He pulled the mask off and stuck it in his jacket. He drove cautiously. God, he needed a fix.

#

The Command Center crew was excited by the outcome of the evening's meeting at the Stennard offices. Along with what Arty had already recorded on the USB drive, they were almost sure to have enough to request the search warrants.

An hour and a half had passed with no word from the team in the surveillance van assigned to debrief Arty and retrieve the USB from him.

MC tapped a pen against her notebook and glanced impatiently at her watch for the forty-fifth time. Her Spidey senses pinged. Something felt off.

The buzz of a cellphone fractured the heavy silence.

Oldfield picked up the phone from a table and answered, listening for a moment. "Dammit! Check his house. All the usual places. Find him. And when you do, bring him here." He paused. "I'm aware this is a secure site, thank you. I don't care. Bring. Him. Here." He threw the phone on the table.

Agent Braun asked, "Bad news?"

Another agent next to Braun said, "Did we lose him?"

Oldfield pivoted to face the team. "Musselman was a no-show for debrief. What's with this guy?"

MC asked, "Has anyone gone back to the Stennard complex to see if he's there? Called his office?"

"All of those things," Oldfield said. "He's not answering his cell nor office phone. No car in the parking lot. The guy Harry Houdini-ed us."

MC glanced at Cam who said, "I don't get it. Arty was solid. The guy was primed to flip."

"I agree," MC said. "His not showing now doesn't make sense. Something's wrong. We need to find him." A trickle of foreboding ran down her spine. She shoved her notebook and pen into her messenger bag. "Cam and I could search for Arty."

Oldfield ran a hand over his face, his fingers scraping stubble. "All right. Go ahead. Keep me posted." He wandered away cursing under his breath.

They fled before Oldfield blew a gasket.

In the twilit evening outside, Cam yanked the keys from his pocket. Smoke signals of frosted air rose when he spoke. "Where to first?"

MC tossed her bag onto the front passenger side floorboard. "Stennard building. Maybe we'll find someone who noticed Arty leave." She wondered about security cameras. And if Stennard security would share.

At the Stennard complex Cam cased both front and rear lots. Arty's parking spot was glaringly empty. Only ice crystals sparkled on the frozen asphalt where his car would have been. Cam steered into an empty slot at the end of the row facing the front corner of the building. He left the Explorer idling but shut off the lights.

"SHIT," MC said. "Do we even want to bother entering the building?" She checked the clock on the dashboard. "Eight-thirty. Not many lights on. The cars in this front lot may be cleaning crew, or maybe some workers left their cars with the intention to pick them up later."

"True. You catch the black SUV in the slot marked Head of Security?"

MC shook her head.

"In the back lot, the first spot near that side door. Someone from security must still be on site."

"Slimy Len, probably."

"Guess the guy made an impression on you."

"He did." MC replayed her encounter with Len. "At some point it might be a good idea to have a sit-down with his ass."

Cam sat up in his seat. "Lights coming." He pointed toward the side of the building.

A black Escalade tore around the corner from the back lot into the front lot where they were parked, tires squealing.

"Someone's in a big hurry." MC leaned toward the windshield to get a glimpse of the driver. "Too dark to see who's behind the wheel."

The SUV barreled out the parking lot exit without so much as a tap on the brakes.

Cam quickly followed. "Whoever it was couldn't have noticed us or they'd have slowed down. Let's see what we can see."

"Turned left up ahead."

"Roger that."

They trailed the Escalade through Wayzata and into Spring Park. Traffic was fairly heavy for a Monday evening, which provided good cover for them. Cam dropped back when the driver turned into an industrial area.

MC visually tracked the car and indicated a gravel road to their left. "Down the hill. Did you see him go down the hill?"

"Yep. Got him." Cam killed the headlights.

"Johnson's Boat and RV Storage." MC read a giant sign outside a huge cyclone-fence surrounding a white cement-block building on the left side of the road. A yellow sign posted at the mouth of the gravel road running parallel to the fence proclaimed it a dead end. Shrubs and trees lined the right side of the hard-packed rocky lane.

"Odd area to go at this time," Cam said. "Maybe there's a spot to park nearby."

They drove past the dead end and down a hill. Only one way to turn at the bottom of the hill so they took a left. A couple of derelict structures, maybe abandoned, lined the otherwise quiet street. A weed-choked hill led back up to the boat storage site.

Cam parked in front of a building with a faded "For Sale" sign on the door.

MC said, "He can't get out any other way than the way he went in."

"Let's hang back here and see what happens."

"I hope we're not out here waiting around the whole damn night."

"I bet not," Cam said. The wind had kicked up, dusting the windshield with spent leaves.

"They're predicting a huge storm on Thanksgiving night into Friday." MC shivered. "I used to be able to handle the winter, but I swear the older I get, the more Barb and I talk about moving south."

"What, and give up your North Shore haven?"

"Hell, no. We'd go south for the really brutal months, come back for the rest of the year. We've had the cabin renovated for year-round living, so we're all set."

"I'm so jealous. Jane and I will never be able to afford a second home, what with two kids to put through college and all."

"You wouldn't trade those kids for anything. You and Jane have the perfect life."

"We do. But I can still live vicariously through you and Barb."

MC peeked at her watch. "That SUV's been gone a while. You think we ought to check things out on foot?"

"Maybe. I guess you're right."

They quietly exited the vehicle. MC had a love/hate relationship with the wind—it provided some sound cover, but froze her ass.

Careful to tread lightly, she crept, with Cam at her back, along dense, nearly leafless shrubbery lining the gravel road above the side street where they'd parked.

When they reached the end of the shrub line they darted behind a huge elm.

Cam tugged on MC's coat sleeve and whispered, "How about I go toward where the road begins and you climb up closer to the shrubs and see what you can see?" He pointed straight up from where they huddled against the tree.

MC nodded.

Cam took off to the left.

MC traversed the incline and peered through the gnarled gray-brown fingers of the shrubs. She was surprised to see the Escalade parked only twenty feet away with the driver's window down. She went completely still and stooped as low to the ground as possible.

Beyond the Escalade, the gravel ended and turned into a weedy flat area. More bushes and shrubs extended away, swallowed up by the night. The security lights inside the fenced area illuminated roughly half the gravel road. She focused on two men standing next to the Escalade, about ten feet from a small white SUV, a Ford Escape, maybe.

A lull in the wind allowed MC to pick up some of the conversation. Lo and behold, the voice coming from the Escalade was Klein's.

"Gimme that." Klein reached for some sort of case from one of the men. He stood next to the open window, the top of his head even with the top of the car, and he wore a dark knit cap pulled tight over his round head.

Klein leaned out the window and poked a finger toward the two guys, but the wind gusted and MC couldn't hear what he said. Then Klein rummaged around inside the cab before sticking a hand back out and giving Round Head a fist-sized object.

The man stepped away from Klein and unfurled whatever he held.

MC squinted, eyes watering from the wind.

Round Head shifted to show the object to the guy he was with.

Holy shit. It appeared to be a roll of money about four inches thick.

He thrust the roll at his companion and pulled out a phone. He checked the screen and shoved it back in his pocket and pulled another from his other pocket. This one he clamped to one ear and slapped his free hand over his other ear, presumably to block the whipping wind.

"Yeah!" he hollered. "I told you we took care of—" His words were swallowed by the squall. "—the fuck? I told you we didn't find no phone. You were there, why didn't you ask him first. You think—"

Whatever else he said was blown away.

The other guy fidgeted with the money roll and glanced between Round Head and Klein, who was preoccupied with something inside his car. He gripped the roll of money and wrapped his arms around himself.

"Fuck!" Round Head returned to Klein's car. "We done?"

Without waiting for a response, Round Head spun around and grabbed his partner by the arm. "C'mon. We're outta here."

Klein stuck his head out the window again. "You keep in mind what I told you. Wooly! You hear me? Yo, Wooly!"

Round Head, or rather, Wooly, raised his hand in a wave, probably acknowledging he'd heard, loud and clear. The sidekick, a skinny guy a couple inches shorter than Wooly, wearing a hoodie under a puffy winter jacket, hustled to the passenger side of the white SUV and quickly climbed in. The driver hit the accelerator, spitting gravel, and leaving Klein sputtering in a gritty cloud.

MC could see Klein was still absorbed with something before he closed his window.

She trekked back to the tree, and Cam joined her moments later.

"It's Klein," she said. "And I think he called one of the guys Wooly or Worly, maybe. Let's roll. I think ol' Len will be leaving any second."

Back in the car and shivering, they followed Klein to a condo complex in Spring Park less than a mile away.

The red brick building and surrounding grounds of the complex were tidy and newer. An expansive turnaround driveway with a lighted fountain that still spouted water decorated the front.

They watched Klein pull around the far side of the building.

"Wait here." She jumped from the Explorer before Cam could say a word and followed the driveway around to the right. She peeked around the corner of the building. Klein was leaning out the open window and waving a card in front of a reader posted at the top of a ramp that she assumed led to an underground parking garage.

She jogged back to the car.

"What the hell, MC? Give a guy some notice before you bail, huh?" His brows furrowed. "I can't back you up when you take off like that."

"Sorry. Klein must live here. He rolled into a secured underground parking area."

"Back to the command center?" Cam still scowled.

"Better hope your face doesn't freeze like that." MC suppressed a grin. "Don't be mad."

Cam heaved a sigh. "Seriously, don't jump ship again. Okay?"

"Okay." MC crossed the fingers of her right hand, which rested on the seat next to her leg out of Cam's line of sight.

"And don't think I'm oblivious to your childish stunt of crossing your fingers when you agreed." Cam fixed his gaze on her as he stopped at a red light. "I know you better than you think, MC."

⌗

When they pulled into Command it was after ten. Agent Braun let them in, and they joined a couple other agents at the PC table.

Oldfield was on the phone behind his desk in his makeshift office. He quickly ended the call as they entered. "You're back. Good." He called out, "Braun. Roberts. In here. Bring chairs."

The two FBI agents dragged in chairs to flank MC and Cam.

"Tell me you have good news." Oldfield said.

MC said, "No Arty."

"No one else has found him either," Braun said.

Roberts shook her head. "Not one peep out of him."

Oldfield leaned back and rubbed his hands over his fatigue-plagued face.

"We did, however, see Len Klein." Cam filled in the FBI agents on the details of the odd meeting between Klein and the two other men.

Oldfield tapped a finger against his chin. "Wonder what that was all about. You're certain you weren't spotted by any of them?" He leaned forward, elbows on the desktop, and pinned MC with an intense stare.

MC said, "One hundred percent positive. No one saw us."

"I didn't notice anyone else in the vicinity," Cam said. "I'm certain we weren't seen at any point."

"I think we'll call it a night." Oldfield stood, stifling a yawn. "We'll reconvene here tomorrow morning at nine. White, McCall, I'll clear it with Sanchez and Chrapkowski. We need all eyes and ears on this until we locate Musselman. I can't believe he rabbited on us." Oldfield waved a hand. "Go home."

MC and Cam said goodnight to the agents and hustled from the building.

"Arty didn't rabbit. I'm sure of it." Cam started the car.

"I agree. Something, or someone, happened to him. And I have a terrible feeling Len Klein had a hand in it." MC gazed out into the inky forbidding night. "And what was in the case Klein got from those two tonight? The roll of cash he handed over was thick. A giant fistful of bills."

Chapter Five
Tuesday, November 18

The blaring of the alarm woke MC at six a.m.

"Is it really only Tuesday?" She rubbed grit from the corners of her eyes and rolled to spoon Barb from behind.

"Yes." Barb tugged the blanket under her chin and snuggled into MC. "Will you be late again tonight?"

"Don't know. Cam and I report to the command center this morning. Not sure what's on the agenda other than tracking down our whistleblower." MC let her eyes slip closed for a few moments.

"I thought we'd have dinner with Dara and Meg tonight and help close up the shop."

"You know I'm all about hanging at Flannel."

"Unless you can't get away from work. Big important case and all." Barb disentangled from MC. "I'll get the coffee started."

"I'm sorry."

"I know you are." Barb disappeared out the bedroom door.

MC made the bed and hopped into the shower. Fifteen minutes later, freshly cleansed and dressed in a white button-down oxford shirt and black chinos, she padded down the stairs in stocking feet.

Barb sat in the breakfast nook tucked in the corner of the kitchen. The bright yellow leather booth and retro Formica-topped table was one of their favorite places in their tiny one-and-a-half-story bungalow. Barb sat with the *New York Times* spread open before her, a mug of coffee sending plumes of aromatic steam drifting upward.

MC kissed Barb's cheek. "Please don't be mad. I promise I'll do my best to be at dinner tonight. You know my family is important to me."

Barb grabbed MC's hand and put it to her cheek. "I know. Sometimes the job seems to suck the life out of you. Especially your cranky supervisor. Misogynistic asshole."

MC cupped both hands around Barb's face. "Ooh, them's fighting words."

Barb knit her brows together, and a pinkish tinge crept across her rounded cheeks. "I don't know why they don't force him to retire." She heaved a sigh. "His crappy attitude, no pun intended, is not your fault. You're the best inspector in the damn agency. And I love you for being so dedicated. Maybe

I have the pre-holiday blues or something." She clasped MC's hand and planted a kiss in her palm.

MC's hand tingled where Barb had kissed it. "How about some toast with peanut butter?"

"I'd love some, but can I grab a shower first?"

"Of course. Holler down when you want me to pop the bread in." MC prepped a mug of coffee at the counter as Barb headed upstairs.

She contemplated Barb's description of Roland Chrapkowski. Aloud she said, "Truth." Then she refocused her energies by grabbing the *Times* and reading a story about yet another corrupt New York City official.

#

MC gathered the collar of her black wool coat tighter as she battled the frigid wall of wind and lurched from the parking lot to Flannel. The meteorologist on NPR had said the temp was twenty-three degrees, a record low for this date. Winter was definitely baring its icy fangs.

Chimes announced her entrance to the crowded coffee shop. She waved to a flushed Meg behind the cash register and stepped into line, five not-quite-awake customers in front of her.

She finally reached the counter. "MC, the usual?"

MC handed over her travel mug. "Yes, please. Busy morning. I guess the huddled masses require your exquisite caffeinated blend to thaw their frozen bones."

Meg passed the cup to Dara. "Fill 'er up with the usual."

Dara propped an enormous silver tower into place on the back counter and flipped the tap open. "You got it. Whew. What a rush." She took a blue bandana from the back pocket of her cargo pants and swiped her forehead. "And now I'm slaving away for the esteemed Inspector McCall." She pressed the back of the hand holding the bandana to her brow in faux dramatic fashion. "Will it never end?" She stuffed the kerchief back in her pocket and held the mug in one hand and the lid in the other.

"You're hilarious, Dara." MC reached for her coffee.

Dara held the twenty-ounce silver travel mug out of MC's reach. "In a hurry for your caffeine infusion? Let me make sure I've put in the right amount of coffee. Need room for cream. Maybe—"

Meg slapped Dara's shoulder. "Stop your blustering and give MC her coffee before you make her late for work."

"I wouldn't want to make her late for her very important job." Dara dumped in a half inch of cream and added a sweetener packet. "Here you go, Inspector McCall. May you have a safe and productive day." She handed the coffee to MC and bowed.

MC snapped the lid onto the cup. "You're quite the comedian." She took a cautious sip. "Delicious, as always. Thanks."

Meg smiled. "Will we see you and Barb for dinner tonight?"

"Or will you be too busy hunting down the bad guys?" Dara did air quotes on her last two words.

"We'll be there, barring unforeseen circumstances."

Dara said, "I bet Barb loved that response."

MC narrowed her eyes. "Don't go there. I'm already in the doghouse. I don't need you fueling the fire." She pulled the collar of her coat up around her ears. "Thanks again, you two."

"Be safe," Meg said.

A gust of chilly air billowed into the shop as MC pulled the door closed behind her.

H

MC met Cam at eight sharp in the parking lot of the sandy-colored stone one-story annex building housing the Twin Cities IS offices.

Cam dangled a set of keys from his right hand. "No need for you to go inside. Thought I'd save you the hassle of a run in with Crapper this morning."

"Thank you from the bottom of my heart. I've got to bite the bullet and schedule a meeting with him, though. You don't mind driving all the time, do you?"

"I'm good with being your chauffer."

"Just say the word and I'm happy to take the wheel."

At the command center, MC and Cam chatted with Agent Braun before ASAC Oldfield pulled them into his office.

Oldfield paged through a stack of documents on his desk. "Minneapolis PD found Arty's car, or rather what's left of Arty's car, in Northeast Minneapolis. Corner of a parking lot in Ridgway Park near the Honeywell building."

MC scribbled the information in her notebook.

"And?" Cam asked.

"The car's been stripped. Stereo. Wheels. License plates. The inside of the car was torn to shreds. Seats slashed. Papers strewn all over. Used the VIN to ID it as Arty's." He tapped a finger on the stack of papers. "No sign of Arty."

MC asked, "Any signs of foul play?"

"Not sure."

"Shit." Cam blew out a frustrated breath. "I knew Arty didn't run."

Oldfield held up a hand. "We don't have proof of anything. Let's not jump to conclusions."

MC asked, "Why aren't you sure?"

"Too soon to tell. The MPD Crime Scene Investigators haven't finished processing the vehicle."

MC asked, "Will Minneapolis PD let us have a look-see at the car?"

Oldfield flipped another couple of pages in the file. "Minneapolis CSI hauled the carcass to the Crime Lab-Forensic Garage. They'll go over it with a fine-tooth comb. I'll call and ask if you two can take a peek." He placed the call and waited while the phone rang.

MC leaned toward Cam. "I know the Minneapolis team is good, but maybe we can find the USB drive. Or something. Anything." She chewed on her bottom lip, and they watched Oldfield wait for someone to answer.

"Hello, Chief? ASAC Oldfield. Listen, I have a team running an investigation in conjunction with the US Attorney's office, and it seems your Crime Lab has possession of a vehicle belonging to one of our witnesses." Oldfield switched the handset to his left ear. "A BMW found in northeast." Long pause. "Yes. That's the one. I've got two postal inspectors I'd like to send over to give the vehicle a once over."

MC's eyes were riveted on Oldfield.

Cam's knee bounced like a pogo stick.

"No, not at all. I know your CSIs are very thorough. We just want to doubly cross our T's and doubly dot those I's."

Oldfield's brows rose. He glanced at MC and Cam. "Right. I agree. Sure do appreciate it." Oldfield hung up the phone.

"Are we good to go?"

"Chief Morton wasn't too keen on the idea at first, as you may have gathered." Oldfield leaned back in his chair. "But she agreed you could take a gander. She'll have one of the two CSIs who are processing the car meet you at the front desk." He glanced down at his notes. "Sergeant Bonnie Wilcox."

"Hot damn! Great news." Cam stood up and grabbed his coat.

MC stowed her stuff. "We can head over now?"

Oldfield nodded. "Let me know if you find anything."

In the car, Cam pummeled an erratic beat on the steering wheel as he waited for traffic to clear.

"Maybe I should have driven." MC eyed Cam's hands. "You're a ragtag bag of nervous energy."

"My gut is telling me something's rotten in Denmark." He glanced at MC. "You, on the other hand, are Cool Hand Luke."

"Time will tell us what we need to know. And believe me, I'm happy to be out of the office and away from Crapper's critical eye." She stared at the cluster of vehicles gathered like a steel herd on a blacktop ferry to nowhere. "We can only do what we can do."

"Philosophical pronouncements so early on a Tuesday morning." Cam laughed. "I should take lessons from you, I suppose." Traffic crawled along a few hundred feet and stopped again. "I swear we could walk to the Forensic Garage faster than driving."

♯

Cam parked in the City Hall parking ramp. He fell into step alongside MC, their footsteps echoing in the ramp. Fog hung in dreary strips from the moisture in the cold air meeting the heat blowing from ceiling vents.

They hustled to the smudged glass doors for the skyway across to the City Hall building. They quickly found the front desk and Sergeant Bonnie Wilcox.

"Heya." With a friendly smile, she introduced herself. "You must be the two postal inspectors."

MC assessed the cop, and her gaydar pinged. "Hi, I'm Inspector McCall and this is Inspector White." MC jerked a thumb at Cam.

Wilcox led the way through a maze of hallways to an elevator bank and once inside pushed the lowest level button. "Down to the bowels we go." A grin split her round face, golden-brown eyes dancing with glee. "Heard you want to see the Beemer we hauled in. Mind if I ask what you're hoping to find?"

MC took an instant liking to Wilcox. "The car belongs to the missing star witness in a case being investigated by a joint task force from the US Attorney, FBI, and the US Postal Inspection Service."

"Wow, a lot of the alphabet agencies. And now MPD, too."

The elevator came to a jarring halt.

"Here we go." The doors slid open and Wilcox led them down a dimly lit hallway to a metal door, light brown ponytail swaying like a pendulum across her shoulders. She swiped a plastic keycard through a reader and a pea-sized light at the top of the white box changed from red to green, followed by a click.

"C'mon in."

They followed her into a room nearly as big as a football field with bright lights and whitewashed concrete walls and floors.

"Impressive," Cam said.

"Over this way." Wilcox led them down a wide aisle and stopped at an alcove tucked next to the first of two rolling garage doors. She provided them with all the coverings to keep from contaminating evidence, and they all suited up.

Wilcox rolled up the garage door, and they followed her into the bay where the ravaged remains of Arty's car sat. The doors were laid out on plastic tarps on the floor.

"We removed them so we can go over them more easily. We checked for hidden compartments, if anything had been stashed behind the panels, and dusted for prints. So far nothing. We pulled all the floor mats and sent them to the lab. The driver's side mat had specks of what appeared to be blood and some other unidentified matter."

MC said, "Blood, huh? Doesn't bode well."

Cam had his gloved hands propped on the roof over the passenger-side front seat. "The glove compartment is empty." He scrunched down and felt under the passenger seat. "Nothing." He checked in the backseat. "More nothing."

MC mirrored his moves on the driver's side. "You haven't found anything of interest? What about the keys?"

"Nothing interesting about the keys." Wilcox stood aside and watched them go over the car without changing her placid expression. She was either a very good sport or had a great poker face. It was never easy when an agency questioned the capability of another agency. MC gave her mental props for her professionalism.

"Nothing out of the ordinary," Wilcox said. "Dealership sticker and handbook, probably been in the glove compartment since he bought the car. Two maps, Minnesota and Wisconsin. In the center console we found a car charger for an iPhone along with an open bag of cough drops and a receipt from a Holiday gas station in Wayzata. The keys were in the ignition and have been sent to the lab for DNA and fingerprint analysis. We have photos of everything."

"No USB drive?" MC gingerly pushed her hand into the shredded mess of the rear seat.

"No USB. We also vacuumed the carpet. Obviously, someone did a number on the seats. Papers tossed everywhere and empty briefcase on the floor. We've got those in the lab, testing them for prints."

MC frowned in frustration. She jammed her arm under the driver's seat, feeling along into the sides where the seat was bolted to the floorboards. "Nothing. Damn. Can we see the photos you took? Maybe get electronic copies?"

Wilcox said, "I'll get the digital camera I used, and we can view the pics. I can email whatever you need."

MC and Cam stood behind Wilcox as she brought up the photographs of the BMW. Nothing jumped out at MC until Wilcox scrolled to the pictures of the keys in the ignition. MC focused on the plain silver ring that held several keys. One of them caught her eye. MC opened her mouth to say something, but Wilcox's cell phone rang.

She answered and swung away from MC and Cam. "I'm down in the garage with the inspectors." She slowly turned back. "Uh-huh. Yep. Got it. No, I'll take care of it." She ended the call.

"What's up?" Cam asked.

"Trouble?" MC asked Wilcox.

"Not to sound like a sad cliché, but I've got good news and bad news. Good news is they've found your guy, Arty Musselman. The bad news is—he's dead."

"Shit," Cam said.

"Is Minneapolis the lead on the homicide?" MC stripped the gloves from her hands.

"Don't know who's got lead at this point. Goldstein—one of our homicide guys—called me, told me the deceased was found in Spring Park. Over near Wayzata. So Spring Park PD, or maybe BCA or Hennepin County."

MC turned to Wilcox. "Thanks for your help. Here's my card. If you could email the photos ASAP, I'd appreciate it."

"No problem."

Wilcox ushered them out of the garage, closed the overhead door, and stood waiting while MC and Cam removed their contamination gear.

MC deposited her gloves in a container marked for disposal. "Maybe the FBI will take over the case because of the crossover with the ongoing investigation." She leaned back against a counter. "Either way, partner, we need to give Oldfield a call."

Cam retrieved their coats, and they followed Wilcox to the elevator. "Like I kept sayin', I knew Arty wouldn't freak on us. This is bad."

MC pulled her coat on. "I have a hunch it's about to get a whole lot worse."

ℋ

MC and Cam sat in front of ASAC Oldfield's desk, backs straight, eyes focused on the blank white sheetrocked wall behind the empty office chair on the other side of the desk.

Oldfield paced back and forth behind said desk, hands in pockets.

Cam said, "Arty's murder has to be directly related to the Stennard investigation."

Oldfield. "Yes. But we've got us quite a clusterfuck, don't we? More hands in the cookie jar. Because Arty was key to the fraud case, his homicide is considered extenuating circumstances. The investigation jumps up to high profile status, so the FBI—this task force—will be taking on Musselman's homicide. I've requested more agents to help out, and we need to move fast."

MC stood. "What can we do? Request a search warrant? We should keep pounding the pavement until someone throws a roadblock at us."

"My partner," Cam smiled. "Relentless."

Oldfield smacked both hands on his desk, head down. "You two ought to be FBI agents. You'd fit right in. I'm submitting the request for the search warrant on Stennard's business based on the recording we have from the meeting. We don't have enough, I don't think, to go after his private properties yet, but this should be enough to get us inside the offices. The USB drive with the other private conversations between Arty and Mike and Gavin would give us the boost we need to search their residences. But until we have that device, we're stuck with what we have."

MC said, "Assign us to the house cleaning team."

Oldfield locked gazes with MC. "Yes, you two can assist. Now get out of here for the day. We won't see a warrant until tomorrow or Thursday."

♯

MC jotted a few notes in her notebook before tucking it away. She then surveyed the late afternoon traffic on eastbound I-494. "I swear driving on the freeway is like playing a video game."

Cam grinned. "I was pretty good at Frogger back in the day."

"Of course you were. No wonder you always want to drive."

He whipped the wheel to the right and tucked in behind a semi. "Gotta keep those mad skills alive somehow."

"So you can pass them along to Ben."

"Unfortunately, Jane won't allow me to even talk about video games in front of our young lad. She thinks five-year-olds should be using their brain cells on more productive endeavors, like reading and math."

"Smart woman, your wife." MC checked the time on her phone and noticed an email from Roland Chrapkowski. "Ugh."

"What?"

"Email from He Who Shall Remain Nameless." MC tapped the email icon and scanned the message. "He's asking for an update on two of my cases. The newest ones, of course. He knows how busy we've been with Stennard, but he hounds me on new stuff. I can't win."

"He is the denizen of doom. Jamie approved my request to cut out early this afternoon, depending on whether or not Oldfield needed us."

"I'd like, just once, for him not to ride my ass." MC blew out a breath. "So, you're leaving early, huh?"

"I told Jane I'd meet her to take the kids shopping for clothes."

"Sounds like good times."

"Believe me, it's more like a tag-team sport."

"I'm so beyond glad I never had any rugrats. I wouldn't have the patience to deal with half of what you and Jane have on your plate. Have you thought of bribery? They're never too young, right?"

"Bribery is one of the first parenting techniques I learned. A cookie goes a long way sometimes."

MC grinned. "Blasphemy! You'll go straight to hell for not following the almighty Doctor Spock's playbook."

"You do know that most of that Spock child-raising stuff is outdated now?"

MC didn't respond. As far as she was concerned, *Mister* Spock was a much more interesting character.

Cam navigated the lanes leading to the one-story office and quickly parked. "I'll go in with you."

"You don't need to run interference for me, Cam. Give me the keys. I'll check us back in, and you can be on your way."

Cam handed over the car keys. "You sure?"

"Yep. I'm a big girl. And Jane's probably tearing her hair out waiting for you."

"Thanks. Have a good night. Catch ya tomorrow."

MC adjusted the messenger bag on her shoulder and headed into the building.

A bullet-resistant glass enclosure housed their receptionist, Chelsea. All visitors had to sign-in and have a good reason to get past Chelsea. Usually no appointment with an inspector or investigator meant no admittance.

MC waved at Chelsea, swiped her badge, and stepped inside. The heavy metal door thunked closed behind her.

Chrapkowski's was the corner office at the far end of the hall. MC's own office was half the distance, and she was grateful she didn't have to pass him to access her own space. She quickly ducked inside and closed her door.

She'd barely hung her coat on the wobbly wooden coatrack before someone thumped on her door. Goddamn. Not one second to breathe. She called out, "Come in."

The door swung open and Chrapkowski's bulk filled her doorway. "McCall."

Chrapkowski's crap brown suit and white—edging toward gray— button-down shirt gave him the appearance of someone just this side of homeless.

"Yes?" She started the computer and thought that his ex-wife had been smart to call it quits with this guy. "What can I do for you?"

Chrapkowski crossed his lumpy arms. "What you can do for me, Inspector McCall, is get me the two case files that were due on my desk this morning." He lumbered farther into the office.

The computer wheezed its way through the startup program in tandem with Chrapkowski's gasping breaths and she launched Outlook to check her Tasks list. She'd closed both cases and planned to scan all her case notes into the system this afternoon.

MC said, "The Dillinger Realty mail theft and the parcel sorter unknown powder assignment due dates are close of business tomorrow."

"I don't care about the due dates. I wanted the cases this morning, and I didn't get them. Maybe this Ponzi gig is too much for you." He raised his steel-wool eyebrows at her. "If you can't handle the work I'll gladly pull you off the Stennard assignment. I'm sure ASAC Oldfield won't mind."

MC took a deep breath. "I do not purposely avoid my work or push it off on other inspectors, like some do around here. I was given assignment end dates. I always meet my assignment end dates, and I fully intend to meet these." MC tamped down the fury burning inside. She held out two files to Chrapkowski. "If you'd prefer to inspect the hard copy files, please feel free. I can always scan the documents after you've reviewed them."

Chrapkowski leveled his dead-fish eyes at her. He snorted air through his bulbous red-veined nose, nostrils flaring, and reached a chunky paw out to snatch the folders from MC's grasp. "You're teetering on the edge, McCall. I suggest you tread lightly or you may find yourself going down hard." He spun on his heel and took a step toward the door.

MC planted both hands flat on the desk and leaned forward. "Are you threatening me?"

Chrapkowski halted. He executed an elephantine pirouette to face MC, his face turning the color of eggplant.

MC refused to back down.

Chrapkowski stuck a porky pointer toward her. "Do your damn job, McCall. And know I'm watching your every move." He spun back around and trundled out the door.

The air had barely settled before Jamie Sanchez poked his blond crewcut head inside her office. "Sorry, MC. I'll work on him. He's a royal pain in the ass. Thank God he's on the home stretch to retirement." He rolled the sleeves of his typical crisp white dress shirt neatly above his wrists.

"Still doesn't give him the right to treat me differently." She met Jamie's eyes. He was only a couple inches taller than her. "I've been adamant about riding it out, but lately he's gotten worse." She sat in her creaky chair and ran a hand through her spiky hair. "Like I don't have enough on my plate. I don't need his bullshit."

"Hang in there. You're one of the best inspectors I've ever worked with. He wouldn't have a leg to stand on if he tried to discipline you. I'll speak to him. Hopefully I can put it in simple enough words for him." Jamie smiled, perfect white teeth glinting against a still slightly tanned face.

"Thanks, Jamie. I appreciate you having my back. Now, I better get back to it before the wild boar stampedes back down this way." She felt some catharsis having Jamie's support, but stopped short of asking about a transfer to his team.

Jamie did an about face and closed the door behind him.

She reviewed her calendar and task items. She was on track with everything. And since it was only twenty after three, she had time to get started on a mailbox vandalism case Crapper had assigned her late yesterday.

After two no answer, no voicemail calls, four no answer, but messages left calls, and one frail-sounding, extremely lonely, very upset postal customer, MC had had enough.

She glanced at the silver government-issue clock on the wall above her door, ticking the seconds away. Four o'clock. She decided to call it a day and, for once, get home early.

♯

MC pulled into the detached two-car garage off the alley of their Highland Park house right after Barb rolled in.

"Hi, gorgeous," MC said.

"Look what the cat dragged in." Barb beamed as she exited her Outback, a cloth tote bag in one hand and a navy-blue Coach tote in the other.

MC had given her the Coach bag as a Christmas gift two years earlier. Barb never would've spent three hundred dollars on something like that for herself. MC had been harping at her for years to get rid of the worn, ratty bag she used for school practically since she'd begun teaching, so she'd splurged on the Coach. Initially, Barb fussed over the expense, but MC knew that deep down, she loved it.

MC kissed Barb. "I deserve that. Hand me one of the bags so you can lock up."

Barb handed over the cloth carryall. "Thanks, hon." She secured the car and shut the garage door.

They entered through the back door and passed through the entry space they called a mudroom and into the kitchen.

MC set Barb's bag on the short end of the L-shaped counter. "We've got plenty of time before we have to meet Dara and Meg for dinner. How about a pre-dinner cocktail?"

"Sounds good. The kids ran me ragged today. I'm ready for Thanksgiving break." She unzipped her puffy jacket.

MC took her jacket. "You go sit in the living room. Turn on some classical on the iPod. Relax. I'll get our drinks and join you."

MC headed down the hallway toward the front of the house and hung up their coats in the entryway closet and secured her handgun in the shoebox-sized safe on the closet floor.

Classical music drifted from the speakers in the living room and MC returned to the kitchen. She poured a glass of white wine for Barb and opened a can of Surly Hell craft beer for herself.

She slid onto the couch next to Barb and handed her the glass of wine. "Cheers."

Barb smiled and took a sip. "Ah. Nice." She rested the glass on her thigh and leaned her head against the back of the couch. "I'm so glad to be off my feet for a few minutes."

"You know, we can cancel with Dara and Meg. They'd understand." MC took a gulp of cold beer and slid her gaze sideways to gauge Barb's reaction.

One eyelid snapped open, and Barb fixed her one-eyed gaze on MC. "Oh, no you don't. You're always ready to cancel. I know you prefer the solitude of our humble abode, but our friends are counting on dinner. And we'll be there." She opened the other eye and took a drink of wine. "But as long as we have some time, maybe we can talk about getting married." She tucked one leg under her and leaned sideways toward MC.

Marriage was a recurring discussion MC tried to avoid, and Barb kept bringing up. "Um. Okay." MC swallowed some more beer and swiped a hand across her suddenly clammy forehead. "Feels warmish in here."

"Come on, MC. You avoid this topic every time I bring it up. Don't you love me?" Barb set her wineglass on the coffee table.

MC fortified herself with another healthy slug of liquid courage then set the can on the table. "I love you. With all my heart. More than life itself." She twisted to face Barb. "Loving you is not the issue. You know that."

"Then what is? Please clue me in."

"I . . . it's . . . I can't bear the thought of some Kardashian-esque event. You know how I feel about family gatherings. And I don't want our getting married to be a disappointment to you by only being the two of us." MC blurted out, "Yet at the same time I'd rather crawl into a hole and be covered by a million fire ants than have some giant gala." The beer left a sour taste in the back of her throat and she lowered her head, an internal battle waging over whether to finally share Cindy's story with Barb.

Barb grasped MC's hands in hers. "Take a breath, MC. Tell me what's up." Her teacher voice commanded immediate response.

But MC couldn't speak Cindy's name. The words lodged in her throat. Instead she said, "There's nothing I want more than to spend my life with you. You, Dara and Meg are my family. I do want to marry you. I can't handle a Lollapalooza-size shindig. Can we keep it just the four of us?" She searched Barb's face for the signs of disappointment she was certain would appear.

"You know I'd love to have my family present, except for Jules, to celebrate our commitment. But I understand. We can limit the invitees. We need Dara and Meg, though, to act as our witnesses. It's the law." She leaned in close. "I've told you this before."

MC kissed Barb. "How do you put up with me?" She touched her forehead to Barb's and closed her eyes, biting her lip to swallow back the tears threatening to shatter her butch façade.

Barb pulled back. "Believe me, it's not easy."

MC's eyes widened. She opened her mouth to respond, but was interrupted by her cell vibrating in her pocket.

"Saved by the cell." Barb reached for her wine and sat back against the arm of the couch, a twinkle in her eye as she watched MC struggle to extract her phone.

MC freed it and glanced at the screen. "Of course. A text from Dara. She says, 'Yo, you better be dragging your sorry butt to dinner tonight. I want the latest scoop on your epic investigation.' I guess it's a good thing I didn't have to work late. You would've had to listen to Dara whine all through dinner about my not being there to update her. I swear, she's worse than Crapper."

"MC! Bite your tongue."

MC held up her hands. "Maybe that was a bit over the top." She sent a quick text back to Dara.

"I'll change into jeans. Then we should get on the road so we're not late. Do you want to call in our usual order to Thai Kitchen?"

"Sure. Two orders of Shrimp Pad Thai, one Green Curry with Chicken, and one Thai Fried Rice with Chicken coming up."

"How about adding a couple orders of Cream Cheese Wontons?"

"Sounds good. I'll be up to change as soon as I call it in."

♯

MC watched as Dara crunched on a perfectly-browned cream cheese wonton. A fluff of white cream cheese squirted out the opposite end. "Geez, Dara." MC snickered. "Take it easy on the poor wonton and—." Barb's elbow in her side cut her off. "Ow!"

"Play nice." Barb eyed MC and Dara.

The foursome had pushed two tables together near the counter and spread out their Thai feast. Cartons, plates, and napkins littered every available inch of space.

MC loved these weekly dinners, even if her initial inclination was to cancel. They'd started the tradition more years ago than she could remember now. MC and Barb would bring takeout from a favorite restaurant to the shop, and they'd enjoy a tasty meal in between waiting on customers. At nine, when

Meg flipped the sign on the door to "Closed" the four made quick work of cleaning up the shop and readying it for the next day.

To MC these people were her family.

Dara nudged MC's foot. "Hello. What's up? Where are you?"

"What?"

"I asked if you'd share the latest on your super-secret case." Dara slurped a forkful of Pad Thai and blinked expectantly at MC.

MC swallowed her chicken and washed it down with a sip of water. "I'll tell you what I can. Confidentiality and all."

"Whatever." Dara waved her fork in the air. "Dish the dirt."

Meg returned from waiting on a customer and took her seat next to Dara. "Stop waving your fork before you poke someone's eye out, and let MC eat her meal in peace."

"Sound advice. I'll give you an update over coffee after we eat. Deal?" MC raised an eyebrow at Dara, daring her to argue.

"Oh, crap, I'm outnumbered. Deal."

♯

Meal clutter cleared and the six current customers sufficiently waited upon, the foursome settled at the table with mugs of coffee and tea.

Dara pulled her chair closer to the table, wrapped her hands around her coffee cup, and leaned toward MC. "Okay, McCall. Spill it." Her brown eyes sparkled.

MC sipped her coffee and focused on Dara. "I'll tell you what I can, but if you tell anyone, I'll have to kill you."

"Out with it."

"News flash. We now have a dead whistleblower."

Three sets of eyes widened.

Barb's mug thumped down on the table, Earl Gray sloshing over the rim. "What are you saying?"

"The guy who we've been working with was found toes up today. Because of this new wrinkle, the team is scrambling to decide how to proceed."

"Wrinkle?" Barb slowly folded her napkin. Her voice rose an octave. "You refer to a man being murdered as a *wrinkle?*"

"Shhh." MC glanced around the café. Barb's exclamation had drawn people's attention. MC reached for Barb's hand, held it and said in a low tone, "I was never in any danger. No need to worry."

Barb leaned back in her chair. "Why didn't you tell me this earlier?"

"We got sidetracked with our other discussion. And I didn't want you to start stressing, which you tend to do when bad things happen." MC tried out a smile. "And then it was time to leave."

"I would think you'd find this tidbit a tad important." She blew out a breath. "What happens now? Do you and Cam suddenly become homicide detectives?"

MC kept her voice matter-of-fact and squeezed Barb's hand. "We don't even know who will be lead on the homicide. Could be Hennepin County, could be Minneapolis, or could be the FBI. Nothing's certain at this point, except that Cam and I will go on investigating the fraud case."

Meg set her cup on the table. "MC, you be careful."

Dara said, "Totally. We love ya. Hey, do you guys wanna go see the new Meryl Streep movie, *The Homesman,* this weekend?" She glanced from Barb to MC and back.

MC mouthed, "Thanks," at Dara and perked up. "Sounds good to me. And Hilary Swank is in it too, right? Gotta be a winner with those two." She raised her coffee cup and took a sip. "How about it, sweetie?"

A deep sigh escaped Barb's lips. "Sure. Why not?"

"Yes!" Dara said. "Should be awesome."

Meg said, "We should make it a double date night and do dinner and a movie on Saturday. We've got the shop covered, so we're free all evening."

Barb whispered to MC, "We're not finished talking about this."

The aftertaste of coffee gone bitter filled MC's mouth.

Chapter Six
Thursday, November 20

"You okay?" Cam weaved in and out of semi-heavy mid-morning traffic on westbound I-494.

MC gazed out the window, watching the menagerie of vehicles howl past, shooting up rooster tails of ashen slush. "I'm feeling the pressure. Barb is freaked out by our dead guy. And Crapper keeps riding my ass. And where are we, or rather, where are they with Arty's homicide? We need a break on this thing, quick."

"Don't worry, I'm sure Oldfield's got irons in the fire." Cam navigated off the freeway. "Barb will come around. She always does. Remember a couple years ago when we investigated that suspicious powder incident at the St. Cloud facility? She wanted you to be tested for exposure to Anthrax, even after you assured her it was only baby powder."

"God, yes. She refused to believe me. Wanted me to bring home lab results to prove I wasn't keeping something from her."

"She loves you. We're both lucky. Could be worse. At least she's not threatening to leave you."

"Leave me? Ha! Far from it. She's talking about marriage again. When I'm hopeful she's forgotten about it, up it comes, like a loaded semi barreling down a mountain road."

"MC, bite the bullet. Do it already."

"It's not that I don't want to marry her. I just don't want it to be some overblown extravaganza. I can't deal with crowds. You know?" MC drummed her fingers on the door's armrest. "I'd be a blithering babbling boob."

"Go online, apply for a license, pick a judge, and go to the government center. Short and sweet. No fuss. No muss. Bada bing, bada boom, you're hitched." Cam snapped his fingers in the air.

"But Barb wants to have her family there, except for her sister-in-law, Jules. We've talked about Jules ad nauseum. Not inviting her wouldn't work because if Jules isn't invited Barb's brother and the kids wouldn't come either. Then her parents would be mad at her. It would be a vicious cycle of resentment. Not worth the trouble. If I could convince her to keep it at Dara and Meg as our witnesses and the two of us, we could be in and out in fifteen minutes."

MC couldn't deal. Weddings were a painful reminder that she had no family. After losing them, MC boycotted celebratory gatherings. She'd tried attending a few times early on, but ended up dissociating. She correlated the feeling to what blacking out must be like. One minute she'd be involved in a discussion and the next she'd be in the passenger seat of Barb's—or Dara and Meg's—car heading home without any recollection of how she'd got there.

"Hello?" Cam waved a hand in front of MC's face. "Where'd you go?"

"Sorry. Lost in thought." MC noticed they'd arrived at their destination. "Let's hope for some good news."

ASAC Oldfield buzzed them in. "McCall, White, gather round the conference table. We have a couple of new additions who will bring us up to speed on a few items." He waved them toward a long table near his office where five people were already seated.

Two women she'd not seen before were seated at the table. Oldfield introduced them as Special Agent Teri Young and Special Agent Alexis Trinh. "They've been added from our Chicago office."

Agent Steve Braun introduced the other two people as Special Agent Sebastian Ferndale, a youngish tall beanstalk of a guy, his skin dark brown and a voice so deep he could beat out James Earl Jones for the voice of Darth Vader. The other man was Special Agent Walt Andrews, a middle-aged white dude with reddish-silver hair, a face full of freckles, and washed out blue eyes. Both were from the FBI's Minneapolis office.

Oldfield stood at the head of the table as MC and Cam sat. "Here's where we're at. I had Cyber ping Arty's phone. The last known location was in Spring Park. I sent Young and Trinh to the site yesterday.

"The location was in the area of a boat storage business. When they noticed the fence had been cut, they called in backup. Orono PD was closest, so they sent a squad to help secure the area. And Hennepin County Crime Scene was called in. We've got lead on Musselman's homicide. All the talking heads at the top want results as soon as possible on both the homicide and the fraud case, which works to our advantage." Oldfield nodded toward Young. "I'll turn the floor over to you."

Agent Teri Young appeared to be in her mid-thirties. Lean and tall, she stood at least six feet. Her blond hair was secured in a very tight ponytail, and she wore a light blue oxford shirt under a dark blue blazer and matching pants.

Young said, "Trinh, wanna set it up?"

"Sure." Trinh, who sported short-cropped, coal black hair, much like MC's, quickly arranged a rip chart on a tripod and angled it so everyone could see. She stepped aside and Young took point.

"As ASAC Oldfield stated, the Hennepin County Sheriff's Department handled the crime scene investigation. We've also been brought up to speed

on the fraud case. Here's what we have so far on the Musselman homicide."
She nodded at her partner, who flipped the top sheet over to display a
timeline.

"We believe the victim was last seen alive at the meeting in the Stennard
building. There's no indication he made it home. The Hennepin County
Medical Examiner will be performing the autopsy tomorrow afternoon
and then we'll have a better idea of time of death. We've questioned
Stennard employees, starting with Michael Stennard and Gavin Thomson.
Neither heard from Musselman after he left work on Monday evening.
They both seemed pretty shocked and torn up over his demise. If it's a
cover, they're good actors."

MC asked, "What about the head of security? Len Klein? Cam and I
followed him, Klein that is, Monday night after Arty didn't appear for
debriefing." She glanced at Cam.

He said, "Klein was driving a black Escalade and hustled to an apparent
pre-set meeting near a local recreational vehicle and boat storage business.
Very clandestine. MC managed to eavesdrop and hear bits and pieces of
what was said."

All eyes fixed on MC. She said, "I was able to get close enough to catch
some of the conversation. Klein met up with two men, maybe mid-
twenties. One was quiet, don't remember him saying anything, in fact. The
other was loud and obnoxious, and I think Klein called him Wooly or
Worley. This Wooly character received a phone call which riled him up."

MC pulled her notebook from her messenger bag. "Let's see, there's
something he said." She flipped pages and ran a finger down her notes and
tapped the page with a fingertip. "This Wooly character said something
about not finding a phone. This was in his conversation with whoever he
was talking to on the cell." MC paused and then, "'Didn't find no phone.'
That's what I heard him say."

Cam rubbed his temples. "Shit. Phone. Boat storage. Do you suppose?"

MC said, "How could it not be?"

Young gazed from one to the other. "You suppose what? Please
enlighten the rest of us."

"The phone this Wooly guy was talking about, what if he was talking
about Arty's phone? What if he had something to do with Arty's murder?"

Young checked through notes she had in a folder. "Hennepin County
found an iPhone at the crime scene. All the earmarks of having been
tossed away. Dead battery, but Cyber is working to revive it and retrieve
the data. The body was found rolled in a blue tarp, tied with a length of
rope and dumped in a boat."

Cam said, "Harsh."

MC asked, "If data from the phone is recovered, can we get copies of everything? Voice recordings, text messages, et cetera?"

"Yes," Oldfield said, "and a list of the last incoming and outgoing numbers. The sooner we get it the better."

Young jotted notes as fast as the team fired requests at her. "I'll set it up. Anything else?"

MC said, "Cam and I inspected Musselman's car. Wilcox at the MPD's Forensic Garage told us they'd found what appeared to be blood on the driver's side front floor mat. No wallet. No phone. Glove box contents tossed around inside the car: maps, insurance docs, registration, and owner's manual. Nothing interesting. Seats were shredded. Tires gone. Some work-related papers scattered about, and his briefcase. Stuff is being tested for DNA and prints."

Oldfield asked, "Are we thinking this was a carjacking? Or is it related to the task force investigation?"

"Who knows," MC said. "Maybe the car stripping was random and not connected to Arty. Or a diversion."

Oldfield cupped his chin in a hand. "Go on, McCall. Never rule out anything until you can prove it."

"Right. First, I had Klein pegged as the guy who took out Arty. But why the secret huddle with Wooly and friend? Do we know what time Arty was killed? Because if he died earlier than the meeting, then Klein could be involved. But if it was later than the clandestine meetup, then it's less likely because we followed him home." She thought for a moment. "Or maybe Klein hired those two creeps to off Arty, and the big exchange was a payoff."

MC hesitated and reread her notes while the agents waited. "But what was in the briefcase Wooly gave to Klein before Klein handed over the money? The briefcase wasn't Arty's, so that doesn't fit. The case the guy gave to Klein was silver or gray, definitely a lighter color, and shiny like plastic or fiberglass or maybe metal. Not leather like Arty's."

Cam said, "Something's not clicking."

MC said, "Agreed. And the fact the rendezvous happened at the same place Arty was dumped? Doesn't make sense. So maybe Klein and those guys had no connection to Arty."

Young said, "We can review the employee list and search for the name you heard. Wooly." She wrote in the file. "We've interviewed Len Klein, but he claimed he worked late and afterwards he went right home. Said he was alone all night. Neither Stennard nor Thomson saw Klein after their meeting with Arty. Appears Mister Klein wasn't being completely truthful. Deserves a closer look."

Oldfield said, "Question Mister Klein again. Delve deeper."

MC drummed her fingertips on the table. "If we don't find a name matching Wooly, whoever re-interviews Klein can maybe work it backwards with him. Ask him what time he got home. We followed him to the complex he lives in, so we know he arrived home around nine forty-five. We were back here by ten to check in. You could work him through his night in reverse. Maybe toss him a question about Johnson's Boat and RV Storage, see if that lights a fire under him."

The agents continued to run down the sparse information they had and then turned the meeting back over to Oldfield.

"Thank you, Young. Trinh. Now on to some good news for the fraud case. Agent Braun," Oldfield nodded at him, "has drawn up a request for a search warrant for Stennard Global Enterprises. Braun, would you like to brief the team?"

Braun stood and tucked his hands into the pockets of his khakis. "We reviewed the footage from the smoke detector camera. The audio was a bit wonky, but we got excellent video, clearly showing the three men at various points. The evidence was enough to convince a district court judge to sign a search warrant, which covers all offices and all files within the Stennard building. We're executing over the weekend. Fewer employees on site, less hassle. The judge didn't think we had enough, though, to include Stennard and Thomson's residences and personal vehicles."

Oldfield said, "If we could locate the elusive USB drive Arty was supposed to hand over we'd probably have enough to cover the personal residences, too. It's unfortunate that we don't have it."

Agent Ferndale interrupted. "Andrews and I, along with Hennepin County, searched Musselman's residence yesterday. We didn't find a USB drive, and believe me, we took the place apart."

MC said, "Minneapolis didn't find a thumb drive in the car either. They even disassembled the doors."

Oldfield nodded. "So, we still have a missing USB drive which, according to Arty, contains many recorded conversations implicating Stennard and Thomson. We need to find that drive. Braun, please continue."

"We'll execute the warrant this weekend. If we have enough people, we may be able to get it done on Saturday. All hands on deck. We meet at seven Saturday morning at the Stennard building. Questions?" He surveyed the others around the table, then sat.

Oldfield stood. "Good plan. McCall and White, I've checked with Chrapkowski and Sanchez and you're both cleared to assist. Sanchez also said he'd arrange for use of one the Postal Service's three-quarter-ton trucks to transport boxes. I appreciate the spirit of cooperation from all agencies involved."

He fixed his gaze on each of the attendees around the table. "For now, I'd like Young and Trinh to search employee records for this Wooly and also the phone numbers from Musselman's cell. McCall and White, I'd like you to find that damn USB drive. Braun will continue to coordinate the search. And you two," he pointed at Ferndale and Andrews "re-interview Klein. Hopefully something or someone will crawl out from under the proverbial rock and shed some light on what happened with our star witness."

The meeting over, everyone dispersed to work their assigned duties. MC and Cam hustled out to the car and headed back to the office.

♯

MC kept her office door closed until about one o'clock. By then the hungry bear hibernating in her stomach woke and roared. She donned her coat and shoved her wallet into a pocket. Like a kid wanting to avoid the playground bully, she opened her door and checked the hallway in both directions before leaving. No sign of Roland Chrapkowski.

"Thank god," she mumbled, and hurried down the hall toward Reception. She poked her head into the tiny room serving as Chelsea Gray's office. "Hey, Chels, I'm running out to grab lunch. Can I bring you anything?"

Chelsea turned from her computer screen and tucked a stray strand behind one ear. "Hey, MC. Nah, I'm good. I had a salad earlier, but thanks for the offer."

"Okay. Be back in a few."

The afternoon tasted of bitter cold and a fast-approaching winter. Thanksgiving was only a week away. She picked up her food and returned to the office to eat a bowl of potato soup and a handful of cellophane-wrapped soda crackers. With a large dark roast coffee in hand, she composed an email to Barb between slurps and sips. Their schedules didn't allow for texting or phone conversations during the work day, so email was the default mode of communication.

She let Barb know she'd be home at her normal time the next two days, but then dropped the bomb about having to work on Saturday. She softened the blow by emphasizing she'd mostly be packing and moving boxes of files, nothing remotely dangerous. She reassured Barb the workday probably wouldn't interfere with their dinner and movie plans with Dara and Meg.

Task completed, she finished off her soup and set to work scanning and uploading the final work papers on a couple cases, closing them out.

She hoped those might keep Chrapkowski at bay for at least a day, maybe longer. MC grimaced, and the recently ingested food roiled and gurgled in her gut. She reviewed the material on the Stennard case, then called Cam.

"Hey," MC said when Cam picked up, "is now a good time to chat about the Stennard case?"

"Sure. Be right there."

Within seconds Cam appeared. "Time flies. Can't believe how much backlog I had on some of my stuff." He stretched and yawned. "Talking about it makes me weary. How about you? Did the big kahuna leave you in peace?"

"I've not seen or heard from He Who Shall Remain Nameless. I don't want to jinx my good fortune. Got a couple things done, and damn it feels good. Clearing cases helps clear my head. Now I feel ready to focus on Arty."

Cam slid into one of her visitor's chairs. He pushed it back so he could straighten his legs out. "Let's rehash what we've got."

They reviewed the information from tailing Len Klein the night Arty disappeared including the rendezvous he had with the two miscreants in the boat storage lot.

MC said, "Klein meeting with the two goons on the same night Arty disappears, the same night he's murdered, seems like a big coincidence, and I don't believe in coincidences."

Cam said, "The more I think about it, I don't see Klein as Arty's doer. Seems unlikely he'd show up back at the scene. That would be ballsy."

"Klein seems stealthy. Black Ops background probably. Yeah, less likely to be anywhere near the scene of a crime he's committed."

Cam said, "Let's go with Klein isn't the killer. Then who?"

MC thought back to Klein's clandestine meeting. "One of the two characters Klein met? They seemed like lowlifes. But quiet guy didn't strike me as having the fortitude or wherewithal to kill someone. The one called Wooly, though, he had a short fuse. He was riled up on the phone." She'd overheard the Wooly guy mention a phone. If he'd not talked about a phone would she even be trying to make a connection between him and Arty?

Almost as if reading her thoughts Cam said, "We don't know Wooly was talking about Arty's phone. You only heard bits of his side of the convo."

"True. But, again, I don't believe in coincidences. He, or the caller, was flipping out about a phone." MC sat back and percolated the facts.

"What are you thinking?" Cam asked.

MC said, "The phone. Maybe I'm too obsessed with the phone."

Cam sat up in his chair. "Let's call Ferndale and Andrews and see if they've interviewed Klein yet."

When the agent answered the call, MC said, "Hi, Ferndale, McCall and White here. We've got you on speakerphone."

"How're you guys? I'll put my phone on speaker so Andrews can listen, too. Got something good for us? Cuz we sure could use some good news."

MC glanced across the desk at Cam. "We're bothered by the fact Klein had a meeting at the same spot Arty's body was dumped." She reiterated all she'd heard of the conversation Wooly held via cell phone out of earshot of Klein and hoodie guy.

Silence filled the air followed by a muted rustling of paper. "Right. You mentioned the location was the same."

MC said, "At first we thought it implicated Klein, but we reconsidered and decided he doesn't seem the type to return to the scene of a crime he's committed."

"Umm . . . okay. Duly noted. We've got an interview scheduled with Klein tomorrow morning, but we're not quite ready to write him off as the killer."

Cam said, "Let us know if you get anything good?"

"Will do. And thanks for the share."

MC hit the button to disconnect the call. "I doubt Klein will spill any beans, but we can always hope. I'm calling it a day. I'd like to go home and get dinner started."

"Barb will faint from shock if she sees you cooking." His blue eyes gleamed and two dimples appeared on either side of his smiling mouth.

"Funny. You should give it a shot sometime. Jane would probably welcome you taking a turn at kitchen duty."

"Trust me, the last thing my family needs is me cooking. We'd all be at the emergency room with food poisoning." He heaved himself out of the chair. "Have a great night. Tell Barb hello."

ℋ

MC stopped at Kowalski's Market on the way home. She picked up a roasted chicken, a mixed greens salad, and some sautéed green beans. She tried to hurry home, fighting the glut of traffic, mumbling about morons learning how to drive in winter.

Once home, she changed into a faded sweatshirt and plaid pajama pants and set the dining room table with place mats, cloth napkins and a rainbow of Fiestaware plates, glasses and utensils. She put the chicken on a serving platter and stuck it in the oven to keep it warm. Then she dumped the salad and green beans in serving bowls.

5:21 p.m. Perfect. Barb would be home soon from her monthly faculty meeting, and everything was ready.

MC nabbed a can of beer from the fridge and wandered into the living room. She turned on the news, mostly to catch the weather, and opened the can. Tiny bubbles teased her nostrils as she sipped the cold beer.

There was no good news. The sports guy was predicting a Vikings loss in the upcoming Sunday game against the Packers. MC had given up on the Vikings years ago. She much preferred to invest her time and energy in following the Minnesota Lynx, the WNBA team that had garnered two championships in the franchise's fifteen-year existence.

"Hello." Barb's voice floated in from the kitchen.

MC abandoned the news and met Barb as she set her school bag on the table in the breakfast nook. "Hi, babe." She kissed her and gave her a hug.

"That's quite the greeting. And it smells like my grandma's kitchen on Sunday afternoons." Barb's apple cheeks shone under the domed ceiling light.

"I'm not your grandma, but I've prepared a dinner fit for a queen." MC pulled on an oven mitt and removed the bird. With a flourish, she presented it to Barb.

"Perfectly crisped and browned. Good job. I couldn't have done it better myself." Her eyes sparkled.

"You know I bought the Six Buck Cluck, right? I didn't actually roast this fowl myself."

"Of course. Even I couldn't produce such a work of near perfection."

"Ha ha. And to go along with our chicken, I also procured sautéed green beans and a brilliant mixed greens salad. I'll set out the food while you hang up your coat. Can I get you something to drink?" MC asked over her shoulder.

Barb made her way down the hall toward the front closet. "A glass of wine would be awesome."

"Red or white?"

"White's great. I'm running upstairs to change."

MC poured the wine and set the food out. She sipped her beer and watched the weather guy drone on about computer models indicating a huge snow storm headed their way for Thanksgiving night.

"How can they possibly know a week in advance what the weather will do?" Barb kissed the top of MC's head as she passed behind her and took her seat at the table.

"I know, right? They love to ramp up the worry factor and nothing happens." She held up a knife. "Wanna carve? I'm horrible at it."

Barb made short work of carving the bird down to its carcass. "May I serve you some breast meat?" She waggled her eyebrows at MC suggestively.

"You are so funny. Yes, please." She held up a cerulean blue plate.

MC scooped some salad on Barb's plate. "How was your day? Did all the rugrats behave themselves?"

"The rugrats were darling. The adults, that's another story. The faculty meeting wasn't as productive as it should've been." She cut some green beans in half and forked them into her mouth. "How about you?"

"My day was pretty good compared to some. I didn't see Crapper, thank the goddess. The FBI is hitting the homicide investigation on all cylinders, with additional agents. Cam and I called them with some info this afternoon. Hopefully, they'll find it useful."

"I'm glad you aren't in the thick of the murder. And I read your email about Saturday. Are you sure we won't have to cancel with Dara and Meg?" Barb picked up her wine glass.

MC watched Barb prepare her cloak of disappointment. "I'm fairly certain we'll be able to keep our date plans. There's a boatload of people assigned to this search warrant, and it's only one building. We're starting at seven in the morning. I predict we finish by three, if not earlier."

"That'd be great. We'd be able to do an earlier show and a late dinner. We'll have more time to visit if we do dinner last." Barb entwined her fingers with MC's. "I love you."

"I love you, too." She lifted Barb's hand and pressed a soft kiss into her palm. "Here's to us and a nice uninterrupted evening out with our friends. She clinked her beer against Barb's wine glass with a tiny ting. A happy sound.

Chapter Seven
Saturday, November 22

Barb mumbled, "Be careful today."

"I will." She kissed Barb's soft, sleep-flushed cheek, gathered her clothes, and crept quietly out of the bedroom.

A quick shower and a cup of coffee later she was out the door, clad in navy sweatshirt, navy cargo pants, and black tactical boots.

The Inspection Service issued winter jackets, navy blue nylon with gold lettering across the back—US POSTAL INSPECTOR POLICE—which she threw into the back seat in case she needed it.

Brilliant sapphire skies held puffs of cottony clouds that floated lazily, unaware Father Winter was about to roar. The dashboard indicated the outdoor temp was thirty degrees.

Could be worse, MC thought. We could be in the middle of a blizzard or freezing rain.

She parked the Camry and met Cam at the company car. "Morning."

"Morning." He let forth a bear-sized yawn. "Sorry." He shook his head to clear out the cobwebs.

"Not enough sleep last night? You and Jane paint the town red?"

"God, I wish. No, Hailey picked last night to wake up with a raging fever. When she's sick she wants her dad. And she's one stubborn two-year-old. I've been up since two."

"A strong cup of coffee will get your motor running. We'll stop on the way."

En route, MC busied herself checking her work email on her phone. "Email from Ferndale." She scanned the message. "Nothing new from Klein. He swears he went home Monday, no stops. Doesn't know the boat storage business. Ferndale and Andrews told him they had witnesses placing him at the storage place and he clammed up. But his story didn't change."

"We shouldn't have expected anything different. He won't fold easily. If they could get enough to get a search warrant for his home, they might be able to find the briefcase."

"Or not. He's had plenty of time to get rid of any evidence—cover his tracks." MC read on. "He's unfazed by Arty's departure from the here and now. Barely acknowledged the guy's dead."

"Liar and a cold fish."

"I didn't detect any camaraderie between Arty and Klein, but you'd think when a coworker is killed there'd be some emotion."

"No shit."

"Oh, hey. This is interesting. They obtained records showing Klein owns a handgun and a couple of rifles. All legally purchased and registered. He's a card-carrying member of the NRA and has a permit to carry concealed."

"What type of handgun?"

"Nine-millimeter semi-auto. No thirty-eight-caliber revolver, which offed Arty, according to info Ferndale and Andrews received from the ME."

"Shit."

"Nailing Klein would've been too easy. Nothing about this case has been easy." She scrolled to another email. "Agents Young and Trinh sent an update—they've gone over the current employee roster and didn't find anyone with a name even close to Wooly or Worley."

"Once we get these records hauled out and someone starts sifting through the crap, something is bound to rear its ugly head."

"I hope you're right." MC pulled her notebook out and jotted some notes.

"Here we are." Cam pulled into an empty slot in the employee parking area at the front of Stennard Global Enterprises.

MC eyed the lot. "It's a veritable circus. Come one, come all to the really big show."

A platoon of vehicles lined the lot. Several reporter types and camera people pressed as close to the front entrance as they could get, barely acknowledging the yellow and black plastic ribbon cordoning off a path from the front door to where the trucks were lined up to take on the boxes of documents.

MC said, "I wonder who tipped off the media. There must be five, six vans here. Every affiliate in the Twin Cities."

They joined the FBI team milling around outside the front entrance. All wore blue jackets with "FBI" prominently displayed in giant yellow letters across their backs.

"Good morning," Oldfield said. "Welcome to the zoo."

"Morning." Cam jerked a thumb over his shoulder. "Zoo seems fitting."

Behind Oldfield the glass front door of the building flew open. Len Klein barreled through the line of agents from various agencies and local police departments. "What's going on here?" Klein shouted.

He was dressed all in black—military style sweater, cargo pants, and combat boots. He folded thick arms across his chest and stood with his feet shoulder width apart to block forward progress of the waiting troops.

"Who's in charge of this show?" Klein bellowed at one of the FBI agents nearby.

Voices hushed and Oldfield pivoted slowly to face the obnoxious asshole. "And you would be?"

"Len Klein, head of security. You're trespassing on private property."

"Good enough for me." Oldfield nodded at Braun.

Braun stepped forward and handed a document to Klein. "Sir, this is a search warrant allowing us to remove any and all records associated with Stennard Global Enterprises and any subsidiaries. We'll need every office door, file cabinet, and desk unlocked. Anything we feel is relevant will be boxed and removed from the premises."

Klein's mouth dropped open. He snatched the paper from Braun's hand and flipped through the pages. "I'll have to contact Mister Stennard and Mister Thomson before you can go in."

"We won't be waiting. You have the warrant, and we are now legally free to enter the building." Oldfield waved the troops forward. "Let's do this."

The blue line surged ahead. MC, with Cam behind her, moved past Len Klein, who was sputtering and waving the search warrant around.

The press crammed closer to the cordoned-off area, cameras hoisted onto shoulders, microphones at the ready.

Inside the reception area, Oldfield gathered the troops. Braun produced a clipboard from which he read off names and assigned everyone specific rooms. Several stacks of folded boxes and rolls of packing tape sat on the reception counter. Each team grabbed boxes and tape and hurried off to their assigned areas.

Braun directed Cam and MC to the security office. MC grabbed the packing supplies, and they marched down the hallway behind the reception desk to the office.

The door was propped open.

"I'd have thought this would've been high tech." She glanced around the ten-by-fifteen-foot room housing one desk and five vertical five-drawer file cabinets. All were standard cabinets in a drab taupe color. A safe the size of a mini fridge hunkered on the floor next to the desk. She dropped the boxes on the floor, pulled off her jacket, and tossed it on a chair next to the desk.

"A multi-billion-dollar corporation and the security office isn't much bigger than one of our offices." Cam scratched his head. "Seems odd, only one office? Wouldn't you think there'd be more security staff?"

MC shrugged. "Whatever. We should be able to clear this out in no time. I'll start with Klein's desk. You want to take the file cabinets?"

"Sure."

"I'll let Oldfield know we'll need Klein to open this safe."

"Okay."

MC sent a quick text to the ASAC while Cam assembled a few boxes and got to work on the first cabinet.

She pulled desk drawers open and rifled through the junk: a mishmash of pens, half packs of gum, pain relievers, and rolls of antacid tablets. In the third drawer, she found an array of hanging files.

She skimmed each before dropping them into a box on top of the desk. The last file in the drawer was a manila folder. She opened it and found a torn sheet of plain, white, unlined paper with "Nick" and "Quentin" scrawled across the middle. She flipped the paper over. Nothing on the back. She turned the folder over, also blank. "Check this out." She showed Cam the half page.

"Nick and Quentin? Could be something—or maybe nothing."

"It's odd. This lonely scrap of paper in an unmarked folder." She found a block of yellow Post-It notes, pulled the top one off and stuck it to the file folder with a note to crosscheck the names against current and former employees. Then she grabbed her notebook from her coat and recorded the info in there as well.

They filled and labeled two boxes with files. The file cabinets were mostly empty. Only the safe was left, but Klein hadn't shown up yet to unlock it.

Cam surveyed the room, hands on his hips. "Let's haul these boxes out."

They each took a box out of the building. A three-quarter-ton postal collection van was backed into the first parking slot, rear door open. They stashed their load inside.

MC wiped her hands on her cargo pants and scanned the growing jabbering crowd. "More than media posted up out here now."

"Do you see Klein anywhere?" Cam asked.

MC craned her neck in every direction searching for the barrel-chested head of security. "Nope. Let's check with Braun for our next assignment."

♯

Len Klein exited the rear of the building, not bothering to zip his black parka. He checked the five vehicles parked in the back lot. Three compact, white, relatively inexpensive SUVs served Stennard security. The other two vehicles were massive Cadillac Escalades. One was his to drive, and the other was used by Stennard executives, or, rarely, by other security staff when necessary. He found no one skulking in the shrubbery behind the row of parking spaces.

He pulled out his cell phone and made a call. "You and Stennard better hotfoot it to the office. Pack of fuckin' law dogs have stormed the gates."

Klein paced back and forth, bits of gravel skittering with every step. "I know it's Saturday, Gavin, but law enforcement doesn't care what day of the week it is. When they have a search warrant, they take care of business."

He pulled the phone away from his ear for a moment, then cautiously replaced it.

"Exactly my point. Some young FBI stud presented me with a book-length warrant stating they can remove every scrap of paper contained within the walls of this here building." Klein switched the device to speakerphone since no one else was around to overhear.

Gavin's tinny voice shot through the speaker. "How extensive is this search warrant? Shit! I *told* Mike we could have trouble."

Klein pulled a rolled document from the inside pocket of his jacket. "The document is a fucking bible, Gavin. And as I said, it gives them free rein to take everything. There are fucking cops and Feds crawling in every corner of this place as we speak. The good news is the search is confined to this building. No personal residences or vehicles."

"Good news? You call that good news, Klein? What the fuck did we hire you for? Do something. Shit! I told dumbass Mike we needed to be more careful. Arty's dead, and now this. Have they questioned you about Arty?"

"They've interviewed me twice. First a coupla local cops. Then the Feds. I told them I have no idea what happened to him. I'm telling the truth. I don't have a fucking clue. Although, the sniveling bastard was acting skittish on Monday night when I saw him leaving after the meeting with you and Mike."

Klein neglected to confess he'd been listening at Mike's office door during some of the meeting, and he'd heard some interesting tidbits, like Gavin saying he basically didn't trust Arty.

Gavin was silent, then his voice slithered, cool as a snake through the phone. "You were in the building Monday evening? I thought Arty, Mike, and I were the only ones on site. What time did you leave?"

"I hightailed it outta here after Arty left. I assumed you and Mike were still here because your cars were parked out front." Klein wondered about Gavin's interest in him being on site the night of the meeting. "Is there a problem? When I heard a meeting was scheduled, I thought I'd stick around in case you guys needed something. I didn't have any plans anyway."

"No problem. I was curious." Gavin sounded preoccupied. "I'll call Mikey and we'll be there soon. Hold down the fort or whatever." Gavin disconnected.

Klein thought Gavin sounded almost worried that he was in the building Monday night. Odd. But Klein had bigger fish to fry right now. He scrolled through his contacts and tapped the one labeled, "Wooly."

Klein kept the phone on speaker and waited for Nick to pick up. Nick Wooler, a/k/a Wooly, and Quentin Laird were due to pick up one of the SUVs later in the afternoon.

Nick Wooler was the leader of the duo. The guy was psycho and Klein used it to his advantage. He was a tough guy with a short fuse, which had come in handy a few times when partygoers got rowdy. He kept Nick in line because he paid both Nick and Quentin very well for their services. And Nick loved money.

Klein worried about Quentin, though. He hardly ever said anything. At first Klein thought the guy was slow or something, but he'd watched and learned Quentin was actually smart. Much smarter than Nick would ever be, and he didn't have a hair-trigger temper like Nick. He thought Quentin's blue eyes probably held secrets—and ugly secrets at that.

Nick had mentioned to Klein that Quentin had family issues, his father had abused him and his mom, and now his mom was on life support in some nursing home, and Quentin had to foot the bill. So, Quentin was willing to do what needed to be done to get his share of the take.

And tonight, Stennard was throwing a party of epic proportions. Unless today's events caused Mike to rethink it, Klein was planning on business, or rather pleasure, as usual, which meant he needed Nick and Quentin to get some good cocaine, heroin, pot, and any happy pills they could round up, along with some hot women. However, Klein didn't want Nick and Quentin showing up at the office while the place was crawling with law enforcement.

"Yo."

"Wooly? Is that you?" Klein stood still to get the best reception.

"Who the fuck you think it is, the president of the United States?"

"I'm not in a joking mood this morning. We need to pick a new meeting place. You and Quentin stay the hell away from the Stennard building. You feel me? There are Feds all over this place like flies on cow shit."

"What?" Wooly's voice got louder. "What the fuck's going on?"

"You don't need to worry about what's happening here. You stay focused on the goodies for tonight's gig at Stennard's house."

"No sweat. I'll round up Quentin and we'll make our pickups. Text me later what time we should come pick up a set of wheels. Do you need us to hang around at the party?"

"Yeah. If I hear different, I'll let you know. You keep your nose clean and wait for my text. Make sure you're locked and loaded. Remember, for now, steer clear of this place. Get my drift?"

"I get it Einstein." Nick let loose a giant yawn. "I'm catching a few more Zs. Hit me up later."

Klein hurried along the side of the building and checked the action out front. A postal van the size of a tank and a fleet of smaller white panel vans were backed into parking spaces. Blue-jacketed agents loaded boxes into the vehicles. So many boxes. Klein gripped his phone in one hand and had to force himself to ease up before he crushed the phone into bits.

"Len Klein?" A hand clamped down on his shoulder from behind. "I'm Agent Braun."

Klein whipped around. The man wore a navy jacket with "FBI" embroidered in yellow across the left chest area. "Yeah?" He scowled at the agent. "Whaddaya want? Need more boxes?"

"Sarcasm will get you nowhere, Mister Klein."

Another person stood a few feet behind Braun. He leaned over the agent's shoulder. "Don't I know you?"

Agent Braun stepped aside. "Inspector McCall would like you to open the safe in your office. If you don't mind, please come with us."

"McCall? Have we met? What's the US Postal Service got to do with whatever's going on here?" Klein shoved his hands into his coat pockets and stared at McCall, ignoring Braun.

She returned Klein's stare. "Mister Klein, if you'd please come and open the safe, we'd appreciate it."

Klein felt Agent Braun's hand on his upper arm. He twisted away from the grip. "Get your hands off me." He strode past Braun and McCall and entered the building through the rear door.

He stomped his feet on the mat inside the door and continued down the hallway toward the security office without checking to see if the two officers followed.

Inside the office, Klein stopped. He spun in a slow circle, taking in the open, empty drawers of his desk and file cabinets.

"What the actual fuck? I don't know what you're hoping to find, but you could've asked, and I'd given it to you. Did you have to destroy the place?" He glared at Braun and McCall.

Braun said, "The safe, please?"

Klein unzipped and shucked his coat, tossing it on top of his desk. He bent down in front of the safe and spun the dial left, right, then left again before yanking on the handle and pulling the door open.

He stood aside and swept his hand in a grand gesture. "It's all yours."

McCall hunched down, pulled files off the top shelf, and handed them back to Braun. Then she reached into the bottom shelf, which contained a holstered handgun, three extra magazines, and several boxes of ammunition.

She pulled nitrile gloves from an outside coat pocket and Braun provided a brown paper sack. MC checked to make sure it wasn't loaded, then slid the handgun into the bag. "Is this your weapon, Mister Klein?"

"Yes, it is. And I have a permit. All legal. I do work security." He frowned. "Why would you need to take my gun?"

"Because it's on the premises," McCall said. "Nothing else in here, Braun." She addressed Klein. "We appreciate your cooperation, Mister Klein."

McCall tugged the blue gloves off her hands and stuffed them into a different pocket. "We're finished with this office."

She nodded at Klein and followed Agent Braun out.

Klein sat in his chair, and in a fit of rage whipped his arm across his desk, sending pens, paperclips, and various bits and pieces flying across the room.

"Fuck!" He grabbed his jacket off the floor and jammed his hands into the pockets, searching until he located his cell phone.

He scrolled through his contacts until he found the one he wanted. Inspector MC McCall and a phone number. US Postal Inspection Service. She'd been here earlier, was it this week or last? He'd picked up her business card off the floor near Taylor's desk in reception.

Klein recalled how he'd asked the inspector what she was doing at Stennard, and she'd given him some story about a mail theft investigation. What the hell? Did they think Stennard was stealing mail? He contemplated the situation and wished he'd heard more of the Monday night conference in Mike's office.

♯

MC and Cam were paired up with two FBI Special Agents, Gary Shaw and Anne Gardner, to pack boxes of files in the accounting offices.

Arty's old office, a tiny broom-closet-sized room off the main accounting office, was packed up separately. The crossover between the homicide investigation and the search warrant for the fraud case was a fine line.

MC sealed up another box. She grabbed a two-wheeled dolly and loaded up a stack of boxes. "I'll take these down to the trucks."

Gardner crouched over a file cabinet drawer, a fistful of manila folders in her hand. "We're about finished. I think Shaw's on the final drawer of the last cabinet. Right?"

"Right you are," Shaw said.

Cam straightened up and cracked his back. "I'm getting too old for this stuff."

MC rolled her eyes at him. "Don't even start." She indicated another dolly. "C'mon Gramps, grab some boxes and let's move 'em out."

"Right behind you."

MC hit the elevator button for first floor and waited for Cam to catch up. "No sign of the USB drive anywhere in Arty's office. I even took out the desk drawers and checked the sides and underneath to see if he'd hidden it. I searched the underside of the desk, too. Nada."

"Nothing in the outer office either. One desk hadn't ever been used and zilch in the other two."

"Where the hell can it be? Wasn't in his car. Wasn't at his house. And it's not here."

"I'm sure as the FBI interviews the employees, they'll ask about it. But it would be nice if we could find it."

The doors slid open and there wasn't a soul in sight.

"Kinda quiet." Cam steered the dolly around the reception desk.

They were mere steps from the front door when it flew inward, and two men strode in as if they owned the place.

MC and Cam pulled their two-wheelers aside to avoid being run down.

The first one was a couple inches shorter than Cam and around two hundred pounds, raven-haired with brown eyes. The other sported brown wavy hair, dark hazel eyes, and was maybe an inch shorter, but he was trimmer than the other man.

Both were dressed like they'd just left a country club.

"Who's in charge here?" the darker-haired man bellowed.

MC said, "And you are?"

"Michael Stennard. This is my business. Who the hell are you?" He leaned forward, his face uncomfortably close to hers.

She took a step back and tilted her head up at him. "Inspector McCall. US Postal Inspection Service." She jerked a thumb at Cam. "My partner, Inspector White. Mister Stennard, you'll want to direct any questions you have to FBI Assistant Special Agent-in-Charge Oldfield."

Stennard let out a string of curses and lurched toward her knocking the top carton off the cart. MC thought he was going to hit her. If the other man hadn't yanked him back by the arm, MC might have had the satisfaction of arresting the bastard.

MC retrieved the box off the floor and restacked it before wheeling around the two men.

Outside, as he held the door for her, Cam said under his breath, "There's about to be some fireworks."

"I'm so glad we got this detail. This asshole is going down. Hard. And we'll be able to say we helped." She wedged her load onto the back of the nearest van and Cam followed suit.

"We've got to be close to finished." He checked his watch. "Almost noon. I'd be happy if we finished soon and I could get home to Jane and the kids. She was not pleased about my short weekend." Puffs of air punctuated his words. "I swear it's colder now than it was at seven this morning."

MC headed back to the entrance. "C'mon, whiner, let's schlep those other boxes out." She glanced to her left and stopped.

Cam almost ran his cart into her heel. "Hey."

"I thought I saw something." She pointed to the corner of the building. "Out of the corner of my eye."

He studied the area she indicated. "Nothing there now. Probably a bird or something."

"I guess." She followed him back inside the building.

ℋ

Klein's phone buzzed with a text from Nick to meet them behind the Stennard building. He charged out of his office, hastening to make sure no one saw him, and made a beeline for the rear entrance.

Nick and Quentin were standing right outside the back door.

"What are you assholes doing here? I told you to stay the fuck away from here today. What if someone sees you?" Klein's breath was a foggy trail in the frosty air.

Nick hooked his thumbs into the front pockets of his jeans. "Relax, bro. We parked a couple blocks away and jumped the fence back here. No one seen us."

Quentin stood silent, a University of Oregon Ducks ball cap clamped down on his head. He was wrapped in a puffy black down jacket that gave him the appearance of an evil Stay Puft Marshmallow Man.

"What, you don't have anything to say?" Klein jabbed a finger in Quentin's face.

Nick sidled toward the side of the building. "Leave him alone. I wanna check out the action."

"Jesus Christ! Have you lost your fucking mind?" Klein felt lightheaded.

"Chill. You'll give yourself a heart attack or something." Nick held a hand palm out toward him. "Be cool. I'll take a quick peek. No one will see me."

Klein had no choice but to follow Nick and Quentin around the side of the building and toward the front.

Nick was in the lead and stopped just shy of the front corner. He stuck his head around the edge and remained there for what seemed like minutes to Klein, but was probably only a few seconds.

"Why is the post office here?" Nick's flat gray gaze fixed on Klein.

"How the fuck should I know why any of them are here? A postal inspector broad was here last week spouting off about mail theft. Gave Taylor her business card. Don't know why she'd be here now, though. This can't be about mail theft." He kicked some loose rocks up against the side of the building. "Nothing's making any sense." He tugged at Nick's coat sleeve. "Come on, let's get the fuck outta here before someone sees you."

Nick pulled his arm from Klein's grasp. "Hold your horses." He pulled out his cell. "I need a snap of the lady inspector." He angled the phone around the building.

Quentin leaned against the wall and stared at the ground. He didn't utter a sound. Not one peep.

The kid gave Klein the creeps. He shivered. "Enough Nick. Stand there much longer and they may come over and drag you inside and start asking questions. Seriously, man. Let's get the hell out of here."

"Hold on. I'm waiting for her to show her pretty face. I see two jackets with postal inspector written on the back. Show me the money, honey. Perfect, that's the ticket." He tapped the phone screen several times. "She's kinda hot." He showed the photos to Klein and Quentin.

Klein waved his hand. "Great. You happy you got something to whack off to now?" He did an about face. "Move out. Now."

Quentin fell in beside Nick. "Why'd you need her pic?"

Klein said over his shoulder, "He does speak. Here I thought the cat got his tongue."

"Leave him be, Klein." Nick slid his thumb across the phone's screen. "Never know when a picture might come in handy. Maybe I want to get to know her better." He leered and clapped a hand on Quentin's shoulder. "Dig it, my man?"

"Whatever," Quentin said.

"You two get lost. Now." Klein hooked a thumb over his shoulder toward the shrubbery lining the back parking lot. "Make like a baby and head out. And for Christ's sake don't let anyone fucking see you."

"Don't get your panties in a twist," Nick said. "What's the plan for tonight? Should we show up at Stennard's house or what? And are we taking one of the SUVs?" He pointed at the Ford Escapes.

Klein checked the time on his phone. "No, you're not taking a car today. I can't take any chances with all those cops around. It's almost noon now. I've no idea how much longer these yahoos will be here. I'll ask Mister Stennard when he and Mister Thomson get here what the plan is for tonight. Far as I know it's still on. Keep your phone handy. I'll text or call. Now get lost!" He pulled the door open and slammed it shut behind him, leaving the two drug dealers in the cold.

Klein went to an empty break room about twenty feet from the back door. He pulled aside the blinds and watched Nick and Quentin climb the fence and disappear.

"Fucking idiots." He dropped the blinds back into place and went in search of Mike Stennard and Gavin Thomson.

#

By two p.m. the team had packed every scrap of paper they could find inside the Stennard building. ASAC Oldfield had been holed up in a conference room next to Michael Stennard's office for most of the afternoon.

MC passed the partially open conference room door with a final load of boxes. A booming baritone caught her attention. She slowed outside the door and snuck a peek in.

"How are we supposed to operate a business without our files?" Michael Stennard slammed a hand down on the table and stood up from his chair.

"Mike. Calm down." Gavin Thomson's even-keeled voice contrasted to Stennard's over-the-top bleating.

Thomson motioned Stennard back into his seat. "Agent Oldfield, I'm sure you can understand the importance of keeping our business running and our employees gainfully employed. What can we do to achieve our goal?"

Oldfield leaned forward and rested his arms on the gigantic conference table. "Mister Thomson, I don't know there's much you can do to keep the wheels in motion at this point. Any new records would also be seized under the parameters of the search warrant."

"And where is this search warrant?" Stennard demanded.

MC sidled closer. Len Klein came into view from further down the table.

"I've, ah, got the document right here, Mike." Klein handed the papers to Stennard. "What he says is true." When Mike glared at him, he lowered his head.

Serves you right, you bastard, MC thought.

"We're fucked then, aren't we, Gavin?" Stennard tossed the sheaf of papers at Thomson.

Gavin Thomson shuffled through the pages and let them drop onto the tabletop. "It appears our hands are tied for now. We'll get our attorneys working on this right away. Hopefully things will be cleared up before we've lost any business." Thomson rubbed his eyes.

"Fine. Gavin, get on the horn with the lawyers. I'll call Linda and have her contact the rest of the staff. Len, you're in charge of notifying your people about the shutdown."

"Will do, Mike." Klein scooted toward the door.

MC hustled toward the elevator. She peered back as the door opened behind her. Klein stared. MC stood her ground.

ASAC Oldfield stepped around Klein. "Pardon me. Hey, McCall, are you finished?"

MC shook her head as if ridding herself of a demon. She tapped the cart handle. "This is the last load."

"Excellent. I'll meet everyone down front in ten. Would you let Braun know?"

"Will do." MC continued to the elevator.

Klein slithered up behind her. "Mind if I tag along?"

"Not at all." She craned her neck to peer down the hall but saw Oldfield was engaged in a discussion with Stennard and Thomson.

"Hope you find what you think you're looking for," Klein said.

MC refused to take the bait. She tapped a booted foot on the carpet wishing the damn elevator would arrive.

Klein positioned himself between her and the elevator doors. He stretched his arm across the doors blocking her way. "Exactly what evidence are you after anyway?"

"I'm not at liberty to discuss an ongoing investigation."

"Oh, come on. I'm ex-military. I've heard that song and dance too many times. Spare me the play-by-the book." He leaned into her personal space.

"Being ex-military, you should know better than to even ask." The elevator dinged.

"Hold the door, McCall," Oldfield hollered down the hall.

"You got it." MC eyed Klein. "You may want to take the stairs if you're in a hurry." She wheeled the dolly inside the elevator and held the open button.

"I think I will." Klein tossed a glare her way and disappeared around the corner.

"Thanks." Oldfield hastened into the elevator. "I want the team to get the vehicles to the secure storage facility. Monday the forensic accountants will start sifting through the materials."

"Got it," she said.

Out in the parking lot, MC stowed her boxes in the last open truck, closed and latched the door. She stepped back and Oldfield signaled for the caravan of vehicles to head out.

He addressed the remaining agents. "Thank you for your hard work. I appreciate your efficiency. Enjoy what's left of your weekend. Remember to not say anything to the press, or anyone."

MC and Cam headed for their car. They skirted the media, waving off a particularly persistent microphone-bearing reporter.

"No comment," MC said as she and Cam hustled to get the hell out of the maelstrom.

She glanced back once to take in the mayhem, and a white Ford Escape momentarily blocked her view as it fell in behind them. "I wonder how the press will spin this," MC said.

Cam said, "Those fucking vultures are like a tornado, they'll have Stennard and company all twisted up in no time. And, mark my words, the debris field will reach far and wide."

♯

Klein sent Nick a text message at around five. *You and Quentin meet me at the bottom of the driveway to Stennard's house tonight at ten sharp. Do NOT be late. Bring ALL the stuff. Plan on staying until the end. You will be adequately compensated.*

Within thirty seconds Nick's response appeared on his screen. *Chill out. Have everything. Need our pieces?*

"Jesus Christ." Klein rolled his eyes. "What a dumb question." He fumbled with the keypad and finally typed an answer to Nick. *YES!*

Nick's text appeared: *K.*

Michael Stennard, twice divorced, owned a home on Bay View Lane on Lake Minnetonka. Bay View Lane was a horseshoe-shaped cul-de-sac and Stennard's residence sat prominently on the crown of the curve. The five-bedroom, six-bathroom house also showcased a full theater in the lower level and a sunken pool in the backyard despite the fact Stennard owned four hundred feet of beachfront.

Klein wondered how Mike could pay alimony to two wives and child support for two kids with wife number one and still afford Chez Stennard.

The most stunning feature was a breathtaking view, from the glass wall at the rear of the main level family room, of Lake Minnetonka.

The liquor store delivery was due at six, which left Klein less than an hour to run home and change. He drove up the winding driveway to the brick and stone mansion, left the Escalade running, jogged up to the front door and rang the bell. A full thirty seconds went by. He was about to punch the button again when one of the double doors opened.

Tall, model-thin, blond-haired, and blue-eyed Tori something or other stood in the doorway. She wore a blindingly white cashmere turtleneck sweater over black leggings that looked painted on. "Yes?"

Klein remembered Stennard's current flame was a woman of few words. "Is Mike around?"

"He's indisposed." She rested a skeletal claw on a bony hip. Her talon-like nails could be registered as lethal weapons.

"Tell him I'll be back by six to oversee the liquor delivery. And security has been lined up for tonight."

"Okay." She began to close the door.

"Wait." He stuck his hand out to stop the door's movement.

She eyed him up and down and sniffed as though she smelled something foul. "Problem?"

Klein clenched his jaw. "Why are you so rude? You act like you're queen of the castle. I got news for you, honey, you're nothing more than the dame of the moment. Don't get too comfortable."

"Such wise words from a security boy who's on the back end of forty sliding into fifty. Please do dish out more advice. I'm sure you're full of it. Full of something, anyway." She shoved the door closed and slammed home the deadbolt.

"Fucking bitch." Klein marched back to his car. "I don't know where Mike finds these broads." His fists white-knuckled the steering wheel. "I'd love to teach her a lesson."

H

"I'm turning up the heat before we leave," Barb called up the stairs to MC. "It's chilly in here."

MC brushed her teeth in the upstairs bathroom and did a quick check of her hair in the mirror. Dressed in a white tee under a plum colored chamois shirt and well-worn jeans, she decided she was ready to face the world. She shut off the light and headed down the steps.

"If you're cold now, then yes, turn up the heat. Temp is supposed to nosedive tonight—low around twenty."

Barb was at the thermostat in the dining room. MC stepped up behind her and wrapped her arms around Barb's mid-section. She eyed her partner's strong, smooth hand working the dial. "Exactly how cold are you?"

"Why? Do you think seventy will be too warm?"

"We'll roast like turkeys in an oven."

"Oh." Barb reached for the dial again.

MC laughed. "I'm kidding."

Barb twisted around to face her. "Smartass."

"I love you, too. Now let's go before we're late for the movie."

"Better hustle, if we're late Dara will never let us hear the end of it."

MC grabbed their jackets. She wrapped a favorite soft gray cashmere scarf around her neck.

Barb fixed the scarf and straightened the collar on MC's pea coat. "You're quite dashing. All the gals will be so jealous." She laid a warm hand on MC's cheek.

"Oh, puhleeze." MC felt the heat of a blush creep up her neck and bleed onto her cheeks. "Let's go before Dara starts texting me." She turned Barb around by the shoulders and guided her out the back door.

Fifteen minutes later, they found Dara and Meg waiting outside the Grandview Theater.

"You're lucky you showed up when you did. I was about to send you a text, MC." Dara waggled her cell phone in MC's face.

MC said, "You're the picture of patience—not. Let's get inside and get tickets. Remind me again what we're seeing."

"We talked about seeing *The Homesman*," Meg said. "Unless you want to see something else?" She surveyed the threesome, with a poor attempt at a frown.

Barb linked her arm through Meg's. "I'm not one for the life story of some gangster and how he became an FBI informant in order to take down a Mafia family invading his so-called turf. Do you two have anything to add?" She pinned MC and Dara with her silvery-gray gaze, wind ruffling her short blond hair.

Dara said, "I got nothing. *The Homesman* sounds dandy. I don't know about MC, though. Maybe she feels the need for more intrigue. I'm not sure she's got enough in her own life."

MC elbowed Dara. Even through her winter jacket, the move hit its mark. "Yow!" Dara dramatically grabbed her side.

"You're fine, Dara." Meg rolled her eyes at MC. "Let's take this party inside before we all turn into human popsicles."

Barb stepped back and threw an arm around MC. "You two are like siblings, I swear. Or like a couple of my students." She laughed, sending misty puffs of vapor twirling off on the wind.

MC's heart swelled as she surveyed her self-made family. This is what life was all about.

By just after nine o'clock the foursome was seated in a cozy corner booth at Rosa's Mexican Restaurant, located a few blocks from the movie theater.

Everyone ordered a margarita, except Dara who ordered a glass of horchata—a rice milk beverage with cinnamon and vanilla. And fresh guacamole and chips for the table.

Meg and Barb were deep into a dissection of the movie, so Dara leaned across the table toward MC. "I saw the news earlier. Stennard, huh?" She raised one eyebrow. "Saw a bunch of trucks and a whole slew of law enforcement out there. Didn't actually see you, though. I guess you're not famous, yet."

"I still can't talk much about it. But yes, we were on site removing potential evidence. Amidst a not so happy contingent of the upper echelon."

MC dipped a chip into the guac. She chewed and considered all the events of the day, including her run-in with asshole Len Klein. His assholery made her wonder if he had, indeed, played a role in Arty's murder. She'd love if he were put away for the crime, but something didn't fit. Klein's meeting with the two unknown men didn't mesh with the timeline for Arty's demise.

Dara asked, "What's next for you guys on this Stennard deal?"

"Not sure. We'll find out more on Monday. Hopefully the forensic accountants will be able to sift through the documents and piece together the necessary evidence, now that we don't have a whistleblower any longer."

"Hey, you two, enough talk about MC's work." Meg grabbed a couple chips. "Let's talk about something fun and cheery."

"I second that." Barb slid a hand onto MC's knee under the table and gently squeezed it. With her other she lifted her margarita, took a sip, and leaned into MC. "How about those Vikings?"

"Argh." A chorus of disappointment from the other three women set the whole group laughing.

The waiter, one of Rosa's many relatives, arrived bearing platters of burritos, chimichangas and enchiladas. Sides of refried beans and sour-cream-topped shredded lettuce and tomatoes garnished each plate. They all dug in with gusto.

#

Barb and MC hugged Dara and Meg and the two couples split off toward their respective cars with a final wave good-bye. MC pulled Barb's arm through the crook of her own, and they strolled the two blocks to where the Camry was parked.

The inky night spit shards of sleet at them. "I didn't know it was supposed to snizzle," Barb said. "I didn't even think to bring gloves. They must be in my other coat."

MC covered Barb's hand with her own. "Snizzle—you're hilarious."

"What? It's not really snow. And it's not really drizzle. More a combination of the two."

"Hence, snizzle."

"Before you know it, we'll be buried in two feet of snow."

"Which reminds me, I should start the snow blower tomorrow. Make sure it's working. They keep talking about a possible Thanksgiving night storm."

"I hope they're wrong because I don't want to miss my Black Friday shopping." Barb shivered. "I can't wait to get some good deals."

"Don't get me anything. I don't need anything."

"Don't tell me what to do, missy. You know better."

MC held up a hand. "No need to go all teacher on me." She leaned over and gave Barb a quick kiss. "How about I get us home. I'm sure the house will be toasty as a wood-fired pizza oven by the time we get there." She laughed as Barb took a swipe at her arm.

#

Safely ensconced in their warm snug bungalow, MC hung their coats in the front closet and locked up. Barb made a beeline up the stairs. "Gonna get my jammies and slippers on. I'll be right back."

MC pulled her work phone from her messenger bag and checked email. Nothing pressing.

She remembered Sergeant Wilcox from MPD was supposed to email copies of the photos of Arty's car. She scrolled back through and didn't see anything from MPD or Wilcox. She was about to compose a message when she heard Barb coming down the stairs.

She pocketed her phone. No sense in ruffling feathers by letting Barb know she'd been doing some work-related stuff. She rose from the couch as Barb hit the bottom of the staircase.

Barb asked, "Cup of hot tea?"

MC considered how incredibly lucky she was to have this beautiful person in her life. "Yes, please."

She pulled Barb into an embrace and kissed her. Slow. Deep. They ended the kiss, and she leaned her forehead on Barb's.

Barb said, "I love you."

"I love you, too. Thank you."

Barb stepped back and gazed into MC's eyes. "What are you thanking me for?"

"For being you. For putting up with me. For loving me." MC kissed her again. "Now I'll go change quick."

"I'll meet you in the living room."

Barb hummed along to Amy Ray's "Goodnight Tender." This particular song fit MC's current mood, and she quietly sang along as she climbed the stairs to their bedroom to change into her flannel pajama pants and a faded Minnesota Lynx T-shirt. She grabbed her phone and composed a quick message to Wilcox.

"MC? What are you doing up there? Tea's ready." A creak sounded.

MC quickly finished and sent the email. She tossed the phone on the dresser. "Coming."

𝓗

By ten p.m., Len Klein noted that the rabble rousers were really winding up. The high-end chic caterer Mike had hired was running ragged keeping the platters of food filled on the dining room table.

Klein figured another hour and the party would be in full swing and by midnight, nearly out of control. He'd dispatched Nick and Quentin to patrol the property and make sure no one accidentally wandered into the frigid lake. The last thing he needed was some dumbass drowning. They were due to check in with him in thirty minutes.

Klein stood near the bar and watched Mike weave his way from the front door across the family room to him.

"Len, at around eleven, herd people back into this area. I'm making an announcement, and I'd like as many people gathered as are able to still stand. You'll handle it?"

"Sure will, boss."

He clapped a hand on Klein's shoulder. "Have you seen Gavin?" Mike wiped his nose on the back of his hand. A whitish residue lingered beneath his boss's nose.

"I haven't seen Gavin. Maybe he's downstairs. I think there's a bunch in the theater and another group playing pool."

"Excellent." Mike stumbled a bit, but quickly regained his balance. "Now, where is Tori? I need more of that kickass white powder. Tori?" He waved his arm and made a beeline for the living room where Tori was holding court with four or five of her Barbie-doll friends. They were sprawled out on a couple of black leather sofas on either side of an enormous oak coffee table that had a glass top. The surface was perfect for the lines of coke waiting to be huffed up someone's nose.

Klein wandered down to the theater. A curtain of marijuana smoke hung heavy in the air and a dozen people guffawed over the movie, *Pineapple Express*. He scanned the attendees. No sign of Gavin. He didn't figure the movie as Gavin's cup of tea, anyway.

Klein felt his cell vibrate and found a text from Nick. *Q and me by lake. F'n freezing! Chk pool/hot tub next.*

He responded using voice dictation. *"Make double damn sure no one is skinny dipping or doing anything stupid. The last thing we need is someone stoned out of their gourd wandering naked into the lake and dying from exposure or drowning. Be back inside by eleven. Stennard is making some big announcement and I want you two close by."*

Nick: *K.*

At five minutes past eleven Gavin Thomson stood in front of the guests, his voice booming over the din. "Everyone! Can I have your attention?"

He set his highball glass on a nearby side table. "Hey! Everyone! Please quiet down!"

Someone from the other side of the room tittered, followed by several giggles.

Klein glanced around, searching for the location of the disruption. He spotted Tori and one of her ditzy friends in a corner of a sofa, high off their asses, and behaving like a couple of sixteen-year-olds. He leveled his gaze right at Tori, willing her to notice him. When she did, she flipped him the bird, but elbowed her friend and shushed her.

Gavin gave it another shot. "Everyone, please be quiet. My friend and our gracious host this evening, Michael Stennard, wants to make a very important announcement."

The stoned group from the theater filed into the family room along the far wall. Klein also noticed Nick and Quentin standing midway up the stairs leading from the lower level. He nodded at them and signaled for them to stay where they were.

Gavin shouted again, "Please! Quiet!"

The noise fell to a dull roar.

"Thank you." Gavin picked up his drink and took a healthy slug. "Without further ado—Mister Michael Stennard." He clapped.

Some people followed Gavin's lead and politely clapped. Others seemed confused. Most simply sat or stood, waiting.

Mike shook hands with Gavin and did the unbearable-to-watch one-armed bro hug.

"Thanks, buddy. Is everyone having a good time?"

This drew a few wolf whistles and a smattering of applause.

Mike beamed and raised both arms in the air like a champ. "Super! I know I'm having fun." He cleared his throat and tossed a quick glance at Gavin, who almost imperceptibly inclined his head. "I'm glad you're having a good time. The good news is we're here to have the best party ever. The bad news is, well, the bad news is this is the last party I'll be hosting for a while."

Groans rippled through the throng. The volume increased as people absorbed Mike's words.

Someone from the crowd hollered out, "Why?"

"I'll tell you why. Today was a dark day for Stennard Global Enterprises. A shitload of cops and feds showed up bright and early this morning and executed a search warrant on our business. There's talk of a federal investigation, so we're taking a temporary hiatus. Our attorneys are working around the clock to resolve the issue." He stopped and guzzled from a bottle of beer someone handed him. The drink tipped his speech into slurred territory.

"Bullshit is shwat . . . what . . . it is."

Klein swore he saw tears glimmering in Stennard's eyes. He wrote it off to the intensely bright track lighting hanging above Mike's head.

Mike continued. "Gavin and I discused," he coughed, "discussed our current state of affairs and decided it would be best to keep a low profile while the situation plays out. No more parties."

"That's fucked up." A shout from the crowd.

"Yesh. It's fucked up. But this ish . . . is . . . really a time to lie low and get our ducks in a row. We appreshate your support. Things'll clear quickly and we'll be back at it. But for tonight—party on!" Mike held up the beer bottle and the crowd whooped in response.

Klein watched as Nick disappeared down the stairs to the lower level. Quentin followed suit, shoulders hunched up around his ears.

"You fucker!" A high-pitched voice behind Klein screamed, followed by the crash of glass.

He spun around in time to see Tori, claws extended, flailing at Mike. "You lied to me. You said there wouldn't be any trouble. We'd be able to go to Vegas for Thanksgiving." She tried to slap Mike and tripped over her friend's foot, taking a header into a couch.

Mike staggered and bent to help her up. "Tori, baby, trush me. This will blow over and we'll be right as rain before you know it. I have it all figured out. Gotta trush me."

Tori slapped his hand away. "Get away from me. You're an asshole." She stood up, wobbling on five-inch stiletto heels. "I wanna leave. And next time, find someone else to cover for you."

Mike reached for her. "Tori, sweetheart, you're drunk and high."

"Fuck you! Whose fault is that? If you didn't have all this coke," she whipped her hand through the remaining snowy lines on the glass-topped table, sending a cloud into the air, "I wouldn't be fucked up."

"No one forced you to snort it, darling." Mike's face was turning as red as Rudolph's nose. "You're a big girl. You made your choices."

"Fuck you! C'mon, Misty." She reached for her blond-haired friend's hand. "Let's get our stuff and get the hell outta here."

"You're not driving anywhere." Mike tried to grab Tori's arm.

She shook him off. "Misty can drive."

"Yeah." Misty weaved back and forth. "Misty can drive. Oh, maybe not." She tittered and put a hand over her mouth. "I feel kind of light and floaty, Tori."

Mike spun around and locked eyes with Klein. He waved him over. "Len will drive you both home."

Klein said, "Mister Stennard, I can have one of my guys drive them. I should really stay here and monitor your security."

Mike put an arm across Klein's shoulders and guided him away from the renegade women. "Listen, Len, I'd much rather you take care of this pershonally. I trush . . . trust . . . you implishitly." He covered a belch. "But those other goons—I dunno 'em so well. I hope you can apprshate why I want you on da job for thish . . . this . . . one. Loyalty is important." He jabbed his pointer finger up in the air.

Klein realized Stennard was beyond shitfaced and gave in. "Sure, Mister Stennard. I'll handle it. I'll get my guys up to speed. Then I'll escort the ladies home."

He tracked down Nick and Quentin. "I have to run an errand for Mister Stennard. You two watch over things and call me immediately if something happens. I shouldn't be gone long. I'll meet up with you when I get back."

Nick asked, "What you gotta do? Need more coke? Someone said a chick threw a hissy fit and sent a bunch of snow flying everywhere."

"No. I'm not getting more fucking coke. Don't worry about what I'm doing. Keep your eyes and ears open for trouble while I'm gone."

Nick said, "Is the big boss up there? I wanna chat with him."

Klein said, "You stay away from Stennard. He doesn't have time to talk to lowlifes. Steer clear."

"Okay, okay. We got it. Right, Q?" Nick stuck a cigarette in his mouth.

"Got it," Quentin said.

"I'm stepping out for a smoke." Nick grabbed Quentin's arm pulling him along.

"Great, I'm feeling so relieved." Klein's sarcasm was lost as the two men wandered toward the door. "Fuck me."

He ducked out through the three-car garage and jogged down the long driveway to where he'd parked his Escalade. He actually felt a giddy-up in his step at the thought of dragging Tori away from the fun. The party would probably be more enjoyable for everyone with her out of the picture.

He drove up to the front entrance, left the car running, and found Tori and her goofy cohort tottering on their stilts in the foyer. "Your chariot awaits, ladies." He mock bowed and held the front door open as the two inebriated dimwits wobbled down the stone steps, holding each other up.

Tori tried to spin around and lost her balance. "Holy hell!" Misty grabbed her arm, saving her from sprawling face first on the driveway. "How're we supposed to get up into this monster truck?"

"Take a running start and leap for all I care." Klein stood stunned at the ridiculous scene unfolding before him. "Get the fuck in, already."

Misty boosted Tori into the backseat and held down her own micro-mini skirt with one hand as she tried to hoist herself up with the other. "A little help, Tor?"

"Gimme your hand." Tori grabbed Misty's hand and pulled. Like Winnie-the-Pooh stuck in the honeypot, Misty jettisoned through the door and sprawled on top of Tori across the backseat.

Klein stuffed Misty's feet inside and slammed the door closed. "Fucking worthless twits," he muttered.

⚡

When he returned to the party, Klein was pleased to find his parking spot still open. He let himself back into the house. The noise hit him like a sonic boom.

He stepped on a half-eaten sandwich lying on a paper plate in the middle of the ceramic tile foyer.

"Shit!" He shook his foot to get the goo off. He picked up the plate and wound his way through the undulating humans and into the kitchen to toss the mess.

He washed his hands and dried them on a towel he found bunched up on the Titanic-sized butcher block center island. He sent Nick a text. *Where are you?*

Nick: *Patio.*

Stay put, I'll be right there. Klein grabbed a roast beef sandwich and wolfed it down on his way to meet Nick and Quentin.

He found his two hired flunkies pacing on the patio, or, rather, Nick was pacing, and Quentin stood robotically smoking a cigarette.

"Everything okay?"

Nick said, "Coupla loud mouths tried punching each other over who won a pool game. We split 'em up. Everything's cool."

"Good. So, here's the deal. You guys can take a break, grab some grub—from the kitchen, not the dining room—and chill 'til midnight. But first I need to let you know that after tonight I probably won't have any work for you, at least for a while. You heard Mister Stennard's spiel earlier."

Nick kicked at some shrubbery next to the patio. "You kidding me? I fuckin' need this job. We need this job."

"Keep it down, Wooly. And stop destroying property. Don't make me boot you tonight without pay."

"I bet it's all the damn postal chick cop's fault. She needs to be taught a lesson." Nick paced in circles on the patio, arms waving like pinwheels. "We're the perfect ones to do it."

"Wooly. Fucking lower your voice," Klein said. "You don't want to go making threats where people can hear you. Don't be a dumb shit. This isn't any one cop's fault. Something big is going down."

Nick leaned into Quentin. "Man, we gotta do something here. This broad cost us our bankroll. No more parties, no more payout. Think about it, bro. Who's gonna foot the bill for your momma's nursing home?"

Quentin twitched and tossed his cigarette butt into the landscape rocks. "Nick's right. If I don't have a job, I can't pay my mom's bills. She'll become a ward of the county in some dump. I need the money."

Nick said, "We'll find out where she lives. This cop—"

"She's not a cop, dumbass." Klein sighed. "She's a lousy postal inspector. And you best stay away. Mister Stennard doesn't need any more trouble than he's already got. Let him handle it. You make matters worse and you'll never get another penny out of me."

"Whatever," Nick said. "She owes us. Thanks to her, our golden goose has flown the coop. Maybe we find out where she lives and ransack the place. She must have some good shit we could pawn for some dough. Maybe she's even got a wad of cash stashed." He gnawed at his thumbnail.

"Help tide us over until things are back to normal. Pay your mom's bills, Q."

"You been sampling the product inside, Nick?" Klein got up in Nick's face. "Stop talking like a fool or I'll toss your ass outta here. I mean it, Wooly. Keep your nose clean and stay away from the inspector. Do. Not. Make. Trouble. Got it?"

Quentin stepped in front of Klein. "C'mon, man. Tell me you got something else for us. I really need the money."

"Listen, kid, if I had anything, I'd have you on it in a heartbeat. I don't even have a job myself at the moment. Not after tonight. Not until this situation is cleared up. I'll put out some feelers, see if there's any security gigs I could get for you guys. Best I can do. Sorry."

"Anything," Quentin said. "I need the money."

Klein laid a hand on Quentin's shoulder. "I know, kid. I heard you. I'll let you know if I find anything. But in the meantime, go grab some food and drink—not too much drink though—and after everyone's cleared out I'll get your dough for tonight. It should be substantial. This is one of the biggest shindigs Mister Stennard has hosted and the guests are all enjoying themselves. Maybe you'll make some extra ching in tips. So, mind your manners and be helpful. And smile, for Christ's sake. You both look like someone shit on your new kicks."

Klein left them on the patio and went to see how the guests were faring inside and wondered where his next paycheck would come from if Stennard went under.

Chapter Eight
Thursday, November 27

Not one speck of light bled under the drawn shade on the east-facing window across the room.

MC rolled over and snuggled against Barb's back, carefully draping an arm over her hip. She felt Barb's hand cover hers and pull her closer. MC considered how lucky she was to have Barb as her partner. Her mind turned to thoughts of a wedding—the kind Barb yearned for. A leap she couldn't quite make.

MC had much to be thankful for on this Thanksgiving morning. Work had been good this week. Less face time with Crapper always made for a good work week. The Stennard thing was moving along nicely, despite the setback with Arty's murder and the missing USB.

FBI Computer Analysis Response Team examiners were combing through all the computers, external hard drives and USB drives seized from the Stennard offices last Saturday. FBI forensic accountants along with Internal Revenue Service Criminal Investigation Division Special Agents were sifting through piles of records, piecing together a tale many speculated could be the largest financial fraud in state history.

If they could locate the USB drive Arty was supposed to turn in, along with the findings from the items seized on Saturday, it would provide enough for additional search warrants to cover all residences, and all Stennard vehicles.

The positives far outweighed the negatives on the side of the good guys.

But Arty's unsolved murder remained a thorn in MC's side. She and Cam weren't directly involved in the murder investigation, but she felt the need to keep a hand in the game. She wanted to find whoever was responsible for Arty's death. Justice for Arty's sacrifice weighed heavily on her.

Arty wasn't a horrible deviant. He was a guy who allowed friendship-fueled greed to cloud his decisions for several years, and when he decided to do the right thing, he'd been snuffed out, like a candle in a jack-o-lantern on a pitch dark All Hallows Eve. No one was all good or all bad.

"Hmmm." Barb mumbled. "What time zit?"

"Shhhh. It's early still. Go back to sleep."

"Few more minutes." Barb backed closer into MC.

MC pulled the blanket up over them and held tight to her partner. Her mind resumed processing, the details a tsunami in her head.

She'd received a short email from Agent Ferndale on Tuesday. They wanted to re-interview Gavin Thomson but had been unable to locate him. The last anyone had seen him was at some hoopla at Stennard's private residence on Lake Minnetonka on Saturday night.

Contact had been made with Michael Stennard, who claimed he'd been suffering from some undisclosed illness and hadn't seen his business partner since late Saturday night.

Ferndale said they'd continue to pursue the Thomson thread. He thought the guy was acting too slick.

MC felt justified in her involvement in finding Arty's killer because of the tie-in to the fraud.

But today she was ready to let go of work, for a day anyway. She and Barb would prepare their Thanksgiving feast and watch the Thanksgiving Day parade on TV. Neither of them was a huge football fan, but they'd probably turn on whatever game was televised. She eagerly anticipated a quiet day with her love.

And now was as good a time as any to wake Barb, in a special holiday way. She nuzzled her nose gently in Barb's exposed ear and placed a soft kiss on her neck. "Wakey. Wakey."

"I'm definitely awake." Barb rolled onto her back and pulled MC in for a warm hug. "Happy Thanksgiving, honey."

ℋ

By eight, they'd emerged from their cocoon ready to take on the day.

MC switched her work cell phone to ring instead of vibrate and set it on the coffee table in the living room. The joy of being on-call on a holiday.

"I'll get the paper." She opened the front door, and a lash of cold slapped her. "Feels like the North Pole." She hauled the newspaper in from the front stoop and slammed the door on the arctic air. "I swear there are more sales ads than actual newspaper in this edition. This thing must weigh fifty pounds." She hefted the *Minneapolis Star Tribune* in both hands and dropped it on the coffee table with a thunk, then slumped onto the couch.

She picked up the remote and found the channel broadcasting the parade.

The south-facing picture window behind the TV framed a sky quickly filling with grayish white clouds. The pallid sun, barely risen, was fading quickly. Shadows hunkered down for a lengthy stay.

Barb came through the dining room carrying two steaming cups of coffee. "That sky is downright apocalyptic." She handed a cup to MC, leaned in for a kiss and sat next to her on the sofa. "Here's to an already wonderful morning, despite the impending gloom."

"No gloom in here. We've got nothing but rays of sunshine and rainbows going on." MC clinked her mug against Barb's. "Although, I think I may need a dose of pain reliever. That newspaper weighed as much as a ship's anchor." She propped her slippered feet on the coffee table.

"Oh, the hyperbole." Barb rolled her eyes and reached for the paper. "Let's see what sales I'll be hitting tomorrow." She set her mug on a coaster on the side table and dug into the three-inch stack.

"Good God, how many ads can there possibly be?"

"Not nearly enough." Barb was giddy with delight. "L.L.Bean, Eddie Bauer, Macy's."

MC laid a hand over her chest. "Be still my heart."

"You should be happy instead of making fun. You'll benefit the most from my forays."

"True. Too bad I have to work or I could go with you." MC sipped her coffee and pulled the local news section from under the stack of colored glossies.

"As if. You hate shopping. I don't understand how anyone can hate shopping."

"I hate crowds and getting trampled in order to save a couple of bucks." MC glanced at the TV. "*Underdog.* I loved *Underdog* when I was a kid. Did you know the first year this cartoon character appeared in the parade was the same year we were born—1965? The cartoon debuted on TV in 1964 with Minnesota's own General Mills as the primary sponsor."

"Mmm-hmmm." Barb rummaged in the drawer of the end table. "Is there a Sharpie in the table next to you?"

MC checked. "Here."

"Thanks." Barb uncapped the marker and began circling items in large black swoops.

"You approach shopping like a well-plotted attack."

"I need to know where I'm going and what I want at each place. The best defense is a good offense, right?" She raised an eyebrow at MC.

"Um, yeah, sure."

"Think about it like a game plan for football. You always see the coaches on the sidelines holding shiny play cards with X's and arrows and whatnot. And you spout things about bootlicks and drags."

MC laughed. "You mean bootlegs and draws?"

"Yes. Those. These pages with circles are my bootlegs and draws. They get me in and out of stores, hopefully unharmed. I don't hear you complaining when I come home with new clothes for you."

"You take very good care of me, and I appreciate all you do."

Barb eyeballed her. "Uh-huh."

"I'm serious. You're the best. I totally don't deserve you."

"A bit over the top, but I love you, too." Barb focused on the ads again.

MC watched her, head bent over the stack of flyers, black marker whisking across pages. Her heart swelled with love. The past nineteen years had been the best of her life, and she counted her blessings every day. Without Barb she'd have a lot less light and love. She'd either have drunk herself into oblivion or immersed herself so deep in her job her social life would've been nonexistent.

Now would be the perfect time to surprise Barb by proposing. Saying to her, easy-peasey, let's get hitched. Let's have a celebration because I love you to the moon and back.

She set the newspaper aside, having no desire to read about the latest homicide, rape, or political jousting match. The colorful parade of balloons, floats, and marching bands engendered a sense of lighthearted merriment. Life should always feel this good, she thought. Then she remembered her parents and Cindy. The holidays were difficult for her, even with Barb at her side. She missed Bobby and Patty McCall profoundly, even twenty-five years after their deaths. And suddenly, the sparks of a wedding flamed out, settling into a pile of ashes. She choked down the proposal, the unspoken words an immobile lump in her throat.

The hardest piece to accept was they had been ripped from her life without warning. She'd not had a chance to say good-bye.

MC found a smidgen of solace only in knowing they'd died coming back from the cabin on Lake Superior, which they loved so dearly. She mourned their never having lived long enough to retire and fully enjoy their favorite spot. Surprisingly, MC yearned to be at the cabin as frequently as she could, but they were almost never able to go. Only there did she feel as though she captured the spirit of her parents. The fun. The love. The peace.

She and Barb had taken a chunk of their investment money and renovated the cabin. MC's parents had installed a heating system sufficient enough to allow for the occasional winter weekend in milder weather, but now the place was ready for living year-round, which was MC and Barb's grand plan when they retired in a few years. They'd even added an additional suite: bedroom, bathroom, and tiny den so Meg and Dara could come stay with them once in a while. Definitely not full-time, though, because as much as MC loved the couple, having Dara on endless loop would be enough to drive her insane.

Regardless, Barb, Dara and Meg, they were MC's family now. So why couldn't she make the leap to the big wedding Barb yearned for?

"Penny for your thoughts." Barb nudged MC's foot with her toes.

"What?"

"You were lost there for a while. Everything okay?"

"Just memories."

Barb huddled closer to MC and wrapped her arms around her. "I know you miss them. But you have me and Dara and Meg. We love you very much." Barb planted a kiss on her cheek. "Now, let's watch the rest of this silly parade. I'll need to get started on our meal soon if we're shooting for dinner at four."

"Four's perfect. And we can have dessert back in here and watch *It's a Wonderful Life* on Netflix."

MC hugged Barb.

"Do we have to watch such a depressing movie?"

"I guess not, but—"

"Thanksgiving tradition."

"A custom started by my parents. I feel like it's one last vestige of them. Besides, we can watch *Christmas Vacation* afterward to cleanse our movie palates. You always laugh, even though it's stupid." MC smiled. "The perfect Thanksgiving."

#

MC gathered their dirty dishes from the breakfast nook. "Can I get you anything?" She rinsed the bowls and loaded them into the dishwasher.

"No, thanks. I'll get started on the pie. It's almost noon." Barb pulled a cookbook from a cupboard shelf above the stove.

"What can I do to help?"

"Go watch TV or read or something." Barb paged through the cookbook until she found the recipe she needed.

"I could get potatoes ready. Or chop veggies for salad."

"No. Really. I can handle this. We'd be tripping over each other." She herded MC back toward the living room. "And I enjoy my cooking therapy."

"Like you need therapy." MC squeezed Barb's hand. "I think I'll go for a run before I vegetate. With work being so crazy the past couple weeks, I haven't had time to get out. I need to get back on track. That's my therapy."

"Bundle up."

MC grabbed her work phone from the living room and tapped the weather app. Cloudy and twenty-four degrees. North winds five to ten miles per hour. Definitely brisk.

She went upstairs and changed into running tights, thermal running shirt, and dug her Saucony running shoes from the closet floor. She pulled on her balaclava and a jacket to ward off the wind.

MC went back down to the kitchen and stuck her hands into a pair of gloves. "I should be back in forty-five minutes or so."

"You're positively villainous. Hopefully you won't freak out any of the neighbors."

"I'm more likely to be stopped by a local patrol than one of our neighbors. I've got my work phone on me." She patted her jacket pocket.

"Enjoy your run."

MC did a few quick stretches in the driveway before heading down the alley. Her head cleared with each puff of air she exhaled.

She jogged over to Highland Parkway and followed it down to Mississippi River Boulevard. The burn in her quads was a stark reminder she'd gone far too long without exercise. The brown river gurgled on her left.

MC dangled her arms loosely at her sides to relax her form for a few strides before shaking them out and resuming her normal running position. She followed the frosted asphalt path along the river to Summit Avenue and headed east on Summit to Cleveland. Going south on Cleveland. From there she traversed the west side of the St. Catherine University campus to the homestretch back along Pinehurst.

At the mouth of the alley she slowed her pace. Back in her own driveway she bent over, hands planted on her knees, and sucked in crystalline air, clearing her lungs. She checked her phone. The run had taken her forty-seven minutes. Not bad for being off her normal routine.

After a few post-run stretches, she found the back door locked. She knocked, and Barb was there in an instant, disengaging the deadbolt.

Warm pumpkin and spices welcomed her home.

"Smells yummy." She kicked her shoes off onto the all-weather mat inside the door, pulled the balaclava from her head, and ran her hand over her sweat-flattened hair.

"Pie's in the oven. How was your run?" Barb leaned over the sink and washed a ceramic mixing bowl. Steam painted patterns on the window above the sink.

"Good. I was off pace, though. And my quads screamed before I was even halfway through the run." MC stuffed her gloves inside the balaclava. "I need a glass of water and a warm shower." She grabbed a glass from the cupboard and stood waiting for Barb to finish rinsing the bowl and utensils.

She filled the glass and leaned back against the counter, drinking water and wiggling her toes to warm them.

"The pie has another forty minutes. I'll prep the turkey breast and work on the sweet potatoes."

"I can pitch in after my shower." MC rinsed her glass and put it in the dishwasher.

"I have it covered. You rest and get warm."

"Holler if you change your mind." MC gave Barb a quick peck on her cheek.

# #

Freshly showered, dressed in jeans and a clean flannel shirt, MC sprawled across the couch and surfed the TV channels. Against her better judgment she decided to give football a chance and selected the Chicago Bears and Detroit Lions game.

At halftime, MC punched the remote until she landed on reruns of *The Big Bang Theory*, one of her favorite shows. The motley group of nerds never failed to make her laugh.

She related to their patched together family. Penny was in the middle of serenading Sheldon with "Soft Kitty" while applying vapor rub to his chest when MC's cell emitted an annoying old-fashioned ringtone. She reached over the arm of the couch and grabbed her personal cell. "Barb, it's Dara on FaceTime."

"Hey, Dara."

"How you doing, buddy? Happy gobble gobble day and all that happy crap." Dara panned the phone and Meg appeared on the tiny screen.

"Hi, MC." Meg waved. "Happy Thanksgiving. Where's Barb?"

"I'm here!" Barb ran into the room wiping her hands on a towel. "I've been slaving away in the kitchen while MC lounges in front of the TV eating bonbons."

"Some things never change," Dara said.

"Ease up will ya? I did go for a run earlier. What have you done?" MC asked.

Dara said, "I've been working at retaining my sanity, which is a brain drain of epic proportions. We needed a break from my folks, so we snuck into my old room, which, as you can see, is now my mother's sewing room slash reading hideaway." Dara shifted the phone to give them a three-hundred-sixty-degree view of the ten-by-twelve-foot room. A sewing machine was shoved in one corner and a giant plush recliner, reading lamp, and table sat in the center of the room. Every wall was lined with bookcases crammed full of books and magazines.

"Your mom sure has a lot of books. How's the family time?" MC asked. "You two don't appear too worse for wear."

"Ha ha," Dara said. "You're a real card, McCall. Actually, they've been pretty okay. My dad's only referred to Meg as my friend once."

"I'm slowly winning him over," Meg said. "Give me another ten years, and I'll have him calling me his daughter-in-law."

"Don't hold your breath," Dara said. "How're you two? Are you watching the Bears-Lions game? Boring. Chicago can't stop turning over the damn ball."

MC rubbed her eyes. "I think I may have dozed off." She yawned and peeled herself off the couch.

"Nice ploy to get out of setting the table," Barb teased.

"Why didn't you wake me?" MC felt guilty for snoozing while Barb worked so hard preparing their meal.

"Oh, stop it and get yourself to the table. Do you want a glass of wine with dinner?"

"I better not, in case I get a call." MC shut off the TV.

Barb had covered the dining room table with an autumnal patterned tablecloth—burnt orange, brown, and gold leaves interspersed with scattered acorns. The centerpiece was a giant cornucopia with two ivory candles set on either end.

Two place settings, one on the end and the other at the first chair to the right, waited for them. Barb set out two orange Fiestaware plates to coordinate with the rest of the table decor. One wineglass stood guard over the place at the head of the table.

"The table is beautiful. You've outdone yourself." MC caught Barb on her way back to the kitchen and pulled her in for a kiss. "Happy Thanksgiving. I'm very thankful for you."

"And I'm thankful for you. Would you light the candles for me? I'll bring the food in before it gets cold."

They plowed through turkey, gravy, and all the usual Thanksgiving accoutrements. Barb enjoyed a couple glasses of wine. Then they quickly cleared the table and stowed the leftovers.

After loading the dishwasher MC carried the pie into the dining room. Barb followed with plates and forks.

MC served up two generous slices and settled back into her chair. "Wait. Whipped cream." She launched herself from her chair and hustled to the kitchen for the whipped topping.

"You're zippy." Barb held a forkful of pie. "I swear you were out of your chair and back in before I blinked."

"Smart aleck. Whipped cream?" She wiggled the red and white spray can over Barb's plate.

"Yes, please." Barb leaned back.

MC pushed the spray top and white globules splayed across the table down the front of Barb's shirt and one tiny dot clung to Barb's chin. "Oops. Sorry. I'll get it." She wiped a finger across Barb's chin and scooped the blob of cream into Barb's mouth.

"I should know better than to let you operate the spray can." Barb wiped the table and her shirt. "Give me the can before you cover the whole room." She snatched it away, deftly covered their slices of pie, and set the can out of MC's reach.

MC scrunched her nose and pretended to pout. "One teeny tiny squirt?"

"Oh, for God's sake. Here." Barb placed the can next to MC's plate. "Please confine the mess to your side of the table."

MC proceeded to make a snow-white mountain on top of her pumpkin pie. "Now this is what I call dessert." She plunged her fork in and dug out a great scoop of creamy-coated pie and shoveled it into her mouth. "Yum. Perfection."

Later MC made coffee and Barb queued up *It's a Wonderful Life*. MC brought them each a cup of decaf. She joined Barb on the couch.

Night had fallen. Inky darkness was broken only by the sodium vapor streetlamp on the boulevard outside their house. Wind bent the arthritic branches of the trees and howled a woeful song. MC said, "Perfect night to be inside with hot coffee and a hot woman."

"Indeed." Barb snuggled into MC's side and pulled the afghan from the back of the couch to cover their legs. "Ready for the movie?"

"Roll it."

Barb fell asleep halfway through and stirred next to MC at the tinkling of bells and ZuZu Bailey saying, "Teacher says, every time a bell rings, an angel gets his wings."

"Rise and shine." MC kissed the tip of Barb's nose. "You didn't even drink your coffee before you zonked out."

Barb stretched. "Sorry. Guess I was tired. I'm getting a fresh cup. Want one?"

"Sure. Are you still up for *Christmas Vacation*? I know it's getting late, almost ten already. Maybe cousin Eddie will keep you from falling asleep."

"He's so disgusting."

"He is disgusting, but also freakin' hilarious," MC said. "But if you'd rather not—"

"I think I can make it through, but then I've got to get to bed because I need to be up at three so I can be at Macy's by four and hopefully back home around seven."

"Sounds so enticing. Not." MC hit the play button to start the movie.

No sooner had the relatives started piling into the Griswold's house than MC's cellphone rang. "Damn. It's work."

Barb hit the pause button and eyed MC and then the clock on the wall. "It's after ten."

MC nodded. "McCall. Hey, Jamie." MC got up and rummaged around in her messenger bag on the floor. Notebook and pen in hand she sat in the Stickley Eastman chair, the worn tan leather cushion sinking comfortably in all the right places. "Yep. Got it. I'll meet him at the facility ASAP."

Barb's eyebrows rose at the last words.

MC held a finger up, pen in hand. "Yes, we'll keep you informed. Bye." MC scribbled a few more notes and set the pen down.

"You've got to leave, right?" Disappointment colored Barb's tone.

"I'm sorry. An employee attacked a supervisor at the Saint Paul processing center. Cam and I are both on-call, so Jamie is sending us both. I'll probably be gone all night by the sounds of it." MC rose from the chair and reached for Barb. "Cheer up. Now you can hit the hay earlier because we don't have to watch the movie."

She shot a thumb over her shoulder at the frozen screen showing a whale-eyed Chevy Chase, mouth hanging open.

"I guess there's a silver lining in every dark cloud." Barb worked at, but didn't quite achieve, a smile. "Be careful. Please." She placed a hand on MC's cheek.

MC covered Barb's hand with her own and planted a soft kiss in the palm. "I'm always careful. And so is Cam. You be careful tomorrow. I don't want you getting trampled by the herd of shoppers hoarding all the deals. We can swap war stories over leftovers tomorrow night and maybe watch this here movie."

"Sounds like a plan." Barb followed MC into the hallway.

"I've got to change." MC ran up the stairs and quickly dressed in navy tactical pants and layered a T-shirt under her navy sweatshirt with the Inspection Service badge on the left front and US Postal Inspector Police on the back, exactly like her jacket. She stuffed her feet into a pair of black tactical boots.

Back down in the front hallway she squatted in the closet to retrieve her handgun and shoulder holster. She ejected the magazine and checked it and pulled two extra fifteen round magazines from the safe and jammed them into the double magazine pouches on the other side of the harness. She draped the contraption over her shoulders and secured it into place.

She yanked her jacket off a hanger and stuck her arms through the sleeves. Messenger bag over one shoulder, she met Barb in the kitchen.

Barb had switched on the iPod in the kitchen. She held the keys to MC's car in one hand and a travel mug of coffee in the other. "Be safe and come home to me." She leaned in for a kiss.

Lucinda Williams crooned "Blue" from the iHome speaker as MC palmed the keys and swooped Barb into a one-armed hug for another kiss. "You're the best." Insulated mug in hand, she moved toward the door. "Love you. Lock the door behind me."

The air smelled fresh and clear. Tiny crystals, not quite fully matured snowflakes, spilled lightly from the leaden belly of the sky. Within the evening silence, MC heard the sharp tap of the granules hitting the pavement.

The icy wind numbed her ears. She never wore a hat in winter, except for running, a bone of contention between her and Barb. But MC had never been much of a hat wearer. Even as a kid, she hated the confined feel around her head, not to mention hat hair.

MC's mind veered to the earlier missed opportunity to surprise Barb with a marriage proposal. Even though Barb understood about MC's hesitation, MC knew how much Barb wanted to get married and share the event with family and friends. She couldn't bite the bullet.

MC's stomach clenched at the thought of inviting Barb's whole family and however many of their friends. She opened the gate and latched it closed behind her. Her head throbbed and she broke out in a sweat despite the raw air.

The ice pellets had evolved into light fluffy snow floating down as she backed the car from the garage. She hit the remote to close the rolling door and leaned over to wave at Barb who was watching out the back door. Barb blew her a kiss, which MC made a huge production over catching before she drove down the alley.

#

Cam and MC met outside the processing center in Eagan. They entered the building through the loading dock doors.

They met a supervisor who had taken control of the situation and separated the parties involved.

Cam left to interview the wounded supervisor in an office before EMTs took him to have the wound stitched up.

MC interviewed the mail handler and reminded him of the zero-tolerance policy regarding violence in the workplace. A couple of patrol officers from St. Paul PD arrived and transported the employee to the Ramsey County Jail. The county prosecutor would decide on state charges to file.

MC and Cam split up and took statements from another five or six employees who'd witnessed the altercation. They all confirmed that the mail handler had totally lost his shit and cut the supervisor.

They notified the other supervisor that the inspection service would issue an investigative summary report to postal management regarding the incident.

A long night of interviews and bad coffee at the postal facility was followed by a slog of early morning paperwork and building a case file back at their office.

#

Just before seven in the morning MC set the file prominently on the center of Jamie Sanchez's desk. Because Jamie had been the Team Leader that called them out, he got to deal with the case file. She found Cam in his office, phone to his ear saying, "I think we're about finished. I'll be leaving soon. Within the next fifteen minutes or so."

He covered the mouthpiece and said to MC, "Talking to Jane."

"I put the file on Jamie's desk. I'm calling it a day. I don't know if Crapper's coming in today, and I'd rather be gone before he gets here."

"Right on. No sense in making a long night even longer. Have a good weekend."

"Tell Jane I said hello and give those kids a hug from me when you get home. You guys have a good weekend, too."

"Will do. Tell Barb hello from us. We should make plans to have you guys over for dinner soon."

MC gave him a thumbs up and left. Back in her office she shut down her computer and checked her phone. Nothing from Barb. She thought about calling her and decided against it because she'd either be knee deep in battling other shoppers or lugging bags into the house and as long as she was heading home, she could wait.

♯

MC was stunned when she stepped outside. Suburbia mimicked a snow globe in the gray light of dawn. Every surface was buried in brilliant white and the sky still shed snow. When she inhaled through her mouth, the air shot daggers into her lungs. Stifling a yawn, she reminded herself she'd heard on NPR recently that if you breathed through your nose, by the time the air hit the back of your nose, it was fully humidified and much easier on the lungs.

Breathing through her nose, she trudged across the unshoveled parking lot, let the car warm up, and checked her cell. Nothing from Barb. Seven a.m. and she decided a cup of French roast from Flannel would be the ticket to help propel her homeward. She put the car in gear and puttered through the parking lot out onto mostly deserted streets. She wound her way eastward, tires squelching over wet, sticky snow. Twenty minutes later she found a parking spot on the street in front of the coffee shop.

Inside, Kate, the young college student Dara and Meg employed, bagged a blueberry scone for a woman and handed her a cup of coffee.

"Hey, MC. You know Dara and Meg are still out of town, right?"

"We actually talked to them yesterday. How was your Thanksgiving?"

"Good. I have a pretty big family and we were all at my grandma's. There were thirty of us. Enough for a couple of touch football teams."

"Sounds fun," MC said. Sounds like a nightmare is what she thought, then chastised herself for being sardonic. Not everyone had adverse reactions to family gatherings.

"What can I get you?"

"I'll take a cup of the dark roast with room and one of those blueberry scones. They look fabulous."

"For here?"

"Please. Barb probably isn't home yet. I'll enjoy breakfast before I brave the elements again."

"Where's Barb? Oh, wait, don't tell me she's one of those Black Friday shoppers."

"Yes, indeed. It's like a religion. May I not be struck by lightning for such blasphemy."

Kate scooped a scone onto a plate and set it on the counter then she poured MC's coffee. "I know Meg was upset about being up north and missing all the big sales today."

"I know. She and Barb had quite the discussion about it." MC paid and dropped a couple bucks into the glass tip jar next to the register.

Kate responded with a hearty thank you.

MC pulled out a chair at the first table. "So, tell me, what are you doing to stay in shape during the winter so you're ready for softball in the spring?"

"I go in a couple times a week and lift weights and do cardio." Kate came out to wipe down the table. She brushed crumbs off a couple chairs at the high-top counter along the front windows. "I've been thinking about doing a kickboxing class. Maybe work on my balance."

"Nice. I hadn't thought about kickboxing." MC ate half her scone and chased it with some coffee.

"I can't take credit for the idea. My cousin told me she took a class last year and it really helped her."

The door opened and two women entered followed by a cyclone of snow. "This weather is really something," the first one said. Her hat was covered in snow, and glops of slush dropped from the bottom of her boots onto the industrial runner inside the door.

MC finished eating, snagged her coffee, and put the plate in the plastic dirty dish bin at the end of the counter. She waved goodbye to Kate and leaned into the blustery squall.

In an effort to keep herself alert, she found the all Christmas FM radio station and cranked the volume up, driving home through the snow-clogged streets to the tune of "Rudolph the Red-Nosed Reindeer", "Here Comes Santa Claus," and all the usual kitschy Christmas tunes.

No sign of plows yet, which indicated the storm was not letting up any time soon. She turned onto Summit, deciding it would be easier to navigate than Grand. She estimated there must be a good three inches accumulated already and no sign of slowing down. She was thankful she wasn't driving the other way, as traffic was much heavier going toward downtown. An added bonus, because she and Cam had pulled an all-nighter they were off until Monday morning. Barb would be happy. MC slid to a stop for a red light at Snelling, the anti-lock brakes shuddering and groaning. She took the opportunity to drink the last dregs of her coffee and think about all the bags and packages she'd find strewn across the kitchen, with Barb happily in the midst of the chaos. MC smiled at the image.

Chapter Nine
Friday, November 28

The long wearisome night was catching up to MC. The weather showed no signs of improvement. Bloated white flakes floated downward like tiny parachutes. Grimy nuggets of ice hugged car wheels. Tree branches wept with frosty wet weight, like soldiers resigned to a long battle looming ahead.

Black Friday morning, the shopaholic's annual championship match. She hoped Barb was home safe and sound. All she could think about was a hot shower, fresh coffee, and a huge hug from Barb. The caffeine infusion from the stop at Flannel was fading and she was losing patience with idiot drivers. Cranky didn't begin to describe how she felt. At this point, she was ready to give the Grinch a run for his money.

MC dug a knuckle into her gritty eyes. She made the final turn onto Pinehurst, her street, and noticed a conglomeration of emergency vehicles a block ahead. She crept down the street, wondering what the commotion was all about.

When she reached the corner, her eyes widened and she slammed on the brakes. The car skidded and the front tire slammed into the curb.

A lightshow painted houses, trees, and snow in a dreadful carnival of red and blue.

Squad cars were parked haphazardly directly in front of MC's house. A paramedic unit sat idling in the mix. The falling snow slowed, revealing the hulking SPPD Forensic Services vehicle, an oversized white cargo van.

MC abandoned her car and scrambled across the greasy road. A flame-haired Saint Paul police officer attempted to stop her. She tried an end run around him, but he grabbed her arm. "No one is allowed beyond this point."

Another officer tied yellow crime scene tape between the two pine trees in her front yard and up the walk toward her front door.

MC was caught halfway between fury and terror. "That's my freaking house! What's going on?"

The cop stood his ground, a human blockade on the snow-covered curb.

MC yanked her cell phone from her coat pocket and turned away.

She heard the cop talking behind her. "Sir, there's a female out front wearing a jacket with US Postal Inspector on the back."

She frantically scrolled through her texts. Nothing from Barb. She called her. The phone connected and rang. And rang. And rang. After the fourth ring Barb's voicemail kicked in. "Babe, please call me when you get this." MC's voice shook.

A pear-shaped man of mature years wearing a trench coat stepped out of MC's front door and bumbled down the walkway. He tilted his charcoal fedora back on his head, nodded at the red-haired officer, and fixed his pale blue gaze on her. "Good morning. I'm Detective Sergeant Sharpe."

"MC McCall, Inspector MC McCall, and that's my house." She thrust her finger at the tiny bungalow and vibrated with a mixture of anger, dread and the desperate need to know what the fuck was going on. She struggled to breathe, to control her wild imaginings. "Will someone please tell me what the hell is happening?"

"I've got it from here, Red. Thanks." Sharpe dismissed the young officer.

"Thanks a bunch, Red," MC said sarcastically. She glared at the young cop as Sharpe guided her onto the sidewalk, but on the public side of the yellow line.

"Easy now, Ms. McCall. He's only doing his job. May I see some identification?" Sharpe pulled a pair of leather gloves from his coat pocket and stuffed his hands in them. His words sent a ghostly plume into the morning air. They stood out in front of god and every neighbor on the street, as he patiently waited for proof she was who she claimed to be.

MC knew he was right. She tried to reel in her anger, unzipped her jacket, showed him her gold shield and ID.

He squinted. "US Postal Inspector. You armed?" One grayish eyebrow inched up toward where his hairline used to be. His face sagged in folds as if weighed down by years of dealing with others' suffering.

"Yes." Huffing out a breath, she yanked the jacket away from her left side and revealed the sidearm in the shoulder holster. "Now, how about telling me what the hell is going on in my house?" So much for self-control, she thought. Was he purposely ignoring her question?

"I'll need your firearm, please. Sorry. Protocol. You understand?"

"Protocol, I understand." She couldn't contain the disdainful sound of her words. "Not much more, so maybe you could find a way to start explaining the situation to me." She yanked her gun from the shoulder holster, ejected the magazine and the round in the chamber, and handed everything to him.

A voice in the far reaches of her mind told her to take a breath and calm down, but her emotions overrode reason.

He seemed unperturbed by her caustic tone. Sharpe waved at the young officer. "Hey, Red. Get me an evidence bag from forensics."

Sharpe said to MC, "The forensic investigators are doing their work. Until the scene is cleared, I'm afraid I can't allow you inside. I do have a few questions to ask you. Let's step over to my car, and I'll drive you to headquarters where we can talk in a place out of the elements."

He held out his hand and directed her toward a black Mark IV sedan speckled with gray and white salt stains, parked at the curb beyond the behemoth van.

The officer caught up with them and handed Sharpe the evidence bag.

Sharpe dropped her SIG Sauer and ammo into the brown bag, sealed, and signed and dated it. "We'll take this downtown with us." He opened the trunk and dropped the bag in.

"Can't we talk here?" MC asked. "My car—" She pointed at her Camry, still running, door open.

The harshness of high wattage flashing lights dimmed the brilliant white of the falling snow. MC's mind spun dark thoughts and her stomach somersaulted.

The blueberry scone threatened to make a reappearance, along with the coffee. She held her breath and swallowed bitter bile, breathing slowly through her nose. "Wait. What scene? What the fuck is going on here?" Her insides turned to Jell-O. Her mouth went dry as a lizard baking in the Arizona sun.

"Do you live here alone, Inspector McCall?" Sharpe's gaze was unwavering.

"Do I? Alone? No. My—I live here with my partner, Barb. Barb Wheatley."

"When was the last time you saw your, er—partner?"

"Why? What's going on? Where is she? Please. Has something happened to Barb?" MC's legs quivered; her body was slick with cold sweat. She spun around to take a step toward the house.

"Listen." He blocked her passage, leaning into her space with the brim of his fedora nearly touching her forehead. "I'm sorry. We found her by the back door. The ID in her wallet matches the name you gave. I'm afraid she's . . ."

"She's what? For Christ's sake tell me."

He opened the door, guided MC into the passenger seat, and hustled around the other side. After he cranked the heat, he pulled off his gloves and tossed them on the dashboard. He retrieved a spiral notebook with a worn red cardboard cover from an inner pocket, clicked his pen.

"Inspector McCall, there's no easy way to tell you this. Your partner has been killed. She was shot. And now I have the unpleasant task of requiring you to answer questions."

Mouth agape, she stared at him. "Dead?"

He pulled out a pack of chewing gum and pushed a white square from the foil. "Quitting smoking. It's tough." He offered MC the gum.

"No," she said, unable to process the combination of gum and gunshots. "Are you saying Barb is dead? Someone killed her? Shot her?"

Maybe repetition would make her brain, and her heart, process and accept the news.

"Yes. I'm so sorry for your loss, Inspector."

"How? What? What the hell happened?"

"We're in the early stages of this." He stopped writing and focused on her. "In the meantime, I need to ask you some questions. So, we'll be taking a ride to the station."

MC grabbed her head with both hands and leaned into the dashboard, holding her tears in check. She felt as though her life was pouring out of her. Barb was dead?

She sat back and took a deep breath, realizing she was the number one suspect. If they'd ruled her out, he wouldn't be taking her downtown and asking her questions.

With anguish, she said, "If only I'd gotten home sooner."

"You also could've been a victim."

"No!" Her scream echoed inside the car and she pounded her fist on the dash. She wanted to beat on something—or someone. She yearned to hunt down the maggot who murdered Barb. But the fight drained out of her, much as she imagined Barb's blood draining out of her.

After a moment, she swiped a hand across her eyes and sucked in a ragged breath. "I'm sorry, Detective. I didn't catch your name."

"Sharpe. I'm a detective with the Saint Paul Police Department, Homicide."

"Detective Sharpe. Let me articulate clearly, I would've been armed, so she might've had a fighting chance had I been here."

"Not unless you make a habit of wearing your gun around the house in your pajamas. You don't want to go down that road, but now you mention it, why weren't you home? Where were you?"

She'd given him the opening he needed to begin mining for information. "I was called in to work last night."

"Last night was Thanksgiving."

Thank you, Detective Obvious, was on the tip of her tongue, but she withered beneath his steely gaze.

MC gave him a brief rundown of her case and Cam's name and number so he could corroborate her whereabouts. She also gave him Jamie's contact information.

He said, "You won't be able to stay here until we've cleared the scene. And I need to get a statement from you." He raised an eyebrow at her. "Let's go right now. Get it over with. The sooner the better. Don't you agree?"

"Yes." The word fell from numb lips.

"And don't worry about your car. I'll have one of the investigators park it down the street. I can drive you back when we've finished. Sit tight, and I'll be right back." He pushed himself out of the car and waved Red over.

MC watched as he pointed to the Camry, then a spot further up the street. The young officer nodded and hoofed it toward her car.

Sharpe returned. "Ready?"

"Yes."

He continued to speak, but tremors shook her, and the drone of his voice was like a cloud of bees swarming her head.

Barb was gone.

Her life—their life together—gone.

Chapter Ten
Friday, November 28

The trek through morning traffic from her Highland Park neighborhood to Lowertown Saint Paul via Interstate 35-E was interminable. MC suffered chills and sweats, in turn zipping and unzipping her jacket and wrapping her arms around herself.

Sharpe kept his eyes on the highway. "Sorry for the defunct heater. These older model cars get finicky after so many years of abuse."

MC unzipped her jacket again. "We have similar issues with our fleet." She watched the parade of vehicles navigating the season's first substantial snowfall. Her breath fogged the inside of the window. Part of her was tempted to draw a heart and put her and Barb's initials inside.

Sharpe veered off the freeway at Seventh Street. "Almost there." He pulled into a parking lot behind a reddish-brown brick building.

MC followed Sharpe across the Saint Paul Police Department lot. Her legs felt weak, as though she were recovering from anesthesia. She waited while he swiped a card to unlock a heavy metal door. She was familiar with this cop shop, but hadn't spent much time there over the years, so when Sharpe led her down a series of hallways and up two flights of stairs to the second floor, it was all new to her.

Before she even unzipped her jacket, Sharpe was shucking off his trench coat to reveal a neat but worn brown suit, white dress shirt, and mustard yellow tie. Detective Sergeant Sharpe was definitely not a fashionista.

Sharpe hung his coat and hat on a metal coat rack inside a room containing six sets of desks in groups of two facing each other. Vertical blinds covered the windows, blocking out the falling curtain of white outside. The Commander's glass enclosed office was located at the opposite end of the room.

Inside the white walls took on an aged hue under the sterilizing florescent lights. Thankfully, no one else was in the area. "Nice digs." MC leaned against the door frame, hoping to appear casual, but feeling like she might collapse.

Sharpe sorted through piles of paper on one of the desks. "This is much better than the old place. Not top of the line, but we can't complain. Although, some do." He pushed aside a stack of files and pulled a pen from the detritus, opened a drawer, and withdrew a yellow legal pad. "How about we find a quiet room and get your statement?"

MC tried to swallow, but her throat wouldn't cooperate. She simply nodded her assent.

"Follow me." Sharpe plodded down a hallway. He took a right and stopped at the second door down.

"This should work." He flipped a switch on the wall outside the door. MC knew it activated the recording system. Sharpe entered and flicked on the lights to reveal a ten-by-ten-foot room.

The walls were two-tone, white on the top and a dusky blue on the bottom. Dark blue industrial carpeting covered the floor of a space that was barren save for a table and two metal-framed tan chairs.

Two dome cameras hung from the ceiling: one beside the door, and one in the far corner of the room.

She removed her jacket and hung it on the back of one of the chairs and sat. With a weary sigh, she covered her face with her hands, then dragged them back through her hair.

"Can I bring you something to drink before we begin?" Sharpe asked. "Water? Coffee? Soda?"

MC cleared her throat. "Water would be nice. Thanks."

"I'll be right back." Sharpe left, closing the door behind him.

MC stared at the door, wondering if it was locked, but not caring.

Waves of grief washed over her and suddenly she was freezing again. She scrubbed her hands up and down her arms, seeking an elusive warmth.

After what seemed like an hour but was probably only a minute or two, Sharpe returned. He slid a plastic bottle of water across the table to her and set a steaming mug of coffee on his side. Oddly enough, the smell from the burnt wisps wafting from his cup caused bile to rise in MC's throat. Her forehead felt clammy. She quickly uncapped the bottle and chugged several gulps of cold water.

Sharpe sipped his coffee and eyed her. "Thirsty, huh?"

MC brushed a stray droplet from her upper lip. "Feeling a bit nauseated." She capped the bottle and set it aside. "Can we please get on with this?"

"Sure. Why don't you begin with yesterday? Guide me through your day and night, then we'll go through this morning when you arrived at your residence."

He clicked the ballpoint pen and scribbled the date and time on the yellow legal pad, then waited, pen poised.

MC stared at the notepad, transfixed. Flashes of coppery red flamed before her eyes.

She flinched.

A metallic scent tickled her nostrils.

She coughed.

Where was she?

Something was wrong.

Barb was in trouble, needed MC's help.

MC reached out a hand, searching in a snowy haze. Seeking the warmth of her partner's hand in her own.

She felt nothing but cold.

"Inspector McCall?"

She'd knocked over the bottle of water. "Sorry. Guess I lost it for a second." She dug her fingers into her thigh. The pressure helped her focus.

Sharpe set the bottle of water upright. "The sooner we get through this, the sooner you'll be able to leave. Okay?" He inclined his head toward her. "From the beginning. Take your time."

MC described their Thanksgiving day and later the call from Jamie about the incident at the Saint Paul processing center. She sketched out the details of the incident, those involved, including her partner, Cam.

She drank down the remaining water, then told him about the time-consuming paperwork she'd filled out, her departure from work, and stopping at Flannel before heading to her house. "And you know more than I do from this point on."

During her statement, Sharpe filled multiple pages on the pad in front of him.

MC said, "Lots of notes."

"I'm old school. Writing things down helps me cogitate the details."

MC gave him a lopsided half-smile. "Nice use of linguistics. I feel the same way." Her ability to smile faded as quickly as it had appeared. "Now what?"

"We go through it all again. Start to finish. Sometimes people forget details which may be important. Someone you may have seen lurking when you were out running or when you left the house. You know the drill."

MC shifted in her chair uncomfortable as interviewee. She leaned her elbows on the table, dropping her head into her hands. "Could I please use the restroom?" She eyed the empty water bottle on the table. "And maybe get another bottle of water?"

"Certainly." Sharpe directed MC to the women's restroom at the end of the hall. "I need to make a couple calls, then we'll resume."

MC felt like a dead woman walking.

She quickly took care of business and splashed cold water on her face. She'd never felt so tired in her life. The face in the mirror—dark circles around lifeless blue eyes, red splotches on pale, white skin—was not one she recognized.

Just past the bathroom, a window at the end of the hall overlooked the public parking lot. She leaned her forehead against the icy glass, watching the snow accumulate outside.

Who would kill Barb? And why? She was the sweetest, kindest person on the face of the earth. She was the type to hand a five-dollar bill—or her own coffee or snack—to a homeless person on a street corner and tell them to have a wonderful day. Why on earth would anyone shoot her?

MC blamed herself. This was her fault. She should've been home to protect Barb.

"Inspector McCall?" Sharpe called from down the hall behind her. "Ready?"

Turning around to face him made her feel slightly dizzy. She put a hand on the window sill to ground herself.

He stood in front of the interview room, hands in his pants pockets.

MC returned to the room and took her seat. A new bottle of water waited for her on the table. "Thanks for the water."

Sharpe closed the door. "You're welcome." He sat, another cup of coffee at his elbow.

The new brew smelled almost palatable. MC watched him flip through his notes. "I made a few calls while you were indisposed. I've got four detectives on site at your house. The forensic team is making good progress in processing the scene. We want to be thorough so I've requested a Crash and Crime Scene Reconstruction team do a 3-D computer animation of the scene. Everything should be done by late this afternoon." He paused and met MC's gaze. "I need one more thing from you, Inspector."

What more could he take from her, she wondered. An arm? A leg? "And what would that be?"

"Your cell phone. One of our analysts will check it. Standard procedure."

"Phones," MC said.

"Pardon?"

"Phones, plural. I have a personal cell and a work-issued cell." MC reached into her jacket pocket and retrieved two iPhones. She slid both devices across the table to Sharpe.

"The purple one is my personal phone and the blue is my work one. You'll notice a call to Barb from my personal phone not long after I . . . after I . . . " She swallowed hard. "Um, after I arrived on scene this morning."

"Sit tight. I'll run these to cyber." Sharpe left the room, closing the door behind him.

MC slumped in her chair and picked up the water bottle. This day was surreal. She felt bereft—hollow.

Her mind whirred with snippets of her life with Barb. People claimed their life flashed before their eyes when they thought they were dying. She might as well be dying because her life as she knew it was definitely over.

A string of vignettes played from the night they first met all the way through their good-bye the previous night. Was it just last night? She whipped a hand through her hair. Tears she'd been working so hard to hold back rolled down her face unfettered. Without warning, gut wrenching, heart-rending sobs exploded out of her. She grabbed a couple tissues from the box at the far end of the table, wiping ineffectually at the streaks running down her face.

Control, McCall. Gotta get control. Get through this and get out of here. She sucked in a lungful of air. Unscrewed the cap on the water and drank half the bottle down. She inhaled as she swallowed and choked, coughing hard. Blew her nose, wadded up the tissues in her hand. She swiped some more at her face, which she imagined would be puffy and blotchy, but at this point she didn't care. She'd barely managed to regain control when Sharpe reappeared.

"Back to business." He took one look at her and quickly sat down. "You doing okay?"

"Fine."

"Good. Let's do this. One more time from the beginning. You both had the day off yesterday. You got up. Watched the parade . . . "

MC ran through the details, point by point, her voice a disembodied drone in her ears. Inside her head a monotone voice chanted, "Barb is dead. Barb is dead" over and over.

She stuttered when the inner voice got mixed in with the outer voice. She stopped and took a sip of water and continued.

"Pretty much the same as the first go-round." He laid the pen down and folded his hands over the notepad. He stole a glance at the watch on his wrist. "It's almost noon. I know we've been at this for a long time. Would you like something to eat?"

MC felt flayed. Her eyes were gritty. She had zero appetite. "No. Thank you. I'd really like to leave."

"I'm sorry, but I need your cooperation for a little while longer."

Her ire was on the rise. A tidal wave of emotions: devastation, anger, impatience, and numbness washed over her. She closed her eyes and muttered, "I can't take much more, Detective."

"I understand. I have a few more questions. And I'd like to take you back to the house and go through it with you. If you feel up to it."

Did she? Feel up to it? "I don't know if feel up to it is the right terminology, but I need to pack some stuff."

Someone knocked. Sharpe rose and left the room. He returned holding her cell phones. "The analysts didn't detect anything questionable on either device, so you can have these back."

MC checked her personal phone first, almost expecting a missed call, a text, or a voicemail message from Barb. Only several missed calls, all from Cam. "Would you mind if I return a call? To my work partner?"

"Go ahead. I'll be down in the squad room. Come find me when you're finished." He gathered his notes and left, leaving the door open. Sharpe reached to his left, most likely cutting the switch on the recording system.

MC detected a low-level buzz of voices, probably from other offices or people in the hallways. She skirted the table and closed the door. She took a deep breath and called Cam.

Cam picked up halfway through the second ring. "MC. I'm so sorry. I don't even know what else to say."

The flow of words fell over MC like a bucket of ice. "I'm not saying I'm okay because I'm definitely not. I'm still at SPPD. I've been here all morning being interviewed. Cam—I—"

"I know, partner. Shit. This is fucked up. What the hell happened?"

"Has SPPD interviewed you?"

"Yes. A detective came by the house a few hours ago. I've been calling you ever since. MC, what the hell?"

"She's dead, Cam. Gone." She choked back a sob. "I don't know. A home invasion gone bad? No one's telling me anything. They're asking me all kinds of questions, but not giving me any answers. I can't be a viable suspect, especially after they've talked to you, but here I am."

"Do you want me to come down there?" Cam asked.

"No. Stay home with your family. Nothing you can do here." She felt a stab of pain as the words fell from her lips. Her family—her Barb—had been wiped out.

"You know you're family to us, MC." Cam's voice cracked. "Ah. God. I can't believe this." He blew out a breath. "How much longer will you be there?"

"Sharpe, the detective in charge, told me he wants to take me back to the house soon. Check it out. And I need to pack some stuff because I have no idea when they'll clear the scene. Could be days, I suppose."

"Shit. That's harsh. You need company? I can meet you there at the PD. And you'll come stay with us." Jane's voice echoed the sentiment in the background. "See, Jane agrees."

"I appreciate the offers, both the company and the place to stay. I don't think Detective Sharpe will allow you to be at the house, though. And you guys are sweet to invite me to stay with you, but you have your hands full with those two beautiful kids. You don't need me moping around, getting in the way. I'll find a place. Don't worry."

Cam said, "I talked to Jamie. He said SPPD interviewed him, too. I'm sure he'll be calling you, if he hasn't already. I don't know what to say. They gotta get whoever did this. Shit, we should take this on. We'll nail him, whoever he is. Fuck." He blew out another breath and MC could tell he was pacing.

"Cam, I gotta get going. Sharpe will probably be back any second." She couldn't stay on the line any longer without losing it. "I, ah, I'll be in touch, okay?" She sniffed and tears filled her eyes, the dam threatening to burst again.

"Call me if you need anything. Anything. Anytime."

"Thanks. Bye." She disconnected, let the phone slip through her fingers onto the table. She covered her eyes with both hands, working to keep it together.

Another thought hit her like a sucker punch. Barb's family. Her parents. Her brothers. She needed to notify them. How on earth would she explain that their daughter and sister was dead? Shit. Shit. Shit. The shit kept rolling over her, threatening to bury her.

Something vibrated. Incoming call from Jamie Sanchez.

"Heya, Jamie." MC's voice wobbled.

"MC. I am so sorry." Jamie's voice eased into her ear, a soothing balm after the shocking realization she'd been contemplating.

"Thanks. So, I um, I guess I'll be—"

"Don't worry about work. Take all the time you need. I'll talk to Chrapkowski. He may want to call you, who knows with him, but I'll be your point of contact. No worries." His words settled the dread she'd felt at the mention of Crapper.

"Okay, good." She didn't even want to think about Roland Chrapkowski and hoped to hell he didn't call her. "SPPD talked to you?"

"A detective dropped by the office. I answered all his questions and even had the case file you left on my desk to further corroborate. So where are you now?"

"I'm still at SPPD. I've been with a detective here all morning, day, whatever. He finally gave me back my phones and left me to make some calls. He wants to take me back to the house to do a walk-through."

"Shit."

Silence filled the air. "About sums it up."

"I'll fill out a leave request for you starting on Monday, leave it open-ended. We'll do what we can to help you on our end. The agency is here for you."

"Thanks. I appreciate it. I should go. Before Sharpe comes back." Her energy was completely sapped. The hand holding the phone shook.

"I'll be in touch. Take care."

"Bye." She set the phone on the table.

Sharpe opened the door mere seconds later. He sat across from her. "How you doing?"

She eyeballed him, a sarcastic response on the tip of her tongue, despite her exhaustion.

He held up a hand. "Sorry. Stupid question. I'll cut to the chase. I got word they'll be ready to allow us back into the house in an hour. We'll drive over and I'd like you to guide me through. Pay close attention to things missing. And anything else you notice which could be relevant. I have a few more questions before we end the interview, okay?"

"Sure."

He flipped to a fresh page on his notepad. "Can you give me the name and address of Barb's workplace?"

MC said, "She's a . . . was . . . a teacher." She gave him the name of the school and the address.

"Are you aware of any enemies she might have? Anyone who'd want to cause her harm?"

"Enemies? Are you serious?" MC clenched her fists. "Detective, Barb taught second-graders. I doubt any of them had her on a hit list." Easy on the sarcasm, McCall.

"I had to ask. What about you? Any cases you've handled lately where someone might be out to get you?"

"Not that I can think of off the top of my head. I am working on a task force right now. We're in the middle of an investigation on a Ponzi scheme. But the wheels are still turning on that one. Nothing else comes to mind."

Sharpe finished writing and set his pen down. "If you do think of anything later, please let me know. Otherwise, we're done for now. Ready to return to your house?"

MC focused on taking slow deep breaths. The thought of entering what used to be their home weighed on her, an anvil of grief.

Home no more.

H

On the way back to her Highland Park neighborhood giant orange snow plows chugged two or three abreast on the highway clearing the lanes, sand and salt spinning out in their wake.

MC sat in the passenger seat, facing the side window. She felt like the car was moving in slow motion while the world around her ran on fast forward. People hurried home or to meet friends for happy hour while she was being driven toward a black morass of hell.

The temperature had warmed a few degrees, but she felt like her bones were made of ice.

Sharpe adjusted the defrost with one hand as he navigated the interstate. "We'll go in the front. I'd like to start at the top and work our way down."

The ensuing silence was disrupted by the repetitive scrape of the wiper blades across the windshield.

"Do you understand the plan?" Sharpe switched to the far left lane and passed the plows.

"Plan? What?" MC glanced at him, then focused on the three hulking orange trucks they passed. "Must have every plow in the state out."

Sharpe took a measured breath. "One more time. You with me, Inspector McCall?"

"Sure."

He ran through his spiel again and signaled his exit from the highway. "We good?"

MC concentrated on keeping the immensity of her grief at bay. "We're dandy. And you'll allow me to pack some things before we depart, correct?"

"Yes. You'll be allowed to remove belongings. The scene will be considered cleared after we finish."

They parked in front of her house. The engine ticked like a bomb timer counting down the final seconds before an explosion, interrupting the silence that hung heavy in the air.

Sharpe cracked his door open. "Ready?"

MC stared straight ahead. "Do you know why there is so much silence when it snows? Fresh snow absorbs sound, lowering ambient noise because trapped air between snowflakes reduces vibration."

"I had no idea."

She took a breath and opened her door. "I heard it on public radio or something. Let's do this."

They reached the front porch and Sharpe brushed aside the fluttering yellow plastic tape and opened the door. The runner in the entryway was askew and dark with grimy footprints. The prints carried over onto the normally glossy oak floor.

Barb would not be happy about this mess, MC thought.

"Let's begin upstairs." Sharpe had removed his hat and held it out toward the stairs on the right.

MC unzipped her jacket and trooped up the stairs, Sharpe on her heels. She made her way through the master bedroom where all the drawers of both dressers were pulled halfway out, with various articles of clothing hanging from a few.

"I don't think there's anything missing from here. We never kept anything in the dressers except clothes, so there wouldn't be anything of value to a thief."

"Explains why all the drawers are pulled open and left hanging." Sharpe jotted something in his ratty notebook.

MC peeked in her jewelry box. She picked up her dad's gold Bulova wristwatch with the worn black leather band. She and her mom had shopped for this watch and surprised her dad on his birthday. He'd been thrilled about the gift and worn it every day. He had it on the day he'd died.

"Inspector McCall?" Sharpe cleared his throat. "Everything okay?"

"Okay? No, nothing is okay, Detective." She waved the watch at him. "This was my dad's watch, a gift on his fortieth birthday. I'm glad it's still here." She tucked the watch into her pants pocket and poked through the rest of her box. She kept a stash of two hundred dollars in twenties inside a velvet bag which contained her mother's rosary. She lifted the black bag from the bottom of the box. She tipped it upside down, and a rosary with pale blue glass beads and a silver crucifix fell into the palm of her hand.

No money.

She reached into the bag with her fingers and encountered nothing but empty bag. "Here's the first item for your list." She held the empty bag toward him.

Sharpe noted the bag and raised an eyebrow. "Missing a rosary?"

"Nope. Cash. I keep two hundred dollars in here. I know the money was here yesterday because I moved the bag when I dug out my watch before I went running."

"And Barb wouldn't have taken it?"

"Not without telling me. We keep an emergency stash handy and neither of us depletes it without letting the other know."

"Hmmm." Sharpe noted it.

"I don't see anything else missing. I don't have a whole lot, but it appears to all be here."

Next they checked out the bathroom, which was a disaster. The contents of the medicine cabinet above the sink were strewn every which way. A plastic jar of TUMS antacid tablets, a half empty tube of toothpaste, pain reliever, a tube of Barb's lipstick, cotton swabs. MC sifted through the debris. "Two prescription bottles missing."

"Really? You can tell so quickly?"

"Yes, because they were brown plastic bottles. One had my name on it. Percocet. I had my gallbladder out last year and they sent me home with pain meds. I only took two or three, so there were probably nine left in the bottle."

"And the other?"

"Barb's. Oxycodone. She'd twisted her back gardening this past summer. The doctor gave her a prescription for oxy. I think there were twelve or fourteen left of the original twenty."

"Seems likely they'd take those. Probably for themselves, though. Not much street value for so few pills."

In the spare room, which they used as an office, MC found several items gone. "Our MacBook Pro laptop is missing. Normally, it sits on the desk. Also, a Bose wireless speaker, black. And our wireless HP printer." MC pointed at the table next to the desk where the printer usually sat. A half ream of paper remained on the bottom shelf under the table.

Sharpe scribbled as MC talked. "Anything else?"

"No." She ran her hand over the framed photo of her and Barb taken up north at the cabin this past summer. They'd been so excited by the renovation and were celebrating with Dara and Meg. MC picked up the photo and drifted out of the room.

Back on the main floor they entered the living room. "Flat screen TV is gone, an LG forty-six inch. DVD Blu-ray player is gone, too." She scrutinized the CD tower next to the bookcase. "I can't be certain without picking through all the DVDs on the floor, but I think there are several missing." She stepped gingerly around the cases tossed about the room. "I don't think any books are missing. I guess the asshole didn't care much for reading."

In the dining room, MC took stock. Her grandma's silver was gone from the hutch. Otherwise, nothing else appeared to be missing. She set the framed photo on the table and angled toward the kitchen.

Sharpe stepped in front of her. "Are you ready to continue?"

She locked gazes with him. "I have to." She stepped around him and entered the kitchen from the dining room.

The breakfast nook was to her left and the back door was almost directly across from her.

"Looks like World War Three." She leaned against the door frame.

Sharpe stopped behind her.

MC smelled gun powder. She coughed and gagged.

Sharpe asked, "Are you okay?"

She held up a hand. "Fine." She knew the tastes and odors weren't really present, they'd dissipated hours earlier.

"Take your time."

"So much blood." MC hunkered down near the counter at the back door. She held her fingers over the maroon Rorschach blots on the white tile kitchen floor. She watched as her hand, of its own volition, reached out to a spot smaller than her palm. MC rested a finger on the stain and felt a spark that immediately faded, much as she imagined Barb's life had faded from her as she lay alone on the cold floor. MC examined her finger. The blood had congealed, but something red glinted.

Sharpe stepped forward. "What's that?"

They both scanned the floor.

"Jesus. Ornaments. She bought more." MC pointed to where the floor was littered with colored glass shards and glitter sparkling in the late afternoon sun. She twisted her feet and heard a crunch beneath her boot. "We didn't need any more ornaments."

The ornaments had been massacred, like Barb.

Tears rolled slowly down MC's face and dropped onto her thighs to create darker blue marks on her pants. She stood up and went to the sink where a roll of paper towels stood in a holder on the counter. She rinsed her hands, tore a sheet from the roll, and blew her nose.

Sharpe said, "We're pretty much done here. We checked the basement and it didn't seem like anyone had even been down there. Laundry room and utility room doors were closed and nothing appears to have been disturbed."

"We use it mainly for storage. Decorations. Old clothes to be donated." MC leaned her hands on the counter and stared out at the backyard. The clotheslines had a layer of snow on them, as did the t-shaped poles on either end. "Her car?"

"Nothing. The garage was closed, and nothing inside seemed to be messed with, including her car. The keys were on the floor not far from her right hand, so we bagged them, and we'll test for prints."

"I can drive her car?" MC asked.

"I don't see a problem with it. Do you have a set of keys?"

"Yes." MC pulled open a cupboard. She'd installed a few small hooks for the extra keys, and the cabin keys. "All present and accounted for." She collected all the keys and dropped them into her jacket pocket.

"You have a house key?"

MC dangled the plain silver key ring with Barb's Subaru key, her Camry key and front and back door keys. "Right here."

"Go ahead and pack up what you want to take. Unless you want to stay here?" Sharpe tucked his pen in a pocket. "Up to you at this point."

"No." She didn't elaborate. Nor did she tell him she wouldn't ever stay here, ever again.

Sharpe pulled out his wallet. He extracted a business card and handed it to her. "My contact information. Call me if you need anything."

She accepted the card and stuck it in her pocket. "Thanks."

"I'm very sorry for your loss Inspector McCall."

"When can I see her?" MC croaked. She coughed to clear her throat. "I want to see her."

"The medical examiner has to perform an autopsy. I'll find out when it's scheduled and let you know."

"We have a will. I'm her beneficiary and her executor. I'm sure you want to know, if you don't already. I'll be the one making all the arrangements."

"I'll want a copy of the will."

"Hang on. We keep a copy in the safe."

Sharpe had his notebook out again and jotted a bunch of chicken scratch on a page before he flipped it closed and stowed it away.

She retrieved and handed him a sheaf of papers. "I have another in a safe deposit box at the bank and our attorney has the original."

Sharpe accepted the packet. "Thank you. I'll be in touch after I speak with the ME."

"I'll be waiting for your call." MC accompanied him to the front door. "Oh, Detective, one more question."

Sharpe stopped halfway out the storm door.

"Barb's parents." MC took a deep breath. "They need to know." She blinked. "And as much as I don't want to do it, I need to be the one to tell them."

Sharpe pushed his hat back slightly. "I understand. Family death notification is difficult. Good luck."

"Thank you." MC's voice was so faint she wondered if she'd even spoken the words aloud.

"Call me if you think of anything else that could help."

Sharpe appeared to be contemplating saying something further, but he went outside and let the door close.

MC pulled the storm door until it latched shut. She watched Sharpe amble to the street. He sat in his car for several minutes before he started it and drove off. Only then did MC notice her car parked across the street and covered in snow. She'd move it to the garage before she left, she thought, then locked the deadbolt on the inside door.

MC returned to the bedroom and dragged the two suitcases from the closet and quickly filled them with clothes, toiletries and other necessities. She carried them downstairs, grabbed the framed photo of her and Barb, and a few other things from the hallway closet and jammed them in, too.

She made a final run upstairs for her favorite pillow and took stock of the space where love had lived for so long. She felt her heart fracture a bit more.

Back in the front hallway she emptied the safe of all their important documents. She crammed all the papers into her messenger bag, which Sharpe had returned to her before they'd left SPPD.

She gazed around the shambles she and Barb had called home and felt a seed of anger squeezing through the anguish inside her.

In two trips, she loaded everything into Barb's Subaru. Then she parked her own car in the garage and shifted over into the Subaru where she sat weeping in the driver's seat.

In that crushing moment, she vowed to herself and to Barb that she'd find out who was responsible and hunt them down.

H

MC checked into the tired Best Western hotel on the outskirts of downtown a little before five-thirty. Her boots scraped over dull worn crap-colored hall carpet, one sole sticking to a blackened blob she hoped was gum.

The building was redolent with the thick, cloying scent of body odor mixed with mold and wet stale heat.

The building and the people in it needed a complete overhaul but she didn't care. Nothing mattered. Barb was gone. Barb ripped from her—from life itself. Some faceless phantom—or multiple phantoms—slipped away afterwards, a snowy curtain covering the escape.

Jangling the well-used gold key attached to a green plastic four-leaf clover, MC unlocked the door to her temporary digs, feeling anything but lucky. Sad, moss-colored drapes covered the window overlooking the parking lot where hulking gray mounds of plowed snow moped in the corners.

MC hoisted her suitcases onto one bed and found the remote and switched on the TV. She shucked her jacket and tossed it over the suitcases.

On the edge of the second bed with her pillow squished in her lap, she channel surfed. She hoped for—dreaded—the six o'clock news. She landed on channel four and watched the *CBS Evening News*.

At six the local news came on. The anchor made mention of another homicide in Minneapolis the previous night and another in Saint Paul early this morning.

Video snippets of the Minneapolis incident flashed by. The MPD Public Information Officer repeated the usual song and dance about keeping the community safe and asking anyone with information to contact MPD.

Next came the SPPD Public Information Officer. He stood on the corner of Pinehurst and Howell, just down from her house. He talked about a suspected burglary and a victim who undoubtedly surprised whomever was inside. There were no further details of the incident or suspects. The name of the victim was being withheld pending notification of family.

She knew, with a part of her barely functioning cerebral cortex she needed to phone Barb's parents who were still down in Mankato with Barb's oldest brother, Father Tom, the priest. And she also had to phone Dara and Meg.

How the fuck could she survive this horror? A kaleidoscope of anger, fear, loss, and grief exploded. Her world slipped sideways and she fell over on the garish comforter-clad bed. She sobbed, battered and broken, as an advertisement for Black Friday sales blared from the TV.

Eventually, MC sat up and pushed her sodden pillow aside. She couldn't put off the inevitable any longer. Time to suck it up. She dug her phone from her jacket pocket with shaky fingers and stared at the dark screen.

Best to get it over with. MC pushed the round button at the bottom of the screen and brought the phone to life. Navigating to her contacts she found the entry for Francis and Peg Wheatley and selected Francis's cell number. On the second ring he answered. MC sucked in a shaky breath and forged ahead before she lost her nerve.

"Hi, Francis, this is MC." A frog took up residence in her throat and she coughed.

"MC? You sound terrible. Are you ill?"

"Um, no. I'm not ill. Hey, Francis, I'm afraid I've got some bad news." MC gently conveyed the details, tears rolling down her cheeks.

MC listened as Francis broke the news to Peg.

"No. No. No. I don't believe you." Peg's stunned voice filled MC's ear.

They sounded heartbroken, understandably so. Their world had been thrown off its axis, just like MC's.

MC swallowed and swiped her sleeve across her face. She got up and stumbled to the bathroom for tissues.

"I'm so sorry." She assured Francis and Peg she had no details other than what she'd shared with them and also warned them a detective from SPPD would more than likely contact them and Barb's two older brothers, Dave and Father Tom. MC asked Francis if he felt up to telling the brothers the news.

"Yes, I can."

MC heard Peg's steady sobbing in the background. "I have to wait to make any arrangements until the medical examiner releases her—body. She has specific instructions in her will. I'll share all the details with you and the rest of the family as soon as I can."

"I understand," he said.

With nothing more to say on either side, MC ended the call and let the phone slip onto the bed. She needed a drink in the worst way.

Unfortunately, no mini-bar existed at this grand establishment. Still dressed in her tactical gear, she grabbed her wallet and keys and found her navy pea coat in one of the suitcases.

Ten minutes later she pulled into the parking lot of a ramshackle liquor store located a couple blocks west of the hotel on University Avenue. She purchased a bottle and drove back to the hotel.

The pearlescent blanket of snow offset the murky darkness of the night. She drove with extra caution wary of erratic drivers.

The TV greeted her as she unlocked the door. *Wheel of Fortune* was in full swing. The spinning wheel of gaudy colors and giddy contestants spewing noise didn't distract from her mission. She found a black plastic ice bucket and flipped the security latch out to keep the door from closing as she hunted down the nearest ice machine.

A humming followed by the sound of dropping ice drew her attention to the far end of the hallway where she found the machine in an alcove. She pushed the button and the machine groaned, but no ice spewed forth.

MC kicked the ice-maker and slammed her fist on the button. One cube clattered into the bucket. "Goddamit! C'mon, you fucker!" She kicked the machine again and this time it belched out a bucketful of ice.

Back in the room, she pulled a plastic cup from its cellophane wrapper, filled it with ice and vodka. Without stopping to think, she tipped her head back. The alcohol cascaded down her throat, the icy burn doing nothing to numb the pain that seared every inch of her.

She recognized that pain—the crushing, sinking sensation—the same feeling she'd had when she learned her parents had been killed in a car crash. And a black hole like after Cindy was gone.

MC served herself another round as the colored wheel spun on the television screen. Plastic cup in hand, she veered to the built-in desk across the room and pulled out the dilapidated black faux leather office chair.

She sank onto the cracked seat. Cup in one hand and phone in the other, she placed the next most difficult call of the evening, using the FaceTime app on her device. She slugged back a chilled mouthful of vodka as the call connected.

"Yo." Dara's voice echoed from the tiny iPhone speaker and her face flickered on the screen.

"Hey."

"What are you doing? And where the hell are you? That's a no-tell motel room if ever I've seen one. What happened? You and Barb have a fight and she kicked you out?" Dara laughed.

"I wish it were so simple." MC swallowed. She set the plastic cup on the dark wood desk. Her tears blurred Dara's face, and a sob escaped her lips.

Dara dropped the comic shtick. "What's wrong?"

"Dara. It's about Barb."

"What's about Barb?" Dara's voice was low and serious. She strode to a door across the room, yanked it open and hollered for Meg to join her, pronto. "MC. You're freaking me out."

Meg came running into the room. "What's happening? What are you yelling about?"

Dara motioned for her to close the door and pointed to the phone. "Something's wrong with Barb is all I know. MC?"

Meg hit Dara on the shoulder. "Let her gather her thoughts. MC, hon. Tell us."

"She's gone. Barb. Gone. She's—"

"What the hell do you mean she's gone?" Dara's deep voice rose.

"Dead is what I mean." There she'd actually said the word. "Someone . . . oh, God help me . . . someone shot her this morning. Home invasion, the cops think. I came home . . . " The waterworks made a grand reappearance, and she could no longer speak.

Meg grabbed the phone from Dara's hand, and her face in the camera frame shook. "We're packing up right now to drive back to the Cities. Dara's parents will understand. We'll be home in a couple of hours."

Dara was busy in the background gathering clothes and opening suitcases.

"No." MC's voice was shaky. She wet her throat with a swallow from her cup and leaned her elbows on her knees. "Don't come back now. The roads are terrible because of all the snow. Let the plows do their work. Come back tomorrow."

"No way, buddy." Dara's head appeared over Meg's shoulder. "The troops are rallying right now."

"Tomorrow is soon enough. There's nothing you can do tonight. I need you two to be safe. And I need to be alone—at least for tonight."

"Alone is the last thing you need to be." Dara's face came closer, blocking out most of Meg's concerned expression. "I can see how you're handling alone. Whatchu drinkin' there? Huh? A triple shot of the gotcha Goose?"

"Dara. Now's not the time," Meg said.

"The hell it isn't," Dara said. "The slope is slippery. I should know. Right, MC?"

MC knew Dara struggled every day to remain sober. She attended AA meetings when life became overwhelming, though those instances had become fewer and farther apart as the years rolled by. Dara had been sober for as long as MC and Barb had been together. She was pushing the twenty-year mark, and MC admired her perseverance. But tonight she couldn't mirror her good friend's behavior. She needed something to deaden the pain. The Goose fit the bill.

"I'll be fine. I'm at a hotel. I couldn't stay at the house."

"I can imagine why you'd feel that way." Meg's voice was quiet, soothing, a salve on MC's exposed wounds. Almost.

"You two stay there tonight. Promise me. Driving will be better in daylight. And I'll be right here."

Meg and Dara put her on mute. Finally, after about thirty seconds of hyperbolic gyrations and arguing MC couldn't hear, Meg unmuted the phone. "We won't run out tonight, but we'll be on the road bright and early in the morning."

"We're coming home to take care of you, pal." Dara's husky voice filled the room and tears spilled from her eyes.

Meg's voice broke and she bit off a sob. "You'll come home with us." Her tone left no room for argument.

Frankly, at this point, MC was out of energy to fight anybody. She thanked her two best friends, told them she loved them and ended the call.

She found her phone charger and plugged in her phone, flicked the ringer on, and cranked the volume up so she'd hear if it rang during the night. But who'd be calling her anyway, she wondered, as she drained the remaining liquid from her cup. No one.

She contemplated food as the Friday night lineup on CBS began.

On second thought, another glass, or two, of mother Goose would serve her purposes better. She flipped the deadbolt and secured the door with the chain, then kicked off her boots.

She dug around in the suitcases until she found her flannel pajama pants and her favorite Popeye sweatshirt. She also pulled on a pair of thick socks, leaving her discarded clothes in a heap on the floor. With more ice in her cup, she grabbed the Goose by the neck and crawled into bed.

Three pillows stacked behind her, she rested against the headboard and sucked down the vodka. Slow and steady. Liquid lava caressed her tongue and coated her insides.

Remote in hand, she toggled up the volume on the TV. *The Amazing Race* melted into *Hawaii Five-O* followed by *Blue Bloods*.

Unfocused.

Welcome numbness settled in, making itself at home.

Chapter Eleven
Saturday, November 29

An old-fashioned phone rang, the type they'd had when MC was growing up.

MC fought through the fog. She couldn't move her arms and legs. What the hell? She opened her mouth to ask Barb to help her.

The incessant ringing blazed through the haze in her head. She struggled to open her eyes. She glanced at the clock on the bedside table.

The teal numbers blurred in and out of focus.

7:01 a.m.

Suddenly she felt like her body was dropping off a cliff. She grabbed to get hold of something, anything, as the ringing pinged around in her skull like pinballs in a machine.

Phone. Cell phone. She reached out and her fingers crabbed across the table, finally locating the demon device.

"'Lo?" Was that croak actually her voice?

Dara's deep voice boomed in her ear. "How you doing?"

MC pulled the phone away from her face. "No need to yell. I can hear you fine."

She kicked at the bedclothes snaked around her legs and rolled to a sitting position, which made instantly clear she was in need of about a gallon of water and a fistful of ibuprofen.

Dara said, "We're about an hour away from the Cities. Meg's driving, so don't get your undies in a knot because I'm talking on the cell."

"Good to know." MC thought about standing, but her head thumped when she shifted so she remained still, perched on the edge of the bed. "I'm not sure what's going on yet. I guess I'll need to contact a cleaning service for the house. And wait to hear from Sharpe about when the ME will release—" Barb's name caught in her throat.

"Ah, Jesus. Okay. One thing at a time. Should we pick you up at the hotel? Or do you want to meet at our house?"

MC's throat burned, a sourness roiling up from her gut. Lack of food? She glanced at the Grey Goose bottle, now only one-third full, next to the empty cup on the table and decided lack of food was the least contributor to her current physical state.

"Hello?" Dara yelled. "MC?"

"Dara. Please. Use your inside voice." MC rubbed her temple with two fingers. "I need to grab a shower and some food. You or Meg call me when you're home, and I'll come to your place."

"Hung over, aren't ya?"

"I don't need a lecture this morning."

"No lecture—an observation." Dara's voice took on an unaccustomed softness. "Hopefully, it won't snowball into—"

"Don't worry." Her phone vibrated. She pulled it away, another call with a 651 area code. "Dara, I gotta go. Incoming call and I should take it. Let me know when you get home." She hit the accept icon without waiting for Dara's acknowledgement.

"McCall."

"Inspector McCall, it's Detective Sharpe. Sorry to be calling so early. How are you this morning?"

"Considering the circumstances, I'm surviving. What can I do for you?" She closed her eyes and focused on keeping the bitterness at bay and her stomach contents inside her body.

"I spoke with the ME and they'll release your partner's body to the funeral home of your choice late this afternoon or early tomorrow morning."

"Do you have the ME's contact info?"

"Yes." He rattled off the number.

"Thank you. I appreciate the call."

"I'll be in touch, as necessary."

"Understood. Do you have any, uh, leads? I know it's early."

His tone softened. "You know I'm not at liberty to say, but between you, me, and the snowbank, we have shit so far."

MC clenched her jaw and bit back the anger and disappointment. "Got it. Thanks for the call. Goodbye." She disconnected and tossed the phone onto the wood table.

The new day had dawned. Her first day without Barb. Yet the previous day had a hold on her, and she felt it wouldn't let her go any time soon.

MC dug in the desk drawer for paper and pen. She scrawled the phone number Sharpe had given her before she forgot it. She considered the bottle of vodka and opted for a shower and clean clothes instead.

By eight, dressed in jeans, her tactical boots, and a white T-shirt under a gray thermal crew neck, MC decided food was a necessity.

She donned her coat, grabbed her wallet and keys and headed for the door. Hand on the deadbolt, she stopped and returned to the desk where her messenger bag drooped on the floor next to the chair. She found her notebook and pen and pocketed the items.

Fifteen minutes later she occupied a tiny back corner booth of a greasy spoon diner halfway between the hotel and her home. The place was fairly crowded. Saturday morning tended to be big go-out-for-breakfast time, and she hoped like hell she didn't run into anyone she knew.

While she ate, she ran through her notes on the Stennard case. If she couldn't broker any info on Barb, she decided she'd focus her energy on Arty. Ferndale and Andrews seemed open to MC's input, but still focused on Len Klein as the killer.

She was doubtful of Klein's involvement mostly due to the fact that she and Cam had seen him with the two questionable characters the night of the meeting. Klein seemed more the type to have someone else do the dirty work, keeping his hands squeaky clean. Despite those factors, she had a nagging feeling that he could somehow be the killer. She made a note to question Klein, then remembered she wouldn't be at work for a while. Maybe Cam would pay Klein a visit. Or she would do it without telling anyone.

She forked eggs into her mouth and crunched a slice of bacon while she contemplated how long she should take off work.

A week? Two? She had a lot to do. For a moment, her mind went blank, and she couldn't recall what she'd just been thinking. A baby started crying from somewhere near the back of the café, and the sound made her head throb.

What was I thinking? Oh, yeah. Things to do. Arrange Barb's memorial. Hire a crew to clean the house. Pack up the place and put it on the market. No way could she live in the house ever again.

She'd need to find a storage facility. Maybe move to the cabin? The cabin was their haven. Maybe that's where she needed to be.

Couldn't someone shut that baby up? Her head was pounding, and suddenly, the food tasted like cardboard. She left the remaining half-slice of bacon on the plate and watched the congealed yellow mass of yolk running into the wall of toast. She pushed the half-eaten breakfast aside. How could she have just had all these thoughts, so clinical, so matter-of-fact? What was wrong with her?

Maybe there was nothing wrong. Didn't she have the right to compartmentalize?

The server approached and asked, "Everything okay?"

"I'm not very hungry." MC rubbed her temples.

The waitress picked up the plate. "No problem. Can I get you anything else?"

"A refill on the coffee and the check, please."

The waitress filled her cup and left the check on the corner of the table. MC sipped her coffee. She felt antsy. Needed to do something. She pulled her phone from her coat pocket and called Cam.

"Hello." Squeals of laughter sounded in the background.

MC smiled. "Sounds like the kids are having a good time."

Cam groaned. "They wear me out. How are you doing? Hold on a sec." The background sounds muffled and disappeared. "Sorry. I diverted the munchkins toward Jane, and now I can hear."

"Things could be worse, Cam. Enjoy the kids."

"I do. Every moment I can. So? How are you?" His voice dropped a notch.

MC filled him in on the latest and told him she'd let him know the date and time for the memorial as soon as she'd set it all up.

Then she dumped her thoughts about Arty.

As soon as she finished, Cam said, "You need to focus on you. Forget about work."

"I swear if I don't do something to occupy my mind I'll curl up in a corner and become a blathering babbling idiot. And then what?"

Cam sighed. "I get it. You've got a point about Klein. He's dirty, but he doesn't do the dirty work. I can talk to him. I'll check in with Oldfield."

"You know what else is stuck in my craw? Thomson and Stennard."

"How so?"

"What do we know about Gavin Thomson? I haven't heard Ferndale or Andrews mention anything about him. Seems he's low on the totem pole as a person of interest, but I have a funny feeling. He's shifty. And Stennard seems wild. Drugs? They both need to be checked out."

"We'll handle them. You have other things to worry about right now. This case shouldn't be your priority."

"What should be my priority?" She gulped a mouthful of cooling coffee to wash away the ashen taste of grief. "I need to do *something*. SPPD won't tell me anything about Barb. I get it, but at the same time I want to scream at them to let me help."

"It's rough. I'm here for you. Whatever you need. You need to take time, though. Grieve. Grieving is a healthy step in getting through this."

"I will. But keeping up on the Stennard thing will help me through. I'll probably request two weeks' leave. Should be enough time for me to get my life back in some semblance of order. But two weeks is a long time to be away. You'll be my eyes and ears, right?" She felt tears threatening and swallowed hard. "Don't shut me out, Cam."

"I won't but only two weeks? I'm sure Crapper would let you take more time. For god's sake. Barb was murdered. Take some time off. Recover."

"Actually, Jamie told me he would be my contact, so I don't have to deal with Crapper. The best thing for me is to stay busy. I need to move forward. And, no, this is not shock talking. It's how I'm wired."

"You have to promise me you'll let me know how we can help you, in your personal life. Jane and I—we love you guys like family. We still haven't told the kids Auntie Barb is gone." His voice cracked. "Going to be a tough talk. They loved her so much."

MC smiled. "And she adored them. Tell them she's gone, but she loved them and she'll be watching over them from heaven. I don't believe in the whole heaven and watching over deal, but I think it might be the easiest for the kids."

"I'm with you."

"I gotta go, but we'll talk soon. And let me know—email or call—after you talk to Klein. Okay?"

"Yep. Take care."

She disconnected, left enough cash to cover the check and a hefty tip, and exited the diner.

The day was brilliant. Bright. Sunny. Mild. The high was expected to be near forty. Yesterday's snow was destined to diminish considerably by day's end, probably changing sidewalks and streets into slushy rivers.

MC checked the time on her phone. It was creeping up on ten already.

She decided to hit up a local bookstore. She needed to buy a new Moleskine notebook. A special one, for a special investigation. Sharpe be damned. She'd figure out who the fuck killed Barb herself.

She drove out to Roseville, a northern suburb of Saint Paul, where she was certain she wouldn't run into anyone she knew. She found the Moleskine display and knew the minute she laid eyes on the perfect notebook to chronicle Barb's case: a five-by-eight-inch Oxide Green hardbound leather notebook with ruled pages. She quickly made her purchase.

MC started up the Subaru and NPR's Saturday lineup filled the inside of the car. She tore the wrapper off the new notebook and cracked the cover. Pen in hand, she recorded the details she knew about the previous day's events, including her own schedule and timeline and Barb's intended plans. She narrowed down the time Barb was killed to between six and seven yesterday morning.

Her calculations were more than she'd gotten out of Sharpe. She tapped the tip of the pen against the steering wheel as she stewed. Her phone rang, jolting her out of her reverie. Dara's name appeared on the screen.

She answered, "Hi, Dara."

"We're home. Where are you?"

"Parking lot of Barnes and Noble in Roseville."

"Okay. Do you want to come over?"

"Yes. I need to run some things by you and Meg." She blew out a breath. "God. Is this real? I feel like I'm in a dream."

"More like a nightmare. Come over. Coffee's on."

"On my way." MC set the phone on the passenger seat and noticed a sheet of paper between the seat and the center console.

She slipped it out and was greeted by a child-sized outline of a hand decorated to be a Thanksgiving turkey. Emmy Carson was printed at a downward slant in the upper right corner. It must've fallen out of Barb's bag earlier in the week.

Her heart shattered like an icicle dropping to the pavement from a gutter. Barb's students would be devastated. She made a mental note to go through Barb's bag and bring any papers to the school. Whoever they got to replace Barb should have the kids' work. She traced the fingers, a rainbow of colors representing the turkey's feathers.

Tears dripped from her chin, and a splash of water stained the bottom corner of the sheet. The thought of the kids not seeing Barb again was enough to shove her off the edge. She couldn't control her sobbing.

Two teen-aged girls scampered past her car and gawped at her before tripping each other and moving on in a fit of giggles.

"Real nice. You've never seen a grown woman cry?" She tossed the paper on the seat, planted her phone on top to hold it in place. She found a napkin in the glove box and blew her nose. MC picked up the green notebook and on the page that read, "In Case of loss, please return to:" she wrote *Black Friday* instead of her name.

Then she pointed her car in the direction of the only family she had left.

ℋ

At her friends' house, MC picked up Dara, and they returned to the Best Western to grab her belongings. She checked out and settled the bill while Dara loaded the suitcases into the car.

Dara and Meg's peach-colored clapboard house was located in the Grand-Dale neighborhood of Saint Paul. White rails ran along the front porch, and teal trim offset the peach nicely. They had replaced the sidewalk with gray hexagon-shaped paving stones, which gave great curb appeal but were hell to shovel in the winter.

Meg came out to help haul MC's luggage in and up to the second-floor guest room at the back of the house overlooking the yard and the alley.

MC peered out the window. "Slushy mess out there."

Meg opened the closet and pushed aside some old coats. "I really should donate these. We don't wear them anymore."

"I've been telling you to do that for two years." Dara heaved one of MC's suitcases on the bed.

"Oh, you," Meg said. "Blah blah blah."

MC listened to her two best friends bicker. Her shoulders were hunched, coat still on, and she leaned her head against the windowpane, barely registering the burn of the frigid glass against her skin. What she wouldn't give to be having a similar exchange with Barb. Tears filled her eyes, and drops lazily snaked down her cheeks.

Meg came up behind MC and drew her into a hug. "I'm so sorry. I want to say it'll be all right."

"I don't know if things will ever be all right." She hiccupped. "Tell me how I go on without her, Meg. Please, tell me."

"You'll be the strong woman you've always been. You go on living. She'd want all of us to do the same. Cherish and gain strength from the memories."

Dara joined in the hug. "Yeah, what my better half said." She smiled through her own tears. "We'll get through this together. We're family."

"Family." MC broke their circle and sat heavily on the edge of the chenille-covered double bed. The bright dandelion-colored walls belied the mood in the room.

Meg swiped at her own face with both hands. "You settle in. I'll go downstairs and make some lunch. Use the closet and the chest of drawers. If you need extra blankets or pillows you know where they are." She rattled on about towels and such in the linen closet, and MC tuned out her well-meaning friend.

Over lunch, the three friends put their heads together and came up with a list of tasks, which they divided up.

MC took on the arrangements for Barb's cremation and memorial service to be handled by Sunset Cremation Society in Highland Park. Sunset's chapel would hold at least one hundred people. A few years before, MC and Barb had set up and paid for their funerals, so all MC had to do was confirm the following Saturday afternoon from one to three would work, and the rest was taken care of, including an obituary notice in the *Saint Paul Pioneer Press* newspaper. Then she got hold of the ME's office to let them know someone from Sunset would be there to take Barb to her final resting place.

Meg contacted a local caterer and placed an order for sandwiches, salads, and cookies to be delivered to Flannel where MC wanted to have their few close friends and family gather after the memorial service.

Dara researched accredited crime scene cleanup companies in Saint Paul. She found three to propose to MC, and they settled on a company called In the Midnight Hour, Inc., because the name seemed discreet, and they had immediate availability for crime and trauma scene decontamination.

When MC gave her the go-ahead, Dara scheduled the crew for that evening. MC hoped having them show up after dark would lessen the chance of gawkers.

Dara asked, "Do you want to be there when they arrive or would you like me to go?"

MC considered the list on the table in front of her. She sipped from a cup of lukewarm coffee and then rubbed her temples. "I didn't even think about having to be there, but I suppose someone needs to let them in and lock up afterwards."

"I can do it," Dara said. "You don't need to put yourself through that."

MC glanced from Dara to Meg and back. "You guys are the best." She bit back a sob. "Would you mind, Dara? I know it's a lot to ask. The scene isn't pretty."

"Don't worry about me." The pool of tears gathering in Dara's eyes contradicted her bold words.

"Promise me if it's too hard, you'll call and I'll come right away."

"You got it. I've still got time before I head over there, so what can I do next?"

MC reviewed the list in front of her. "Nothing else right now. I've got to get to the post office and rent a post office box. I don't want mail delivered to the house."

Because I don't ever want to go back there again is what she didn't add.

Chapter Twelve
November 29 – December 7

The next few days were a blur. November bled into December.

MC finalized details for Barb's memorial and managed to coordinate everything with Barb's parents and brothers.

They'd put together an amazing photo array and each of the family members, along with MC, Dara, and Meg, were getting up to speak. Some folks might refer to their comments as eulogies, but MC preferred to think of them as Barb's life stories and the sharing of the legacy she left behind.

Dara and Meg closed Flannel at noon on Saturday, December sixth, for Barb's memorial. Barb's family and MC and Barb's closest friends and co-workers were invited to attend the luncheon. Meg set up photo collections and piped all Barb's favorite music through the café's speakers.

MC somehow made it through the day. She reminisced with friends and cried with Barb's mother.

She laughed with Cam and Jane as they watched their two beautiful, vibrant children, Ben and Hailey, chase Dara around the tables and chairs. Her heart broke and swelled at the same time with all the love this group shared for a woman who'd been the brightest star in the darkest of nights.

♯

Mid-morning on the Sunday after Barb's memorial, Dara, Meg, and MC piled into Dara's blue Jeep Grand Cherokee and made the two-and-a-half-hour drive north to MC's cabin.

She sat in the back seat cradling Barb's bronze urn. Dara had NPR on the radio, and they were silent as the inside of a church during the ride.

With only one stop in Hinckley for gas and a restroom break, they made excellent time. The day was mild, near forty degrees, and lemony-light colored a pallid blue sky overhead.

MC fought the demon inside screaming for a drink. She'd not touched vodka since her bender in the hotel over a week earlier, but the evil tempter pecked at her brain daily. The thought of the fine French vodka, created from winter wheat instead of Russian potatoes, made her toes tingle. Of course her wallet tingled too. Grey Goose was expensive.

Determined not to think about alcohol, she listened to the replay of the weekly radio show, _A Prairie Home Companion_, and absorbed the steady thrum of the tires on the road.

At noon Dara drove through the virgin snow covering the driveway to the two-car garage fronting MC's cabin north of Two Harbors.

The crunching sound set MC's teeth on edge. "Sounds like fingernails on a chalkboard."

"I agree." Meg opened her door, dangling her short legs before dropping to the snow-covered driveway. "Snow's almost up to the tops of my boots."

"I'll shovel us a path to the house." Dara regarded MC in the rearview mirror. "Toss me your keys and I'll get the shovel from the garage."

In short order, Dara had cleared the snow from the garage to the house and trudged around to the lake-facing side and made a trail from the cabin's sliding glass doors to the steps leading down to the lake.

MC didn't own a boat, so instead of a dock she had a patio with a bench near the shoreline on Lake Superior. The gales of November had given way to the squalls of December, carrying the steely taste of ice and snow. The threesome huddled on the patio and watched the whitecaps soar and recede, the sharp tips sparkling like diamonds.

Meg linked her arm through MC's. "I know it's hard to let go, but she'll always be with us." She dabbed her eyes with a gloved finger.

"Yes." MC lifted the heavy round top off the container. "And she wanted to be here, where we both found so much peace." MC slipped as close to the water's edge as she could and tipped the urn and dumped about half the contents. A gust of wind wound up and the waves crashed, grabbed Barb's ashes and rolled away.

MC said good-bye as the turbulent waters cradled Barb and retreated, leaving a lacy froth in their wake. She contemplated the irony of Barb's violent death culminating in their committing her ashes into the tempestuous Great Lake, where she would find eternal peace in its frigid depths.

They hugged and cried. Eventually, MC led the way back up the stairs to the corner of the yard that held Barb's garden.

She upended the urn at the same time another brisk, pine-scented breeze kicked up. MC squinted in the sun's glare as swirls of ash climbed upward, and she lost sight of them before some slowly drifted back down, dotting the whitescape of the garden. MC plugged the cover back onto the now-empty urn and traced Barb's name, etched on the container. She drew in a ragged breath through her mouth, freezing her lungs.

"We should probably get back." Dara held a hand to her forehead, shading her eyes. "Fuckin'-A, trouble's brewing." She pointed out over the lake.

MC followed the direction of Dara's finger. Great hulking black and gray clouds appeared to be marching across Lake Superior. "You're right. We should get out ahead of the storm."

Chapter Thirteen
Monday, December 8

MC's first of two recommended appointments with Doctor Emily Zaulk, a police psychologist, was scheduled for one o'clock. Jamie convinced her to complete the visits prior to her return to duty. He wanted to ensure she wasn't returning to work too soon.

Although MC understood, and mostly agreed with the logic, the last thing she wanted to do was rehash Barb's murder with the psychologist. She left Dara and Meg's house and stopped at a corner bar about two blocks from Doctor Zaulk's Grand Avenue location where she slipped onto a cracked leather stool at the bar and ordered a double Grey Goose on the rocks.

The bartender asked, "Rough Monday?"

"You might say." MC took a healthy swallow. She absorbed the cool burn and finished the drink.

MC paid her tab and thanked the bartender. She stuck a stick of spearmint gum into her mouth and slogged the two blocks to her appointment.

Doctor Zaulk's office was in a refurbished brown brick duplex on Grand Avenue. The doctor lived on the upper floor and her practice was on the lower level.

MC hung her coat on the empty rack in the front foyer. No other coats on the rack must mean no one else was around. She stepped into the waiting room and closed the door. Doctor Zaulk's rules, posted clearly on the wall, were that patients remain in the waiting room until the doctor came for them.

MC was about to sit when a door on the other side of the room opened and a woman wearing a green cashmere sweater over black wool slacks came in. "Good afternoon, I'm Doctor Zaulk. You must be Mary McCall?"

MC stood. "I actually go by MC, not Mary. No one's called me Mary in years."

Doctor Zaulk was about her same height. She had a helmet of sturdy gray hair and wore no jewelry. Her green eyes were a shade that reminded MC of a forest filled with shade-drenched pine trees. Calming was the word that registered in MC's mind.

"MC it is. Follow me and we'll get started." Doctor Zaulk led her down a short hallway and through a set of French doors.

The room was spacious. Muted daylight filtered in through heavy, sheer curtains covering a curved bay window overlooking Grand Avenue. Strategically placed floor lamps made the lighting cozy and inviting.

"Where should I sit?"

"You choose." Doctor Zaulk retreated to her desk in a back corner of the room to pick up a notebook.

MC considered the choices: mission-style wood rocker; an armchair with golden corduroy cushions and wide sturdy arms; a green beanbag; and two ivory-colored wingback chairs. The seating arrangement was set up around an eight-by-ten-foot rug with soft teals and pops of yellow woven throughout.

MC sat in one of the wingback chairs.

Dr. Zaulk chose the other wingback chair. A round cherry accent table between the two chairs made the setup feel like an afternoon gabfest between two friends.

Doctor Zaulk opened a notebook, a Moleskine, MC noticed.

She studied MC. "Tell me about Barb. And what you're doing to cope."

"I guess you know the gist of what happened."

"I do. But I want to hear your version."

MC blew out a sigh. She shared the events, beginning with getting called into work on Thanksgiving, the horror show the next morning, and ended with the previous day's trip to the cabin where she, Dara, and Meg had spread Barb's ashes. She left out her self-medicating via Grey Goose and the fierceness with which she craved an infusion at this very moment.

"I'm so sorry all of this has happened to you and your beloved partner, MC. You're going through a most difficult situation, and I'm here to help you navigate through it."

"Thanks."

"Are you aware, there are stages of grief you'll experience? You're likely to feel a great many uncontrollable emotions in the coming weeks and months. And though this is only our first session so it's too early to tell, we may find you'll suffer from PTS. While the incident was not work-related, it was violent and very personal. Are you familiar with PTS—post-traumatic stress?"

"I've been to a couple of training sessions about psychology and dealing with people who have it."

The doctor made a note. "This is good. Let's talk about some steps you can take to combat the difficulties that lie ahead."

MC nodded and stared at the butterscotch wood flooring surrounding the woven rug island upon which they were moored. Though the room was steady, she could almost imagine being on a ship chugging off somewhere, waves cresting all around. In her head, birds shrieked and the smell of rotten fish made her head ache. She closed her eyes for a moment. She wanted the session to be done so she could settle the turbulent waves inside her with a drink.

"What do you think? Can you commit to these things?"

Heat rose to her face. Embarrassed she said, "What? Sorry. I missed that."

"Daily journaling and weekly sessions. At least for the next few weeks." Doctor Zaulk paused. "Research has proven journaling about one's feelings is a great form of therapy. Helps the mind process the events and the related emotions."

"I'm not much for journaling. My job requires so much writing as it is, I don't see how personal journaling will help me." She didn't share the fact she'd already begun recording the events surrounding Barb's death. A sort of homemade murder book.

Facts.

Details.

Suppositions and theories.

No feelings.

"I hope you'll reconsider."

She tightened her hands into fists. "I probably won't."

"Could you let me know why you feel that way?"

MC forced her hands to relax. Through a tight jaw, she said, "I don't think it'll work for me."

The doctor frowned. "Writing down your personal feelings can be clarifying, a cleansing of sorts. And believe it or not, it will help your healing. Would you be willing to at least give it a try?"

MC had nothing more to say.

After a moment, the doctor jotted a few more notes. "Our time is up. Shall we meet again next Monday? Same time?"

MC agreed. Anything to get away from the good doctor.

She practically ran from the building and hurried the two blocks to her car. Once inside, she dug out the green notebook from her messenger bag and opened it to the title page. Next to Black Friday she carefully wrote, "Life after Barb."

Why had she argued with Doctor Zaulk about journaling? She could easily have acquiesced and shared that she'd begun her own version of writing therapy. On second thought, she doubted a murder book would qualify as writing therapy in Doctor Zaulk's estimation. With a grimace she stashed the book and started the car.

Now that she had escaped the therapy session, she found some energy flowing back, and some of the stress she'd been feeling slipped away. She skipped the bar and moved on to the next in an endless series of tasks.

These tasks felt like the Labors of Hercules, countless and all-encompassing, and seemed to be happening in a completely different dimension of space and time. The world surrounding her was real enough, but she felt like she was living her life frame by frame, through a Viewmaster, a jerky one-dimensional existence.

♯

Back at Dara and Meg's house, MC found Dara at the kitchen table with the newspaper and Meg busy at the stove surrounded by delicious wafts of steam. "Mmm. Chicken soup, Meg?"

"Yes. It should be ready for supper."

"How ya doing?" Dara peered over the paper as MC slid into a chair across the table.

"Fine. I had an appointment with a therapist. Guess I'll be seeing her once a week for a while. Part of my return to work deal with Jamie."

"Good," Meg said. "Someone to help you sort things out."

"I guess." MC flipped through a manila folder of documents.

"You sound less than thrilled," Dara said.

"Can we talk about something else?" MC wished she had a drink.

"Whatever you want is what we'll do." Meg shot Dara a scowl. "Right, Dara?"

MC knew Dara wouldn't dare argue. "So, I've been thinking."

"I recognize that tone," Dara said.

"I've signed with Midwest Realty to sell the house. Spencer Douglas will handle the sale. We've gone through, and he decided what items need to remain for staging. I've hired a company to come move the rest to storage."

"We could've helped," Dara said.

"You two have been generous enough, putting me up for the last ten days. Which brings me to the next task on my list—I need to find a place of my own."

Meg sat in a chair next to MC and grabbed her hand. "Stay here with us for as long as you need. We're family."

"Meg, you're a sweetheart, and I love you to pieces, but I need to put on my big girl pants and move on." She was antsy for privacy and itchy for a drink, preferably in her own space.

Dara stared at the newspaper.

Meg stood. "You can be so damned stubborn, MC." She was only five-foot-three, but she was a force and MC knew to tread carefully.

Dara peeked over the top of the newspaper. "Now you've gone and done it, McCall. You know better than to get Meg upset." She lowered the paper and leaned toward MC, a glint of devilishness flashing in her eyes. "Besides, she's right. What's your hurry? We've plenty of space and we're happy to have you here. Where're you planning to go?"

MC glared at Dara before turning her attention to Meg. "I don't want to be the constant boarder. You've been so supportive, opening your home to me. But I need my own place. Maybe you guys can help me find something?"

She watched Meg's facial expression fade from consternation to contemplation.

"Suck up," Dara mumbled.

Meg said, "We will most certainly help you find a place." She wiped her hands on a dishtowel and rummaged for pen and paper in a drawer. "What are your requirements, madam?" She slipped into a chair. "And you, be quiet." She pointed her pen at Dara. "I heard your snide comment."

"Busted." MC elbowed Dara's arm.

Dara raised the paper. "I'll go back to the news and keep my mouth shut."

MC said, "That'll be the day." She pushed aside the folder of papers and pulled from her messenger bag the green hardbound notebook, her "Life after Barb," the record of navigating through the minutes, hours, and days without Barb.

Dara folded the newspaper in half and sat back in her chair. "Whatcha got there?"

"My life. Literally. I process better when I write stuff down." MC turned through the many pages of notes she'd made in the aftermath of Barb's murder, recognizing the irony of her words after her response to Doctor Zaulk's recommendation.

Pieces of evidence she knew of.

Records of the daily calls to Detective Sharpe, which had elicited nothing more than "Sorry. No news."

After her session with Doctor Zaulk, she'd added feelings and thoughts.

Lastly, every task or step toward her existence without the love of her life.

"All righty. Carry on." Dara fingered the newspaper but didn't open it.

Meg scribbled notes on her own pad of paper. "House? Apartment? Condo?"

MC got up and poured a cup of coffee. "Something simple, Meg. Small. I think an apartment."

"Okay. Apartment." Meg crossed off the other options. "We have a start."

"Wait a sec." Dara tossed the paper aside. "The manager of those two buildings on Grand and Dale stopped in for a coffee a couple weeks ago, and he mentioned he'd listed a one-bedroom apartment."

Meg said, "A couple weeks ago? It's probably been rented by now."

Dara said, "I guess."

MC said, "It's worth checking out. Good location."

"And close to us." Dara thumped MC's arm.

Meg rolled her eyes. "Dara, don't scare her off."

MC said, "Dara's right. For once in her life."

They all laughed.

"I'll get my laptop and search the net. See if I can find a listing." MC grabbed her piles and stowed everything in her messenger bag and hustled up to her room.

She was able to locate a contact online and to her amazement, the apartment was still available. She set up an appointment to see the place next Monday morning.

Then she phoned Jamie and asked to extend her time off work until the following Thursday, December eighteenth, a week before Christmas.

That taken care of, she checked her email and sifted through condolence messages from co-workers and found an email from Sergeant Wilcox at the MPD Forensic Garage. The email had come in the Monday after Thanksgiving.

She opened the message and scanned it. Wilcox had been on vacation and apologized for not sending the photos before leaving. She opened the file containing images of Arty's BMW. She scoured each photo.

Nothing stuck out. She viewed the pictures again and stopped at the one showing the keys in the ignition. She zoomed in on a gold key that caught her attention.

MC retrieved her keys from her coat pocket and held up a key she'd recently obtained. "USPS 342840" was stamped on hers, which was very much like the one in the picture. Clearly a post office box key.

She enlarged the image and squinted. The key on Arty's ring was a similar gold key, but she couldn't see if there were any identifying numbers or letters on it. "Damn." Still she thought the keys were enough alike that it warranted investigating.

She saved the photo of the keys to her desktop and sent an email to Cam with the picture and her thoughts. Then she called him.

"Hey," Cam answered. "How are you doing?"

"I'm okay. Busy. Had my first psych appointment today." She took a deep breath. "I was going through my email and Wilcox had sent me pics of Arty's car a week ago."

"MC, you shouldn't be thinking about work. Focus on you."

"We've had this discussion already. Don't shut me out. I need this. Call it part of my healing process. I could investigate stuff on my own and not involve you if you prefer." She may have come across too harsh, but she wasn't about to back down.

After a long pause, he said, "Jesus. Okay. But we better not let Jamie or Crapper know. What've you got?"

"Keys. Or rather a key. I think Arty may have a PO Box somewhere. When I reviewed the photo of his keys, there's one like the one I have for my PO Box. Gold. Mine has USPS and a six-digit number stamped on it."

"You want me to put in a request with postal management to search the post office box database?"

MC said, "You're a mind reader. Email's already in your inbox. And you'll let me know as soon as you hear, right? Promise me, Cam."

"I'll see what I can find out. I promise."

"You're the best. Give Jane and the kiddos a hug for me."

"Will do. Take care."

"Thanks. Talk soon." She disconnected and studied the photo one more time. Fingers crossed they'd get a hit from the database search.

Chapter Fourteen
Monday, December 15

Stewie Levine, the apartment building manager, met MC at nine Monday morning. A Danny DeVito doppelganger, Stewie heaved his stubby bulk up to the third floor with MC hot on his heels.

"These stairs are gonna be the death of me," he huffed.

"No elevator?" MC didn't mind, but without an elevator moving furniture up to the third floor would be a bitch.

"Not in this old place." He stopped at the second door on the right. "It's a one bedroom." Stewie unlocked the old worn oak door. "Solid construction." He tapped his knuckles on the jamb and stepped inside.

"Yes, I can see." She followed him into a living room with maple wood floors shining in the morning sun.

"Closet?" She opened a door directly behind the entrance.

"Yep. Eat-in kitchen. Stove and refrigerator are new."

MC trailed Stewie into the living room and down a short hallway. The bathroom had a claw foot tub with shower, and the bedroom was sizable.

He said, "Wood floors throughout."

"I'll take it."

"I'll need first and last month's rent along with a three-hundred-dollar damage deposit. Total is nineteen hundred and thirty bucks. Rent's eight-fifteen a month. We should talk about how long a lease you're looking for, and will you be the only tenant?" His beady eyes gazed up at her like a ratty pup, then flashed on the ring on her left hand.

Jesus, was he hitting on her? "For now, I'm interested in a six-month lease. I'll be the only tenant."

"Had to ask. Noticed the ring and all."

"My partner died recently, so like I said, it'll just be me."

Cherries bloomed on his cheeks. "Oh, God. I'm sorry. Ah. Six months is good. I can get the paperwork from my car if you want to wait here. Shoulda brought it with me so I could avoid those stairs a second time and . . . "

When he returned, out of breath and sweating, MC signed the required documents and wrote him a check.

Stewie gave her two sets of keys. "I'll let you have 'em now even though the lease technically starts on Wednesday."

"You're very kind. I can start moving in right away?"

"Have at it. Oh! And there's a parking lot in the back. No assigned spots, but usually there's enough room for all the residents."

"Thanks, Mister Levine." MC pocketed the keys.

"Stewie. Please. Mister Levine is my ninety-year-old father."

"Stewie." MC shook his pudgy paw and ushered him to the door. "Thank you."

"My pleasure. Call me if you have any problems." He fumbled a business card from his wallet and dropped it, picked it up, and crammed it into MC's hand.

She stood in the barren living room as the winter sun painted her shadow across the floor. She tried to envision what the future held in store, and grief twisted her heart like someone wringing out a wet dishcloth.

No rest for the weary, she thought. She sat on the windowsill above a hot and clanking metal register to make a few calls.

With a deep breath she put her phone away, closed and locked the door to her new home, and strolled the short distance to Flannel. The one bright spot in this dark phase was she had Dara and Meg, and she'd be close to their house and the café.

Over a steaming cup of dark roast MC filled them in on her day.

"The moving company process was easier than I expected. Truck will be at the house at eight tomorrow morning. I guess a middle-of-the-month move is a good thing. I decided not to stage the house, so when the place sells everything will be out. What I don't use in the apartment will go into storage. I have an appointment at one today with the therapist. Afterward I'll be at the house."

Meg said, "We'll come help you this afternoon when Kate comes in, sometime after two."

"I don't know what I'd do without you." MC swallowed back sudden tears. Both her friends wore similar expressions of dismay and helplessness. She couldn't take their pity, and had no idea how to comfort them from their own loss. She rose. "I've got to get going. See you later."

Back in her car, MC played a voicemail from Sharpe informing her she could pick up her duty firearm.

She called him and made the short trip to SPPD.

A uniformed officer escorted MC up two flights and through the maze of hallways to the Homicide office and turned her over to Sharpe.

Sharpe said, "Thanks for coming in so quickly. I've got everything right here." He unlocked a file cabinet and handed MC her gun and magazine.

MC took the items checking to ensure all was as it should be before stowing them in her messenger bag. "So, anything new?"

He sighed, "No. I'm afraid not."

"Right," she said. "Well, thanks for getting the gun back to me." Fat chance he'd tell her even if something new arose. She refused to give up, though. She had her own agenda, and it didn't necessarily correlate with SPPD rules.

Her next stop was Louie's Liquors on Grand and Snelling. She ran in and purchased a bottle of Goose. Back in the car, the brown paper wrapper crinkled in her gloved fist as she laid it inside a box of towels she'd packed a couple days earlier at the house.

She made a mental note to purchase other freezer items to mask the bottle's presence should Dara or Meg happen to peek inside the cold zone later.

#

MC chomped a couple pieces of gum as she trudged from her car to Doctor Zaulk's building. She settled into her spot in one of the wingback chairs and waited for the doc to open up the session.

"MC, I know you weren't interested in journaling, but did you make an effort?"

"Funny you should ask. I want to come clean about something. The day after Barb's, ah, death, I bought a notebook. A special notebook, in Barb's favorite color." A shade slightly lighter than the doctor's eyes, MC realized.

"Have you been writing in it?"

More than you could ever imagine, MC didn't say out loud. "Bits and pieces. Details I don't want to forget." Details about her bloody murder. MC shook her head to clear the images.

Doctor Zaulk scrutinized her. "You've made progress." She wrote some notes. "Keep with it. Write as much as you feel able to. The more you let out, the better."

They talked about MC's support team: Meg and Dara; Cam and Jane. MC confessed to having no communication with Barb's family after the memorial.

"Do you get along with Barb's family?"

"For the most part. There is . . . Barb's sister-in-law, Jules, is a homophobe. I could ignore her at the few family functions we attended, but Barb couldn't stand her. Family events were hard sometimes. It put Barb and her brother Dave at odds. But that's not why I haven't talked to them."

Doctor Zaulk asked, "Why then?"

"I feel too raw yet. Like I'm responsible for their daughter's death and they'll blame me, not want to talk to me or see me. How can they not condemn me?"

"You aren't culpable. Barb's death was not your fault. I understand needing some distance from her family, but I hope you'll be able to come together at some point in your healing."

"So, doc, I can return to work on Thursday, right?" She felt a desperate need to be busy.

"I think one more week off might do you some good."

"No. Please. I need to get back to my job." She stopped and took a deep breath, steadying her racing heart, then calmly said, "I'm moving into an apartment on Wednesday, and I'll be ready for work bright and early Thursday. I don't want more time off. What will do me good is to immerse myself in something productive instead of having time to sit around and dwell on the current state of my personal life."

MC held her breath, waiting for the final verdict, ready to dive deeper into battle.

Doctor Zaulk tapped a finger on her open notebook. "I'd rather you take the extra time, but I can't force you."

She signed a basic Fitness for Duty form and handed it to MC. "I'll agree as long as you continue weekly appointments for at least six months, as I've noted on the form."

MC stood. "Wait. Six—"

"Non-negotiable, MC. These sessions are not a punishment. I'm here to help you. We've got lots of hard work ahead of us."

MC sank back into the chair. "Okay."

"We'll reassess at the six-month mark." Doctor Zaulk closed her notebook.

"Reassess." MC folded her get-out-of-jail form and scheduled her next appointment.

She drove to the post office. Her PO box held a six-inch stack of mail, of which most appeared to be cards. MC asked for a bag at the window and dumped the envelopes in. She tossed the bag on the backseat and drove to the house, pushing from her mind all thought of opening and responding to sympathy cards.

She parked in the garage and bolstered herself with a quick slug from the bottle, feeling like one of those folks she'd seen countless times in dank doorways along the city's streets. She stashed the bottle in the back of the Subaru. MC hoped she'd be able to make it through the packing session without losing her mind—or at least until Dara and Meg arrived to prop her up.

Chapter Fifteen
Wednesday, December 17 – Thursday December 18

Wednesday evening Dara and Meg helped MC move the last of the boxes from her house to the apartment. The mover had dropped all the items MC didn't need at the public storage space she'd rented.

The house was now completely cleaned out. MC had argued with Spencer, her realtor, about not staging the house, and she put her foot down. She needed distance. Needed to be out, once and for all. He finally gave in after Meg stepped in and read him the riot act.

The three women worked in the apartment all day, unpacking, cleaning, and moving furniture around. They finally collapsed on the couch as the sun painted the western sky orange.

"Supposed to snow tonight." Dara covered a yawn.

"Are you sure you're ready to go back to work?" Meg asked MC, a frown creasing her brow. "You could put it off until Monday, start the week fresh."

"Ready as I'll ever be." MC stared out the window at the yellow glow of the street lamps reflected on the road below. "I have to go back. I need to work or I'll go crazy. And the case is breaking wide open."

She didn't mention she'd be doing her own sleuthing on Barb's murder. Her gut told her Dara and Meg wouldn't understand.

Her insides itched. She needed something, a quick icy dollop from her friend the Goose. She licked her parched lips with an even drier tongue.

Dara clapped a hand on MC's shoulder and pushed herself up from the couch. "I guess we should head back to the shop."

"I can help you close later." Even as she uttered the words, she prayed they'd decline. She needed a drink, and Dara would know immediately. She always did. "It's the least I can do for all you've done for me these past couple of weeks."

"No way." Meg stood, hands on hips. "You have enough to deal with. You can help us some other time."

"You heard the boss." Dara smirked. "I think we both know better than to argue. Right?" She hugged MC. "Love you."

Meg grabbed hold of MC. "I love you. I didn't mean to be so feisty with you, but I know how stubborn you get. Someone has to keep you in line." She bit her lip. "I'm sorry." She brushed a tear away.

"It's okay, Meg. You're right. Barb was my North Star. Sometimes I feel like a buoy afloat on this giant ocean of life. Nothing's anchoring me." She pulled them into a group hug. "I love you guys. But right now, I need you to leave so I can get ready for tomorrow."

And have a drink or two.

MC ushered them toward the door and locked up behind them. She left the shade up on the middle window and pulled the two side ones down. Dara and Meg stepped down the stairs from her building.

They turned and waved. She waved back and decided on some soup for supper. While the soup warmed in the microwave, MC poured frosty vodka into a coffee mug. The quicksilver heated her from chest to belly.

She sat at the kitchen table and spooned cream of broccoli soup into her mouth as she reviewed notes on the Stennard case. The empty coffee mug beckoned from the middle of the table.

MC ignored it and continued to peruse her notes. Cam hadn't let her know if he'd talked to Gavin or if he'd found out about Arty's post office box. She made the PO box her first priority for the following day, unless Crapper had other plans for her. Jamie hadn't mentioned anything specific when she called to let him know Doctor Zaulk had released her and now that she'd be back in the saddle, she'd be under Crapper's supervision still.

She closed the work notebook and opened "Life after Barb," the green notebook. She decided her plan would be to start at ground zero.

Who called 9-1-1? Maybe Sharpe would tell her. Even if he did, she concluded that interviewing her old neighbors was a must. Not a task she relished. Maybe she'd be able to find an ally in SPPD willing to score her some inside info.

She cleared the table and washed the dish and spoon. Thirsty work. She opened the freezer in search of something to take the edge off. The long, pearly neck of the Grey Goose bottle pointed at her, luring her in. The bottle seared her fingertips.

She pulled back and opted for the safer, though more calorie-laden, Dove bar. Mint swirl ice cream surrounded by silky Dove dark chocolate would suffice.

She slammed the freezer closed before the demon could change her mind and savored the chocolatey minty sweetness, feeling a sort of victory. She'd be going back to work with a clear head in the morning, though she swore she heard a scratching sound from the wintry confines of the freezer.

"Come back, MC. One more won't hurt."

She picked up the notebook, shut off the lights and concentrated on the ice cream, drowning out the wicked whispers as she headed toward the bedroom.

Chalk one up for the good guys.

She tossed the green notebook and pen on the nightstand. She kept the log close in case something came to her during the night, or as in most cases lately, to help fill the dark sleepless hours.

Her journal, her murder book, not only her means of chronicling her investigation, she also filled the pages with entries in which she swore to Barb she would find whoever was responsible and bring them to justice.

Or better yet, retribution.

H

The next morning, MC woke before the alarm sounded. She showered, dressed, and strapped on her gun. A surreal feeling engulfed her as she packed up her messenger bag and opted to stop at Flannel for coffee.

Her actions felt rote, like someone else was performing them. The streets and sidewalks bore a pristine Christmastime snow covering the dirty underlayer. She scraped ice and snow off the car, and the tires crunched frozen slush as she eased out of the parking lot.

She arrived at Flannel within minutes.

"Morning, sunshine. The usual?" Dara's gravelly voice carried over the hum of early morning caffeine seekers and the holiday music piped over the cafe's speakers.

"Please." MC forced a smile onto her face.

"You ready?" Dara handed MC a twenty-ounce white cardboard cup and a sleeve with the word Flannel imprinted in black watch plaid.

"For the coffee? Why, did you poison it?" MC meandered to the end of the counter and dumped cream and a packet of sweetener into the cup. She held it to her nose and breathed in. "Used hemlock, eh?" She set it on the counter and snapped a black plastic lid on top.

A customer standing in line regarded the two, eyes wide.

"Always the comedian. Don't listen to her." Dara served the customer, who quickly left the shop. She wandered down to where MC stood pulling her gloves on. "Seriously. Going back to work, I'm—"

"Worried about me. I'll be fine. And with this jolt," she raised the cup, "I can handle anything they throw my way. Give Meg a hug." She met Dara's eyes. "I'm okay."

"I don't believe you. You're a good liar, MC. Always have been. How about dinner here tonight? Seven? Maybe we can entice you into helping close."

"Bribery by food. Tempting." MC sipped her coffee. "Let me get back to you once I have an idea of what's on my plate at work. Deal?" The last thing she wanted was dinner with her friends. Much as she appreciated them she had a need to pull back a bit. They weren't exactly suffocating her—okay, yeah, they were suffocating her.

"Let us know. We can order Thai and eat here. Or maybe some Chicago-style pizza?"

"I'll call later. Love you guys." MC waved and held the door as a threesome entered, stomping snow from booted feet.

H

MC arrived at work by seven and swiped her badge to enter the office suite. Chelsea didn't come in until eight, so the Reception bubble was empty.

She hung her coat on the skeletal rack in the corner behind her desk. One day she fully expected the assemblage to collapse, scattering its bones every which way. She thought about buying a new one herself, since multiple requests for a replacement had been denied. Budgetary constraints.

Ensconced behind her desk, computer humming, MC drank her coffee and plowed through the hundreds of emails in her Outlook account, mostly moving condolence messages to a separate folder to deal with later. The mind-numbingly boring task was exactly what she needed to start the day.

She'd just opened an email from Agent Ferndale when someone knocked on her door.

"Come in." She hit reply as Jamie Sanchez entered.

"Welcome back. Mind if I sit?"

"Thanks, Jamie. Sure, have a seat." She pushed her keyboard aside.

He smiled. "How you doing?" His brown puppy dog eyes showed concern.

If she had a dollar for every time someone said "How you doing," she could retire. "Good as can be expected." She reached for her coffee.

"MC, if you need more time—"

"Jamie, thank you. I don't. Honestly, I need to work." Offset my nightmarish life, she thought. "At this point even dealing with Chrapkowski is better than not being here." She took a mouthful of coffee and swallowed hard.

"Okay, then. You're still on Stennard. Cam will bring you up to speed. Priority one. Work your other cases as you have time." He stood up.

MC rose. She was afraid he'd hug her if she stepped around so she stayed rooted behind her desk. "I'll get with Cam as soon as he's in." And avoid Crapper as long as I can, she thought. "Wait. Why are you giving me assignments and not Chrapkowski?" She stuck her hands in her pants pockets.

Jamie said, "I almost forgot. Chrapkowski is out on indefinite medical leave. He suffered a heart attack almost a week ago. I've heard from the

Assistant Inspector in Charge his prognosis isn't good. He may retire rather than return to work. Time will tell."

MC knew she should feel something—empathy, concern, maybe even jubilation—but she couldn't muster the energy or the will to express emotions for Roland Chrapkowski. Instead she let the silence build up around her, a padded wall of protection, allowing feelings to bounce off it. Heartless Crapper incapacitated by his heart. The forces of the world were exacting a fitting payback.

Jamie had his hand on the doorknob. "I'm sorry for the way he's treated you. The teams have your back. You're one of the most respected inspectors in this domicile."

MC blinked. To hold the tears in check, she focused on the chipped eggshell-colored paint above the doorframe. "I appreciate that, Jamie. I hope Chrapkowski gets what he needs." Even though the asshole doesn't deserve it.

"I don't know if he's got any friends left. He's burned plenty of bridges over the years. Still, I guess everyone deserves a modicum of peace in life."

"Right." She couldn't quite keep the sarcasm out of her tone.

"I'll let you get back to work. Let me know if you need anything. I'll keep the wolves at bay. Give you a chance to reacclimate."

"Thanks. I don't know how much sympathy talk I can stand. Know what I mean?"

"I do." Jamie exited, closing the door behind him.

MC settled back in her chair and ran her hands through her hair. She glanced at the time on her computer screen, seven twenty-three.

Cam usually rolled in around eight so she had time to get through more email.

Instead she reached for her desk phone. She quickly punched the numbers she'd memorized.

"Sharpe."

"Morning, Detective. This is MC McCall."

"Inspector McCall, what can I do for you?"

"Checking in. Anything?"

"Nothing."

She yearned for an ice-cold vodka to bulldoze the pain blaring in her skull and wet the dustbin that was her mouth.

He blew out a breath, charging the phone line with crackles. "Inspector McCall. Trust we are doing everything in our power to solve the case."

"Have you talked to the neighbors? All of them? Did anyone see or hear anything?" MC was a pitbull, latched on and refusing to let go.

"I can't go into specifics about the investigation." His voice softened. "You will be the first to know if anything of relevance is discovered. I know how hard this must be for you."

"I understand." She didn't. "Thank you for talking to me."

"Anytime. Have a good day." He hung up.

After work she'd go back to her old neighborhood and do some door-to-door chats with the neighbors. She remembered the email from Agent Ferndale and returned her attention to the computer. She read through the message. Ferndale wrote they were interviewing Klein yet again. He and Andrews seemed hellbent on Klein as Arty's killer.

MC disagreed. But she decided to hold off on a response until after she and Cam discussed what was going on.

As if on cue, her door swung open and there he was.

"Partner!" He hustled around the desk to give her a hug.

"Hey, Cam." He was the younger brother she never had. "How're you? How're Jane and the kids?"

"We're all fine. More importantly, how are you?" He stepped back, hands on her shoulders. "You've lost some weight. Have you been sleeping?"

"Gee, don't hold back." She sat. "I'm as good as I can be, considering. Grab a chair."

"How about I get us some coffee? Unless you don't need more."

"You know I do." She sucked down the cold remnants and handed over her cup. "Please and thank you." She sent a sheepish grin his way as the headache pounded behind her eyes.

"You got it. Be right back."

MC swallowed a couple ibuprofen before he returned.

Hunkered down over her desk they went through the file on Arty.

MC said, "Ferndale and Andrews think it's Len Klein. They're interviewing him again." She scrolled down through the emails trolling for any other related messages. "Hey, what's this?" She hovered the cursor over an email from late the previous day from Agent Teri Young, the FBI agent partnered with Agent Alexis Trinh. MC clicked it open.

Cam stepped behind her and read over her shoulder. "The cyber team found no text or emails of concern on the phone, but they found a couple audio files, including one from after Arty's meeting with Stennard. And no go on any "Wooly" or "Worley" in any of the employee records."

"We were there, Cam. At the dump site. Why didn't I find the damn phone when I was skulking along the shrubs?"

"We were too late to save Arty. And you managed to get some good intel on Klein and his buddies. Besides, the phone was found at the end of that road, if you can call it a road. In the darkest area of the scene."

"Still, I should've noticed something." She hit the reply button on the email. "I wish we could find that damn USB drive. Then at least we'd be able to push ahead on more search warrants for the fraud case. I'll ask Young to send us the MP3 files."

MC and Cam had settled back in their seats when MC's desk phone rang. "Inspector McCall. Agent Young, hello." MC's gaze lifted to Cam.

"Right. You think the last recording makes Klein more of a suspect?" MC flipped open her notebook and started scribbling. "Because Klein's SUV matches the one described? But you know there are two black Escalades in the Stennard security fleet, right?" MC scrunched her eyebrows together and squinted at her computer screen. "Yes, it showed up in my inbox. Cam is here with me. We'll listen to the recordings and get back to you. Thanks, bye." She hung up.

Cam leaned back in his chair and crossed his arms. "Sounds like the FBI is all over Klein. First Ferndale and Andrews and now Young."

"They think the recording, the last one on Arty's phone, nails Klein. Let's listen."

Cam scooted his chair to sit next to MC. She opened the audio file. They sat through it once and then played it again. MC scrawled notes as Arty and another man's voice droned from the tinny computer speaker.

"Impressive," Cam said. "Someone tailed him, and Arty had the presence of mind to make a recording."

"And to think fast enough to get rid of the phone before the bad guy or guys found it."

"No kidding. All Jack Reacher."

"The timeline doesn't fit with Klein as the doer, though. I don't buy it." She spun the notebook so Cam could see. "The second voice is not Klein's. I'm no voice expert but Klein's voice is more baritone, this guy sounds more tenor. Seems younger to me. And the other voice, the shooter, doesn't sound like Klein either."

"The shooter's voice is harder to pinpoint. Probably because the phone is farther away from the group by then. Maybe Klein was the driver who let the masked guy out?"

"Could be, I guess. But why would Klein go back to the Stennard building? Why not go home?"

"Because he had the meeting with the two doofuses."

MC shook her head. "Also bothersome. Why would Klein set up a meeting at the boat storage lot, the same place he'd just dumped Arty's body? He's not stupid. Arty's wallet was gone, but his briefcase and a ream of papers were strewn all over the car. Too sloppy for someone with Klein's background."

"Good point."

"Gavin Thomson, on the other hand, Mister Sleek Businessman, might not be as thorough." MC hesitated. "Maybe he was the driver? He let the henchman off on that frontage road with instructions to take care of Arty?

He had access to the company vehicles, same as Klein. Let's listen to the recording of the meeting again."

Cam leaned forward in his seat, his face the picture of concentration. "Thomson definitely sounds like he wants Stennard to do something about Arty. He would've had to have someone on speed dial to set this all up so quickly."

"Or he had it pre-arranged." MC stared at the computer screen. "I think Gavin was at the end of his rope with Arty. The guy is cool as a cucumber, and his voice is chilling. I wish I could've seen his eyes. The eyes tell so much."

"True. But the timeline?"

"He had time. Think about it. Gavin left before Arty did. Arty thought he heard someone in the hall so he checks it out. Next, he has a run-in with Klein on the first floor. This gives Gavin plenty of time to grab one of the SUVs from the back lot and follow Arty when he departs."

"Do you think Klein and Gavin are in this together? Is Klein the masked guy? Oh, wait. The voice doesn't match. Is Gavin the masked guy and Len Klein the driver?"

"Possible. Not probable. We don't have any indication Klein and Gavin have contact. Seems like Stennard has most of the interaction with Klein. And I don't see Gavin pulling on a black mask and wielding a gun. The effort would entail getting his hands very, very dirty. Guys like him, the high-class sociopaths, want to keep themselves clean. Someone else handles the wet work. We need to talk to both Klein and Gavin. I'd love to convince Ferndale and Andrews to let us interview these two."

Cam stood. "Let's do it. I bet Klein is at the Stennard building guarding the fortress even though nothing's going on."

"And Thomson is probably holed up in his fancy house on Lake Minnetonka. Hatches battened down. Waiting for the waves to recede. I'll call Oldfield and let him know what we're doing."

"I'll grab my coat and sign out a car. Meet you by the bubble."

MC dialed Oldfield's cell. He picked up after the first ring. "Oldfield."

"ASAC Oldfield, this is MC McCall."

"McCall, hello. How are you?" Oldfield's voice lost its edge. "I'm sorry for your loss."

"Thank you." MC gripped the phone tighter, gritting her teeth against the swampy fog of grief threatening to descend. "I'm calling because Cam and I decided to interview Len Klein and hopefully Gavin Thomson about Arty." She quickly dished the dirt on their suspicions.

"I've listened to the recording, too. I like the plan. Keep me posted, and loop Ferndale and Andrews in, too. They've been interviewing people all over the place. Glad to hear you're back on the job. You good?"

"I'm good. Thank you for your concern." MC hung up and expelled a huge gust of air, not realizing she'd been holding her breath.

𝓗

Cam parked in front of Stennard Global Enterprises. Bright light reflected off the glass doors and bounced off white snowbanks.

The lot wasn't quite deserted, but close. MC counted three vehicles, all parked in the section designated for employees. Stennard and Thomson's spots were empty.

Taylor, the receptionist, sat behind the reception desk in the lobby. "Good morning. Do you have an appointment with someone?"

MC flashed her badge. "You don't remember us, Taylor?"

"Oh, hi." Her face flushed. "Sorry, there's been so much going on the last couple weeks. No one is really here. I mean no one important, except I guess Mister Klein." She twisted her blond hair around a finger.

"Lucky for us, we're here to see Mister Klein." MC smiled, hoping to put her at ease.

"I'll let him know you're here." Taylor reached for her phone.

Cam stretched his arm over the desk and stopped her. "We know the way to his office."

"Thanks, Taylor," MC said.

They angled around the reception desk and down the hall toward the security office.

The door was propped open. No need to lock doors when there wasn't anything to secure. MC knocked on the doorframe.

Len Klein sat texting on a cell phone and paused when he saw them. "What do you two want? Didn't you get everything during the raid last month?"

"Touchy, Len." Cam wandered into the office. He moved into position behind him.

Klein tucked his cell into his pocket and craned his neck to locate Cam. MC shifted to the front of the desk. She leaned down, her hands on the barren desktop. She said, "We've got a few more questions for you."

"I already told the FBI everything I know, which is nothing," Klein said. "They asked me about Musselman."

"Now *we're* here to ask you *our* questions." MC hooked a folding chair with a foot and sat. She pulled out her green notebook and a pen. She crossed her legs, pen poised over the notebook, then realized she had the wrong one. Her stomach took a dive and she swallowed the bile rising in her throat as she stared at Barb's name on the page before her.

Klein let out a growling sound of exasperation. "You gonna ask your freakin' questions or sit there all day staring at the damn note pad?"

Cam said, "Why don't you shut your yap, Klein."

MC bent to her bag and swapped the green for the black notebook. She took a deep breath. "Tell us about November seventeenth. Clue us in on what you did that entire day—from waking up to when you arrived back home."

Klein eyed Cam over his shoulder. "Don't you want a chair, too?"

"Nope. I'm good right here. Why don't you go ahead and answer the question?"

Klein told them about his day. He mentioned seeing Arty both before and after the meeting with Stennard and Thomson. "I think it was around six forty-five when I ran into Musselman getting off the elevator down here. He left and I went back to my office and did the schedule for the next two weeks. I never saw him again after he went out the door."

"Did you make any calls after Arty left?" MC asked.

"Calls? Uh, no." Klein shifted in his seat, not making eye contact with MC. He focused on Cam again. "Sure you wouldn't be more comfortable sitting?"

"Do I make you nervous?" Cam asked.

"To be honest, yes." Klein shifted his gaze back and forth between Cam and MC.

"I'll stay right here."

MC said, "You didn't make any calls after you saw Arty leave. What time did you leave?" She settled her gaze on Klein, enjoying the sight of him twitching in his seat.

He stared at some place above MC's head. "I think around nine. Maybe a bit after."

His answer certainly correlated with what they knew. "Where did you go after you left here?"

"Where did I go?" Klein asked. "I, um, I think I went home."

"You think?" MC stared at him. "You're not certain? Maybe you followed Arty. Maybe you left earlier than you're telling us."

"No way." He raised his voice. "I didn't follow the twerp. Why would I? I was here until nine, then I went home."

MC said, "Relax. We're just chatting, nailing down the timeline."

Klein leaned back in his chair. "Sure doesn't feel like no chat."

MC asked, "How long does it take you to get home from here?"

He took a moment before answering. "Fifteen minutes with no traffic. Twenty-five or so if traffic is heavy."

"You left here at nine, which puts you home at nine fifteen, right?"

"Sounds about right."

"What if we told you we know you didn't get home until nine forty-five?" MC folded her hands over the notebook in her lap. Do it, Klein, she thought. Hang yourself.

Klein screwed his eyebrows together. "Maybe it was nine forty-five. Wait. I think you're right. I met a couple of business associates after I left here. A quick meeting and I went right home." He nodded. "Definitely home in time to watch the late news."

"And who might these business associates be?" MC leaned forward.

"They were referred to me by someone else. I'd never met them before. Now I think back, they were supposed to meet me, but they didn't show up. And geez, I can't remember their names." He stared up at the ceiling. "Damn. Wish I could help you out, but I can't."

MC stowed her notebook, removed a business card from the pocket in her bag, and slid it across the desk. "Give me a call if you remember anything, especially if you remember the names of those business associates."

Cam reached over Klein's shoulder and tossed his card onto the desktop. "Here's my card, too. You contact either one of us posthaste if your amnesia clears up." He clapped a hand on Klein's shoulder. "You hear me?"

"I hear ya. You're practically screaming in my ear." Klein tipped the chair over as he stood, Cam's hand slid from his shoulder.

"We'll see ourselves out," MC said.

As they strode through the reception area toward the front door, MC waved at Taylor.

"Nice to see you again," Taylor said.

"Nice to see you again." Len Klein's voice mimicked Taylor from behind.

Outside Cam said, "I think we got to him."

MC said, "He knows we know something, but he's not sure what. I still don't think he was involved in Arty's kidnapping and murder, but he's up to something." She settled into the passenger seat and found the Map app on her phone. "Gavin Thomson's?"

"Yep. So, what happened with you in there?" Cam started the engine and flipped the heater on high. He held his hands in front of the dash vents as lukewarm air huffed out.

"I grabbed the wrong notebook and was confused for a second." MC hoped he'd let it drop.

Her need for a drink was ramping up, and Cam's concern nudged the craving up a notch. She scanned the pages in her notebook until she found the one with Gavin's home address and typed it into the app.

She said, "You know, there are these amazing new things called gloves. They work wonders to keep your hands warm when it's cold outside."

"How about you read me the directions and keep the commentary to yourself?" He frowned. "You sure you're all right? You'll tell me if you need a break, right?"

"Cam, I don't need a break."

Thirty minutes later they pulled up to a McMansion on Bohn's Point on Lake Minnetonka. They parked on the brick driveway in front of a three-car attached garage. The house was a mammoth two-story structure of wood, shakes, brick, and stone.

Cam whistled. "Impressive. Think they have a pool and lakeshore?"

"Green isn't a good color on you."

"I'm not envious. Not much. How do you suppose they keep the driveway so clean? No snow. No ice. Underground heating? The one percent, huh?"

"Yep, the one percent. Shall we see if His Excellency will grant us an audience?"

A man about Cam's height with dark brown hair and hazel eyes answered the door. "Yes?"

"Gavin Thomson?" MC recognized him from the day they'd enacted the search warrant at the company.

"Who's asking?"

"I'm Inspector McCall and this is Inspector White." They flashed their IDs. "We're with the US Postal Inspection Service. We'd like to ask you a few questions, if you have time." MC refrained from stamping her feet as the chill wind whipped a dervish of ice crystals past them. "Are you Gavin Thomson?"

"Yes." Thomson scowled. "Come in." He stood aside so they could pass.

"We can talk in my office. This way." Down the hall, Thomson opened a set of sliding wooden doors, exposing an office about the size of MC's apartment.

"Nice office," MC said. "Maple?" She pointed at the built-in bookshelves behind the monstrous desk.

"Did you come here to inquire about the design of my home, Inspector, uh, sorry. What was the name again?"

"McCall, Inspector McCall." The smell of money emanated from every surface in the room.

Thomson settled in the leather executive chair behind his desk and motioned MC and Cam to less comfortable chairs across from him.

MC sat in a brown leather chair on wheels and placed her feet firmly in place to avoid moving back and forth. She wondered how many people had betrayed their nervousness by rolling the chair around while sweating under Thomson's scrutiny.

Cam took the other chair and wheeled closer to the desk. He crossed one ankle over the opposite knee and unbuttoned his coat, exposing his SIG Sauer in shoulder holster. "Mister Thomson, we'd like to talk to you about Arty Musselman."

MC opened her coat and prepared to take notes. She leaned back in the chair, waiting.

Thomson eyeballed them. "Why are postal inspectors asking about Arty?" His voice was smooth as single malt scotch. "He's been murdered. Isn't murder the cops' jurisdiction?"

"When was the last time you saw Arty?" With his thumbnail, Cam scraped at a spot on the desktop.

Thomson seemed transfixed by the movement of Cam's thumb. "Would you mind not doing that?" He nodded his head at Cam's hand.

"Sorry." Cam tapped on the desktop instead. "So? Arty?"

"We had a meeting with Mike in Mike's office on November seventeenth." He looked directly at Cam without blinking.

"How was the meeting? Everyone left on good terms?" Cam continued tapping on the desktop.

"The meeting went fine. I'm sure you know what happened since then, which is why we're here and not at Stennard Global Enterprises having this discussion."

Thomson narrowed his eyes and fixated on Cam's finger movements. MC bit back a smile, pleased that her partner was getting the better of Mr. Sleek Businessman. She wondered if he was the type to blow up and yell. Or maybe he was a low simmering antagonist who didn't get mad—he just got even.

Thomson said, "I left before either Mike or Arty. The last time I saw Musselman was a few minutes before seven, when the meeting ended. I had a dinner engagement with my wife at seven-fifteen, so I left right away. Never saw Arty again. Poor guy."

MC studied Thomson's face as he spoke. His eyes were dull, his voice flat, face like granite. The guy was one cold-ass character. Sociopath.

Cam raised his eyebrows. "Why do you say 'poor guy'?"

"For the obvious reason, Inspector. Arty's dead, isn't he? I regret the fate that befell Arty. He, Mike, and I have known each other since college, almost thirty years."

MC noted he didn't say they'd been friends since college.

Cam said, "You feel bad because Arty was killed. Did you notice anything suspicious when you left that night? See anyone lurking inside or outside the building?"

"Nothing out of the ordinary. I took the elevator down to the lobby and left through the front door. Got in my car and drove away."

Cam asked, "Who do you think killed Arty? Did he have any enemies?"

"Enemies? I don't really know. Not that I know about. Maybe he had some secret gambling addiction and got in over his head. I can't say I'm privy to goings-on in his personal life."

"What kind of vehicle do you drive?" MC asked.

Thomson's head swiveled slowly toward her, his blank unblinking gaze fixed on her, like he'd forgotten her presence. "Gray SUV. A BMW, X5." He refocused on Cam.

MC glanced at Cam, whose eyes were locked on Thomson. She asked, "Light gray? Dark gray?"

"Metallic gray, to be precise." He quirked one eyebrow at her. "I could show it to you if you're interested in the exact shade."

"Thank you," MC said. "We'll examine the vehicle before we leave."

Cam resumed his questioning. "You left and came home?"

"I went to meet my wife for a dinner engagement. She drove separately as I wasn't certain how long our meeting would last."

"And where was this dinner?" Cam asked. "What does your wife drive?"

"Dinner was to be at CoV restaurant, on the shores of Lake Minnetonka. You should stop in sometime. They serve a great prime rib and the grilled salmon isn't half bad."

"I'll keep that in mind if I'm ever in the neighborhood. If we ask at the restaurant, they'll vouch for you and your wife?"

"Actually, I'd intended to meet my wife. However, she called me as I was driving and told me she'd come down with a migraine and wanted to stay home. Told me to pick up some takeout for myself because she was taking some meds, which would knock her out for the night."

Cam kept tap-tap-tapping his fingertip on the desk without taking his eyes off Thomson. "The dinner at CoV never happened? What did you do next?"

"I drove to Katsana's Thai in Plymouth. Bought an order of beef curry and their Three Special Egg Rolls. I came home and ate by myself in the media room and watched a basketball game on ESPN. Not the Timberwolves. Can't remember who was playing, but you should be able to Google it."

Thomson's smug tone wasn't lost on MC. She despised this type of guy, a captain of industry who thought he was better than everyone else.

Cam asked, "Do you have proof of the time you were at the Thai restaurant?"

"Not really. I paid cash for the food. The whole order was less than twenty bucks."

"Anyone see you?" Cam asked, still tap-tap-tapping. "Your wife? Kids? Anyone?"

"My wife was in bed. I told you she had a migraine. We don't have kids, and the housekeeper was away visiting her sister. So no, no one saw me. What are you getting at? Do I need to call my lawyer?"

MC said, "We're piecing together Arty's last hours. Who saw what and when. If you feel the need to have your attorney present, we can certainly take this discussion somewhere more official and Mirandize you. I'm certain the local police department would have an interview room we could use."

"Who's running this show, you or her?" Thomson hooked a thumb toward MC as he faced Cam.

"Mister Thomson, we're both here to find out what we can about the death of your friend. I'd think you'd want to cooperate. Now, shall we move this show, as my partner said? Or continue our discussion here?"

MC said, "Maybe you have something to hide."

Thomson glared. "No need to Mirandize me or to change locations. We'll continue the discourse here. No one else saw me. I checked on my wife after I ate. She was asleep with one of those mask things on." He waved a hand around his eyes. "To keep out light. I slept in one of the other bedrooms, which is a common practice when she has one of her headaches." He stood. "Now, if you don't mind, I have some work to do."

"Work? Really?" MC asked. "Stennard is pretty much shut down. I'm surprised you have work to do."

"My work is none of your concern, Detective."

MC said, "Inspector."

"Whatever. I'll see you out." He waved for them to precede him.

MC stopped at the front doorway. "You mentioned we could see your vehicle."

"Wait outside the garage. I'll open the door from the inside and meet you." He held the front door open and closed it firmly behind them.

"What are the chances he'll open the garage?" MC pulled up her collar against the blustery mid-day wind.

"What's he got to lose? He'll let us in."

As if on cue, the door on the first garage bay began rolling upwards. MC said, "Not a sound. Good equipment."

Thomson stood next to a mid-size gray SUV parked nose-out with the BMW logo on the hood. "Here you go."

MC stepped in out of the wind. "Nice."

She glanced to the next stall and noticed a white Volvo SUV and in a third stall, a sleek black sporty Porsche. Mid-life crisis car?

"The Volvo is my wife's and the Porsche I drive during the non-winter months. I don't like to get sand and salt all over it. Besides, this baby is safer to drive in snow and ice." He patted the front fender of the BMW.

"I'm sure," MC said. "Thank you for your time, Mister Thomson." She handed him a business card. "Please contact us if you think of anything that may help us."

Cam also handed him a card. "Have a good day."

MC and Cam climbed back into their crappy Impala. Thomson stood inside the garage watching them. Cam executed a three-point turn, headed down the driveway, and glanced in the rearview mirror. "He's only now closing the door. He's way too chill for my taste."

"He's a sociopath. Through and through." MC stared out the passenger window. "Geez, Louise the money out here." She shook her head. "I don't like him, Cam. My gut tells me he's involved in Arty's demise—or knows who is. We need to prove it."

Chapter Sixteen
Monday, December 22

MC scrubbed off the layer of fuzz coating her teeth and berated herself for drinking the night before. Her weakened psyche called bullshit, and the craving for a morning pick-me-up flared. A vision of the long-necked bottle stowed in the freezer loomed large, jeopardizing her resolve on getting to work clear-headed and on time.

A hot shower started the blood flowing through the highways and byways inside her body. A good cuppa joe to kickstart her system was next on her list.

After the shower, she flipped the coffeemaker on and returned to the bedroom to dress.

Her attire since Barb's funeral tended toward the dark. Navy. Black. Charcoal gray. She'd never been one to wear vibrant colors anyway, but she'd pushed all her bright-colored shirts to the back of the closet. Today she selected a black collared shirt to wear under a gray jacket.

She eyed the empty glass lying on the nightstand and the green notebook next to it.

"Life after Barb" was dark.

Her mind sifted the bits and pieces of info on Barb's murder. She needed to set those thoughts aside and get ready for work, but she knew even when she wasn't consciously considering her partner's death, the details were running in the background computer in her mind. Maybe that was part of the reason she felt slow-witted and foggy-headed at times.

Evenings were reserved for reliving the memories, recording notes, and sometimes leaving messages for Detective Sharpe. She hadn't forgotten her promise to hunt down the killer or killers and see justice was served. Sometimes her late-night notes were indecipherable, which didn't help. And she still needed to interview the neighbors.

MC shook herself out of her reverie. She was running late. She strapped on her shoulder holster, grabbed her coat and messenger bag off the coat tree, tossed in her two notebooks, and headed out. She realized she'd forgotten her gloves and her coffee. She'd make it without gloves, but coffee was essential if she hoped to survive the day. She backed out of the cramped lot and drove the few blocks to Flannel, bracing herself for an encounter with Dara and Meg. She'd been off the grid since the previous Wednesday.

"Yo, MC," Dara greeted her as she entered the shop, "you look like you got the squirts, but you're squeezing hard to hold it in."

MC rolled her eyes at Dara's disgusting reference. "And it's a shock that you're still in business despite the fact there are two Caribous within half a mile of this place."

Meg said, "We've missed you. How are you?"

"I'm good. Busy. Work. The new apartment." And poking into Barb's murder, she didn't add.

Dara grabbed a twenty-ounce cup and filled it with the day's brew. "Here ya go. A rough night, huh?"

MC reached out a trembling hand to take the cup. "You know it. Rough, tough and never enough."

"If you're interested, I'm attending a mee—"

"I'm not interested, Dara. I don't need to go to AA. I'm fine. Not everyone is an alcoholic. End of discussion. I've got to get to work." She slopped coffee as she made several attempts to snap a plastic lid on the steaming cup. "Thanks for the coffee."

"Got the shakes I see," Dara said. "I want to help you. I'm worried."

Meg wound an arm around Dara's waist. "We love you, MC"

"I know. I love you both, too." MC busied herself dabbing at the spilled coffee on the counter, not meeting her friends' eyes. "But I'm fine. Truly fine and now truly late. Gotta run." MC flew out the door, away from the concern and the warmth of their love, back into the bitter cold void of her life.

#

MC fought ice-coated roads out to the southwestern suburbs, not daring to take even one sip of her steaming coffee. Her teeth chattered together, and her hands clenched the steering wheel in a death grip during the stressful drive. Cathy Wurzer's voice on MPR, Minnesota's local public radio affiliate, was a familiar backdrop to her morning commute.

She knew she'd been too harsh with Dara. Her friend possessed the biggest heart to go along with her big mouth. Meg and Dara were MC's rocks now. They did their best to keep her on track, but her life was a gaping windy chasm of nothingness, something she didn't think anyone could fully comprehend.

A horn honked behind her, and she saw the light had turned green. "How about practicing patience, asshole?" She restrained herself, barely, from flipping off the driver.

Wind-whipped and coffee in hand, MC slunk into her office. She'd no sooner sat down when a sharp rap sounded on her door.

"Come in," MC said.

Cam stuck his head inside. "Good morning."

"Is it?" she asked, blowing on her coffee before taking a sip. She wanted to ask if anyone had noted her tardiness, but she didn't.

Cam ignored her sarcasm and sat in a chair. "You feeling okay?"

MC set her cup on the desk. "I'm fine. I didn't sleep much. Got a bit of a headache this morning."

"Need some pain reliever? Maybe you should take a day. Talk to Jamie. I can cover for you."

"No."

Cam held up his hands.

MC rubbed her hands over her face. "Sorry. I didn't mean to bite your head off. I'm in a foul mood because I was late. I forgot my coffee at home, so I stopped at Flannel and traffic was horrific. And on and on."

Cam, being the good friend he was, went along with her story. "Sounds frustrating. All I'm saying is ease into a routine. No need to jump into the deep end."

"But Cam, I *do* need to jump in the deep end. If I don't, I'm afraid I'll float away into oblivion. Work is exactly what I need. Doctor Zaulk cleared me, so it's not like I've made a rash decision to come back."

"I know, I know. I'm just sayin' . . . "

"I appreciate your concern. I won't be a slug, promise. What's on the agenda for today?" She powered up her computer and picked up her cup of coffee.

Cam relaxed. "Diving right in, word has it that Klein is in custody."

MC stopped mid-sip, meeting Cam's eyes over the top of her cup. "As in arrested? Since when?"

"Arrested, but not charged yet, for Arty's murder. About an hour ago."

"He didn't kill Arty. I mean, he couldn't have. Right?" She picked up the phone and dialed Agent Ferndale's number. "Let's find out what's going on."

The call went to voicemail and MC left a message. She hung up and checked her email, finding a brief message informing the task force of Klein's arrest in relation to Arty's homicide.

"What about Thomson?" MC wondered. "After our chat last week, I'm even more convinced he's in this up to his eyeballs." She read the brief email again.

Cam spread his hands wide. "I dunno. We can keep hammering away at the guy. Maybe talk to his wife? Might be worth a shot."

"Good idea. But first I'd like to see if we can sit in on the FBI's interview with Klein. Where are we on the post office box key?"

"I haven't heard back on the PO Box. Maybe we should bring Jamie in. He might be able to push postal management to respond. In the meantime, I've got some paperwork. Holler when you want to roll." He stood, hesitating when MC grabbed her coffee. "You sure you're okay? Your hand is shaking. You cold?"

"Jitters from lack of sleep." MC wouldn't meet his eyes and took a gulp of coffee, thankful it had cooled enough that her mouth wasn't scalded. "See? All better."

"You seem on edge." Cam leaned against the desk.

"I'm fine, Cam. Like I said, I've had trouble sleeping and last night was one of those nights. I woke with a headache, and the drive in was hellacious. Otherwise, I'm good to go." She forced a smile. "How are Jane and the kids?" Redirection never hurt.

"The kids are about out of their minds what with Christmas a few days away. All Santa all the time. Jane and I are barely holding it together." He rolled his eyes. "I get tired listening to them. If only we could bottle their boundless energy."

"Truth. Barb loved teaching because of kids' vivacity." Barb coming home excited about how wonderful the kids were and how she loved their enthusiasm and genuineness flitted through MC's head.

"I get what she meant." Cam cleared his throat. "We all miss her. You know we're here for you."

"Thanks. I'm good. Swear." She held her hand up, palm out. Her phone rang. Literally saved by the literal bell.

"Inspector McCall. Hey, Ferndale."

MC held up a finger to stop Cam from leaving. "Thanks for returning my call. Cam and I are wondering if we could sit in on your interview with Klein, maybe ask a few questions ourselves."

Cam raised an eyebrow.

MC nodded. "You bet. We can be there in an hour."

Cam gave her the thumbs up.

MC hung up. "If we get there in an hour, we can prep with Ferndale and Andrews."

"Meet you at the bubble in half an hour?" Cam asked.

"Yep. I'll send Jamie an email asking for his help expediting the PO Box search. And, Cam?"

He stopped in the doorway.

"Thanks. You're a good friend."

♯

MC called Agent Sebastian Ferndale as she and Cam entered the parking ramp near the Hennepin County Jail in downtown Minneapolis. Ferndale met them at the building entrance and escorted them to an office, an approximately eight-by-ten very beige space that held a desk with a computer and a few chairs.

"County gave us this empty office to use," Ferndale said. "Andrews is set up in an observation room waiting for us."

MC shed her coat and tossed it over the back of one of the chairs. "Thanks for including us."

"No problem. You can leave your stuff here while we do the interview."

MC and Cam followed Ferndale down what seemed, to MC, a never-ending hallway. Echoes of Cam's concern over her wellbeing pinged in MC's head, and she made a conscious effort to repress all of it.

Her thoughts soon flowed toward SPPD's lack of progress on nabbing Barb's killer. MC needed to pound the pavement. Someone had to have seen or heard something. All she needed was one tip, a snippet. Something to wedge the door open and shine some light into the darkness.

"MC?" Cam's voice broke into her musings.

"Sorry. What?"

Ferndale said, "I understand you two had a chat with Thomson." He opened the door to a cubbyhole observation room with a desktop computer and three chairs squeezed around a desk. "Would've been nice to get a heads-up."

Andrews sat in one of the three chairs in front of the computer. "Hi guys."

The others greeted him.

MC said to Ferndale, "My bad. Oldfield asked me to let you know. Slipped my mind. In our defense, after listening to the audio files you sent us, we felt Thomson might be a viable suspect. Especially after talking with Klein first."

Cam said, "The voices in the audio don't sound like Klein." He held up a hand as Ferndale opened his mouth. "Hear me out. The quality isn't the greatest, but I urge you to listen again to see if you change your mind. And the timeline doesn't fit for Klein to be involved."

MC sat in a chair and pulled out her notebook. She paged through it until she found the page she wanted. "Remember we followed Klein the night Arty was killed."

Ferndale said, "Yeah, I remember."

MC continued, "He met with two goons. At the dump site, no less, although at the time we didn't know it. And we followed him home. I've said it before—the timeline doesn't work with him being the killer."

Ferndale said, "You may have valid points. But I can't ixnay Klein quite yet. He was the last person to see Arty alive. We're not ready to clear him. Right, Walt?"

Andrews said, "That's why we brought him in."

Investigating always got MC's mojo running and, thankfully, she felt her focus returning. For the moment, she felt sharp and with-it. She gave Ferndale and Andrews an approving nod. "Maybe we'll get something more concrete from Klein today."

Ferndale dug through a file. "We've had all the voice recordings transcribed. I've also got a stack of photos from Arty's car and from the crime scene. I'll have copies sent to you, as long as you promise to keep me in the loop on what you're doing." He eyed MC. "We're all on the same team."

MC said, "Sure. Great." MC glanced at Cam.

"What?" Ferndale asked. "There's more?"

MC sighed. "Truth is, we already have copies of the photos from Arty's car. Wilcox from MPD sent them to me a couple weeks ago."

Ferndale said, "And?"

MC said, "One of the keys on Arty's keyring resembled one I have. For a PO Box."

Andrews angled away from the computer and toward MC.

Ferndale folded his arms across his chest and leaned a hip against the desk. "You didn't think we needed to know this? What'd you find out?"

Cam said, "We haven't heard anything yet. We escalated the issue to our Team Leader because postal management hasn't responded to my request for information."

MC said, "We're hoping he'll be able to get us what we need."

"And you'll tell us immediately, correct?" Ferndale asked.

His face was flushed, and MC wondered if that was from anger or frustration. She hoped the FBI agent wouldn't blow a gasket and get them booted.

"Ferndale, catching Arty's killer is important to us, too. He was pivotal in our fraud investigation. I think we can all agree the two are tied together." She contemplated Cam, then Ferndale and Andrews. "We really want to see whoever killed Arty pay for the crime."

Ferndale sighed. "I get it. But let's work together. No more secrets. Agreed?"

"Agreed," MC said.

They settled on Cam and Ferndale interviewing Klein, and MC and Andrews observing via computer in the room they were gathered in.

"He doesn't care much for me," MC said. "No sense antagonizing him."

Ferndale stood. "Let's see what Mister Klein's got to tell us."

MC settled in front of the monitor next to Andrews. She was glad she didn't have to interrogate this guy. She'd felt clear-headed when the four of them were planning their tactics, but now her head hurt, and she didn't think she had it in her to stay ahead of the suspect.

Klein was seated in a red chair in the eight-by-eight-foot interview room. Mint green paint adorned the walls. Two dome cameras hung from the ceiling, and microphone plates were embedded in the walls on either side of the interviewee's chair. Cam and Ferndale entered the room. Agent

Ferndale introduced himself, and Cam dragged in an extra chair. He sat on the opposite side of the table from Klein while Ferndale set his chair to the left of the door facing Klein.

Ferndale leaned forward, forearms resting on his thighs. "Len. Is it okay if I call you Len?"

"That's my name." His gaze slid toward Cam. "Why is a postal inspector here? Am I accused of stealing mail?"

"Inspector White is here because of the Inspection Service's involvement in an investigation in which Mister Musselman was a key witness."

A sneer creased Klein's face. "I didn't have nothing to do with killing Musselman. So, I'm not clear why I'm even here."

"Why don't we just dive in?" Ferndale asked and verified that Klein had been Mirandized. "And you're willing to speak without an attorney present?"

"Whatever. I got nothing to hide." Klein tried to move his chair back and almost tipped over when the legs caught on the carpet.

MC leaned toward Andrews. "Our guy appears to be nervous."

"He definitely isn't comfortable." Andrews turned the volume control up a couple clicks. "And he's a giant sweatball."

Ferndale said, "Len, take us through your day on Monday, November seventeenth."

Klein heaved out a sigh. "Again? How many times do I need to tell the same story?" He launched into a monotone description of his day, including the exchange with Arty in the evening after Arty met with Stennard and Thomson.

"You follow Arty when he left the building?" Ferndale asked.

"I've told you people a million times. No. The last time I saw Musselman was when he hightailed it through the front door. He seemed pissed off or scared or something. I didn't think any more of it because I had work to finish and a meeting of my own to get to."

"What type of vehicle were you driving?"

Klein rolled his eyes and puffed out his cheeks. "The same as last time you asked. I drive a black Escalade owned by Stennard Global Enterprises."

"Interesting. Because we have information a black SUV followed Arty after he left the Stennard building. Know anything about that?"

Klein crossed his bulky arms and leaned back in the chair. "I'm not the only person who drives a black SUV."

MC sent Cam a text message. *Ask him who else drives the Escalades owned by Stennard.* She watched as Cam read the text.

"Agent Ferndale? If I may?" Cam asked.

Klein's head whipped to the right as if he'd forgotten Cam was in the room. "Are we doing 'good cop, bad cop' now? Gonna sweat me out?"

Cam leaned forward. "We don't do that shtick. We're here to get your take on what went down. Tell me, how many black SUVs are in the fleet at Stennard?"

"Two. Mine and one extra for when we have important security details."

Cam jotted something in his notebook. "And who has access to those two vehicles?"

"Me, Mister Stennard, and Mister Thomson."

"No one else? The other staff?" Cam glanced up at Klein.

"I mean, other security staff have access when I assign them to a specific detail. But they don't have access to the keys. I'm in charge of the keys."

Cam asked, "Do you have to give Mister Stennard and Mister Thomson keys? Or are they able to take the keys at will?"

"They have access any time. But they hardly ever use the SUV. Usually only if they have a meeting or want to take clients around town and not use their personal vehicles."

Cam asked, "Did either of them use the second SUV on the night Arty went missing?"

Klein stared up at the ceiling as if the correct answer were written on the white tiles. "I don't think so. But I left before them. When I left, both of their vehicles were still out front, and the other Escalade was parked behind the building."

"You were the only one driving an Escalade then." Cam scrawled some more in his notebook.

Klein slammed a hand on the table. "Pay attention. I did not kill Musselman. I told you, I had a meeting. I didn't see Musselman after he left the building. Why the fuck won't you people listen?"

Ferndale said, "Okay, Len. Calm down. We're just talking here. Tell us about your meeting. Who with? Where? How long?"

"Can I get some water?" Klein asked.

"Sure." Ferndale left to find Klein something to drink.

Klein growled out, "I'm telling you people. I didn't f'n off Musselman."

"You need to give us more, Len. I gotta be honest, things are not going your way right now."

Ferndale returned and set a bottle of water in the middle of the table.

Klein reached for the bottle, unscrewed the white plastic cap and sucked down half the liquid. The suction crinkled the flimsy plastic, and the sound bounced off the concrete-block walls. "Thanks."

Ferndale resumed his questioning. "You've quenched your thirst. Now tell us about the meeting."

"Like I said, I met with a couple of business associates. End of story."

Ferndale shook his head like a disappointed parent. "Len. You're facing a possible murder charge. I'd think you'd want to be a bit more forthcoming."

"I didn't kill him!"

"Tell us where you were and who you were with. These associates have names?"

"I had a business meeting."

"Len, you sound like a broken record. Maybe we should leave you to think about things for a while. Some personal reflection may enlighten you. What do you think, Inspector White?"

"I agree."

"Fine by me," Len said, his voice argumentative. "The story will be the same when you come back in here."

Ferndale smiled. "Oh, did I forget to mention we have a special place for those needing alone time?"

"Whaddaya mean?"

"Glad I got your attention," Ferndale continued, "as we'll be moving you to a holding cell. When we're ready to continue the interview, we'll have you brought back here. The digs are a bit more—stark—shall we say?" He gathered his notes.

"You don't scare me," Klein said.

Cam stood. "We don't want to scare you, Len. We want to find the truth. If not today, maybe tomorrow, or the next day."

"I've seen all the tactics. I was in the military."

Ferndale grimaced. "I was, too. But believe me when I tell you the jail holding cells contain more colorful individuals than you saw in the military."

"Guess we're outta here," Cam said.

Ferndale followed him out of the room and into the observation room.

MC glanced up as they filed in and quickly refocused on Klein. "I was hoping for more."

Ferndale came up beside her. "I'll have one of the officers haul him to general holding. Maybe he'll have an epiphany and want to talk after some quality time with the county's other guests." He picked up the phone and made the arrangements.

Within two minutes, a six-foot tall, muscle-bound deputy entered the interview room, cuffed Klein, and hauled him out.

MC's phone vibrated. Email from Jamie. She opened it, scanned the message and then read it again.

Andrews asked, "Everything okay?"

"Sorry, just a message from our boss."

Ferndale said, "We'll take another run at Klein in a couple of hours. If we shake anything from him, we'll let you know." He opened the door. "I'll take you back to the other office. This place can be worse than a corn maze if you're not familiar with it."

♯

On the way to the car Cam asked, "What'd Jamie find out?"

"He wants to talk." MC pulled her phone out and placed the call.

"MC?" Jamie's voice was stern.

"Hey, what's up?" She glanced at Cam.

"Where are you?"

"Cam and I are leaving the Hennepin County Jail. Why?"

"I thought you two were working on the fraud case. Why are you at Hennepin County Detention? And what's with the post office box inquiry?"

"We were helping the FBI re-interview Len Klein about Musselman. And the reason I requested the post office box search was because I noticed a PO Box key on Arty's keychain. I thought we might find something useful in his mail."

"You need to let me know stuff like this instead of barreling ahead with requests. When I said you and Cam were still assigned to the Stennard case I didn't mean the homicide investigation. We've plenty of work if you and Cam have spare time."

"I don't think we can work the two cases separately, boss. They're intertwined, whether we like it or not."

Cam frowned at MC.

"I have to justify the department's activities now that Chrapkowski's out. I need to be in the loop."

"Jamie, I'm sorry we didn't route the initial request through you. Won't happen again."

Jamie blew out a loud breath. "Okay. Your point about the two cases is well-taken. I just want to know what my inspectors are doing."

"Understood."

Jamie said, "You believe this will help the task force investigation?"

"We do," MC said. "And we'll loop Oldfield in if something pans out."

Jamie said, "All right. Arty had a box rented at the Main Post Office, downtown Minneapolis. I gave the supervisor on duty a heads-up you'd be there within the hour."

MC said, "Thanks, Jamie. We're on it." She ended the call and relayed the gist of the conversation to Cam. "He sounded flustered, maybe pissed off."

Cam pulled open the car door. "He's probably having a bad day. It happens. But we probably should've routed the request through him to begin with."

MC said, "We don't usually, though. Maybe he's stressed, and it's coming out sideways."

Cam said, "Forget about it. Let's do this."

They parked at the Minneapolis post office on First Street and went in to find hordes of customers waiting in line, most with stacks of boxes to mail, most likely Christmas gifts. People wait until the last minute, MC thought. I don't get it. Who wants to spend half their day at the PO?

A twenty-something woman, ruddy-faced and exasperated, hollered at a small child, "Zachary, stop!"

Cam barely dodged a toddler with a drooly candy cane stuck in one plump fist. "Yikes. Little Zachary nearly got me with his sticky mess."

MC laughed. "Quick reflexes. I guess having kids trained you for field maneuvers, eh?"

"You know it."

MC used her plastic employee id badge card to open the door from the lobby to the workroom floor. She knew her way around the facility. Both of them had investigated plenty of incidents at most post offices over the years. She led the way through a maze of equipment, some filled with packages and sacks, and others waiting to be filled. Trucks were backed up to the dock to be loaded.

"God," she said, "I'm glad I don't have to work the mail. What a nightmare."

They passed sections of post office boxes to a spot where a woman sat at a desk wedged between a pillar and massive rolling carts. MC flashed her shield. "Postal inspectors. We need to speak with the supervisor of the PO Box Section."

The woman pushed aside a pile of forms. "That's me, Susan Berg. I heard you might be showing up." She pulled a scrap of paper from under the pile of forms. "You want to inspect the Musselman box, right?" She stood, not much taller than a munchkin from *The Wizard of Oz*.

MC said, "Correct."

"This way." She didn't glance back to make sure they followed. "All the mail has been sorted for the day," she called over her shoulder.

She scooted past one cluster and took a right at the beginning of the next section. She stopped and viewed the note in her hand, then surveyed the boxes. "Right here." She pointed at one of the smaller boxes about halfway down. "Number 24418."

MC peered into the box. "One yellow padded envelope." She pulled a pair of gloves from her messenger bag. To Susan Berg she asked, "Do you know the last time anyone picked up mail from this box?"

Berg said, "Couldn't tell you. We have hundreds of boxes, and unless a box is overflowing and we have to notify a customer to come pick up their mail, we don't monitor frequency of pickup."

MC withdrew the envelope. "Addressed to Arty but no return address. We'll need to take this, ma'am." MC dropped the padded envelope into an evidence bag, but didn't seal it.

"I'll get the necessary paperwork for you to sign." Berg hurried back to her desk.

MC and Cam followed, waiting while she clicked on the computer, completed a form and printed it out. Cam signed and dated where Susan Berg indicated. She made them a copy, and handed it to Cam who stuck it in his coat pocket.

MC asked, "Is there an empty office where we can have some privacy?"

"Not out here, but the postmaster's conference room might be available."

Cam said, "Thanks."

In the postmaster's office they were greeted by the executive assistant seated behind a counter. "Hey, MC. Cam." Her voice took on a pleased tone. "How can I help the two of you?"

"Hi, Quinn," MC said. "Can we borrow the conference room?"

"Sure. The weekly managers meeting was canceled, so I know it's free. Let me make sure it's unlocked."

"How are the grandkids?" Cam asked.

"Rambunctious." She pointed to photos in silver frames on her desk.

Cam leaned over the counter and admired the pictures. "They grow up fast."

"Don't I know it." Quinn stepped down the short hallway and stopped at the first door on the left, and opened it for them. "All yours. Please turn out the lights when you're finished."

"You got it." MC set her messenger bag on a chair and the evidence bag on the table.

Cam closed the door and joined her at the conference table. "Let's open that baby up."

MC pulled new gloves from her messenger bag and offered a pair to Cam. "Can I borrow your penknife?"

Cam dug his keys out, flipped open the penknife on the ring, and handed them to her.

MC slowly slit the envelope open. She tipped it upside down over her other hand and a USB drive slid into her gloved palm.

"The elusive drive?" She handed the envelope to Cam. "There's a sheet of paper in there. Can you grab it?"

Cam used two fingers to slide the sheet from the envelope. "A handwritten note."

To Whom It May Concern: If you are reading this note then something has happened to me. Enclosed is a flash drive with phone recordings which are evidence of fraud committed by Michael Stennard and Gavin Thomson. I was supposed to turn the drive over to the FBI. I couldn't meet at the assigned location and time. I'm afraid my associates may be suspicious. I am truly sorry for my involvement in this horrible scheme. So many innocent people were hurt by the actions of Stennard Global Enterprises.

Sincerely,
Arty Musselman

Cam carefully stuck the sheet back into the envelope, his face gleeful. "I guess we have what we need for search warrants on Stennard and Thomson's personal residences."

"Uh huh." MC dropped the flash drive into the envelope and sealed the evidence bag. They both signed and dated the flap.

Cam said, "Let's get this to Oldfield so he can request the search warrants. And we'll call Ferndale from the car."

"Right on," MC said.

They thanked Quinn as they hustled past.

"Happy holidays," Quinn called after them.

"And to you," Cam replied.

In the pit of her stomach, MC felt a lump, like the one chunk of coal Scrooge allowed Bob Cratchit. Christmas was mere days away. Despite the constant reminders all around her she'd managed to ignore the fact. Quinn's simple words hammered her with sadness, guilt, and a glut of other feelings. Barb had loved the holidays. MC dreaded them, now more than ever.

♯

MC was exhausted. She and Cam had traveled from Edina to Minneapolis to Wayzata and back to the Postal Inspection offices, and it felt like they'd flown around the world on the red-eye.

They'd left the evidence bag with Oldfield. He lit up like the proverbial Christmas tree.

Back at the office MC completed a few tasks on a couple open cases before she called it a day. She was packing up to leave when her desk phone rang.

Oldfield wanted to let her know the flash drive yielded several recorded files of phone conversations between Arty, Michael Stennard, and Gavin Thomson, which was more than enough evidence to obtain search warrants for the personal residences and vehicles of both men.

"Good work, McCall. Both you and White. We'll let you know when the search warrants will be executed."

"Thank you. I'll let Cam know."

MC caught Cam as he was leaving and locked up her office.

What a long ass day. They hadn't even had time to stop for lunch. With her messenger bag over her shoulder, she headed for her car. The frigid air whacked her in the face.

Her mind hopped back on the rollercoaster of possibilities of what they might find when they executed search warrants on Stennard and Thomson. The fraud investigation was on solid ground. If they could only be as successful at reeling in Arty's killer, life might be almost tolerable.

Behind the wheel of her car, she checked her phone for messages. Sadness descended on her as she realized yet again there would be nothing from Barb.

Ever.

Tears filled her eyes and she swiped them angrily away.

Instead of heading to her empty apartment, she decided to drive by the old neighborhood. The time had finally come for her to chat with some neighbors.

MC passed the For Sale sign posted in the frozen yard and parked in the driveway behind the garage. A faint glow of light shone inside the house from a floor lamp set to a timer that illuminated at five each evening and switched off at eight in the morning. She wasn't worried about anyone breaking in because the house was empty but decided to play it safe.

She navigated down the alley and through her neighbor's gate. Hank Schmidt had lived in the neighborhood since time immemorial and was always helpful and friendly. He was a seventy-eight-year-old widower who acted as a handyman for whomever needed him. A sweet concerned old guy, MC and Barb always loved him. His house was lit up, so Hank was probably home.

MC knocked on the back door. After a minute or so, she pushed the glowing green doorbell button. She was about to give the button another nudge when the door creaked open.

Hank's slightly hunched frame filled the doorway. He unlocked the outside door and pushed it open. "MC? Is that you?" He squinted rheumy brown eyes under a flop of snow-white hair on his forehead.

"Hi, Hank. I'm sorry to bother you. I hope I'm not interrupting your supper."

He stepped back and waved her in. "Come out of the blasted cold. You're not interrupting anything. I was watching the news."

MC stepped into the narrow alcove which served as a mudroom, closed the door behind her, and slipped off her boots. Hank led the way into the kitchen, lit a buttery yellow by the overhead light.

"Take off your coat and stay a while." Hank pulled out a chair at the kitchen table. "Can I get you something?" His eyebrows, white furry caterpillars, crept upwards. "Coffee? Tea? Beer?"

MC was dying for a drink. "Coffee would be great, if you have some made. Don't to go to any trouble."

Hank crossed the kitchen and pulled a couple mugs from a cupboard and filled them from a silver thermal pot sitting on the coffeemaker. "I've always got coffee going. I live on the stuff, even though I probably should cut back." He set a mug in front of her. "Help yourself to the cream and sugar there on the table"

MC doctored her coffee and took an appreciative sip. "Thanks, Hank, this is the perfect end to a long day."

She tapped the voice recording app on her phone and set the device next to her on the table, the sleeve of her coat partially obscuring it from Hank's view. She didn't tell Hank about the recording, thinking it might upset him or maybe make him not want to talk.

Hank wrapped his gnarled hands around his cup. "I miss you and Barb. Such a terrible tragedy. I'm darn sorry. I never, not in a million years, thought something so awful could happen in our neighborhood." He shook his head. "I noticed you got the place up for sale right quick. Can't say I blame you. How are you holding up?"

His voice conveyed the level of concern and caring she might expect from her dad if he were still alive. MC swallowed hard, fending off the tears that always seemed to lurk just beneath the surface.

"I'm surviving, I guess. Work keeps me busy, but I need some resolution on a personal level. Do you know what I mean?" She stared at him. "I haven't had much chance until now to speak with anyone in the neighborhood about what happened."

"I talked to the police. A detective, Sharpe I believe his name was, paid me a couple visits. Told him everything I know. I don't know what more I can tell you."

MC gripped her mug, contemplating her approach. "Hank, I need you to tell me what you told Detective Sharpe. I know it's redundant, but I need to hear it all and frankly the police don't share their investigative information with outsiders. And I'm considered an outsider. I have to know the details." MC folded her hands on top of the table and waited, working to remain patient with her favorite old neighbor.

"The police don't tell you how the investigation is going?" He sounded surprised. "But you're all law enforcement."

MC tiptoed around the truth. "It's like I said, they consider me an outsider on this—because I'm too close to the circumstances."

Hank reached over and patted her hand. "I understand." He blew out a breath. "Let me think. I remember snow was falling to beat the band, the beginning of a good Alberta clipper. I went to get my paper off the front porch around seven, maybe seven-thirty that morning. No one was out front. I heard a couple pops. Louder than firecrackers. I asked myself, did I hear gunshots? I thought I heard muffled yelling, possibly male voices, then what sounded like a door banging closed."

MC hardly breathed. She was shocked that Hank had actually heard the attack on Barb.

"You didn't see anyone?"

"No one was out front, so I went through my house and out the back. I noticed your gate was wide open and your outside back door was whipping in the wind. I didn't see anyone. Then I heard an engine start, maybe in the alley or down the block, hard to tell because of the wind and snow."

He took a sip from his cup. "I know you and Barb kept the gate closed and the back door open was even more troubling. I went back inside and dialed 9-1-1, then grabbed my jacket thinking I should maybe check out your place. The operator told me not to go in. When the first squad showed up, I flagged down the young, red-haired officer and told him I'd called 9-1-1 and pointed out your back door. He told me to go back inside and he'd come talk to me later. I did as he instructed and stood watching inside my back door there."

Hank pointed to the alcove MC'd entered through earlier. "Before I knew it, there were cops and fire trucks and paramedics and whatnot everywhere in front and back. The red-haired officer appeared within a couple minutes and asked if I knew who lived in the house. I told him I knew you and Barb. I gave him the details of what I'd heard and seen. All he told me was a female appeared to have been shot. Nothing more."

"You heard a car engine though? Before the police arrived?"

"Most definitely. But I didn't see it. About thirty minutes after I spoke with the young officer the detective showed up and I told him the story, like I told the younger cop." His crepey-hands shook as he drank his coffee. "MC, I'm so sorry."

His brown eyes brimmed with unshed tears. She felt bad for him. He'd been a good friend to her and Barb for many years.

"Hank, I appreciate you telling me this. I know it's difficult." She took a swallow of her coffee to tamp down her own emotions. "Who else do you think I should talk to? Did anyone else on the block hear or see anything?"

Hank dug a neatly folded white hanky from his back pocket and wiped his eyes. "Gladys Crandell."

"Please, anyone but her."

"She's a bit of a nosy rosy, but she not only knows what's going on in the neighborhood, she also has the gift of gab. I bet she has a story to tell." He gave MC a half-hearted smile. "Grit your teeth and suffer through a short visit is my suggestion." He patted her hand again.

Thoughts buzzed in MC's head like so many bees in a hive. All information was pertinent. She needed to suck it up and go see Mrs. Crandell. MC stood and reclaimed her coat. Phone in hand she hit the stop button and hugged Hank. "Thank you for being so helpful."

"Don't be a stranger. Come see me anytime. And if you need anything, let me know."

MC headed for the back door and stepped into her boots. "Thanks for the coffee and the talk."

"Take care."

MC returned to her driveway. A quick glance at her phone showed it was still plenty early. She made the decision to continue on through the backyard and out to the front, crossed the street and hiked up to the white stucco bungalow diagonally across from her house. She pushed the doorbell.

A slender, gray-haired woman came to the door. "Oh, goodness, MC, what a surprise to see you!"

"Hello, Mrs. Crandell." MC kept her voice polite. "Do you have a few minutes to talk?"

Mrs. Crandell unlocked the storm door and held it open. "Please, come in." She stood back, rubbing her arms against the chilly air.

MC stepped past and stood on the runner inside the foyer. "I apologize for stopping by unannounced, but I happened to be in the neighborhood, so I thought I'd take a chance on you being home. Would you have time for a quick chat?"

"Of course. Take off your boots and hang your coat on the hook there. Can I get you anything? Tea?" Mrs. Crandell slipped into the living room and muted the television. "Come. Sit. I bet this is a difficult time for you—the holidays."

Mrs. Crandell's eyes were the color of a wintry sky, giving MC shivers that had nothing to do with the wind blowing outside. She followed her into the living room and sat on the sofa, again activating her phone's voice recording app and setting her phone, screen side down, next to her on the couch.

"No, thank you, on the beverage. I promise to not take up too much of your time." MC was determined not to allow the situation to devolve into a gabfest.

Get info. Get out.

"Nonsense. I've got all the time in the world."

Of course, you do, MC thought.

Mrs. Crandell settled into a glider rocker at a right angle to the sofa.

MC gritted her teeth and took a deep breath. "Mrs. Crandell—"

"Gladys. Please stop with the Mrs. Crandell. Good grief, I'm still stunned by the events. How are you doing? Has there been any news?"

MC felt control slipping away. "Gladys, I was just over at Hank's place, and he thought you might have information about the day Barb was killed." Direct, no hedging, take control.

"I didn't arrive home from shopping until almost nine that morning. I don't have any firsthand information."

MC's heart sank. "I see." She started to stand.

Gladys waved her back down. "Now hold on. I didn't say I don't have *any* information. I did speak to the nice man who lives at the end of the block on your side of the street. I can't remember his name right now, but it'll come to me. He told me he'd been out walking his shih tzu. Early. He saw an SUV with two people inside, both wearing dark, maybe black, hats and jackets. The SUV came barreling out the alley and headed south toward Ford Parkway."

The words gushed from Gladys's mouth like water spewing over Minnehaha Falls after a hard spring rain.

MC leaned toward Gladys. "What time was this?"

"He said it was early. Definitely before the police arrived."

"Did he get a license plate number? Or say what type of SUV?"

Gladys tilted her head. "He didn't mention a license number, but he saw a smallish white SUV. Possibly a Ford or what's the other brand? Begins with a K?"

"Kia?" MC asked. A distant pinging sounded inside her brain.

Gladys clapped her hands together. "Yes! A Kia."

"And you're certain this happened before the police arrived? And the vehicle was a white SUV?"

"Definitely before the police showed up. According to Mister Dogwalker. I wish I could remember his name. Can't you confirm all this with the police?"

"I don't want to pester the detective with questions. He's working a lot more than this one case." MC hoped like hell she sounded official enough not to send up red flags. "The more I can find out on my own the better. More efficient." The last thing she needed was Gladys letting Sharpe know she'd come around asking questions. She'd gotten all she could from the woman.

MC checked her phone. "Gee. It's almost seven o'clock. I didn't mean to take up so much of your time, Gladys."

"I'm glad you stopped by. Have they found any suspects?"

"I haven't heard." MC hustled toward the door with Gladys hot on her heels. She pulled her coat on and slid her feet into her boots. With her phone tucked safely in her coat pocket, she reached for the door knob. "Thank you for taking the time to answer my questions."

"I'm happy to help. Would you like to leave your number with me? I could call you if I think of anything else."

"How about if I stop by if I think of anything?" The last thing MC wanted to do was give her number to Gladys Crandell.

"I guess so." Gladys sounded disappointed. "Happy holidays."

"Happy holidays to you. Enjoy the rest of your evening." MC got out of Dodge while the getting was good.

Back in her car she replayed the recording of her conversation with Gladys. Something nagged at her, but she couldn't put a finger on what.

#

Safely situated in her tiny apartment, MC grabbed a crystal rocks glass from the cupboard and rewarded herself with a generous pour from the bottle of Grey Goose.

She settled at the kitchen table with her laptop and notebooks. A pearlescent finger of moonlight reached toward the windowpane only to be squeezed out by a fist of darkness. MC felt insulated and alone. She took a healthy gulp from her glass. The vodka slipped like quicksilver down her throat, tendrils of warmth sliding into her veins.

Another slug made her grimace, but she drained the glass. She pushed the computer away and went to the freezer for a refill, then pulled her work notebook in front of her.

MC sipped her drink and flicked through the pages until she got to the notes on Klein's interview from earlier in the day. She backtracked to the night she and Cam had followed Klein to his meeting at Johnson Boat and RV Storage. She skimmed the pages once, then a second time.

Glass in hand, halfway to her mouth, it finally hit her. Small. White. SUV.

She poured the remaining finger of vodka down her gullet and pawed open her "Life after Barb" notebook where she'd recorded highlights from the evening's confabs with Hank and Gladys.

The words blurred.

She blinked several times to focus.

Small. White. SUV.

There had to be thousands of compact white SUVs in the Twin Cities area, though.

In red ink she wrote: SUV—cross reference with Arty's case also having a white SUV involved.

She needed a refill in order to better process the information. The clear thin liquid poured like water into her glass. Mesmerizing. At the halfway mark she halted the flow, reconsidered, and filled the glass to about three-quarters, then recapped the bottle.

MC grabbed her green notebook and a pen and flipped the kitchen light off, headed for the bedroom.

Back pressed against the headboard, she drank and tried to re-read her notes as drips dotted the page. She wiped her sleeve over the sides of the glass and realized there was no condensation on the glass.

The droplets were her tears.

She finished her drink, turned out the light, and crawled under the covers, wishing she'd wake up from the nightmare and everything would be normal again.

Chapter Seventeen
Tuesday, December 23

Out of the shower, she felt halfway alive. She dressed and ignored breakfast, instead deciding a quick check of email and a dose of antacid to cure the hangover nausea were about all her system could handle at the moment.

The online news was helpful. They'd gotten their search warrants for Stennard and Thomson's residences and vehicles.

Score!

She checked in with Jamie. He was in much better spirits after hearing the news. Next she sent a quick text to Cam suggesting they meet up at the FBI command center.

That done, she retreated to her room to make the bed and spotted the green notebook splayed face down on the floor. The empty glass was shoved against the base of the lamp on her nightstand.

What a night. She scooped up the notebook and tried to press the crinkles out of a couple of bent pages, then picked up the glass and headed to the kitchen. She fully intended to put the glass in the sink. Instead she paused in front of the fridge, hand gripping the plastic handle of the freezer. A tiny voice inside coaxed her to pull the door open. One quickie.

Her phone chimed. She pulled it from a side pocket. Text from Cam. Jesus Christ, she thought. Did he have ESP or what?

I can swing by and pick you up if you don't want to drive.

She swore under her breath. The last thing she needed was jovial Cam so early. *Thanks, but I have some stuff I need to do after work so I'll drive.*

Cam answered right away. *Okay. See you there. Get some coffee into your bad self so you're not grumpy. LOL*

Her fingers flew over the screen. *Smart ass.*

Truth be told, she felt relieved he'd interrupted her. She'd been close to grabbing a Grey Goose eye-opener.

Grief, a sharp pain, drilled her to the core. She fought through it and packed up before the dark voice convinced her to take a dive.

Shoring up her resolve, MC stopped at Flannel and procured a cup of dark roast while deftly dodging questions from Meg and Dara. She hugged them and promised to call later, then she was on the road to Wayzata.

#

The task force members assigned to carry out the search warrants were from the FBI and the US Postal Inspection Service, the group split into two teams. MC and Cam, Agents Andrews and Ferndale, along with two other FBI agents MC didn't know, were the six-person team taking on Gavin Thomson's house. MC rode with Cam from the command center. They drove up the wide swath of driveway in front of the Thomson manor. "Odd. The sidewalk to the door hasn't been cleaned off. Don't rich folks have someone for that?"

MC scoped out the area. "Has a deserted feel." She exited the car, and the team hit the front door. "Has anyone thought about the plan of action if the Thomsons aren't here?"

Ferndale said, "In that case, Oldfield instructed us to head over to the Stennard place."

MC grumbled, "Great. Hope this isn't a fucking waste of time." She tromped through the snow to the door and pushed the doorbell. The chimes reverberated inside the cavernous house, adding to the sense of a place vacated. She checked her watch and half-turned toward the group of five huddled behind her. "Doesn't appear promising." She pounded on the door.

Cam stepped to the slim window to the left of the door and leaned forward, cupping his hands around his face. "I can't see much besides murky shadows through the sheers."

Behind them the door opened. "May I help you?" A gray-haired, stocky woman dressed in a double-breasted, short-sleeved, silvery-gray maid's uniform stood with her hands folded in front of her.

MC glanced at Cam, eyebrows raised, and a smirk pulling her lips upwards. Facing the woman, she thought, *The Brady Bunch*. What was the maid's name? Oh, yes. Alice. But Alice's demeanor on TV was more welcoming than this unsmiling woman in real life.

Ferndale said, "Good morning, we're law enforcement here to see Mister Thomson."

"I'm sorry, Mister Thomson isn't home."

Ferndale persisted. "Is his wife available?"

"No, she isn't here either."

MC, annoyed, stepped up. "When do you expect them to return?"

"I cannot say for certain. May I ask what this is in regards to?"

MC's patience was leaking out of her quicker than oil from a 1998 Chevrolet Lumina. "We need to speak to Mister Thomson. Why don't we step inside and discuss this further?" MC took a step forward, feeling Ferndale and the others close behind her.

The woman, a couple inches shorter than MC, but solidly built, put her hands on her hips and blocked the doorway. "I need to see some identification."

MC unbuttoned her coat to reveal her badge clipped to her belt, which also ensured that she gave the woman a peek at her holstered firearm. "I'm US Postal Inspector McCall. This is my partner, US Postal Inspector White, and the others are FBI agents."

The woman's brown eyes grew slightly wider before she appeared to gather her wits about her. She checked each of the group's identification and allowed them entry to the towering foyer. "I don't know what I can do for you." Her voice echoed. "As I told you, the Thomsons are not here."

MC focused on the maid. "May I ask your name and your relationship to the Thomsons?"

"My name is Ann. Ann Davis. I am the Thomsons' housekeeper. Have been for over twenty years."

MC did a double take at the name. "Ann Davis?"

"Yes. Like the actress who played Alice on *The Brady Bunch*. Don't think I've not heard a few jokes during my life." The woman crossed her arms, a stern gaze fixed on MC.

Truth is stranger than fiction. MC wrote down the info. Definitely not as personable as good ol' Alice had been on the TV show.

"All right Alice—I mean Ann—we have a warrant to search the premises and any vehicles on the property."

Ferndale moved forward with the paperwork and handed it to the maid, who fished a slim eyeglass case from a side pocket and placed a pair of reading glasses on her nose.

She examined the document and attempted to hand it back to the FBI agent.

"You keep it, ma'am. That's the owner's copy."

"I don't understand. Am I supposed to allow you to go through the house? And garage?"

Ferndale responded, "Yes. We'll be conducting a thorough search and removing any items we believe are relevant. We'll provide receipts for anything we remove."

"Oh, goodness." Ann fumbled with her glasses before regaining her composure. "I guess you have to do your job." She turned and marched toward the rear of the house mumbling, crepe soles of her chunky black shoes squeaking on the tile floor.

Ferndale huddled up the team, and split up the search duties. "McCall and White take Thomson's office."

MC nodded. "Cam, I'll meet you in there. I want to check on Ann. Her pallor would impress Dracula."

The others dispersed to various parts of the mansion.

MC strolled down the hall past the living room, dining room, an office half the size of Gavin's, and through the kitchen. Out the window, a four-season porch faced the wooded acreage behind the house.

No sign of Ann.

She noticed a couple doors on the far side of the kitchen and opened the first. A set of stairs led to the basement. The second opened into a hallway with two more doors, one open and the other closed.

She passed the first and discovered a laundry room the size of her living room. High-end stainless-steel front-loading washer and dryer lined one wall with a laundry tub the size of a bathtub at the end. On the other side of the room were racks for hanging wet clothes, an ironing board, and a thirty-two-inch flat screen television mounted high up on the wall. Built-in shelves housed a plethora of detergents, fabric softener, and a couple of irons. She supposed one could never have too many irons.

No sign of Ann.

MC continued down the hallway and stopped outside the closed door, hand raised to knock. She heard a voice.

Ann's.

MC leaned closer and pressed her ear to the door.

"They've been here a few minutes. Asking all sorts of questions. I had to let them in, sir. One of them showed me papers, a warrant. Yes, I'm certain. The document gives them permission to search the house, garage, and vehicles. No sir, I only said you and Mrs. Thomson were not home. I didn't mention you're traveling."

Traveling? Uh-oh. MC's brain went into overdrive. Would Thomson flee the country? During the meeting with Arty, hadn't Stennard mentioned being ready to abscond if things got bad? Maybe Thomson had decided to take flight, too.

She left Ann's door and caught up with Cam in Thomson's study. "I've got a hinky feeling."

"About what?" Cam sat behind Thomson's desk, several file folders in his hand. "Check out this setup. I swear the desk is about the size of a baby grand piano. Definitely the type of place worth keeping someone quiet about the scam you're working so the cash flow stays steady." He waved his free hand over the huge desk. "Give a guy a hard-on, if he were into this kind of gig."

"Stop drooling," MC said. "Listen." She gave him the lowdown on the one-sided conversation she'd overheard.

"You think he's in the wind?"

MC paced back and forth in front of the desk. "I think he knows how close we are to nailing him and Stennard for fraud, and I think he played a part in killing Arty. What I'm really worried about is whether he and the missus are on their way to some obscure country with non-traceable bank accounts loaded with money and no extradition. Fuck. We can't let him get away."

"Calm down." Cam stood. "What if they've gone to visit family? It's the holidays."

"True. But my gut is telling me otherwise." She took out her phone and called Oldfield. "Hey, it's McCall. I'm wondering if you could have someone check flights for the Thomsons?" She filled him in on what she'd heard. "Thanks."

She and Cam made quick work of Thomson's office, boxing up documents from his desk and credenza. The bookshelves didn't yield any secret panels or fake books storing secrets. MC figured that only happened in Sherlock Holmes or Agatha Christie novels.

♯

The boxes of documents were transported to a secure location for the forensic accountants to dig through and analyze. Back at the command center, Cam and MC headed to their vehicles.

"I'm off until Friday," Cam said.

"Why didn't you take Friday, too?"

"You sound like Jane. I don't want to lose the momentum on this case. And I have a couple other irons in the fire needing attention."

"I'll be in tomorrow and Friday," MC said.

"What're your plans for Christmas?"

"Dara and Meg have grand plans for me." MC tried to smile, but failed. "I'll do dinner with them and be back home early evening to decompress."

"You're welcome at our place both Christmas Eve and Christmas Day. Jane wanted me to remind you." Cam scuffed at a chunk of snow hanging from the rear wheel well. "The kids would love to see you. So would Jane's parents and mine."

MC bit her bottom lip. The thought of so many people made her uneasy at best. "I appreciate your offer. But I don't think I'm quite ready to deal with so many folks at one time. Too much, too soon."

"I get it." He hugged MC. "Take care. Call if you need anything."

"Thanks. Give Jane and the kids huge hugs for me." She slipped two envelopes from her coat pocket and gave them to Cam. "A little something for the kids."

Cam stared at the gifts in his hand. "MC you didn't have to—"

"Have a great holiday. I'll see you in the office on Friday. And no checking email while you're off. Be with your family."

Cam jingled his keys. "Same goes for you—no checking email while you're off." He stopped in the open driver's side door and faced MC. "Call, even if you just need to talk. I mean it." He tapped a hand on the rooftop before disappearing inside the vehicle.

She watched Cam drive off, then climbed into her Subaru.

MC picked up the green Moleskin notebook from the passenger seat and flipped through the pages of notes, too many of which were rippled in spots from where late-night tears had fallen. Lots of notes, but nothing pointing her toward the assailant or assailants.

She slapped the notebook down on the seat and noticed the turkey drawing stuck between the seat and console. She pulled out the artwork, folded it, and stuck it in the green notebook. She felt a twinge of guilt over Emmy not getting her turkey back, but not enough to give up the tiny remnant of Barb's life.

MC drove back to the office in the thickening traffic, a few stray snowflakes floating lazily from the ashen sky.

According to the weather report, another storm was barreling down from Canada with a promise of a fresh layer of snow for Christmas.

"Blech." MC pushed buttons on the radio, searching for a station playing anything but holiday music. If she never heard "White Christmas" again it would be too soon.

Back at the office MC flung her coat over the back of a chair. She powered on her desktop computer and worked through a few emails on other assignments before hitting upon one from Agent Ferndale.

Ferndale and Andrews had interrogated Klein again. This time he'd coughed up the names of the two guys he'd met with on the night Arty was killed. Nick Wooler and Quentin Laird.

The FBI had put out BOLOs—be on the look out bulletins—on both men. They wanted to talk to them about their interaction with Klein, including dealing drugs. MC picked up the phone and dialed Ferndale's number.

"Hi, this is McCall. Do you have a few minutes to elaborate on the Klein interview?"

"Sure. What do you want to know?"

"The names he gave you," MC peered at the email on her computer screen, "How does he know these guys, Wooler and Laird? Are they employees of Stennard Global Enterprises? I don't recall hearing those names or seeing them on any documents up to now." MC grabbed a pen and flipped her work notebook open to a fresh page.

"They aren't official employees. I talked to Young and Trinh, and they'd dug through all the employee files. Cross-referenced employees hired through HR and those hired by Security. Funny thing is, Klein was the only Security employee on file."

"Really? How do they get staff then?"

"Klein admitted he worked with local security firms and hired temp personnel, as needed. He also made it sound like Wooler and Laird were off the book extra help whenever Stennard had his infamous house parties. They obtained drugs, you know, ecstasy, pot, cocaine, whatever the flavor of the month was at the time, and handed it over to Klein for a hefty payment. Which, by the way, corresponds with the meeting you saw between him and the two guys. Klein also mentioned he'd used them as extra armed security to keep guests under control. And he'd allow them to drive security vehicles when he needed them to work."

"How long has Klein known them?"

"He couldn't pinpoint an exact date when he started using their services, so to speak. He thought it had been about two years give or take a few months."

"What's your take? You said they were allowed access to the security vehicles. Is it possible one, or both, of them were in a black Escalade? You think they have anything to do with Arty?"

"I asked if they had one of the Escalades the night Arty was killed. Klein said they'd never have been in one of the executive security vehicles. They'd only have used one of the compact SUVs, which are white Ford Escapes. He didn't mention anything more about them than the drugs and extra muscle at the parties."

"Very interesting."

"Obviously, we'd like to talk to these two, but we haven't been able to locate either one."

Pages rustled in the background. "Laird's mother is in a nursing home, but no one at the place has seen him since the day after Thanksgiving. The administrator said Quentin was a quiet guy who visited mom at least once a week and paid the monthly fees on time. She mentioned the last time he was in, he'd paid for six months and told them he'd mail in future payments."

"I wonder what that was about? Sounds like he was planning a trip."

"The last known address the nursing home had for Quentin was a friend's house. An officer spoke with the friend who said Quentin had been couch surfing, but after Thanksgiving he left. The guy assumed Quentin was staying with a different friend because his belongings were gone and he'd not heard from him. We have no phone number for him either."

"No phone number isn't surprising. These guys probably use burners. But leaving a friend's place, I'm not up on proper etiquette, but wouldn't you at least say good-bye and thanks for the hospitality?"

"I know, right?"

"What about the other guy? Wooler?"

"We actually found an address for Nick Wooler via DVS—Driver and Vehicle Services. He has a valid driver's license, according to DVS, and the address was a dumpy apartment in South Minneapolis. His roommate said he hadn't seen Wooler since around Thanksgiving, and most of his stuff was gone. He was ticked off because he'd been calling Wooler, but the phone number wasn't working. The friend is putting a notice on Craigslist for a new roommate if he doesn't hear from Nick by January first."

MC scrawled the info on her notepad, including Wooler's last known phone number. "Sounds like both these guys are a dead end, for now." She blew out a frustrated sigh.

Ferndale said, "We were hoping for some connection to Arty, but it doesn't sound like they even knew him. Klein said he'd tried calling Nick a few times after the last big party. The first couple tries he got voicemail, then the number became a dead end. No service. Probably dumped. Needless to say, we had to cut Klein loose."

"Thanks for sharing," she said. "We'll be in touch after the holiday or if we get anything new on our end."

"Sounds good. Enjoy the holiday."

MC hung up. While her gut told her Klein wasn't their guy, she'd been hopeful he'd point them to a possible suspect.

Her personal cell vibrated. She glanced at the screen, saw it was Dara, and let the call go to voicemail. She wasn't in a mood to fend off Dara's insistence they have dinner or whatever else she had up her sleeve. MC had agreed to do Christmas Day dinner with them, which was the extent of her commitment capabilities.

The dark voice inside her head urged her to finish up and head to the liquor store. The bottle of Grey Goose in the freezer was almost empty.

⌗

MC trudged up the stairs to her apartment, arms full of Thai takeout, a 1.75-liter bottle of Grey Goose, and her messenger bag. Inside, she kicked off her boots and dumped the food and vodka on the kitchen table. She hung up her coat and changed into her flannel pants and sweatshirt, along with a thick pair of hiking socks to ward off the chill from the hardwood floors.

MC picked up her phone and sent Dara a text. *Sorry I missed your call. Work is super busy. Just got home. More work to do tonight. I'll see you and Meg on Xmas Day.*

Her phone buzzed with a response. *No prob. We'll be around if you change your mind. Meg sends a hug. Stay away from the devil juice.*

MC took the new bottle of Grey Goose from its bag and stuck it into the freezer after removing the current almost empty occupant. She pulled a glass from the cupboard and dropped a couple ice cubes into it, and found herself mesmerized by the clear liquid cascading over the ice. "Devil juice. More like liquid courage. Courage to live another day without my heart and soul."

The slow burn spread outward. She finished the drink while leaning against the refrigerator. Ice clinked as she tasted the last of drops on her tongue, sounding like the glass was begging for a refill. MC complied.

Drink replenished, she grabbed a fork and dove into the white container of Thai fried rice with shrimp. She ate a few bites, washing it down with more vodka. She opened the green notebook and tucked the folded turkey drawing into the pocket located inside the notebook's back cover.

For the hundredth time she read through her notes. She continued to eat, read, and drink until her glass was once again empty. She rubbed her hands over her face, glanced at her phone and saw it was almost nine. Outside the windows, white flakes drifted erratically from the glowering sky.

Bone-weary, MC refilled her glass. A soft voice, reminiscent of Barb's, warned she didn't need any more. But her entire body ached, pitchforks of pain digging to the very marrow of her bones. She gulped for air, her chest heaving. Her hand shook as she brought the glass to her lips, the liquid rolling like a wave on a lake. A long swallow washed a trail of numbness down her throat and brought a waterfall of tears from her eyes. Sobs followed, her body a limp lifeless mass puddled on the chair.

Buck up, she thought and reached for the glass. About halfway through her third drink she threw caution to the wind and called Detective Sharpe. The line rang a few times, then voicemail kicked in. She swallowed and croakily identified herself. She asked if he'd checked out a lead on a white SUV spotted by one of the neighbors the morning Barb had been shot. She also asked him to please call her the next day.

Damn Sharpe.

Why hadn't he made any progress?

And why had she been so polite? She was angry. Fucking pissed off.

Alone.

Thirsty.

Food no longer appealed to her, she closed up the carton and tossed it in the almost empty fridge. She placed the fork and glass in the sink. Stared at them for a few seconds. Washed the fork and picked up the glass. One more drink wouldn't hurt. The inner voice chimed in again, admonishing her that she'd had more than enough already.

Fuck the voice.

She dumped out the half-melted ice and ignoring the words of reason poured in about an inch of liquid, and then seeing not much was left, she went whole hog and drained the remaining liquor into her glass and tossed the dead soldier into the recycling bin. She felt ghostlike as she floated to the table and retrieved the green notebook and her phone, leaving her bag and work stuff. MC flicked the light off and fumbled through the darkened apartment to her bedroom.

She set her alarm and plugged her phone into the charger on the nightstand before she crawled into bed and propped herself up against the headboard. Thoughts swirled, a cyclone inside her mind. Her head began to ache. Pain, like a vise, squeezed her temples. She took another swallow in what was proving to be a vain attempt at silencing the demons.

Eventually, the notebook slipped from numb fingers. She sucked down the remainder of her drink, wishing she didn't have to deal with any holiday ever again.

Chapter Eighteen
Wednesday, December 24

By nine, MC was half-assed together and in her car driving to Flannel. She ran in for a coffee. Twinkling strands of holiday lights hanging over the counter burned MC's retinas. Thankfully Dara was nowhere to be seen. Meg was behind the counter and handed her a steaming coffee. MC promised to call later, then realized this promise had gone unfulfilled several times now. She couldn't find it in herself to care.

Before MC could make her escape, Dara came around a corner. She hollered a happy greeting and made a point to look at a non-existent watch on her wrist.

"Looks like someone overslept," Dara said. "Too much of the liquid Goose last night? You know—"

"Dara. Jesus!" MC checked her temper with effort.

"Just sayin'. It might be time for—"

"Stop. I don't have time for a lecture about AA." Dara's chipper voice assaulted MC's eardrums and set a drumbeat thumping in her skull. A cranial orchestra warming up.

"But, wait a minute. You should—"

"Please, please stop!" MC glanced toward the counter where Meg stood silent and anguished. MC took a gulp of air. "Look, I'm sorry. Both of you— I'm sorry, but I just can't…"

She fled.

"Merry Christmas!" Meg's voice followed MC back out into the arctic air.

Oh, my God, she thought. Exactly what I didn't need to begin the day. Why does Dara have to do that? Why?

She sat for a couple of minutes in the car, her forehead against the steering wheel. After a few sips of hot coffee, the banging in her head subsided, and she felt ready to drive.

The late morning traffic was light and she was relieved to make good time to work. Chelsea had the day off as did almost everyone on staff. Lights glowed in two other offices, Jamie's and a newer inspector at the opposite end of the hall from her. She hoped Jamie hadn't noticed she was late. A knock on her door quashed those hopes.

Jamie stuck his head in. "Morning."

MC felt her face flush and busied herself booting up her computer. "Hi. Sorry I was late." Bite the bullet, she thought.

"I got a call about forty-five minutes ago from Oldfield. He said he tried your number first and left a voicemail. They picked up Gavin Thomson and brought back him and his wife."

MC managed to focus on Jamie, which wasn't easy with the steady throbbing behind her eyeballs, her pulse a heavy metal bass beat hammering her brain. "That's great news. I'll call him and see what the game plan is. Hopefully he'll allow me to interview Thomson, or at least sit in on the interview."

She tried to set the coffee cup on her desk and misjudged. The cup fell to the floor, the khaki-colored liquid joining the other stains on the blue gray industrial carpeting.

"Crap!" MC shot up from her chair, sending it flying into the wall behind her.

Jamie stepped farther into the office. "MC? Are you okay? You seem frazzled."

MC opened a desk drawer and grabbed a wad of stockpiled napkins. She dabbed the wet spot, soaking up what she could. "Got a late start."

She didn't add, and I hate the holidays, and someone fucking murdered my partner a month ago, but she wanted to.

"I hate oversleeping. Throws me off my game." Her hands shook as she tossed the dripping brown mass into the trash can.

Jamie sat in one of the two chairs in front of MC's desk. "Maybe you should take a few days off. You've suffered a traumatic experience, and you've worked long hours since you came back. I'll give you as much time as you need."

"Thanks, Jamie. I appreciate your concern, but I don't need more time off. I promise I'll do better at getting here on time. Damn alarm didn't go off this morning." She shifted documents and files around on her desk, not meeting his gaze.

"If you change your mind let me know." He stood. "I'm on call tomorrow, and I'll be leaving at noon today. If you need anything you can reach me on my cell. Don't put in a full day today. Go be with family or friends."

"I'll see what the plans are regarding Thomson first."

Jamie placed a hand on the doorjamb. "I'm serious, MC. Cut out early. Don't make me give you a direct order." His tone was firm, but he gave her a half smile.

"Got it, boss."

She called Oldfield, reaching him on his cell. He told her Thomson and his wife had been escorted back from Atlanta by a couple of agents.

They'd been booked on an outgoing flight to the Bahamas, a country with no extradition. Mrs. Thomson was driven home and questioned there. Gavin was being held at the Hennepin County Jail.

Oldfield asked how soon MC could get to the jail. She told him she needed the next thirty minutes to complete an Investigative Memo on a mail theft complaint and then she'd be freed up. She was glad Crapper wasn't around, he'd be dealing her a rash of shit for not handling the theft complaint faster. She wondered about her ex-boss's circumstances . . . but not enough to go visit. It's not like she'd heard a peep from him after Barb died.

She decided to take her car rather than sign out an official car and have to come back at the end of the day. She let Jamie know her plans and left.

When MC arrived at the Hennepin County Jail in downtown Minneapolis, Ferndale and Oldfield were waiting for her. In the conference room before the interview, MC flipped open her notebook. "Has Thomson said anything to anyone?"

Ferndale laughed. "Sorry, I'm a bit punchy. Running on fumes. He's demanding to know why he's here, why we won't let him go, the usual. Mostly been pacing or drumming his fingers on the tabletop."

MC leaned forward. "I'd like to take a crack at him."

Oldfield pursed his lips.

MC said, "I'm sure I could get him to open up."

Ferndale said, "I think it would be beneficial to have McCall in there. Thomson doesn't seem like he's easily intimidated. I'd like to try a different approach."

Oldfield said, "What are you thinking?"

Ferndale said, "We set up in a less institutional room. He may feel more at ease, which could lead to him giving us what we're after."

"Exactly," MC said.

"I checked and there is a room that's quiet and furnished with a sofa and a fairly comfortable chair, plus a homey-looking floor lamp and low table between the sofa and chair. The camera is up in the corner behind the chair, so that's where you'll want to sit."

"Let's do it," MC said.

Oldfield held up a hand. "Wait." He swiped his phone screen. "New info from the search warrant authorizations. One of the techs finally filed his report on the nav system in both the Escalades owned by Stennard Global Enterprises."

MC asked, "What took so long?"

Oldfield said, "We didn't have access to this data until this latest round of search warrants."

Ferndale chimed in, "Should've had those on the first warrants, but no sense in rehashing the issue now. What does the report show?"

"Hold on a sec," Oldfield slid his finger down the phone screen, "here we go. The vehicle Klein used showed his final route on the last night he drove it. His fingerprints are all over every surface in that particular SUV."

MC said, "Not an unexpected revelation."

"Right, but the really interesting stats are from the second SUV. The last route shown on that navigation system is from the night of November seventeenth and indicates whoever drove the vehicle initiated a route back to the Stennard building from the boat storage site."

Ferndale forward in his seat. "Wait. What time?"

Oldfield read from the email. "The time stamp coincides with the time of Arty's disappearance."

MC said, "I guess I'm not surprised. Cam and I have always believed someone from Stennard knocked off Arty."

Oldfield said, "There's more. A pair of black leather gloves were recovered from the floor on the driver's side and one clear partial print was found on the nav control." He looked up at the others in the room.

MC said, "The report pretty much rules out Klein as Arty's murderer. Right? He couldn't drive both SUVs on the same night."

Oldfield said, "Agreed. And we know Thomson and Stennard were also in the building that night."

MC nodded her head. "My money is on Thomson. Maybe he didn't pull the trigger, but I think he set the wheels in motion. Do we have a match on the partial print?"

"No match yet," Oldfield said. "But they'll run it against Thomson and Stennard. Hopefully we'll get a hit."

Ferndale asked, "Has the lab done any testing on the gloves?"

Oldfield said, "In process. But it could take a couple weeks before we get all results back, even though I asked for expedited service."

MC paged through her notes. "Okay, so we wait on the labs. Let's go back to Klein. Check this out. He admitted in one of his interviews he'd snuck up to Stennard's office the night of the meeting. He'd stood outside the door listening and picked up a couple tidbits. Enough to know Gavin was not pleased with Arty about something."

Ferndale said, "And Klein also said he'd seen Arty talking on his phone after the meeting."

MC said, "I think Arty was recording on his phone, not on a call."

Ferndale pulled his chair closer to the conference table. "We need to chat with Klein again. See if we can shake loose anything more."

MC said, "I agree on taking another crack at the guy. But the gloves in the second SUV bother me. What if whoever owns those gloves didn't realize they'd dropped or misplaced them?"

Ferndale asked, "What's that got to do with Klein?"

MC said, "Nothing. Sorry, about the tangent. I'm back to thinking about another person. Someone like, say, Thomson. If we can tie him to the second SUV and the gloves, we'd be a step closer to proving his involvement in the murder."

Oldfield said, "Even if the shooter wore the gloves, there's a chance any GSR on the gloves could've been washed or wiped off."

MC stood her ground, her gut telling her she was on the right track. "Only if he realized GSR could be present on the gloves. He'd have to have known, then tried to clean them. I don't think we'd have found them lying on the floor of the vehicle if he'd thought about cleaning them."

Agent Ferndale said, "You may be on to something. I liked Klein for the murder, but—"

Oldfield said, "Put a pin in it for now. Let's see if Mister Thomson can enlighten us."

In the homey room, MC sat in the square-shaped chair leaving a loveseat-sized couch for her interviewee. A floor lamp stood behind a table, and a box of tissues was centered on the otherwise empty surface.

MC imagined someone seated on the couch hearing the news that a loved one had died. It would be a more civilized experience than she'd had when Barb was killed. Her chest tightened with pain.

She pushed those thoughts away and flipped open her notebook.

The door opened and a deputy escorted Gavin Thomson into the room. She remained seated, pretending to read some notes.

Thomson settled onto the sofa, a look of distaste on his face. "Where do they buy their furniture? Goodwill?" He picked red fuzz from his perfectly creased black wool dress pants and flicked it to the floor.

"Good morning, Mister Thomson," MC said. "Thank you for agreeing to speak with me."

"I didn't agree to speak with anyone. Perhaps I should call my attorney. Why am I here? Is this about the fabricated charges on Stennard Global Enterprises?"

"We're interviewing people about Arthur Musselman."

He scowled. "Why wouldn't the FBI be talking to me? And what does the postal service have to do with anything?"

She ignored his two questions. "We're building the framework for what happened to Arthur Musselman and I plan to achieve that in a cooperative manner. Standard procedure dictates that I Mirandize you so you are aware of your rights."

She read him the Miranda warning, then met his gaze.

"Do you understand these rights as I've read them to you?"

He scoffed. "Yes. Should I phone my attorney?"

MC said, "If you'd rather have your attorney here, I can let the others know, and we can postpone our talk until your attorney arrives. Since it's Christmas Eve day, I'm guessing he might be busy. Could take a while for him to get here."

Even for someone like you, she didn't say out loud.

Thomson crossed his arms over his chest. "Fine. Get on with it already."

"Great." MC paged back through her notes. "When was the last time you saw Musselman?"

"At a meeting in Mike's office the same evening Arty was killed, I guess."

"Who was at the meeting?"

"Mike, Arty, and me."

MC noted he kept his answers clipped. "No one else?"

"No." Thomson brushed a hand over his pants.

MC wondered if his palms were sweating, or if he was brushing imaginary dust off. "Anyone else in the building?"

"I know the three of us were in Mike's office. I can't speak for staff who may have been in other areas. Although, it was after hours, so I don't imagine there were too many folks around. Maybe security."

MC scribbled a couple of fake notes. "Security?"

"Len Klein's our security. He always seemed to be around."

"But you didn't specifically need him at your meeting? Was there anything else going on which would've required his attention?"

"Agent McCall—"

"Inspector."

"Whatever. I don't know every move our employees make. I trust Len Klein knows his job and does it."

"Klein wasn't attending to something specific in the building?"

"I don't know." He leaned forward. "You're asking a lot of questions about Len Klein. Is he a suspect in Musselman's murder?"

"I'm not at liberty to discuss an ongoing investigation, Mister Thomson." MC felt good being on the giving end instead of the receiving end of those words. "Let's get back to the meeting."

Thomson sat back and let out an impatient sigh. "The meeting was over right around seven. And I left first, so I don't know if Mike and Arty left at the same time or not."

MC took a moment before acknowledging Thomson. "And after the meeting?"

"My wife and I had dinner reservations for seven that evening."

"Which restaurant?" MC didn't move her gaze from him.

"You and your partner already went through this with me at my home last week. Seems redundant to ask the same questions."

"We're interviewing multiple people for second and third times. It's a murder investigation. I would think you'd want to help find your friend's killer."

"We weren't friends. We were business associates." He blew out a breath. "My answers haven't changed."

"Recount it for me, to be sure I didn't miss anything." MC tilted her head slightly, the epitome of patience.

"Why isn't your partner here? He was asking the questions last time. Maybe his memory is better than yours." He crossed his legs.

MC ignored his question and waited.

Finally, Thomson said, "The restaurant was CoV on Lake Minnetonka, but my wife called and said she had a migraine. She told me to pick up some takeout for myself because she'd taken some meds and would be in bed for the night. I went to Katsana's for Thai. Went home and watched a basketball game on TV while I ate. End of story—again."

MC paged back through her notes. Tapped her pen against the notebook. "Interestingly enough, your story pretty much matches what you told us earlier."

"Why wouldn't it?" Thomson glared at her.

"We had some officers show your photo to employees at Katsana's, and no one recognized you. And there's the trifling detail of no receipt as proof you were there. These things puzzle me."

"Maybe you're not cut out for this job." Thomson's face was turning the color of the sofa on which he sat.

"Another thing we discovered is Katsana's has a security camera. They had a rash of robberies early this year and spent extra money to have a high-quality system installed. They were able to show us the video from November seventeenth from open to close. Busy day. Know what the funny thing is?"

"Enlighten me."

"Absolutely no sign of you. We had them go back a couple days and forward a couple days. You never appeared."

She stared at him, thinking *wiggle your way out of this one asshole.*

"I don't understand why you're acting so smug, Inspector. Are you implying I had something to do with what happened to Arty?"

"Did you?"

"I'm done answering your questions. I'd like to leave now. It is Christmas Eve, after all."

MC stood. "Stay put. I'll let the others know we're finished."

She exited and leaned against the wall in the hallway. Thomson's reminder about it being Christmas Eve caused her heart to seize and she felt light-headed. Barb would've had the house decked out all holly and jolly. Instead

MC would go home to her one-bedroom spartan apartment. She took a deep breath and tried to re-center herself.

Ferndale stuck his head out of the next room. "What's going on?"

MC straightened up. "Just thinking." Praying for strength, she followed him into the observation area for the interview room.

Once they were all gathered inside the room Oldfield said, "Here's where we're at. Agent Andrews talked with Mrs. Thomson. She supports Gavin's story about the migraine. She, however, didn't know of any dinner reservations for that evening. Take it away, Ferndale."

Ferndale said, "When asked if they had any plans, she said Gavin told her of the work meeting, and he didn't know how long it might last. She vaguely recalls him telling her things were getting complicated with the business, and he and Mike were worried about Arty's capabilities handling some tough financial issues."

MC asked, "And the headache was real?"

Ferndale reviewed his notes. "She verifies she had a migraine and took meds, which pretty much knocked her out for the night."

MC wrote the details in her notebook. "He lied about dinner reservations and the takeout. Makes him look guilty. Hints at premeditation."

Oldfield nodded. "Yep."

Ferndale continued, "Mrs. Thomson doesn't seem to have a clue what's going on. She knows bare bones, from what I got from Andrews. She knows someone killed Arty. Gavin told her the business is being investigated for, in his words, 'fraud or something.' "

Oldfield asked, "You don't think she's covering for him?"

"No, we don't," Ferndale said.

MC said, "Thomson's a sociopath. Keeping his wife in the dark plays into his mindset. He wouldn't take any chances with her accidentally spilling the beans. He needs complete control."

Ferndale said, "We're keeping him. We'll get his prints and compare to the partial from the SUV. Hopefully it'll be a match."

Oldfield said, "I spoke with AUSA—Assistant US Attorney—Vince Long early this morning. He agreed to stick around today in case we got enough to support a Warrant for Arrest on Thomson."

Ferndale said, "Do you need anything from me?"

Oldfield responded, "No. I've got the Affidavit mostly written up already. I'll fill in the details showing the evidence we have and Thomson's alleged role in the crimes. AUSA Long will file the Complaint and Affidavit with the US District Court and get us the Warrant for Arrest. We'll be good to go on Friday."

While Ferndale and Oldfield continued to confer, MC checked her phone. Almost two. Exhaustion, a heavy cloak, draped over her. The murmur of Oldfield's and Ferndale's voices barely penetrated the fog.

"McCall?" Ferndale's voice was a sharp report in the confined space.

"What?"

Oldfield said, "Let's call it a day. We can pick up again on Friday."

Ferndale said, "Thomson won't be going anywhere because we got a judge to sign off on a seventy-two-hour hold without charges based on his flight risk. It's a godsend he was hightailing it to the Bahamas. And the holiday worked in our favor."

MC stood. "Gives us some breathing room."

Speaking of breathing room, she hoped she'd have some at Meg and Dara's for the Christmas celebration. She'd wracked her brain for ways to avoid attending, but there wasn't an effective enough excuse in the world that could prevent her two friends from coming to roust her out to be with them.

Chapter Nineteen
Friday, December 26

The house was darker than an abandoned well. MC closed her front door and flipped the light switch. Nothing happened. "Barb?"

Muffled sounds, voices from the back of the house. MC edged into the living room and twisted the knob on the floor lamp. Nothing. Had a breaker tripped? "Barb?"

"MC. Help." Barb's voice was faint, but clear and panicked. "Help me."

MC drew her gun and hustled to the hallway leading from the front door to the kitchen. She ran into a wall. Turning this way and that, she realized she was in a maze of hallways she didn't recognize.

"Barb? Where are you?"

"MC! Help. I'm scared."

MC's heart thundered, the thrum ricocheting down her arm, making her gun waver in her hand. She tried to follow Barb's voice.

"Too late . . . "

One gunshot blasted through the house, then another.

MC screamed, "No!"

She sat bolt upright, gasping for air, sweat-soaked sheets in her fists.

She desperately tried to focus. Not her house. Barb wasn't next to her. MC swallowed, realized she was in her bedroom inside her apartment.

She rubbed sleep-crusted eyes and prayed to Jesus Christ the work crew inside her skull would stop their incessant buzzsawing. The upside? Despite the nightmare from which she'd just awakened, the early morning light proved she had managed to get through her first holiday without Barb.

Head pounding, stomach queasy, MC swung her legs over the edge of the bed and stepped on notebooks and a pen lying on the floor. A definite pattern was forming. Barb wouldn't be happy about her newly acquired slovenly habits.

She got ready for work in record time and drove to Flannel. The bright light and subzero temp exacerbated the hammering in her cranial cavity. She parked in front of the coffee shop and sat, unable to erase the feelings and images from her dreams. The remnants of the nightmare slowly fizzled, leaving her worn out and guilt-ridden. She'd again not been able to save Barb.

She exited the car and dashed into the café.

"Good morning, sunshine." Dara's voice boomed across the shop turning the heads of the few customers seated at various tables.

At the counter, MC said, "Cripes, Dara, could you be any louder?"

"Are we feeling under the weather this fine winter's morn?" Dara's voice dropped a couple notches. "You look like you're carrying a couple of overstuffed bags under your eyes, pal."

MC said, "Do not go there. I don't have a problem. I didn't even have a drop to drink at your place yesterday."

"But maybe when you got home—"

"Would you please be a good friend and give me a coffee with a double shot of espresso, to go?" MC retreated to the condiment station where a jug of water sat beside the sweeteners and cream. She filled a plastic cup and swallowed a pill cocktail—ibuprofen and naproxen—she'd stuck in her coat pocket.

"Coffee with dual extra lift," Dara called out.

MC retrieved the high-octane brew. The aroma penetrated her foggy brain. "Sorry for snapping."

"S'okay. But you should know I intend to rag on you whenever I feel it's necessary. We've all lost someone special in Barb, and I don't want to lose you, too."

"You dumb oaf. You're not losing me." MC blinked back tears. "I can handle it."

"Handle what?" Meg came out of the office. "MC, good morning." Meg rushed from behind the corner to give MC a hug. "Handle what?"

MC gave Meg a quick squeeze. "Nothing, we're talking about work stuff." MC glared at Dara.

"I was making sure our girl was keeping safe on the job and whatnot." Dara grabbed a towel and wiped down the counter.

"Gotta run. Time is my nemesis in the mornings. Can't be late...again." MC blew out a breath. "Have a great day."

MC tasted the bite of the windchill as she got back into her car. The task force arrest warrants would be issued today for Michael Stennard and Gavin Thomson, for fraud amongst other charges. MC did not want to miss the action. She buckled up and called Cam.

"Hey." Cam's voice ricocheted off her eardrum.

"No need to yell. I'm on my way in so don't go having all the fun without me."

"No worries. No one else is here yet."

"See you soon. Meet in my office."

H

Cam sipped an energy drink while MC wished she could hook up a coffee IV to her arm. They'd spent the requisite few minutes catching each other up on their holiday experiences and then got down to business. "What's the plan?" she asked over the rim of her cup.

"According to Oldfield we get another shot at Thomson, and then we get to go with the team to pick up Stennard. I can't believe we're finally on the home stretch."

"Cheers." She raised her cup.

"Let's go see what Mister Gavin Thomson has to say." Cam crushed the empty can between his hands and made a two-pointer into the recycling basket next to MC's desk.

At the Hennepin County facility, FBI Agents Sebastian Ferndale and Walt Andrews met up with them, and they all gathered inside one of the observation rooms.

Ferndale said, "They're retrieving Thomson from his cell, and it could take a few minutes." He handed MC a manila folder. "Check this out while we wait. Oldfield is about ten minutes out. By the way, I called Klein."

MC said, "And?" She opened the file and scanned the pages: photos of gloves and fingerprints.

Ferndale said, "He magically remembered that after he saw Arty acting weird, he'd called Mike. Said Mike sounded agitated and told Klein he'd 'take care of it.' Klein wasn't sure what Mike meant and didn't ask."

Cam said, "Interesting he didn't remember calling Mike before now."

MC set the folder aside and opened a file on her cell. She read the transcript of the last recording from Arty's phone. "One of the guys at the shooting says, 'Gimme the gun.' This tells me whoever the masked gunman was ended up not being the shooter."

Cam said, "Okay."

Ferndale nodded.

MC said, "After the gunshot, the guy says, 'Loyalty is everything.' I saw or heard reference to loyalty somewhere else." She went back to a different file. "Here it is. At the meeting, Stennard tells Gavin that Arty is loyal. I'd been thinking Gavin Thomson was the shooter. Could it have been Mike Stennard?"

Ferndale said, "Maybe."

Andrews said, "When we talked to him, he seemed pretty torn up over Arty's death, though. I got the impression he was a grieving friend."

Ferndale said, "Let's see what we get from Thomson."

MC felt her cell buzz and saw a message from Dara. *No hard feelings about earlier. Dinner tonight at the shop? Let me know. Peace out.* MC tapped the corner of the phone against her knee as she considered the offer, then filed the thought away to deal with later.

Agent Ferndale said, "McCall, you ready for another round with Thomson?"

"Definitely."

Cam asked, "Did you guys get much from him the other day?"

Ferndale said, "McCall did the interview and got bits and pieces of a story. But what we didn't have then is confirmation the partial print from the inside of the SUV is a match for him." He pointed to the manila folder he'd given MC.

"Any results on DNA or GSR from the gloves?" MC asked handing the folder to Cam to review.

"Nothing yet. Lab's backed up because of the holiday."

"Having the print gives us leverage." MC reviewed her notes. "I think Cam should be in there with me."

"Okay."

"He wants his lawyer present this time," Andrews said.

"He hasn't been charged yet, right?" Cam asked.

"Correct," Ferndale said. "But I think he knows it's inevitable. He's not sure what we'll throw at him."

MC said, "Let him have his lawyer." Movement on the video monitor got her attention. "Look who the cat dragged in."

Andrews said, "And he's not quite as dapper in his orange scrubs and Jesus sandals."

Ferndale said, "Today the interview room lacks the comfort of the one we used the other day. He must know we're serious."

Cam stood. "Hopefully, he's feeling chatty." He passed the file back to MC.

Ferndale's phone rang. He answered, then held up a finger to MC and Cam. "We'll be here." He hung up. "Oldfield. He's parking and will be right in."

MC said, "If Thomson is unresponsive with us, we can switch out and you and Andrews can take over. We can tag team for as long it takes to break him."

Ferndale said, "Sounds like a plan."

MC focused on Thomson's image on the monitor. "We want him on edge. The fraud and money laundering charges are solid. Maybe we share with him that his bestie Mike will be experiencing a similar wardrobe change sometime today, his house of cards is about to collapse, and he can't do anything to shore up the damage at this point."

The door in the other room opened, and MC watched as the guard allowed a short black man into the room. The man was dressed in an expensive-looking dark charcoal pinstriped suit with black shirt and black and gray striped tie. A matching pocket square peeked out from the chest pocket of his suit jacket.

He carried a gargantuan leather briefcase. MC had never seen one so huge. "Jesus, what's he got in his briefcase, the files from the OJ Simpson trial?"

"Meet the great Fletcher Upton," Ferndale said. "He's well-known in the criminal defense arena."

Cam said, "Briefcase resembles a saddlebag from *The Wild Wild West*."

"How would you know?" MC asked. "You're too young to have seen that show."

"Hell, I used to watch reruns with my grandpa when I was a kid. He was an old westerns junkie. Shall we mosey on into the other room, Miss Emma Valentine, and have a chat with our bad guy?"

Cam had a hand on the door handle as the door was pushed open from the hall and Oldfield entered.

"Whoa there, pardner . . . uh, I mean, good morning, sir."

MC raised an eyebrow at Cam and swallowed her laughter. "Morning, ASAC Oldfield. We're about to have a go at Thomson now that his attorney has shown up."

"Excellent." Oldfield stepped aside to allow them to pass.

ℋ

In the interview room MC and Cam took seats across the table from an orange-clad Gavin Thomson.

"Good morning," Cam said.

"Nothing good about it." Thomson scowled in MC's general direction, then concentrated his attention on Cam. "I hope any repartee about to ensue will be handled by you."

MC refused to take the bait. She opened the file folder containing the photo of the black leather gloves, along with the fingerprint results.

Cam said, "For the record, this session is being recorded. Present are: myself, Inspector Cameron White; Inspector MC McCall; and the subject of our interview, Gavin Thomson and his attorney . . ."

When Cam gazed at the attorney pretending not to know Upton's name, MC had to stifle a laugh.

Upton unloaded a yellow legal pad and a couple of pens from the bowels of his briefcase. He cleared his throat and straightened the cuffs of his shirt sleeves before responding. "Fletcher Xavier Upton, counsel representing Mister Thomson."

"Thank you." MC waited a beat and dove in. "Mister Thomson, would you please run us through your activities on November seventeenth?"

Thomson blew out a huge sigh. "I've been through this with you people how many times? Do you have poor memories? I could refer you to a good memory care facility. Perhaps you utilized defective recording devices during the previous interviews? Or is it an issue of overall incompetence?"

Nothing came from Upton regarding Thomson's rant so MC proceeded. "Tell us what you did on November seventeenth."

With clear reluctance, Thomson repeated what he'd told MC two days earlier.

MC jotted a few notes, then picked up the manila folder. "And you were driving your own car?"

"Yes."

"I see. When was the last time you used one of the black SUVs owned by Stennard Global Enterprises?"

"I don't remember."

MC quirked an eyebrow at him. "You don't want to take a minute or two and think about it?"

"Asked and answered inspector. Move it along." Upton waved a hand in the air. A gold pinky ring on his right hand sported a diamond the size of a grape.

Cam said, "This isn't a deposition or trial testimony, Mister Upton. We'll dictate the pace of the interview."

Thomson said, "I don't need a minute or two. I've answered your question."

MC asked, "Do you know who drove the Escalades owned by Stennard on November seventeenth?"

"I assume the security people. Len Klein and whoever else he gave the keys to."

"No one else?"

"Only security personnel or Mike or I were allowed to drive those vehicles. Of course, I can't confirm or deny Klein didn't let someone else drive them. What's your point?"

MC opened the file folder and slid the fingerprint info out. "This, Mister Thomson, is a fingerprint lifted from a dial inside one of the black SUVs."

"Yeah, so?"

"It's a match—for yours. This leads me to believe you, sir, had been driving the vehicle recently, as no other prints overlay yours."

Silence descended on the room. Thomson stared at her, his eyes like rotted chestnuts. "Maybe I did drive it. I don't remember when, though. I'm sure there are lots of prints inside the company cars. Why don't you ask Klein about it?"

Upton held up a hand. "May I confer with my client a moment, please? Alone."

Thomson started to bluster. "I don't need—"

"Gavin," Upton said, "please. You pay me a lot of money. Let me do my job."

"We'll step out for a minute." MC gathered up her stuff.

They left the room and joined the others in the observation room, where Andrews had paused the recording and muted the sound to ensure there could be no complaint of Thomson's rights being violated.

Oldfield stood at the computer, hands in his pants pockets. "Thomson's not rattled. He definitely prefers to call the shots."

"But Upton seems to know how to lasso him," MC said.

After a few minutes, Andrews restarted the recording and MC and Cam re-entered the interrogation room, taking their places across from Thomson and Upton. MC said, "Mister Thomson, do you have anything further to add about driving the SUV?"

Upton said, "My client has given you all the information he has in regards to the vehicle."

"Fine, let's move on." MC slid the photo of the black leather gloves from inside the folder. "Do you recognize these?"

Thomson leaned forward and appeared to study the photo. "Looks like gloves. I've—"

Upton put a hand on Thomson's arm. "You don't need to elaborate."

"I sure as hell do. So what if I have several pair of gloves similar to those? So do a million other people."

Upton made some notes on a pad in front of him.

Thomson leaned back in his chair. "Why are you showing me these gloves, detective?"

"Inspector," MC said.

"Pardon me?" Thomson asked.

"You said detective. I'm a US Postal Inspector, not a detective."

Thomson flipped a hand in the air. "Inspector, why do you ask?"

"Do you recognize these gloves?"

"I said I own similar gloves."

In a stern voice, Upton said, "Say nothing more." His tone left no doubt he wanted Thomson to close his yap.

MC slid the photo back inside the file. "Ever shoot a gun, Mister Thomson?"

"My client will not answer that question." Upton sat up straighter, fire in his dark brown eyes.

If Gavin was taken aback by the abrupt change in the tone of questioning, he didn't reveal it. "Oh, relax, Fletcher." He turned toward MC. "Not for some time. I've hunted, but only a couple times—many years ago."

"How about handguns?" MC asked.

"Nope, can't say I've ever shot a revolver."

MC fixed her gaze on Cam, widening her eyes slightly and keeping the uptick in her pulse under control.

Cam remained silent.

"What? What're you two ogling about?" Thomson demanded.

"Gavin. Be. Quiet," Upton said. "Any further questions, detectives?"

"Inspectors," MC reminded the lawyer.

"Apologies," Upton said. "Inspectors, do you have more questions for my client? If not, I'd like to speak with him."

"I think we're done for now," MC said.

She and Cam exited again and joined the others in the next room.

"Revolver. He said revolver," MC said.

Cam paced in the room. "He sure did. I about let out a whoop in there."

Ferndale said, "Okay, maybe it wasn't Stennard. Do we have enough to charge Thomson? Maybe we can get him to spill. We could hit him with first degree murder and conspiracy to commit murder along with the fraud and money laundering charges."

MC said, "Dammit, I wish we had the murder weapon. We'd have a rock-solid case then." She scanned through several pages of notes. "We heard two voices, both male, on the final recording on Arty's phone. Who are they? Thomson? Stennard? Klein? John Doe?"

Cam stopped pacing. "We've nailed Thomson. He may think he's above the law or his fancy criminal defense attorney will get him off, but there's enough on him to put him away."

"If for nothing else," Oldfield said, "for the fraud and money laundering. I can work with AUSA Long on other charges."

"I want him to go down for Arty." MC paced. "I don't know, though. We hear on the recording one guy takes the gun away from the other."

Ferndale said, "Correct. And?"

MC said, "And the guy who took the gun killed Arty. Executed him. He then tells the other person to 'clean up the mess,' to which the other guy says 'You got it boss.' Boss." She stopped midstride.

The others stared at her silently.

MC said, "Stennard is the boss. I think Stennard is the person who shot Arty." She didn't disguise the vehemence in her voice.

Oldfield said, "But Thomson is also a boss. And we have a pretty strong case against him with the evidence and his wife's statement. We'll confer with the US Attorney's office on what additional charges to file against both Thomson and Stennard."

"Now what?" MC asked the group.

Oldfield said, "Now you four head out and bring Stennard in, and we'll see what his story is. I've instructed Agents Young and Trinh to meet you at

Stennard's house. Thomson will be charged today on the fraud and money laundering, and the US Attorney will probably go for a no bail request based on flight risk."

Ferndale said, "We should ultimately have enough to also charge Thomson in Arty's murder. Maybe the prosecutor will offer him something if he cooperates."

ℋ

MC and Cam rolled up in the circular driveway right behind the black Chevrolet Suburban driven by Agents Walt Andrews and Sebastian Ferndale.

A twin SUV was already parked. Agents Alexis Trinh and Teri Young exited the front vehicle.

MC heard the crunch of snow and ice as the women moved toward the other two teams. She felt an icy finger trace a trail down her spine.

Anticipation.

She gazed around the silent snowy vista. The nearest neighbor seemed like miles away in this haven of affluence. She began to wonder if Stennard was even home because there hadn't been any movement from inside the palace on the lake.

Ferndale took lead and said, "Young and Trinh you take the back. McCall and White you follow us in the front and take the upper level. Andrews and I will take the main level."

"Copy that," MC said.

Young's blond tightly harnassed ponytail swayed as she and Trinh took off around the side toward the rear of the house.

Andrews, MC, and Cam lined up behind Ferndale at the front.

Ferndale's bass voice shattered the cold quiet, "Michael Stennard! Open up. FBI." Barry White couldn't have issued a more intense-sounding command.

MC's heart hammered in time with Ferndale's thumping fist. Her eyes were laser-focused on the door, ears straining to pick up any hint of sound.

The sharp taste of adrenaline at the back of her throat.

No response from within.

Then Ferndale turned the knob and they were inside Stennard's apparently unlocked home.

MC and Cam climbed the staircase leading from the foyer to the second level and quickly cleared all the rooms except for the back one facing the lake.

The door stood ajar.

MC nudged it with her foot and brought her gun up as the door swung inward to the left.

Michael Stennard sat in what appeared to be his home office, behind a dust-covered wood desk commensurate in size and extravagance to the Resolute Desk in the Oval Office.

She took in the open laptop, a sheet of white paper with text filling about two thirds of the page, and the man sitting in a leather executive chair holding a nine-millimeter handgun.

"Mister Stennard. Drop the gun." MC stepped to the right and sensed Cam behind to her left.

No one else was in the room.

Stennard stared down at the gun in his hand as if bewildered by its presence.

MC kept her weapon trained on Stennard. "Drop the gun. Don't do anything stupid."

Stennard stood slowly, arm at his side, gun dangling from his right hand.

Cam moved behind MC to her right and sidled toward Stennard.

MC said, "Mister Stennard drop the weapon. We don't want to shoot you."

Stennard faced MC as he came alongside his desk, seemingly unaware of Cam creeping toward him. "It's over. All. Over."

"Yes," MC said. "We need to take you in. Put the gun down. Slide it toward me."

To MC's utter surprise Stennard placed the handgun on the desktop and slid it toward the front corner.

Cam holstered his sidearm and grabbed cuffs. He stepped behind Stennard and reached to bring his arm around.

Stennard lurched forward and grabbed the gun off the desk. He whipped around and put the gun against Cam's head.

Shit.

"Don't do this, Stennard," Cam's voice came out a bit raspy. He reached for his weapon.

"Don't." Stennard jammed the barrel of his nine-millimeter hard against the side of Cam's head. "Won't matter if I kill one more at this point."

MC took in Stennard's red, wild eyes and figured he was probably hopped up on something. "It will matter. You don't want to kill a cop. No matter what else you may have done, that will be the end of you." She kept her voice calm and eyes glued on Stennard.

Just then the four FBI agents filed slowly into the room.

"Aw, fuck me," Stennard said. He shook his head and pushed Cam away from him, bringing the gun up to his own head.

"No!" MC's shout stopped Stennard. "Don't be a coward," she said, voice steady, commanding.

Stennard's gaze met hers. He shook his head and dropped the gun.

Cam cuffed him.

MC kicked Stennard's weapon behind her toward the FBI agents.

Young and Trinh took Stennard from Cam and escorted him from the room. Trinh said, "We'll take him downtown. Meet you there?"

"Sounds good," MC said.

She pulled on nitrile gloves and went behind the desk. "I thought the desk was dusty." She pointed to the white powder coating. "Cocaine. I wonder how much he snorted before we got here."

"What's that? A note?" Cam indicated a sheet on the far side of the desk.

MC stepped around the chair and reached for the paper. "Suicide note. He admits to killing Arty. Says he hoped by taking out Arty he'd stop the downfall of his empire. He realized that wasn't how it'd play out so he decided to end his life."

"The gun used on Arty was a thirty-eight, right?"

"Yep."

"He had a nine-millimeter today."

"We know someone else was present the night Arty was killed. Whoever it was probably has the murder weapon or got rid of it."

Cam said, "We may never know then."

"What a clusterfuck."

Chapter Twenty
Friday, January 2

The house sold. The closing was set for the end of January. Another step toward closure.

Dara and Meg begged to help her at the house, but she'd deferred, assuring them not much left called for attention, and she needed to handle it alone. MC could tell Dara was hurt and angry and Meg was worried. She'd not spent time with them since Christmas. Mostly, she didn't want to deal with the accusation coloring Dara's eyes when she asked if MC was hungover, or, worse, if she was drunk. Nope. Didn't need to answer those questions.

The process of cleaning out the home she'd shared with Barb was depressing and not the way MC envisioned beginning 2015.

A random button on the closet floor about undid her. MC remembered when she and Barb had scoured the space last year looking for the dark brown button that had fallen off Barb's favorite pair of worn corduroy pants. She gritted her teeth to prevent unleashing the torrent of anguish washing through her.

Now. Now she'd found the button. What the hell good was it now?

She tossed the piece of plastic into the trash bag and moved on.

In the kitchen, MC checked all the cabinets and drawers to make sure they were cleared and clean. In the last drawer, next to the sink, she found some rolled-up cloth jammed at the back. She tugged the item free.

MC shook, head to toe, as she unrolled the white apron she'd bought for Barb on some Valentine's Day past. "Kiss the Cook" was stenciled in red and images of giant red kissing lips dotted the fabric. A slim pebbled-patterned box fell to the floor with a thud.

MC jumped and let the apron drift free.

She scooped up the box and cracked the lid open.

Inside lay a gorgeous pen nestled in white satiny material. She stared at the resin barrel. Shades of brown with hues of amber and gold reflected the light. The colors evoked warmth and love, and MC was certain this was to have been her Christmas gift from Barb.

She recalled a conversation a few months earlier when she'd seen a fountain pen online and expressed her interest in trying out the sophisticated writing tool. Barb must have found this beautiful pen and then hidden it away so MC wouldn't find it before the holidays.

MC sucked in a shaky breath and had herself a little sobfest.

She wiped her face on her sleeve and grabbed the apron and yanked opened the trash bag. But she couldn't part with the goofy gift. Instead she carefully rewrapped the pen inside the apron and set it aside to place in the box she had at home full of bits and pieces of Barb—birthday and anniversary cards, love notes she'd kept—all the little things over nineteen years that she'd almost tossed away, but decided to keep.

Disheartened, but determined to get through the task, MC moved on to the garage, which held nothing more than cobwebs and chunks of melting snow that had plopped onto the floor from the wheel wells of the Subaru.

MC had sold her Camry and kept Barb's Subaru. She found Barb's car somehow comforting, not to mention it handled much better in the snow than her Camry had.

MC set the apron and its hidden secret on the backseat of the car. She tossed the bag of trash into the barrel outside the garage.

Now on to more important tasks, like finding her lover's murderer.

She spent the afternoon reinterviewing the neighbors, who had nothing new to tell her. Gladys Crandell invited her to stay for dinner, but MC declined and fled like the devil was chasing her. Spending long periods of time with Gladys was enough to make MC's gremlins start grumbling for a dose of the Goose.

To round out the mostly unsuccessful interviews, she stopped at Mr. Dogwalker's (a/k/a Doug Freelander, a dean at Highland Park High School) house. This was the first time she'd caught him at home.

He'd allowed her inside, but was adamant he had no more info than what Gladys had told her, then he started questioning her. All the while his damn shih tzu wouldn't stop yipping.

Why was she interviewing people? Weren't the police supposed to handle the investigation? He intimated he wasn't comfortable talking to her and mentioned maybe he should check with the detective to make sure it was okay.

MC felt a flush heating up her face and flashed him a grim smile as she thanked him for his time. What an uptight asshole.

She went home and dove into the bottle to drown out the demoralizing misery of the day. No closer to any answers.

Perhaps not surprising, that night her nightmare made a second appearance. In the nightmare, she searched for Barb, but she was lost and couldn't get to Barb in time. Two gunshots exploded and then MC awakened, bathed in sweat and hyperventilating.

Chapter Twenty-One
Monday, January 5

MC was the first to arrive at work on the Monday after New Year's Day. She sat in the office and reviewed the notes from the latest round of interviews of her old neighbors.

What she really needed was to know who had killed Barb.

MC was consumed by the need to resolve the case and frustrated by Detective Sharpe's inability to catch the culprit or culprits.

She glanced at the time in the corner of her computer screen. 7:11 a.m. Eight would be a respectable time to call Sharpe.

She pushed the notebook aside and pulled up a file on a revenue investigation Jamie had assigned to her before the holiday. Her attention wandered toward the green notebook staring at her from the corner of her desk. She scooted the notebook back in front of her.

The ping of a calendar reminder roused her from her deep reverie. MC had a meeting with Jamie scheduled for nine-thirty to discuss the status of her assignments.

She decided to wing it. Instead of preparing a solid update for Jamie, she wanted to go through her notes on Barb's case and call Detective Sharpe.

Before she could give it any more thought, and though it was not quite eight, she picked up the desk phone and punched in his number. The phone on the other end rang four times, then went to voicemail. After the standard greeting, she left a message: "Detective Sharpe. Good morning. This is MC McCall. Would you please call me at your earliest convenience?" She left both her work phone and her cell phone numbers.

She dropped the handset back onto the base and paged through her notes. Head in her hands she read every word on every page, including both occurrences of the horrid dream. When she got to the last page, she returned to the first and read it all one more time.

Her head throbbed, and her tongue stuck to her palate, like a bug to flypaper. She'd give anything for an icy pick-me-up. Instead she swallowed a couple aspirin and went in search of another cup of coffee.

"Morning." Cam came into the hall from the entrance bundled in an olive drab parka, scarf, and black knit hat.

"Are you off to duty in Alaska or what?" MC asked. "And do you need to be so jovial so early?" She sipped the mug of coffee in her hand, desperately wishing she had something stronger to bolster her.

"Happy new year to you, too." Cam smiled, though it didn't quite reach his eyes.

Ah, shit. She'd have Cam dogging her too if she wasn't careful. "Sorry, I didn't mean to bite your head off, I've got another headache. Lack of sleep. And I just tried calling Sharpe at SPPD and as usual I had to leave a voicemail. I can't believe after more than a month they have nothing. What the hell, Cam? I don't mean to be a Debbie Downer, but when is something going to break?" She slumped against the hallway wall.

"You've every right to want Barb's case solved. I can't even imagine what I'd be like if Jane—"

She waved a hand. She didn't want his pity. "I want him to listen to what I've learned from some of the neighbors. I swear Sharpe's avoiding me, like the plague."

"You've been talking to the neighbors? When have you had any time? Between the Stennard thing, Arty's murder, not to mention your other assignments, you've been balls to the walls for weeks. No wonder you're not getting any sleep. Burning the candle at both ends isn't a great idea."

"I have more time now since the Stennard investigation is finished. All we need to do is help get the files together for the US Attorney before trial. As gratifying as it is to nail Stennard and Thomson, I'm still pissed over not being able to find the accomplice on Arty's murder."

"But that's not our bailiwick. We gotta let the FBI do their job. You deserve a lot of credit for helping nail Stennard for killing Arty. They were focused on Klein, so kudos to you for getting them to see the light. But we have plenty going on right here."

"Spoken like a true leader-in-the-making." She tried to smile, but her face muscles refused to cooperate. "Jamie gave me a revenue investigation before the holiday. I haven't even cracked the file, and I have a meeting with him this morning."

"If I can help say the word." Cam unzipped his jacket and pulled the cap from his head, leaving his sandy brown hair standing on end.

She contemplated the offer. If she got Cam to help out then she could slip out of the office and pay Sharpe a visit at SPPD. He'd have to talk to her if she showed up in person.

"I appreciate the offer. I'll get back to you after my meeting with Jamie. In the meantime, you may want to take a comb to that hair. You've got the Alfalfa hair style going on."

"Alfalfa? What?"

"From the old-timey show, *The Little Rascals?*" He appeared to be puzzled.

She said, "I guess the extent of your TV oldies knowledge only includes *The Wild Wild West.*"

His gaze remained blank.

"Never mind. I'll catch you after my meeting."

MC felt a twinge of guilt over even considering dumping work on her already over-burdened co-worker, but when she caught sight of the green notebook in the middle of her desk, the feeling was soon replaced by a grim determination.

#

MC got through the meeting with Jamie without incident other than the bad news that Crapper may return to work in a month. He expressed concern over her ability to keep up with work. Asked if she needed more time off. Assured her she could talk to him whenever she needed to, but because they were down a couple people due to vacations and a vacancy, he counted on her pulling her weight.

Meaning, he would be supportive up to the point where it negatively impacted him or others in the office.

She assured him she could handle the workload before her mind wandered to what she'd say to Sharpe. Right after Jamie ended the meeting, she gathered her stuff and let Chelsea know she was going out in the field for a few hours.

She drove to Saint Paul, parked in the public lot next to SPPD headquarters, and grabbed the green notebook from her bag. At the front desk she told the officer she was there to meet with Detective Sharpe.

The young officer instructed her to have a seat while he contacted Sharpe. MC felt like her life was a kite being whipped around on a frenetic wind. Then she was yanked back down to earth by a muffled voice. "Inspector McCall?"

MC stood. "Yes."

The officer said, "I'll take you back to see Detective Sharpe now."

MC followed him through the now-familiar tangle of hallways, unbuttoning her coat as she went. The stale, heavy air felt suffocating.

The cop left her in a tiny interview room. A box of tissues sat on the middle of the table.

Before too long, the door opened and Sharpe entered, closing the door firmly behind him. Dressed in pressed suit pants and a blue shirt with the cuffs rolled to expose hairy wrists, he seemed sharper than she remembered from a month earlier when she likened him to the bumbling TV detective Columbo.

He pulled a pack of gum from his trousers and stuck a white square into his mouth before sitting in the other chair.

"This not smoking business is giving my jaw a workout." He chomped on the gum. "So, Inspector McCall, how are you doing?"

MC wished she'd had the foresight to remove her coat before sitting down. How was she doing? Her life was a never-ending maze of shadow-filled days. What good would come of this visit? Sharpe would think her unhinged. Maybe even be worried enough to contact Jamie and let him know she was teetering on the edge.

"Inspector?" Sharpe leaned forward and touched the back of her hand.

MC lurched backward.

"Sorry!" He held up both hands. "I thought you were about to faint or something."

"I'm fine." McCall get your shit together. She bit the inside of her cheek, hoping the tweak of pain would give her focus. "Have you made any progress?" MC paged through her notebook, finding the entry she needed. "I may have some info you aren't aware of, or maybe you are, and you can enlighten me." She grasped the notepad firmly in both hands.

"MC—may I call you MC?"

She nodded.

"MC, I empathize with your situation. I can't imagine how you must feel, but unfortunately, I don't have any details to share with you."

"Nothing?"

Sharpe's voice was soft. "Truly. Nothing. I wish I could tell you that I had a hot lead. Anything. So far we've got a whole lot of nothing."

MC pushed forward. "I've spoken with several neighbors and learned a compact white SUV was seen that morning. The car came by after the 9-1-1 call but before the first officer arrived on the scene." She angled her notes toward him and pointed to the words as if they were the key to unlocking answers to the investigation.

Sharpe tilted his head to read the notes before leaning back in his seat. "I admire your determination. I assure you we're doing everything in our power to catch whomever committed this heinous act. You should get on with your life, hard as it may be." He pursed his lips as if considering whether to say more, but remained silent.

MC stowed the notebook in her coat, biting back her frustration. She was using substantial mental bandwidth and depleting her system. Now was the time to be strong. Not give in to overwhelming guilt. "Right. Thanks for your time."

Sharpe placed a hand on her arm. "I'm sorry this happened to you. I'm sorry we haven't made progress. I'm sorry for many things. But you going rogue and hunting for suspects won't help either of us. In fact, you could be placing yourself in danger."

"If the incident was a burglary gone bad, what danger would I be in? If the mob contracted out for a hit, then I'd buy your theory, but I believe the odds lean more toward some meth-fueled idiot who was surprised when Barb came home. They panicked and shot her. I find that more plausible. Don't you?"

Sharpe sighed. "I can see we'll not agree on the issue of your safety." He stood, ending the discussion.

MC stood. "I won't take up any more of your time." Sharpe's ever-present banalities did nothing to satiate her. In fact, they only fueled her anger. But anger was better than guilt. Anger could lead to action whereas guilt was passive.

Sharpe got to the door first and opened it. "Please feel free to call me. I caution you to be careful. We really can't be certain who we're dealing with."

"Thanks for your concern." MC fought to keep her voice from shaking. She refused to show him how rattled she was. She pivoted and stepped from the room and collided with an officer coming down the hallway.

"Sorry!" She glanced at a sturdy woman who was about her own height, her hair a short tawny-colored afro. She seemed vaguely familiar. MC read the name tag over the officer's chest pocket, "I apologize, Officer Reece."

"No problem," Reece said. "I should've been paying attention, too." She flashed a one-hundred-watt smile. "Hey, Sarge."

"Reece, what brings you to Homicide?" Sharpe asked.

MC thought she might know the woman, but couldn't place her. She had the most intense emerald-colored eyes. Her skin a smooth coffee and cream hue.

She broke into their exchange, "Have we met before?" she asked Reece.

Reece tilted her head. "I'm not sure. Where do you work?"

Sharpe cut in, "I need to get to a meeting. Reece, would you see Inspector McCall out?"

"Sure, Sarge," Reece said. She scrutinized MC, "Inspector?"

"US Postal Inspector," MC said.

"I doubt we've worked together. Maybe we hang out in some of the same places outside of work?" A smile quirked at the corner of her mouth.

MC's gaydar pinged. "Maybe. Ever go to the Townhouse?"

"Many times. Small world, eh? Kiara Reece. Nice to meet you." They shook hands. "What's up with you and Sharpe? The postal service and homicide don't usually have much in common. Did someone go—"

"Please, spare me the going postal comment. To answer your question, Sharpe and I aren't working together, per se. He's in charge of the investigation into my partner's murder back in November." MC was shocked she'd so easily spilled the information to a virtual stranger.

"I'm sorry. Was it in the line of duty?"

"Not my work partner." MC felt dizzy. "I really should be going. I've got to get back to work." Or better yet, grab a glass of something eighty-proof.

"I'm really sorry." Reece touched MC's coat sleeve. "Trust me, Sharpe is one of the best. If anyone will catch the bad guy, Victor Sharpe will. He's always on point. Get it?"

MC didn't have it in her to laugh. "He doesn't seem to be having much success," MC said bitterly.

"Sorry. Bad attempt at humor on my part. I'll show you out." Reece led MC to the entrance. "Let me know if there's anything I can do to help."

"Thanks," MC buttoned her coat and pulled on gloves. She hesitated, a hand on the glass door leading out. "Be careful what you offer, I may take you up on it."

"Anytime," Reece said with a kind smile.

MC went out into the windswept afternoon. The air burned her nasal passages and brought tears to her eyes. Or maybe it wasn't the cold air.

Damn.

She needed a drink.

Clouds hovered, like the underbelly of the Hindenburg, threatening to unleash a fury of white flakes.

Sharpe was unmovable. Why couldn't he see two heads were better than one?

H

Back at her desk she added the Kiara Reece encounter to the green notebook. She wanted to remember the name. Maybe she could get on the inside via Kiara. MC didn't feel even a tiny smidgen of remorse over involving Officer Reece in her off-the-books probe into Barb's murder.

She got back to work, patently ignoring the email from Jamie asking about her progress on the revenue investigation. She should've gone out and made contact at Galaxy Printing, a mid-size mailer located in Chanhassen, a southwest Minneapolis suburb.

She wrote a message to Cam asking him if he could do a quick call to the postmaster in Chanhassen and get some info about Galaxy. Her mouse hovered for a moment over the send button as a twinge of guilt over using Cam like a personal assistant pinged through her. Was she taking advantage of his generous nature? No doubt. But she had Barb to worry about. She was convinced Sharpe couldn't possibly have the level of focus she had. Or maybe she was just plain feverish. She sent the email.

MC wiped her forehead and noted a glossy sheen on the back of her hand. Maybe she was coming down with a virus. She had no time to be sick.

Take a breath, MC.

She thought she heard Barb's voice. Behind her? She whipped her head around, glancing in all corners of the office. Nothing. Of course not. Jesus. Was she going crazy? The voice sure sounded like Barb's. And that was one of the things Barb constantly told MC: "Take a breath, hon."

Maybe she should go home and medicate herself with a cool glass, or two, of the Goose. She peeked at the clock, almost four, she'd put in more than eight hours. She got ready to leave and opened the door to Jamie standing in front of her, hand poised to knock.

"Shit." MC was so surprised she put a hand to her chest.

"Didn't mean to startle you. You leaving?"

"I am. Came in early, so thought I'd call it a day. Is there a problem?"

"I hoped to get an update on Galaxy Printing and to let you know I'd heard from ASAC Oldfield on the Stennard and Musselman cases. Got a minute, or do you have to leave?"

MC backed up and flipped on the light switch. "Come in." She dropped her messenger bag behind the desk and sat in her chair. "So. Stennard?"

"Oldfield told me the Hennepin County Attorney had filed conspiracy to commit murder charges against Thomson in the death of Arty Musselman. And murder one on Stennard."

"That's good news."

"Thomson had a Come-to-Jesus moment—took a plea deal for a lesser sentence when the AUSA threatened to file the murder on the federal level."

MC said, "Smart move. Federal murder could result in the death penalty."

"Yep. Anyway, he confessed he followed Arty and dropped off the goon with the gun on the frontage road. Claims to not know the guy's name, so the mystery man is still a mystery."

"Well that sucks."

"In addition, the US Attorney has filed wire fraud, three counts of mail fraud, one count of conspiracy to commit mail and wire fraud, one count of conspiracy to commit money laundering, and five counts of money laundering against Thomson. The trial will probably be toward the end of summer or early fall. You and Cam did a great job. You especially, because of the personal struggles you've been through."

"A great job, I'll take it. But it cost me, personally."

"You don't think Barb's murder had anything to do with the task force?"

"No. Maybe. I don't know." Did she think that?

"Regardless, I'm grateful to you for your hard work and dedication. I know how difficult the past couple months have been. ASAC Oldfield said I better watch out because the FBI might be interested in stealing you from us."

MC's first thought was to wonder what Barb would say. Then she remembered the cold hard truth: Barb would never have anything to say ever again.

"Thanks for filling me in," MC said quietly. She counted her blessings Jamie hadn't grilled her on the Galaxy thing. "The joint task force was a well-oiled machine. Credit should go to everyone on the team."

Jamie pushed himself up from the chair. "I wanted to give you the good news. So, would you be interested, if the FBI came calling?" He raised an eyebrow.

"I'm happy right where I am. I'm flattered the FBI might even consider me, but I've been with IS a long time. My career is here."

"Good to know. Now go home. Enjoy your evening. Maybe celebrate. You deserve it."

"Thanks. See you tomorrow."

MC watched him leave. Actively helping to solve a murder had been gratifying, but the feeling of justice served was eclipsed by another murder that remained unsolved.

She resolved to make it her goal—no, not goal, her mission—to find justice for Barb. Barb no longer had a voice, so MC vowed to be the voice that could no longer speak.

MC picked up her bag and shut off the lights. She paused in the open doorway, staring back into the suffocating blackness pushing against the windows behind her desk.

An icy darkness filled her heart, spilling into her veins and threading to her very core.

She knew of only one solution to dispelling that darkness.

Find the person who had taken the light from her life and make them pay.

About The Author

Judy M. Kerr has published short stories in three anthologies. She resides with her extended family in Minneapolis, Minnesota. Judy retired from the US Postal Service in 2017 after thirty-eight years of federal service. *Black Friday* is her first crime fiction novel. Her website is at www.JudyMKerr.com.

Published by:
Launch Point Press
Portland, Oregon
www.LaunchPointPress.com

CPSIA information can be obtained
at www.ICGtesting.com
Printed in the USA
BVHW072355090322
630953BV00001BA/4